PERSUADED

the Story of Nicodemus

PERSUADED

the Story of Nicodemus

a novel

DAVID HARDER

To Malinda Fugate-
Mary Blessings Along
your Journey!

AMBASSADOR INTERNATIONAL
GREENVILLE, SOUTH CAROLINA & BELFAST, NORTHERN IRELAND

www.ambassador-international.com

Persuaded: The Story of Nicodemus, A Novel

ISBN: 978-1-62020-710-9
eISBN: 978-1-62020-734-5
Library of Congress Control Number: 2020938634

Cover Design and Page Layout by Hannah Nichols

Scripture taken from The Passion Translation®. Copyright © 2017, 2018 by Passion & Fire Ministries, Inc. Used by permission. All rights reserved. ThePassionTranslation.com.

AMBASSADOR INTERNATIONAL
Emerald House
411 University Ridge, Suite B14
Greenville, SC 29601, USA
www.ambassador-international.com

AMBASSADOR BOOKS
The Mount
2 Woodstock Link
Belfast, BT6 8DD, Northern Ireland, UK
www.ambassadormedia.co.uk

The colophon is a trademark of Ambassador, a Christian publishing company.

Dedicated to Dr. Emily Weinacker, my wife

who believes in and supports me in so many ways

PREFACE

The Bible is a historical record, a spiritual guide, and a road map to the future. We may discover the Bible in several ways. We study it either as a body of works or the individual words and their meanings. Another method is to read the Scriptures according to a plan, or accomplishing a goal of reading the entire Bible in one year. *Persuaded: The Story of Nicodemus* takes a different approach—by using the words from the Bible and bringing the text and characters to life in a realistic story.

Although *Persuaded* is historical fiction, I base the events and timetables within the pages upon the *Passion Translation* version of the Bible. For two years, material about the Hebrew language, locations in the Holy Land, Roman history in Israel, maps, customs, and even the burial practices of Hebrews became part of the research. The goal of this book is one of historical and spiritual accuracy, and to provide information for the reader. When this project began, I didn't understand the number of research hours required to keep the story true.

Nearly every week, archeological discoveries in the Holy Land shed new light and confirm the truthfulness of the Bible. Scholars, intellects, historians, and religious leaders will endlessly debate the validity of the Bible, but the overwhelming historical evidence supports its truthfulness. Two historians of antiquity, a Roman by the name of Tacitus and a Jewish Priest and historian by the name of Josephus, recorded supporting statements about Jesus, His crucifixion and His miracles. In addition, Hebrew records show Jesus existed and was a man of illegitimate birth. Therefore, *Persuaded* accepts the fact that Jesus is who He says, and that He died and came back to life three days later. Every person who identifies as a follower of Jesus (a Christian) looks to the day when we will see Jesus return and to set up His kingdom on earth for eternity. For us, we believe the words in the Bible as fact and base our belief on the miracles we see and the powerful changes in people.

In the Bible, the Gospel of John mentions Nicodemus only three times. We find the first account during his visit with Jesus (Y'shua) at night. At length, he and Jesus discuss spiritual rebirth and the intimate knowledge of God (YaHoWaH). The second incident occurs on the streets of Jerusalem. The members of the Sanhedrin and Pharisees discuss killing Jesus. Nicodemus asks whether the Jewish Law permits them to condemn a man without a trial and without the chance to face his accusers. Publicly humiliated, they chastise Nicodemus in front of his colleagues, and accuse him of being a follower of Jesus. This public admonishment shows Nicodemus is young and not accepted as a full-fledged Pharisee. Had he been an accepted member of the Pharisees, they would talk with him privately. The Gospel of John records the details of this incident. The last record of Nicodemus comes near the end of John's Gospel and during Jesus' crucifixion. Nicodemus, and his friend Joseph of Arimathea, approach Pontius Pilate and request the body of Jesus following His death.

Please note several important facts regarding the actions of these two men. One, they both were members of the Sanhedrin and their actions were in direct violation to the wishes of the Chief Priests and the Sanhedrin Council. Two, the Passover is the most sacred and holy holiday for Hebrews. This celebration remembers the day the Hebrews achieved their freedom from slavery in Egypt. Every Hebrew looks forward with anticipation to the Passover. When Nicodemus and Joseph performed the tahara (burial rites) for Jesus, they gave up any chance of celebrating in the Passover. Since they touched a corpse (Jesus' body), Mosaic Law required a period of cleansing. Their actions disqualified them from the opportunity to join in Passover functions. It further required them to perform a three day cleansing ritual and then offer a sacrifice in the Temple before they could rejoin their fellow Hebrews. Number three, their choice to honor Jesus at the Tahara, meant they would incur the ire of the Sanhedrin and Pharisees. They could have easily become the same target of the Council's rage against Jesus and His followers. And finally, number four, their livelihood and incomes were no longer supported by the Council. The Sanhedrin was comprised of men who had power, money, and control. For their infractions, Nicodemus and Joseph could no longer enjoy these comforts. For their actions, the leaders would have considered them as outcasts.

Based upon oral and written historical records, Joseph of Arimathea operated a metals business that had strong ties to the Roman Government, which is probably the main reason he felt comfortable approaching Pontius Pilate and asking for the body of Jesus after the crucifixion. It's a miracle Pilate released Jesus because in normal circumstances, the Romans wanted to set an example with public deaths and prolong their agony—as a warning to other citizens. Instead, Pilate allowed the speedy end to the execution. Pilate's action speaks volumes about the relationship between him and Joseph and why he released Jesus' body to two Hebrew men, when the relationship between Romans and Hebrews was fragile.

Historically, *Persuaded* maintains accuracy through written words of the Bible, and extra Biblical writings. A pastor friend who advised and aided me during the development of this book provided the following endorsement:

> "This book is a documentary approach as to how Nicodemus came to know the Apostle John and Jesus. Their history and friendship development was intertwined well in the book. Also, Nicodemus' interaction with all the disciples is well conceived. This is one of those personal involvements that leads them to their faith and actions after the cross and burial of Jesus. The theory in the book covers the possible ways the transmittal of the gospel may have occurred."
>
> —Pastor Robert Koch

CHAPTER ONE

THE SIEGE OF JERUSALEM

THROUGHOUT THE ANCIENT CITY OF Jerusalem, anarchy gripped the city. Roman soldiers laid siege while resistance Hebrew groups inflamed the situation further. The Roman war machine displayed its full might as they sought to eradicate what it considered to be an uncivilized and ungrateful population. Caught between two warring factions were the average citizens, the people just trying to eke out a living and survive.

Central to the town, and clustered among many similar-looking stone structures, sat the simple home of Nicodemus. A descendant of the dominant ruling class of Pharisees, and a member of the religious council known as the Sanhedrin, Nicodemus was destined to rise as a leader. Yet, all of his aspirations were quickly being erased.

In this living anguish, tomorrow was an eternity.

"YaHoWaH, hear my prayers, for I am frightened for my life. Our town, the city of David, is being torn apart. Please provide a miracle and find a way for me to escape. For You are—"

Interrupted, Nicodemus swiveled his head and stared. With their fist, someone pounded on the front door. He stopped breathing, and his eyes narrowed in fright.

The banging repeated.

A voice on the other side of the door shouted, "Nicodemus, open the door!"

Cautious, he arose from his kneeling position of prayer. His knees covered in dust from the dirt, Nicodemus crept slowly and quietly to the door. He peered through the cracks between the boards and spotted two imposing Roman soldiers along with another non-military man.

Terrified, Nicodemus panted and leaned his back against the door.

Think, Nicodemus, think.

The knocking continued, and Nicodemus could feel the vibrations of the door throughout his body.

"Nicodemus, can you hear me? I am a friend of Joseph of Arimathea. Please open this door at once!"

The name Joseph of Arimathea was welcome news. Against all instincts, Nicodemus turned and lifted the weighty beam away from the door. He opened it a mere inch. He saw a physically fit, younger man, in his early twenties with his fist poised to pound on the door once more. The man's blue eyes were filled with trepidation.

His voice hoarse, he whispered. "Nicodemus, you must come with us right now. Joseph says it's not safe for you here in Jerusalem. The Romans have surrounded the city and are destroying everything in their sight. The city will fall by tonight!"

Nicodemus' eyes darted between the two Roman soldiers standing on either side of the man. One a centurion, the other a regular soldier. Muscular, they wore expressions of determination. Their presence seemed ominous. Nicodemus' knees felt weak. The young man followed Nicodemus' gaze and tried to reassure him.

"I am Leontis. Your friend, Joseph of Arimathea, says you must come with these two soldiers and me. They will escort us from the dangers occurring in the city. You must hurry, for there is very little time left. Joseph awaits us in a cart by the Gate of the Essenes. Now, please!"

While Nicodemus contemplated the man's demands, several Roman soldiers ran down the passageway between houses, chasing a woman and small child. Everyone watched in horror as the soldiers seized the fleeing individuals and butchered them instantly in the street. Blood splattered the walls of nearby buildings as one soldier with his sword sliced open both the woman and child in one swoop.

The two escort soldiers with Leontis burst their way into Nicodemus' house. They pulled Leontis inside as they entered and slammed the door shut. One Roman kept watch, his foot bracing the door closed.

He shouted, "In a few moments, it will be too late!"

Screams of terror and the sound of swords terrorizing humanity filled the outside air.

Leontis grabbed Nicodemus by the shoulders. "Do you wish to bring anything important? We have to leave now, or you will die."

Nicodemus hastily seized a large satchel, and set it on his table. He stuffed his scrolls and research papers into the bag. As he reached out for ink jars and stylus pens, the centurion knocked them out of Nicodemus' hand, causing them to spill on the floor.

Stunned by the abruptness, Nicodemus stared with an open mouth.

"Citizen, enough! You can replace them later. We must go now." He roughly grabbed Nicodemus and shoved him toward the door.

The heavy satchel slipped off Nicodemus' shoulder, so he bent over to retrieve it. The Roman centurion snapped the bag up off the floor and pushed the group outside.

Everywhere they looked, crazed Romans killed innocent people in bloodlust. The Roman soldiers escorting Leontis and Nicodemus grabbed an arm of each man and marched them between two buildings.

As the four worked their way through the city, complete pandemonium erupted throughout the streets. Every time Nicodemus looked around he saw nothing but blood and dead bodies. Recognizing a few of the individuals as friends or neighbors, Nicodemus felt sick to his stomach.

The two Roman escorts urgently pulled Nicodemus and Leontis along as they moved closer to the southern wall of the city. When Nicodemus looked over his shoulder in the direction of the temple, he saw thick black smoke rising. Nicodemus lost his footing and stumbled, but Leontis took hold of his other arm. Running, the soldier and Leontis nearly dragged Nicodemus by his arms the last hundred feet.

Nearing the Gate of the Essenes, Nicodemus recognized Joseph hunched over, waiting. When Joseph heard the four men approaching, he looked up and smiled. Leontis pulled back a heavy cloth covering the rear of the cart. Multiple small crates, sacks of grain, and hay littered the floor of the wagon.

One Roman soldier hefted Nicodemus into the back. He then rearranged the cargo and pointed. "You, hide up there below the seat of your friends. Make yourself tight, into a ball. Don't make a sound!"

Without hesitation, Nicodemus did as instructed and pulled his satchel in tight to his body. These notes represented his life's work.

The soldiers and Leontis arranged the cargo and moved the extra hay around Nicodemus. They then pulled the tarp back over the rear area.

The centurion leaned in close to where he suspected Nicodemus lay concealed. "Not a sound or you will die. No matter what happens, the other soldiers cannot know you're back here. Do you understand me?" he demanded.

"Yes," came Nicodemus' clipped reply.

The soldier slapped the donkey's backside, and the cart jerked forward. As the wagon plodded along with Joseph and Leontis driving, the two soldiers walked on either side of the wagon as a protective detail.

As they cleared the gate, a cluster of Roman soldiers nailed a man to a crucifix. He screamed as they drove nails into his wrists. The detail of soldiers stopped their work and watched their two fellow soldiers with the cart. A sizable menacing man approached the four intruders as they departed the city.

"Halt, who goes there?"

The escort centurion stepped forward. "Step aside, Decanus. We are on official business per the legatus, Pontius Pilate."

The lower ranking decanus saluted by striking his fist to his breastplate and then extending his arm forward. "Yes, sir, Centurion." But he was suspicious. "What, if I may ask, is in the cart, sir?"

Irritated, the centurion chastised the soldier, "Supplies for our unit bringing up the rear of this campaign."

The others associated with the cart, watched in shock as the centurion pulled the heavy cloth partially aside revealing the boxed contents. Nicodemus froze, praying no one could see him. After a long pause, the centurion pulled the fabric back over the rear.

With an icy edge in his voice, he barked at the decanus. "Satisfied?"

The Roman nodded. "Yes, sir."

The centurion slapped the donkey's backside again, forcing their journey forward. Leontis started to look back but was abruptly stopped.

"Eyes forward, Leontis. Please," mumbled Joseph.

After about thirty minutes elapsed, the four individuals began to relax when they rounded a small hill and encountered a full Roman detachment blocking the road. Two Roman sentries halted their progress.

Before the sentries could ask, the centurion of the escort group quickly explained to minimize curiosity. "We are conducting official business per the legatus, Pontius Pilate."

"What's in the back?" demanded one the sentries.

"Supplies for our unit bringing up the rear of this campaign," said the centurion.

Joseph pulled out a roll of parchment with a red seal and held it out. The centurion escort took it and showed it to the sentry.

The sentry inspected the parchment roll and saw the official red wax seal, but then refused to touch it.

An officer appeared and dismounted his horse. "Legionnaire, what's going on?" The officer handed the reins to the nearest soldier.

The soldier snapped to attention. "Travelers with supplies to a rear detachment, sir."

The tribuni looked at the escort centurion, "Tell me, to what unit are you assigned?"

The centurion saluted. "The Legio VI Ferrata, sir." He held out the roll of parchment, and the tribuni did not hesitate and opened the wax seal.

After reading the contents, the tribuni handed the document back. "Check the back of their wagon, Legionnaire."

The sentry took his sword and slashed through the cloth cover, letting tip strike wood. Moving around, he stabbed several times. He lifted the tarp and saw crates, small barrels, sacks of grain and scattered hay. Satisfied, he nodded to the tribuni.

Curled tight and barely breathing, Nicodemus watched with horror as the sharp Roman blade pierced the cloth striking the area all around his hidden position. On the last plunge of the sword, the tip nicked Nicodemus' calf, slicing a deep gash into the flesh. Nicodemus squeezed his eyes shut and bit hard into his tongue. He stifled a scream. The searing pain was excruciating.

Joseph kept his face down the entire time and instantly spotted red droplets falling from beneath the cart. Worried, he saw the crimson liquid forming into a small pool. Joseph held his breath.

The tribuni used his riding crop handle and lifted the face of Joseph. "Name?"

"Joseph of Arimathea." He smiled up at the Roman officer.

The tribuni looked at the athletic young man seated alongside Joseph. "What's his story? He looks fit enough to fight for the Romans."

Joseph snatched the left arm of Leontis and thrust it toward the tribuni. When he performed this maneuver, an iron bracelet affixed to the man's wrist revealed in Latin and Greek letters, the man was a slave. "His name is Leontis and he is my servant."

The tribuni gazed into the eyes of the two men seated in the cart, as if gauging whether they were telling the truth. After a brief pause, he remounted his horse.

"Let them pass," commanded the tribuni.

The high-spirited horse, anxious and ready to run, acted like a racehorse ready at the gate. The tribuni pulled on the reins to maintain eye contact with the centurion of the escort. "Give my regards to your praefectus castrorum. Perhaps we can be finished with these savages soon enough and return home to our wives."

"Yes, sir, and thank you," replied the centurion as he saluted.

The Roman encampment contained several thousand men, so the four-person escort gradually navigated the horde as soldiers surrounding their position watched them pass through. When the group neared the edge of the camp, Joseph saw captured Israeli zealots in a holding area.

Without regard for their ghastly screams, the Romans began hacking off the limbs of the Zealots. Once the prisoner was devoid of his arms and legs, the soldiers then decapitated their wailing heads. Other Roman soldiers tossed the severed body parts onto a colossal burning pyre. The stench was retching and the sight even more grotesque.

As the cart with the four individuals detoured around the ghoulish spectacle, Leontis glared at the Roman soldiers.

Joseph raised his eyes just slightly toward his slave and muttered, "Don't watch, Leontis."

"Why on earth are they doing this?" Leontis barely whispered.

Joseph tightly gripped Leontis' wrist.

The two Roman soldiers and their escorts traveled several more miles, and then the centurion stopped their progress. They were now out of sight and far away from the Roman detachment.

"As requested, we've completed our task, per orders of the legatus, Pontius Pilate. Don't think I'm not repulsed by our performance, for I have just lied to a tribuni and several brothers back there. And for what—to save a wealthy citizen, his slave, and this Jew?" The centurion shook his fist at them.

Leontis doubled his hands and tightened his body. Joseph patted Leontis' leg, and then reached under his seat and pulled out a small chest. After unlocking it, he retrieved two purple cloth bags with gold drawstrings. Each bag was the size of two men's fists. He handed them to Leontis.

"Please pay the soldiers."

Leontis vehemently hissed, "Master, one bag equals the wages of a man's lifetime."

Joseph smiled. "Centurion, here is your payment for your services. There are one hundred gold shekels for each of you. May YaHoWaH bless you for what you have done for my friends and me."

The mood instantly shifted as the centurion and the soldier hefted the weight of the bags in their hands. Like gleeful school boys who had escaped punishment for their misdeeds, the two soldiers smiled with pleasure. They grinned at one another. One soldier opened his bag and pulled a gold piece out and laughed.

"Yes, this made our deception worth it. I suggest you never come back this way again," the centurion threatened. "The outcome may not be so favorable."

Both soldiers turned and walked back in the direction of Jerusalem. While they walked, they endlessly congratulated themselves for their new fortunes. Leontis and Joseph watched them disappear over a small rise in the road.

"Master, why so much money. They will just spend it on prostitutes and beer!" objected Leontis.

Joseph half smiled. "I was prepared to spend even more to save my friend's life."

Joseph reached down and patted their stowaway under the cloth. "Nicodemus, it is safe, you may come out. We are now far from the city and any danger."

Nicodemus didn't move.

Leontis jumped from the cart and pulled back the heavy cloth. He sucked air between his teeth when he saw the vast pool of dried blood. Nicodemus was curled into a tight ball, his eyes jammed closed. Leontis shook the man.

"We're out of danger, Nicodemus, can you get up? Are you hurt?" asked Leontis.

Slowly at first, Nicodemus opened one eye then the other. He paused and surveyed their surroundings. He was soaked with sweat.

"Quickly, Leontis, give him some water," commanded Joseph as he handed the clay watering jar to his slave.

The servant helped Nicodemus sit up and let him sip some water. "Let me look at your wound."

Ripping several long narrow strips of cloth from his outer robe, Leontis bandaged Nicodemus' leg. He smiled up at Joseph. "It is a surface cut; not too deep."

Nicodemus winced. "Surface cut? It's not your leg!"

Both Joseph and his servant chuckled.

"You are alive Nicodemus, and you will probably have a nasty reminder once it heals, but you are alive and away from the city," said Joseph.

Nicodemus felt relief. "Thank you, Joseph." He looked at Leontis. "Thank you both for saving my life. You are the answer to my prayers."

When the three men looked back in the direction of Jerusalem, they could see nothing but dark billowing smoke rising to the clouds.

Joseph shuddered and mourned over the destruction. "My friends, we are observing the end of an era for Israel. Our history is forever changed by what we have witnessed here, and I doubt we will recover for several thousand years."

CHAPTER TWO

ARIMATHEA

FOR THE NEXT SEVERAL YEARS, time elapsed swiftly as Nicodemus settled into a new life in the town of Arimathea. Slowly, the tragic events in Jerusalem faded from his memory. Joseph no longer took extended trips to far away cities for business but allowed a younger partner to accomplish these duties. Age took its toll, and Joseph was now content to sit, watching others toil away.

Leontis tended to Joseph's needs and watched over his master with loving care. Nicodemus also lived in the same house and served his elder friend. Finding a position of education in the town, Nicodemus taught young children the words found in the Torah and shared all the stories of Y'shua he could recall from memory.

The children were attentive, listening as Nicodemus told of Lazarus coming to life after being dead for four days. Animated, Nicodemus embellished the story for effect. He delighted to see the children jump when he called out, "Lazarus, come forth!" Nicodemus repeated his stories over and over, but the children never grew tired of his storytelling. Instead, the older children would encourage Nicodemus to retell the accounts for the newer ones.

Nicodemus watched Joseph bend with age and grow frail over time, often panting to make the journey from his bed to a stool on the portico of the house. Joseph would smile and listen, yet sometimes, he would sleep for hours, always with a pleasant look on his face, his hands resting on his walking stick.

"You add something different each time you tell the stories, Nicodemus," teased Joseph during one evening meal.

Nicodemus stared at Joseph and Leontis as the two men grinned. "I . . . I do not!" Nicodemus protested.

Joseph laughed so hard he started choking. Finally, after clearing his throat, he said, "You do, Nicodemus, and it's fine. The children love it, and so do I."

Leontis added, "It is true, Nicodemus, and I enjoy hearing the stories as much as the children. You make me believe I knew Y'shua personally, even though He died long before I was born."

"Does he speak the truth?" asked Nicodemus.

Joseph nodded as he ate his stew. "You should write your stories down, so others may know Y'shua."

"But I was not there for everything, Joseph. We weren't present for many of the days Y'shua walked this earth," lamented Nicodemus.

"Yet, I think you should write down what you know, for future generations. Who will tell your stories once you are gone?" asked Joseph.

For the rest of their meal, Nicodemus was quiet and reflective.

As more people slowly escaped the punishment of the Roman campaigns, they had migrated in different directions, with some settling in Arimathea. Several times, former teachers of the law or scribes challenged Nicodemus concerning his conversion to follow Y'shua. Nicodemus never fully relaxed, and several individuals threatened his life for being a traitor. Nicodemus brought the subject up in the middle of dinner one night.

"Joseph, as more men from the old Sanhedrin move into our town, I am feeling the dangers associated with my name. Many of these men knew my father and connect me with being a traitor to the laws of Moses."

"Nonsense," rebuffed Joseph.

"Perhaps I should change my name?" questioned Nicodemus.

Joseph stopped eating and stared at his younger friend.

In the evening, Joseph called for Nicodemus at bedtime. "Do you think another name will prevent their wrath, Nicodemus?"

"I'm not sure, Joseph. When I was given the name Nicodemus my parents told me it meant *victorious*—to prevail or overcome. When I look back on my life, I don't feel so victorious. In fact, my life has been filled with misery and pain."

Joseph began to speak, but it turned into coughing and choking instead. Eventually, he regained his composure. "Let me sleep and pray about this Nicodemus."

"Of course, my friend," said Nicodemus.

Joseph struggled with his breathing and continued to cough. Once the coughing abated, he bid his friend good night. "Shalom, Nicodemus. YaHoWaH will give us the answer. Now go to sleep."

"Shalom, Joseph."

Nicodemus watched his friend as he backed away from the room. He realized Joseph was becoming increasingly frail and his friend's life was quickly coming to a close. All that night, Nicodemus prayed for Joseph and for wisdom. He eventually fell asleep while praying in bed.

Early the next morning, Leontis urgently cried out. "Arise, Nicodemus, the Master, is calling out for you."

Pulling himself free of his bed, Nicodemus shuffled to the side of Joseph. When he looked at his friend, Joseph appeared ashen, struggling to breathe. Nicodemus pulled a stool alongside Joseph's bed.

"I'm here, my brother."

Joseph took Nicodemus by his arm and feebly called out, "Leontis? Where are you?"

Leontis moved to the opposite side. "Here, Master."

Joseph took hold of Leontis' arm with his free hand. "Nicodemus, you are my witness, Leontis is now a free man and has completed his service to me."

"But, Master," protested Leontis, "my debt is not fully paid."

"You are now a free man, Leontis. Nicodemus, give him seventy gold shekels and remove the iron bracelet. He has a wife and family and must be free to choose his own destiny."

Joseph began coughing again.

Leontis kissed his master's hand and wept. "Master, I do not deserve this. I will serve you until my last breath."

Joseph placed his hand upon Leontis' head and pronounced, "Leontis, go with shalom and serve Y'shua with your life. Worship YaHoWaH with all your heart, soul, and mind. Always be kind to those in need and never ever forget where you started your journey with me."

Through tears, Leontis mumbled, "Thank you, Master, thank you."

Joseph smiled up at his servant. "You are from this day forward called a free man, but remember, you are also my friend." Joseph then looked at Nicodemus. "You are like a son I never had, Nicodemus. I have always cherished our times together. Please promise me. . . "

"Ask what you may, Joseph, and I swear, I will keep my promise," assured Nicodemus.

Joseph patted his friend's hand. "I know you will, Nicodemus, for you are an honorable man and true to your word. From this day forward, you are to be called, Tobias. For this name means *the goodness of YaHoWaH*. Everything you have done is filled with kindness and YaHoWaH has much more to reveal in your life. You must follow His directions and record the stories of Y'shua for future followers. Although you were not victorious earlier in your life under the name of Nicodemus, as Tobias your goodness will shine for the world to see."

Nicodemus mildly protested, "I know so little, Joseph. I know only parts of Y'shua's story, the parts you and I witnessed."

Joseph patted Nicodemus' hand. "You must visit our brother John, the witness. He will give you the words to speak. Seek out John and YaHoWaH will be with you. Now shalom my dearest friend and never stop being curious about the ways of YaHoWaH. My time is close, and I must go home. I am weary. . . ." His voice trailed off.

Nicodemus and Leontis slowly moved to leave, but then Joseph roused one more time. "Leontis?"

"I'm here, Master."

"You must no longer call me *master*. You are a free man and my name is Joseph, my friend."

Leontis released a heavy sigh. "Yes, Joseph." His tongue seemed to stumble over the name after so many years of addressing the man as Master.

"Please retrieve the box hidden in the wall and bring it to me now. You know of what I'm referring?" asked Joseph.

Without pausing, Leontis dashed from the room and returned moments later, out of breath. "Here, Mast. . . I mean Joseph."

Joseph smiled and fumbled with the wooden box, trying to open the lid. After several attempts, he finally pried it open. His hands trembling, Joseph retrieved a Roman spike from the box. Thick, dried red stains caked the edges. He gingerly held the box out for Nicodemus. "Here, take it, Tobias." He addressed him by his new name.

Nicodemus studied the spike with a look of bewilderment. "What is this, Joseph?"

Joseph struggled, trying to explain. "It is from Y'shua's cross."

Nicodemus immediately dropped the spike into the box, and his hands began to shake. "How is this possible?"

"You must keep this safe at all times, Tobias. It is the only reminder I have of the day Y'shua was crucified," said Joseph. "I am now giving it to you. Every time you touch it, you will be reminded of Y'shua's sacrifice for us. It will help you remember to tell His story and write it down for future generations."

Joseph exhaled a long breath, having accomplished the things he wanted to finish. A small smile appeared on his face, and he closed his eyes. As Leontis and Nicodemus watched, Joseph slowly relaxed and sank into the bed. He had stopped breathing and was no longer among the living.

As Nicodemus gazed at the spike in his hands, he wept, recalling the events the day Y'shua died. He also remembered Y'shua came back to life on the third day and was seen by many, many people. He looked up at Leontis and weakly smiled.

"One day, Y'shua said He would return. This symbol reminds me of His death, but His words are a stronger reminder, for one day, Y'shua will return."

Leontis smiled. "Then you must tell the whole story of Y'shua. Just as Joseph said, you must write these things down so those of us who remain, can remember what we are waiting for."

CHAPTER THREE

A STORMY JOURNEY

EARLY ONE MORNING AND MANY years later, by a pier in Joppa, a very elderly shepherd, now curved with age and dressed in shepherd's clothing nervously waited. Two bundled bags hung on his slumped shoulders as he watched the activity around the harbor. Several boats of different sizes sat in slips awaiting cargo transfer or undergoing minor repairs.

A Roman guard of six men stood at the entrance of the pier, patrolling and inspecting patrons and workers alike. The shepherd carefully observed, ensuring it was safe to enter the dock area. He had many reasons to be fearful, yet he steeled himself for the adventure on which he was about to embark.

After a deep breath, the shepherd made his way closer to the boats. People lined up, coins in their hands, waiting to purchase a seat on one of the ships. Joppa, a seaport along the Mediterranean Sea, provided a stopping off point. Goods and passengers were exchanged. Soldiers checked papers, and daily commerce took place. It was a busy port with constant activity. Boisterous sailors, greedy money exchangers, along with a melting pot of inexperienced travelers created a menacing cesspool of humanity. Roman soldiers policed the streets and merchants with Machiavellian tactics.

The old shepherd wanted to travel to the island of Patmos, a small Greek landmass more than a week's journey from Joppa. Patmos was an island under tight Roman control and reserved for prisoners. As the line of people dwindled, the shepherd moved a step closer to his goal. His journey was risky, and he wasn't sure the Romans would let him travel, but he had a significant purpose for this trip.

"State your business," said one of the soldiers.

Startled, the shepherd pulled his attention from the boat activity. "I uh, I would like to hire a boat."

"Destination?" the same Roman soldier demanded.

"I would like to visit Patmos."

The Roman soldier's eyes narrowed. He looked over the shepherd carefully.

The old man hoped the soldier would see the shepherd's hair and beard, streaked in thick tufts of white and grey strands. The shepherd did not want the Romans viewing him as a threat. He held his breath.

The Roman grabbed the lapel of the shepherd's cloak. "And what business does an old shepherd have in Patmos?"

The shepherd weakly smiled. "To visit a brother, sir."

The other soldiers standing nearby laughed. The Roman leaned in close to intimidate the shepherd. "It is an island for prisoners. Who is your *brother*?" The Roman over-emphasized the last word.

"I, uh, what I mean is, his name is John, sir." The shepherd was nervous but steadied himself. "As a Roman citizen, are we not allowed to travel and visit with other citizens of the empire?" The old man stretched Roman law, but no more so than the soldiers. He silently prayed his tactic would work.

The Roman straightened up, taking a guarded stance, resting a hand on his sword. "I'm not sure this applies to enemies or prisoners of the state."

Again, the shepherd smiled. "What harm could it be to visit an old brother waiting to die alone on an isolated island?"

The Roman rubbed his unshaven stubble, considering the shepherd's proposal. "What's in your bags? Open them and show me."

The shepherd knew this might happen and so he had carefully planned for the inspection. As he slowly opened the bags, coins jingled. The Roman roughly pushed the shepherd aside and finished inspecting the bags alone. Several gold coins sparkled in the morning sunlight.

Shoving his hand over the coins, the Roman soldier grasped them in his fist. He hoarsely whispered, "Is this a bribe? Show me your other bag, Shepherd."

Again, the shepherd deliberately opened his other bag revealing more gold coins. "I assumed these are for the travel taxes, kind sir," said the old man.

The Roman snatched the additional coins and greedily smiled. He looked over his shoulder and yelled, "Let this shepherd pass." He leaned in close to the old man and whispered. "The boat in the third slip travels directly to Patmos. Wait for my soldiers to load one of our prisoners before you attempt to board." The Roman stood up straight and pointed at another soldier. "You there, Ignatius, escort this shepherd and make sure he gets on his boat."

"Yes, sir!"

As Ignatius and the shepherd walked toward the boat, the Roman escort asked, "What is your name and where do you come from?"

The questions were inquisitive and not interrogative. Nonetheless, the shepherd remained cautious.

Pulling his hand across his grey beard he said, "My name is Tobias, and I come from Arimathea."

Ignatius nodded. Instantly the two men were interrupted by someone barking orders.

"Stand aside, get out of the way. Move!"

Two Roman soldiers roughly dragged a shackled prisoner to the same boat Tobias was to ride in. The prisoner wore only a loincloth. Flogging marks and dried blood covered the man's back. The Romans were rough in their handling of the prisoner. After a quick verbal exchange with the boat captain, they affixed the prisoner to the side of the boat with his shackles. The lead soldier produced a rolled document containing a red seal and handed it to the captain. With haste, the Roman detachment left the ship and walked back to the pier.

"It is now safe to board the boat, shepherd Tobias," said Ignatius.

Before Tobias could thank Ignatius, the Roman escort disappeared into the crowd of people.

"Your name and destination?" a gritty voice asked.

Tobias turned to face the boat captain who was a rotund man with sunburned skin and white hair. Deep crevices of weathered age lined his face, and his marine blue eyes bore holes into the shepherd's head. "The name is Tobias, and I seek to visit a brother on the island of Patmos."

The portly captain gave Tobias a curious, sideways glance. "Patmos you say? And do you have any papers?"

"I . . . I, uh, I wasn't aware any were required." Tobias turned, nervous and hesitant, and pointed at the man who had granted him passage. "That Roman soldier over there, the tall one, granted me travel permission."

As the captain stared at the Roman, Tobias worried his efforts thus far were for nothing. A long pause ensued when suddenly the captain grabbed Tobias by the shoulder.

"The fee is ten drachma and includes water and food rations, but you're required to lend assistance when called upon."

Reaching into a pouch under his cloak, Tobias retrieved the coins and dropped them into the captain's beefy and calloused palm.

"Stow your bags in the bow and find a comfortable seat on the starboard side."

Tobias stared at the captain in confusion. He had no idea what the captain meant.

Shaking his head in disgust, the captain pointed to the right side of the boat. "Find a seat there and," he then pointed to the front of the boat, "stow your bags up there." The captain walked away with a gruff. After Tobias situated himself, he watched another elderly couple, and then a young teenage man, join him for a ride in the small boat. The abundant cargo, lashed in the center of the ship, required the passengers to climb over crates and parcels to obtain a comfortable seat.

When Tobias surveyed the ship, it seemed small compared to the vast body of water in the west. The lone mast dominated the center, along with a long boom arm and tan sail lashed tightly to the two parts. He looked toward heaven and said a quick, silent prayer. *"YaHoWah protect me, and grant me safe passage to my destination. Make a way for me to meet Your witness, John."*

Another man joined the captain on the pier. He appeared to be a sailor joining the crew. After the captain and the sailor embraced each other's forearms, the lean sailor began untying the boat from the pier. Jumping into the ship, the captain started raising the sail, and the small craft slowly drifted away from the slip. At the last moment, the lanky sailor jumped from the pier and into the ship causing it to lurch forward. The sailor then stowed the ropes that initially held their boat to the dock.

A gentle eastern breeze filled the sail and the worn fabric snapped with a loud thud. The boat quickly lurched forward. Within seconds, the ship drifted out to sea at a steady speed. Tobias watched with fascination as the sailor and the captain moved about the boat, guiding the wooden craft in the proper direction. Keeping his hand on the rudder, the captain squinted toward the horizon and then bellowed at the sailor.

"Trim the sail a bit more; I feel the wind gaining strength."

The lanky sailor dove over the crates and grabbed the lashing that held the horizontal boom of the sail. He began tugging with all his strength, but he was unable to pull it in because the wind was too strong.

"You there, Shepherd, help him!"

Tobias joined the sailor and grasped the lashing. Together they pulled until Tobias sweat.

"That's enough," said the captain as he gazed upward and watched the sail strain tight against the wind.

The boat surged forward, gaining speed, and Tobias could hear the waves lapping against the sides of the ship. Occasionally, one wave would break apart, and a fine salty mist would spray the passengers' faces. Tobias took his sleeve and wiped his face.

"You'll get used to it in a day or two," said the lean sailor. He then chuckled.

Excited and frightened at the same time, Tobias had never traveled the sea in a boat before. He turned to watch the shoreline and Joppa slowly disappear. Within an hour, the small ship was alone, surrounded by blue-green waves in every direction.

Looking at the prisoner, Tobias worried about the man should the boat begin to sink, for the poor man was locked by chains to the sides of the small craft. *He will surely perish.* Tobias felt a shudder move through his body. *What am I thinking; we will all drown.* He leaned over the edge and stared at the water quickly speeding past.

"If you are going to be sick, move aft, so we don't have to share your spoils in our face," roared the captain.

Tobias looked up. "Aft, Captain?" he asked with bewilderment.

Both the sailor and the captain grunted at the same time. The sailor nudged Tobias and pointed toward the captain minding the rudder.

Snarling, the sailor said, "Back there, where the cap'n is standing, that's aft, Shepherd."

Tobias smiled and nodded, but the sailor just shook his head in disgust. Tobias crawled over the cargo and returned to his seat, settling in for the long journey. Hours passed, and Tobias watched the sun gently travel in the sky from east to west. Clouds gathered then disappeared. Seagulls swooped over the boat, circling the small craft. When one attempted to land on the cargo, the lean sailor jumped to his feet and kicked the bird away. Puzzled, Tobias watched the crewmate.

"They leave their foul-smelling droppings all over the cargo. They can cost me money at the market," groaned the captain.

When evening started, Tobias watched with fascination as the sky slowly turned black and stars by the millions dotted the sky above. The rhythm of the movements of the boat, the waves beating against the sides, and the sail occasionally snapping in the wind were hypnotic. Tobias' eyes became heavy, and soon he fell asleep.

A dream concerning children and old friends was interrupted when a torrential downpour rained over the small boat and splashed Tobias in the face. Jerking awake, Tobias stared with dread at the captain.

Yelling above the wind and rain, the captain pointed at Tobias. "You there, come manage the rudder. Now!"

Tobias moved quickly and joined the captain. The portly man roughly pushed Tobias into position and wrapped his arms around the handle of the wooden rudder.

"Grab the stick with all your might and don't let it move right or left. Do you understand?"

Tobias, nodding vigorously, could barely see because the rain ran down his face and blurred his vision.

"You're doing great, Shepherd. Stay here until I come back. We need to drop our sail."

Tobias used all his might to hold the rudder in place. The boat rocked back and forth as the wind and waves easily pushed the small boat around. All the stars were gone, and Tobias could not see beyond the edges of the boat. Tobias wondered how the captain knew if they are going the right direction. Tobias prayed for YaHoWaH's safety and worried about dying at the same time. The boat jerked and thrashed about, causing Tobias to be thrown off balance. He watched the captain and the sailor struggle with the sail. Once the fabric was down and tied to the mast, the captain made his way back to Tobias.

"Go back to your seat and hold on tight."

Tobias nearly crawled across the cargo, fighting his way back to the side of the boat. The small ship thrashed about in the wind and waves. When he arrived at his place, Tobias was exhausted. Taking a loose rope, Tobias wrapped it around his waist and tied himself to the side of the boat. This was the most frightening event he had ever experienced in his entire life.

Whenever lightning flashed, Tobias looked across the sea and saw huge waves, taller than their small boat dancing all around their position. Seawater splashed over the ship and filled the bottom. The sailor came to Tobias with a bucket with a rope attached. The sailor yelled over the sounds of the rain.

"Dump the water out." The lanky sailor lashed the bucket to the side of the boat and roughly thrust it at Tobias.

Tobias could not believe what he heard. "What good will it do? The boat is filling fast," he asked.

"It will keep us from sinking!"

Tobias scooped the bucket through the water in the bottom of the boat and dumped the contents over the side. He looked over and saw the sailor and the young man were doing the same. The elderly couple were huddled in a tight knot, frightened to death. Despite the efforts of Tobias, the sailor, and the young man, it seemed their work was almost fruitless against the rain. Nonetheless, the water in the bottom of the boat never rose higher than a foot.

When the rain finally slowed then stopped, Tobias could barely move his arms. As fast as the storm arose, it subsided, leaving the air cool. Above their heads, the clouds disappeared, and the stars returned to the nighttime sky. Laying his head back, an exhausted Tobias fell asleep, still holding the bucket in his hands.

CHAPTER FOUR

ISLAND OF PRISONERS

FOR ELEVEN DAYS THE SMALL boat traveled across the Mediterranean Sea. During their journey from Joppa, the ship had stopped on the island of Cyprus where the elderly couple disembarked. Goods were exchanged, and the small boat then traveled northwest, arriving near the coastline of Lycia. The captain kept the ship within visual range of land as they headed in a westerly direction toward Greece. Tobias was grateful to have terra firma within sight.

Along the way, they passed many islands, eventually stopping briefly on the island of Rhodes. Here the young teenage man departed from their company.

The journey over the next three days took a zigzag course as they maneuvered around small islands. Tobias was convinced they were lost or going in circles, yet the captain was confident. Glancing at the prisoner, Tobias could see he had become anxious as well.

Weariness overcame Tobias, and the monotony allowed him to rest often. Early one morning, the lanky sailor cried out, which startled Tobias.

"Patmos, just port of the bow!"

Immediately, Tobias gained a renewed vigor and raised his head, straining to see. Glancing at the prisoner, he noticed the man did not lift his head and looked disinterested. Off in the distance, near the horizon, a small dark-blue mountain rose above the fine line of blue-green water. He could not distinguish one island from another, as the water was dotted with islands everywhere.

The sailor pointed in the general direction. Squinting, the captain pulled hard on the rudder causing the boat to aim directly for the declared land. Other than the wind beating against the sail and the sounds of water slapping the sides of the ship, everyone sat quietly, straining to witness the appearance of land. Nearly an hour later the elusive land grew in height. Joy swept over the faces of everyone except the prisoner.

Arriving at Patmos is the simple part. Now I must gain passage to visit John.

Tobias looked in the direction of the captain.

"How much longer, before we arrive?"

Looking up at the sail, the captain then scanned the horizon. "If the wind is steady, we'll be landing by mid-day."

Despite his worry, there was nothing Tobias could do but wait. Time dragged on slowly and the land mass grew wider and only slightly taller. Other landforms of various sizes jutted from the water and appeared on either side of the boat.

Arriving in Patmos, the boat traveled into what appeared to be a massive harbor. The island loomed on either side of the ship, yet their destination seemed further away. Finally, the land on either side of the boat merged encompassing them on all sides except east, from where they originated.

The island was not very tall, perhaps eight-hundred feet. White structures and green vegetation dotted the port of Skala. As the boat neared the docks, the sailor and the captain lowered the sail, allowing the ship to drift in gently.

Tobias noticed limited commerce activity; far less than in Joppa. A large contingent of Romans guarded the port, inspecting every boat as it made shore. Then the captain stood up, cupped hands around his mouth, and called out in a loud voice "Prisoner aboard!"

Tobias saw instant reactions by the Roman soldiers as four men scrambled along the docks, rushing headlong toward their position. As the sailor leaped from the boat to tie the ropes, a Roman soldier stepped aboard at the same time. He scowled at Tobias.

"Here are his papers," said the captain.

He handed the rolled document to the Roman who immediately tore open the red seal. Unrolling the paper, the Roman quickly read the parchment.

"Thank you, Captain." The Roman pointed to a small building. "See the quartermaster for your payment." He then yelled at the other three soldiers, "Take the prisoner to be processed."

Three men unlocked the chained man from the boat and dragged him across the pier, heading to a small building with a Roman flag on its roof.

The boat captain called out to the Roman as he started to step out, "Sir?"

The Roman turned and scowled.

"This passenger wishes to visit another prisoner on the island." The captain pointed at Tobias.

The Roman's eyes narrowed. "State your name."

Nervously standing, Tobias tried to smile. "Tobias, sir."

Moving in closer, standing a few inches from his face, Tobias could smell the man's sweat and the food the soldier had eaten earlier.

"Centurion Laurentius of Joppa granted him passage," said the boat captain.

"He permitted a citizen to come here? Follow me, Shepherd," barked the Roman.

The sailor tossed Tobias his bundles as he climbed out of the boat. He gathered his belongings and dashed to keep up with the Roman.

Once inside the small white building, the warm temperatures dropped precipitously. A Roman officer sat behind his desk sipping wine from a gold challis.

The Roman escorting Tobias called out. "Lieutenant Severinus, a visitor wishing to visit a prisoner, sir."

Casting his hazel eyes at Tobias, the lieutenant smiled.

"Tell me, Shepherd, why do you wish to visit a prisoner on my island?"

Clutching his bundles to his chest, Tobias desperately tried to produce a soft smile so he would not appear nervous. Surely, the lieutenant could see through his futile attempt to mask his fears.

"He is a brother." Tobias knew he misrepresented his relationship since John was a brother in the name of Y'shua and not a member of his family.

"The prisoner's name?" asked Severinus.

"John, sir."

The lieutenant closed his eyes for a moment, frowning.

Another soldier behind the lieutenant leaned forward and softly spoke.

"John, sir, the Christian sent here by Titus Flavius Caesar Domitianus Augustus."

Severinus opened his eyes and smiled. "Ah, yes, sent here nearly seven years ago. Why do you want to visit him?"

For eleven days, Tobias had asked himself the same question. He knew he must produce a reasonable answer to gain access to a Roman prisoner on a remote island. His response rehearsed, he hoped it was convincing. Drawing his hand across his beard, he said, "We are both getting old, and I wish to share the news of our family."

"What is in your bundles, old shepherd?"

"I have writing materials for John, a blanket, and some bread," said Tobias.

Turning to face another soldier, Severinus motioned. "Show me."

The soldier rounded the table and took the bundles from Tobias. Laying them on the lieutenant's workspace, the soldier opened the first bag. Inside sat a neatly folded white blanket with dark blue bands and tied with string. A small stack of writing paper sat on top, also bound. Two vials of ink in ceramic jars and several metal writing styluses were bundled in linen cloth.

The lieutenant picked up a metal stylus.

"These look dangerous, possibly used as weapons."

"He is an old man, nearly ninety years. How dangerous could he be?" Tobias shrugged defensively.

Severinus set the writing instruments down.

"Show me the other bag."

The soldier opened the second bag. Inside were several loaves of thin, flatbread. He handed one to the lieutenant, who leaned over to examine the remaining contents.

"Jewish bread, Shepherd?"

"Yes, sir."

"What is it with you Jews and your ridiculous hard bread?" asked the lieutenant. He then broke the loaf in half. Crumbs scattered in every direction. The lieutenant brushed the crumbs off his uniform. Severinus tossed the two halves into the bag with disgust.

Tobias held his breath. He could see the edge of a folded paper in one side of the bread, and he prayed no one else noticed.

Inside several of the loaves held written messages intended for John, from friends, and writings by the witness Peter. The notes had been folded and baked inside the bread. Tobias quickly gathered the corners of his bag tying them into a knot.

"The bread is from a long line of family traditions which has religious aspects. We bake it for special occasions."

Lieutenant Severinus shook his head in disbelief. "Uncivilized. No wonder you people are still shepherds. Gnaeus?"

A lean and muscular Roman Centurion soldier, in his early twenties, stepped forward, snapped to attention, and saluted. "Yes, sir."

"You are to escort this old shepherd to visit with John the Christian. I believe he is positioned in the grotto and alone. Ensure this information is still true." Turning toward Tobias he said, "You have one day for your visit, Shepherd." He turned back to the Roman. "Gnaeus, if you are not back here in two days with his old man, I'll send a garrison of soldiers to find you and crucify the two of you. Do you understand me?"

In a standard Roman salute, Gnaeus slapped his right arm across his chest striking it with a fist and thrust his arm straight out. "Certe, Lieutenant."

Tobias gathered his belongings while Gnaeus pulled on his shoulder. Tobias looked up. "Thank you, Lieutenant. You are most kind, sir." Tobias smiled.

Severinus dismissed them with the flip of his downturned hand. He returned to his desk and sipped his wine. Just before they disappeared, the lieutenant scorned at his guest and commanded once more, "Only two days, Gnaeus, and I suggest you do not test my patience!"

Scrambling out the door, the Roman soldier dragged Tobias while yelling over his shoulder, "As you command, sir."

Once outside, the soldier picked up two cylindrical clay-watering jars with leather slings, and handed one to Tobias. "Take this, you'll need it. The journey is long and dusty."

Before Tobias could thank the man, the soldier walked away. Tobias hurried to catch up. The hot sun beat down as they walked up a gentle slope and sweat broke out across his skin. He needed the soldier to slow down.

"Where are we headed, Gnaeus?"

The soldier seemed irritated. Stopping, he faced Tobias. "Shepherd, you may address me as Centurion."

"Yes, Centurion, I meant no disrespect." Tobias did his best to look and sound respectful. "Forgive me, sir."

Gnaeus pointed in a south-west direction. Rising from the sea, the land gradually climbed from the shore to the peak of a mountain in the center of the island.

"About halfway up the far mountain, facing the east is a small cave. John the Christian resides there."

"Why does John live alone and not with other prisoners?"

Gnaeus scowled. "He lives alone by decree of Lieutenant Severinus. He was originally placed with a group of harsh criminals in hopes they would eliminate him. Unfortunately, he survived, and in fact, he converted most of the men to his Christian beliefs. We then moved him to another more sinister group, but the same thing happened with those men."

Tobias smiled and then drank some water.

"It's his proselytizing that got him sent to this godless and unforgiving island in the first place." The centurion turned and started walking again.

Tobias scanned the mountainside straining to see if he could spot John's cave, but the low savannah brush disguised the landscape. After several hours of walking, they stopped under the shade of a lone tree to rest.

Gnaeus stared at Tobias, studying him. "You look too old to be a shepherd, yet you're dressed like one."

Tobias felt uncomfortable talking about personal details. He had taken a considerable risk coming to Patmos, and the last thing he needed was a Roman centurion discovering the truth. Drawing his hand across his grey beard, he shifted the conversation.

"How long have you served on this island?" asked Tobias.

Gnaeus frowned. "Too long, almost four years." He reached out and grabbed Tobias by the wrist, turning his hand over, Gnaeus inspected Tobias' palm. "You look like a shepherd, but your hands say otherwise. They're too soft and are unstained." He pushed Tobias' hand away. "Why are you here on Patmos?"

Tobias smiled. "You are correct, I am too old to be a shepherd, but nonetheless, I tell you I am a shepherd." Tobias spoke the truth for he was a shepherd to a *flock of Christians* but not sheep. "The lambs in my care are people."

The centurion could not grasp Tobias' meaning. "When I was a young lad, my family cared for sheep in the northern territory of Rome. It took me years to rid my hands of the oily sheep stains. The stench was worse."

Tobias nodded. "Sheep require effort and diligence to maintain."

The centurion responded in a flat tone of casual disgust. "Yes." Standing, the centurion commanded, "Let's keep walking. You heard the lieutenant's instructions; besides I don't want to be stumbling along this path in the dark."

As the two men walked, Tobias stared at the lean soldier. Looking around, Tobias saw hundreds of tiny islands dotting the sea all around Patmos. The sky was nearly cloudless with occasional tufts of cotton hanging in the light blue haze.

The journey toiled on for a long time, allowing the bright sun to drain all the energy from Tobias. By the third stop for rest, Tobias had nearly finished all his water. Feeling sorry for the old man, Gnaeus walked over to Tobias, shaking his head in disbelief.

"Give me your watering jar."

Embarrassed, Tobias sheepishly handed the jar to the Roman.

Gnaeus poured some of his water into Tobias' jar. After roughly placing the stopper to seal the jar, the Roman said, "Only wet the inside of your mouth, and don't drink so much. You'll get sick and have nothing left for the rest of the journey."

Startled by this information, Tobias gave Gnaeus a shocked look. "I assumed there would be a spring to refill our jars."

Gnaeus snorted. "Well, you assumed wrong. Occasionally, when it's the rainy season, we can obtain water, but not this time of year."

Tobias received the watering jar from the Roman and smiled. "Thank you, Centurion. May YaHoWaH bless you."

The Roman seemed as though he didn't know how to respond, nor how to comprehend Tobias' meaning. He shrugged, instead.

Toward the evening, as the men were nearing their goal, the time between stops grew shorter. Their last break exposed them to the direct sun. The centurion briefly closed his eyes to take a pause. In silence, the two men gathered their thoughts, resting. When Tobias looked at the Roman, he noticed a poisonous snake slithering over the boots of the centurion. The snake paused directly below the centurion's shadow.

Barely whispering, Tobias, called out. "Gnaeus! Don't move a muscle. A venomous snake is on your boot!"

Alarmed, the Roman began to shift his position so he could verify the information.

"Stop, sir!" cried out Tobias.

The snake stirred and slid up the boot, toward the soldier's knee. Gnaeus struggled to remain still as the snake inched up his leg.

Tobias slowly removed himself from his position and crept quietly behind the snake's head, extending his arm with slow movements.

"What are you doing, Shepherd?" asked the Roman, worried.

Tobias never moved his eyes, but stealthily crept closer to the snake. The snake hissed.

The Roman moved slightly, and the snake swung his head around and faced Gnaeus.

Seizing the moment, Tobias lunged forward and grasped the snake behind its head. With the snake in a tight grip, the viper wriggled around Tobias' arm and hissed.

Reaching for his sword, Gnaeus untangled the snake's tail from around Tobias' arm, stretching the snake's body in a straight line.

"What are you going to do, Centurion?" pleaded Tobias.

The Roman moved the blade just below Tobias' fist and cut the snake. Blood splattered both men. The head of the snake flexed its mouth open and fangs poised to strike.

"Whatever you do, don't let him go, Shepherd!" demanded the Roman.

Gnaeus tossed the still wriggling severed body of the snake to the ground. The two men watched the snake writhe aimlessly in the dust until it relaxed and stopped moving. The dusty ground caked with the snake's blood.

Gnaeus took the tip of his sword and tapped the snake's open mouth while Tobias still had a firm grip on it. It didn't move, but small droplets of poison hung on the ends of the sharp fangs.

"Release it. I think it is dead, Shepherd."

Tobias relaxed his grip and quickly cast the snake's head aside. The head fell to the dust near the severed body and didn't move, but the mouth closed partially.

After a lengthy silence, with both men staring at the snake, Gnaeus finally spoke. "Whew, by the name of Zeus, that was close. How did you know what to do?"

"I didn't really," was Tobias' bewildered answer.

"But you were so fast, like lightning." The Roman nervously laughed.

"YaHoWaH was watching over and protecting us," said Tobias.

"I don't know who this YaHoWaH person is, but thank you. You saved my life!" exclaimed the Roman.

"And you saved mine earlier, by sharing your water with me, Centurion."

The Roman slapped the shoulder of Tobias firmly, startling him. "Well done, Shepherd. What did you say your name was, again?"

Smiling, he responded, "Tobias, sir."

"Well then, thank you again, Tobias."

The experience invigorated the two men as they finished their journey. They arrived at the grotto where John was staying, just as the sun was beginning to set. John was not around.

When Tobias surveyed the camp, he saw it was meager. A shallow cave faced the sea and inside was a simple wooden table and bed mat. Various scrolls were curled on rock ledges. A crude handmade stone altar lay against the cave wall, and he spotted two deep impressions in the earth in the shape of a man's knees, just in front of the altar. The round indentations were near a ledge where the scrolls were stacked.

Near the cave opening was a campfire which contained warm coals. A barrel sat in the shade, and when Tobias looked inside, it was filled with collected rainwater. Gnaeus reached into the barrel to fill his ceramic jar.

"I wouldn't drink water from the barrel," said a voice behind the two men.

Tobias and the centurion turned around and saw a weathered old man, bent with age. His hair was grey, long and unkempt, as well as his beard. The rags hanging on his body were worn and threadbare with a piece of rope tied around his waist. His faced, darkened by the sun, radiated a sense of peace and his eyes twinkled in direct contrast to his otherwise miserable physical appearance. In his arms, he carried a bundle of driftwood, and three small fish were on a string hung around his neck.

"Excuse me?" asked Gnaeus.

The old man pointed at the drum. "This is collected rainwater and I nourish my garden with it. The water isn't safe to drink and will make you very sick."

"You have a garden?" asked Tobias in disbelief.

Moving slowly, the old man dropped the wood near the campfire. Despite his age, he was still spry and robust. He then hung the fish on polls near the flames. He methodically broke the twigs and arranged the gathered wood in the fire pit. Stirring, the coals, he kneeled on the ground, bent close to the coals, and began blowing. Within moments, the fire sprang to life, and hot flames flickered as they quickly consumed the new fuel. The old man stood. "Come."

He led them away from the cave and near a shadowed area. There he showed them his tiny garden. Various root vegetables and leeks were sadly clinging to life. The old man picked up a bucket and walked away. When he returned a few minutes later, he slowly dripped measured amounts of water on each plant and nourished them. He smiled. "Are you thirsty?"

"You have drinking water, Prisoner?" asked the centurion.

Again, without saying anything, the old man walked away motioning with his wrinkled hand, indicating they should follow him. The group walked down the hill toward the sea. Near the bottom, clustered in the rough rocks, the old man carefully lifted several stones from a group of boulders. When he revealed his treasure, both Tobias and Gnaeus peered over the old man's shoulder to get a closer look.

Grinning, the old man beamed with pride. "See!"

A small spring bubbled from a tiny pool with a ring of rocks surrounding the spring. The water collected in a small basin and spilled at the edge into a small trickle of fresh liquid. The old man extended his hand toward Gnaeus, asking in silence for his watering jar. The old man then carefully took the soldier's container and filled it with the spring water. He handed it back to the centurion.

Gnaeus lifted the jar to his lips and took a long drink. Smiling, he shook the jar at Tobias. "It's delicious."

Tobias handed his own jar to the old man who filled it as well. The men then walked back to the old man's camp. There the old man motioned for his guests to sit. Tobias sat upon a rock near the fire, but the centurion suddenly looked uncomfortable.

"If it's all the same, I'll be over there," he said, pointing toward a shady spot about twenty yards away.

Tobias and the old man watched the Roman walk away. Then Tobias asked, "What is motivating his aversion now?"

The old man frowned. "He is a Roman soldier and should maintain his position with regards to prisoners, like myself. I suspect he had a momentary lapse of judgment initially."

Tobias nodded while the old man tended to the fish as they were already browning on one side. He lowered himself to a rock and sat staring at Tobias.

"Are you called John, the witness to Y'shua?" Tobias asked.

John grinned and nodded. Then he frowned.

"You look familiar." John studied the face of Tobias. Then he suddenly smiled. "I know you, you are Nicodem—"

"I'm Tobias, your brother!" Tobias asserted, cutting off John's proclamation.

John frowned. "But you remind me of—Tobias, you say?"

Tobias looked around and saw the centurion was far away and reading something in his hands. His voice just above a whisper, Tobias leaned in close to John. "You are correct, I was once called Nicodemus, but my name is now Tobias, and I have come from Arimathea. Please use this new name while I am visiting."

John smiled. "But why all the mystery? What are you afraid of?"

Tobias looked around again and whispered. "The Nicodemus you knew is wanted by the Jewish authorities. I have been living in Arimathea as Tobias, and I tend to a small flock of believers."

"But didn't your friend, Joseph, live in Arimathea?" asked John.

Tobias' quickly turned reflective, and he grimaced. "He did, and I have spent years trying to locate you and fulfill a promise I made to Joseph on the day he died."

"I'm sorry." John reached out with his hand and touched Tobias' shoulder. "So, you have a group of believers?"

Tobias nodded.

"Are they filled with the Holy Spirit?" inquired John.

"We have seen many miracles and wonders! We even had a young man delivered from an awful demon," added Tobias.

The fish were now finished cooking, so John removed them from the fire with his bare fingers, and he offered one to Tobias. Looking up at the centurion, John shouted, "Roman, are you hungry?"

Gnaeus looked up. He stood and slowly walked back toward the camp.

John extended the fish toward him. "Please sit with us and eat."

Gnaeus accepted the offering but stood towering over the two older men. He mumbled, "Thank you."

Tobias looked up at the Roman. "I have bread if you'd like?"

Shaking his head, the centurion said, "No thanks. This will do." He then turned and walked back to his shady spot.

Tobias opened his first bundle and extracted a wafer of bread. Smiling, he handed it to John.

"If only we had some wine," bemused John. "Then we could celebrate our Y'shua's Supper."

"The water will work," assured Tobias.

They bowed their heads and quietly prayed. Then John blessed the meal. "Father in heaven, thank You for my guests and the meal we are about to partake. Bless these meager offerings and glorify Your name in everything we say and do."

Both men said, "Amen."

John then broke the bread. A parchment piece jutted from inside the loaf. Narrowing his eyes, he asked, "What do we have here?"

Carefully pulling the parchment piece free, John handed the bread to Tobias. He then studied the parchment. Slowly unfolding it, John held it near the fire and tried to read the words. Scowling, he handed it back to Tobias. "Can you read it? The light is fading."

Tobias took the parchment and read it out loud. "Our dear brother John. Many blessings from YaHoWaH, our Father in heaven for—"

"What is that?" asked Gnaeus.

Startled, both men jumped, realizing the centurion was now standing near them.

"We are reading from the Torah. Care to join us?" asked John, smiling.

Tobias was petrified and clutched the parchment tightly in his hand.

"No, thanks." Gnaeus then asked, "Do you have more fish? It was good."

Without hesitation, John handed his untouched fish to the centurion. "Yes, here, take mine."

Gnaeus stared at the offering from John for a while. "What will you eat, if I take yours?"

John smiled. "There are more fish in the sea. I am full."

Gnaeus shrugged. "You sure?"

John pushed the fish into the centurion's hands and smiled. "Yes, my son. May you be blessed by YaHoWaH as you eat."

Gnaeus looked down. "Thank you, Prisoner."

After Tobias and John watched the Roman walk away, Tobias realized he was still holding his breath and started breathing hard.

"You must relax Tobias. YaHoWaH is great. He is protecting us."

Tobias split his fish into two parts and handed half to John.

"Thank you, brother. Now, where were we?" John smiled.

Tobias took the parchment and started reading again. "Many blessings from YaHoWaH, our Father in heaven, and for your safety. We pray you are in good health and filled to overflowing with the Holy Spirit."

Startled at a sound nearby, both men glanced up and saw the Roman was standing alongside them again. Tobias froze.

"I've changed my mind. May I have a portion of your bread after all?" the soldier asked.

Tobias' eyes went wide with fright as the Roman bent over the open bundle to take hold of one of the loaves of bread.

John extended the half resting in his hand. He produced a disarming smile and said, "Please take this portion."

The Roman soldier briefly studied the bread before finally taking it from John. "Thank you." Again, the Roman walked away.

"We were nearly exposed," whispered Tobias.

John patted Tobias' knee. "Brother, you worry too much."

Tobias frowned and leaned forward. "You weren't living in Jerusalem when the Romans laid siege to the city. Thousands of innocent people lost their lives. Women and children were butchered, just for being an Israelite! Were it not for Joseph saving me, I might not be alive today."

John smiled broadly, the lines on his face joining, so his entire face formed a huge smile. "But you are alive and here to tell the story. YaHoWaH has been watching over you, protecting you, and I am happy for your visit today."

Tobias nodded slowly, but his eyes began to tear up. "My life is so different now." He hid his face and wept.

John respectfully waited in silence.

When Tobias looked up, his eyes were red. "Forgive my weakness. I never imagined how different my life would be from where I started . . . " His voice trailed off.

John touched Tobias' shoulder. "Believe me, Tobias, you are not alone. All of us, who chose to follow the Teacher, have witnessed dramatic changes."

Realizing his selfish attitude, Tobias quickly agreed, "You're correct, John. Again, I'm sorry."

John leaned forward and embraced Tobias tightly. Tobias could smell fish and body odors mixed with an earthy, salty fragrance. Tobias wrapped his arms around John's neck and hugged firmly.

"I love you, brother," whispered Tobias.

When the moment passed, John looked into Tobias' eyes. "Tell me about your travels, how you came to Arimathea, about the other witnesses."

Tobias gathered himself and weakly smiled. "Originally, I stayed in Jerusalem after Y'shua went up to heaven. I visited the gatherings of the many believers and heard the witness Peter speak with great wisdom. Many, many people joined the believers, but the Pharisees began attacking the meetings.

"Then a man from Tarsus, originally named Saul, arrested many of the believers. We started living in fear. When Saul met Y'shua on the road to Damascus, he was suddenly a changed man."

John became animated. "Yes, yes. I have spoken with Paul, and I believe he is a true convert of Y'shua."

"Paul is an educated man and has started many churches throughout Greece. Men by the name of Luke, Timothy, and Titus are his students, and they continue to spread the good news about Y'shua to the people. But then, the Romans began attacking the believers in Jerusalem. Joseph was continually trying to convince me to join him in Arimathea.

"I didn't want to leave Jerusalem and remained for a while, but when the Romans overthrew the city, the peaceful situation rapidly declined into utter chaos. When the Romans brought all the armies to bear on Jerusalem, the city fell to pieces. They destroyed our beautiful temple. The killings started, and bodies lay in the streets for days. It was awful. I witnessed thousands who were crucified on crosses, both inside and out of the city walls. They were left for weeks without anyone caring for their bodies. With fearful threats of death, the Romans forbade anyone from touching the corpses.

"By a miracle, Joseph came for me and ushered me from the city. He had many connections within the Roman government, and I believe he used every favor they owed him to spare my life. He spent a fortune in gold as bribes, but I'm alive because of him."

John smiled. "No, my brother, you're alive because Y'shua wanted you alive."

Tobias frowned. "Perhaps you're correct."

"Y'shua has always been watching over all of us and planning our steps. The Holy Spirit protects us," said John.

"But some of the believers have died, John. Stephen was stoned to death!"

John softly smiled. "Yes, and some of the original witnesses have perished, but it doesn't mean Y'shua has forgotten us. Remember, it is not my will, but the will of YaHoWaH."

Tobias looked down and stared at his folded hands. Contemplating his life's journey thus far, Tobias could see where YaHoWaH had spared his life, time after time, and guided his steps. Even his trip to Patmos had been covered by YaHoWaH's protection. He suddenly felt weary and tired. Tobias gathered the bread wafers together and tied the bundle. He then handed the wrapped bread to John.

"Thank you, Tobias. I will take my time and read the notes the others have written to me."

Darkness was shading the sky and stars began appearing. Tobias looked up and remembered the nights sailing to the island Patmos.

"Let's gather some more wood for the fire before we make ready for sleeping. We need the fire to last through the night," said John as he stood.

In silence, Tobias followed John as they walked down the hill to the edge of the sea. In the moonlit sky, Tobias could see the sandy beach. The two old men gathered driftwood strewn along the beach. When their arms were full, they shuffled back to the camp.

As they approached the cave, Gnaeus was crouching by the fire, trying to warm himself. He stood when he saw the two older men loaded with wood.

"Why didn't you call me, I could have helped you?" He seemed disappointed that he was excluded.

John started stacking the wood near the fire but stopped to point. "Follow the path down the hill. At the bottom, near the spring we visited, you will see the beach. Gather some driftwood. Your help will be appreciated."

Immediately, the Roman soldier marched off. Tobias and John finished stacking the wood they brought and sat upon the rocks around the fire. John stoked the coals and added more wood. In no time, the flames grew hotter. The two men sat in silence watching small yellow fingers dancing above the pit.

Tobias opened his other satchel. "I have ink and parchment for your writing."

John's eyes gleamed. He held the gift to his chest like a small child.

Then Tobias took the small cloth bundle and held it out.

"What is this?" John asked.

Tobias smiled. "Open it."

John pulled on the string and removed the outer cloth. A neatly folded white blanket with dark blue bands lay in his hands. John began to cry. He opened the white cloth and draped it over his head with the blue bands on the ends along with knotted tassels. "Bless you, Tobias, a prayer tallit." John folded it and set it aside.

Moments later, they heard the Roman walking back. Looking up they saw the soldier with a large bundle of wood in his arms, many times greater than what Tobias and John had brought together. Gnaeus proudly dumped the sticks in a pile and began warming by the fire.

John smiled. "Thank you, Centurion."

The Roman puffed up his chest. "Is this enough to last the night, or shall I gather more?"

John chuckled. "We have enough for several nights. Thank you again."

With pride, the Roman soldier plopped himself onto a rock and smiled. "Excellent."

CHAPTER FIVE

MY BROTHER'S KEEPER

BETWEEN IDLE CHATTER AND LONG periods of silence, the three men sat watching the fire and occasionally gazing up into the night sky. Thousands of stars dotted the clear heavens above. Looking around, Tobias started wondering about where to sleep. He was weary and tired and noticed the others yawning as well.

John retrieved his mat from the cave and brought it near the fire. "I'm afraid I don't have better accommodations," he said as he spread it out for Tobias.

The Roman stood up and stretched. "I'll be fine." He started to walk away.

John stopped him, "Sir, you may sleep near the fire. I believe there is enough room for all of us."

"I wouldn't want to impose, Prisoner," the Roman said.

"Centurion, his name is John," Tobias demanded.

"Fine, John, thank you," Gnaeus said with a slight irritation in his response.

John smiled. "You're a Roman soldier, and I am the prisoner." John extended his hand. "My name is John, and it would be my pleasure to have you stay warm by the fire."

The Roman hesitated at first and then shook John's hand. "Gnaeus, my name is Gnaeus. Thank you for your offer."

John pointed toward Tobias. "And have you met my brother, Tobias?"

The Roman laughed and shook his head. "Yes, I've met Tobias. He doesn't look like he is related to you, though."

Tobias laughed. "None the less, we are brothers."

Gnaeus shook his head again. "So you say."

Encircling the fire pit, the three men arranged themselves and curled up to sleep. In a manner of a few minutes, the Roman was loudly snoring.

John and Tobias looked at one another and burst into laughter.

Jerking awake, the centurion sat up. "What? Why are you laughing?"

John smiled. "You remind me of my dear friend, Peter. He snored loud enough to wake a city."

"Was I snoring? Impossible, I just closed my eyes," protested Gnaeus.

Tobias and John roared with laughter.

The centurion rolled with his back to the fire and curled into a tight ball. "Humph!" he groaned and let out a big sigh. He started snoring again, but not as loud.

Tobias made himself comfortable lying on his back. He pulled his outer cloak in tight. Against the dropping nighttime temperature, the heat of the fire was comforting. He stared at the stars and saw familiar patterns allowing him to orient himself. His eyes drifted east and he recalled many days past when he departed from Joppa. He silently prayed the journey back would be uneventful.

John added more firewood and walked into the cave. Tobias watched John kneel on the ground where he had seen the depressions in the earth. John bent over, folded his hands, and slowly rocked. His lips moved but Tobias heard no sounds.

Tobias closed his eyes and began silently praying. He thanked YaHoWaH for his protection and safe passage. His praises included thanksgiving for the earth, heavens, and the Holy Spirit. As he continued to pray, his thoughts encircled the many friends and believers back in Arimathea. After about a half hour, Tobias then started praying for John. He thanked YaHoWaH for allowing John to live a long life and asked if YaHoWaH could find a way for John to be set free from the island of Patmos. Weariness finally consumed Tobias, and while still praying, he drifted off to sleep.

In the middle of the night, Tobias awakened and saw the fire was quite small. He felt cold and damp. Reaching for the driftwood, Tobias added it to the fire, and after many minutes passed, the wood began burning. Looking around for John, he saw the man was still kneeling and praying in his small cave. The new tallit was draped over John's head. Tobias smiled.

Tobias watched his friend pray for a long while, but then John stopped and slowly stood. It was clear his body was achy and stiff. He set the tallit aside and hobbled near the fire and warmed himself. John looked at the Roman centurion lightly snoring.

John smiled at Tobias. "He sleeps as if nothing mattered."

Tobias sat up. "I'm afraid I don't sleep as much, now that I'm older."

John smiled and nodded. "It gives me more time to pray."

"Have you slept yet, John?" asked Tobias.

"I drift off to sleep while praying many times, but since I'm kneeling before YaHoWaH when I awaken, I simply continue to pray." John rubbed his sore knees and then added more wood to the fire. "How long are you staying, Nicodemus—I mean, Tobias?"

Tobias glanced quickly at the soldier and saw he was fast asleep. "The Romans granted me only one day to visit. The one in charge, Lieutenant Severinus, sternly warned the centurion to make sure we were back in two days or he would crucify us both."

John chuckled. "The lieutenant is young, pompous, and acts as if he were the emperor himself."

Tobias nodded. "Still, I don't think we should test patience. Besides, Gnaeus seems like the no-nonsense type and overly obedient."

John slowly nodded in agreement. "They are all very much alike. It is part of their character, especially the ones who work on this island of prisoners."

"I haven't seen any other prisoners except you. Where are the others?" asked Tobias.

John pointed over his cave. "On the other side of the island. Perhaps three or four groups are living separately, depending on their crimes. I was living with the worst prisoners for a while, but then they moved me here by myself. I think the lieutenant wanted them to kill me, but I kept preaching about YaHoWaH and Y'shua. Many became believers, which is why they moved me here."

"How long have you been in this place, John?"

John frowned, trying to recall the time. "They send a detachment here once a year to make sure I'm alive. They don't ever stop or visit, but simply stand on the rise overlooking my camp and watch me for a few hours. Then they leave without any communication. I believe they have come here five times."

Shocked, Tobias asked, "You've not spoken to another human in over five years?"

John shook his head. "No, but I didn't think I missed people until you came here to visit. I had forgotten how much I enjoyed visiting with a friend."

Tobias was amazed. Any complaint he could ever imagine, paled by comparison. "How do you survive?"

John beamed with a big smile and leaned in close to Tobias. Nearly whispering, John said, "I do have angels visiting me."

Tobias blinked a couple of times, absorbing what John just shared. "Truly?"

Suddenly, John appeared much younger, as he started animatedly explaining, "Y'shua visits me and has me writing down many revelations for the believers. I have lots of pages written."

"In the morning, can you show me?" inquired Tobias.

John whispered, "I need you to carry them out for me and share them with the believers scattered all over."

Tobias became frightened. "What if I get caught? I took a huge risk bringing the notes hidden in the bread. How will I transport them out without someone noticing?"

John smiled. "Tomorrow, I'll show you what I have prepared for you. For now, rest easy. We will sleep until daybreak."

Worried, Tobias was too frightened to sleep. He watched John curl into a ball near the fire. John closed his eyes and drifted off to sleep. Tobias silently fretted. He prayed to YaHoWaH asking for protection and the grace to permit him to carry John's papers off the island in safety. Tobias then tried to sleep, but his mind raced with thousands of thoughts.

No matter how hard he tried, Tobias could not figure out a way to successfully transport John's writings. He exhausted every scenario, frustrated that each attempt in his mind ended in his arrest. He finally muttered aloud, "YaHoWaH, help me find a way!"

The centurion stirred and rolled over, and Tobias held his breath. When the Roman soldier started snoring again, Tobias relaxed. He added more firewood to the fire and curled into a ball near the heat. After an eternity passed, Tobias finally fell asleep.

When the sun crested the rise behind John's camp, the first waves penetrated the low savannah shrubs with white-hot points of light shining into the damp campsite. A single beam landed on Tobias' cheek, and he jerked awake, panting. The Roman soldier was gone, but John was asleep and still in the same position. Tobias added more wood to the fire while searching around for the centurion. He spotted the soldier a distance away, his back to the two men. Tobias stood and walked in the opposite direction to attend to needs.

Both Tobias and the Roman hurried back to the fire and warmed themselves. The centurion quickly rubbed his palms together.

"It's cold and wet here. Did you sleep well?" the soldier asked.

Still nervous from the discussions with John, Tobias just nodded in response.

"We should get an early start back," commanded the Roman.

"I'd like to say goodbye to my brother before we leave," pleaded Tobias, trying to barter for more time.

Annoyed, the centurion scowled. "If we wait too long, the sun will be high in the sky, and it will be sweltering. It is a long walk back, and I don't need Lieutenant Severinus sending more soldiers out to search for us. I assure you, he will not be pleased, and he will follow through on his threats."

Tobias nervously searched the camp, trying to find a way to delay the soldier. In a huff, Gnaeus stormed off while muttering, "Wake him up, and say your goodbyes! We leave within the hour. Right now, I'm going to fill my watering jar."

Tobias watched the soldier gather his belongings and march toward the spring. After the soldier was gone, Tobias rushed at John and awakened the man. He shook John's shoulder.

"John, John, wake up. The centurion says we must go back this instant!"

Slowly lifting his frail body from the ground, John frowned. "I thought you were here for two days?"

Tobias was worried and spoke excitedly. "We journeyed a half a day to get here. One day to visit, and another half a day to walk back. The centurion is worried about Lieutenant Severinus."

John grabbed Tobias by the arm. "Come quick, we must get your things together." John pulled Tobias into the cave. John showed Tobias his scrolls stacked on the ledge above his place of prayer. "All of these are copies, but the originals are inside your watering jar." John picked it up and handed it to Tobias.

The jar was heavy as if it was full of water. Tobias shook the container and could hear something inside. He gave John a puzzled look.

"I tightly rolled the scrolls and stuffed them into the clay jar for safe keeping. While you and the Roman slept, I placed the revelations Y'shua has given me about the future inside. The entire manuscript is hidden in your jar. You must make the soldier think you are drinking from your jar during your journey back, so he doesn't suspect anything. I also have other writings inside, but there are no copies. These are my originals. When you get back to Arimathea, share copies, but you must guard the originals for safe keeping."

Stunned, Tobias tried to absorb everything John was telling him. "How did you have time to get them into the jar? What if someone opens the jar? What if the Romans want to inspect the jar?" He was sweating even though it was still cold.

John placed his hands on Tobias' shoulders. John looked into his eyes carefully. "Listen, my brother, you are a messenger of YaHoWaH and protected by the blood of Y'shua. You are filled with the power of the Holy Spirit. Just remember, if YaHoWaH is for me, who could possibly stand against me?"

Tobias nervously nodded. "Yes, yes, yes. I am YaHoWaH's messenger. I must have faith He will lead and protect me."

John shook him. "Look at me."

Tobias stared at John.

"You are not here by chance. Y'shua told me you were coming and had me make copies. Your journey has been predestined by Y'shua, and He will watch over you. In my younger life, I have eaten with Y'shua, heard Him speak, laid my head on His chest and heard His heartbeat. He is real, and you were there when He ascended into heaven. Have faith, my friend. He is a lamp unto your feet and a light unto your path. Go in peace, my brother."

John pulled Tobias into a tight hug, kissed him on the cheek, and whispered into his ear, "I love you my brother. Shalom."

Tobias wept and kissed John's cheek. "Shalom, my friend. Until we meet again." Although Tobias knew the chance was remote.

"Are you two women finished?" Gnaeus stood at the cave opening, feet apart, one hand resting on his sword hilt. He was grinning.

John walked over to the centurion and grabbed his hand and held it with his two hands. John smiled up at the soldier. "Thank you for bringing my brother to visit me. Go in peace, Gnaeus. May you one day seek Y'shua and find He loves you very much."

The Roman withdrew his hand quickly. "You're a crazy old man, Prisoner."

John bowed. "Thank you, Centurion. May your journey be pleasant and swift."

"Now on this account, I can agree. I don't need Lieutenant Severinus doubting my loyalty. Come, Tobias, we must start."

"Wait, you must fill your watering jars first," John said with concern.

The centurion was miffed. "I have already done so. Go quickly, Shepherd. I haven't all day."

Tobias was dumbfounded, while John pulled him down the path and walked to the spring.

Tobias hoarsely whispered, "We can't fill my watering jar, John, it will destroy your writings!"

John ignored Tobias and quickly marched toward the spring. When they arrived, John told Tobias, "Bend down and drink as much water as you can hold. It will be your last time to get water until you reach your destination. Do it quick, before the Roman comes here!"

Tobias bent over and drank vast gulps of water. When he tried to get up, John pushed him back down. "Drink some more!"

Tobias gulped more water until his belly was full.

"Get up, quick, I see the soldier coming."

Tobias got up and wiped his mouth with the back of his hand.

"There you go, my brother," said John while talking loudly. He handed the watering jar to Tobias but not before wetting the outside from the spring. "Come, we must get you on your long journey."

As they walked up the path, they met the Roman soldier. John and Tobias walked past the centurion. John then hugged Tobias one more time.

John whispered into his ear. "Shalom Nicodemus, peace to you both."

"Move along." Gnaeus lightly shoved Tobias down the path.

The sun hung partly above the horizon, and the temperature was changing just as fast. The Roman squinted at the sun. "It will be mid-day soon enough. I want to be back so I can get a bath and a good meal. We won't be stopping much."

His statement was more of a command and not a request. Tobias made a note of the centurion's shift in demeanor, making sure he would not provoke the soldier. He clutched the clay watering jar tightly.

CHAPTER SIX
A HORRIBLE DILEMMA

AS PLANNED BEFORE HE STARTED walking back with the soldier, Tobias would lift his watering jar to his lips whenever the Roman stopped for a drink. The midday sun was hot, and each time Tobias performed the maneuver, he worried he was being watched.

Tobias' mouth felt like cotton and his tongue stuck to the roof of his mouth. No matter how hard he tried, he could not stop thinking about the cool liquid of John's spring. *I wish I could have drunk more.*

"Are you all right?" asked the Roman. He was standing near Tobias and inspecting his face.

Tobias lied, "I'm fine, why?"

"You're sweating a lot and red in the face. Don't go and get sun sickness on me, because I'll let you die out here and tell Lieutenant Severinus I could not drag your old body back."

Tobias tried to smile. "I'm fine. Perhaps we could rest a moment. I'm not a young man."

The soldier narrowed his eyes. "Take a minute to catch your breath."

There was no shade anywhere, so Tobias knelt on the dirt and bent over with his back to the sun. He quietly prayed. After several minutes passed, he felt better. Tobias slowly stood, and the Roman reached out to help him to his feet.

"Thank you, kind sir," Tobias mumbled.

The Roman studied Tobias' face.

"I'm fine. Let's go," said Tobias as he brushed past the centurion.

The Roman shrugged.

Pushing his body beyond his limits, Tobias continuously prayed for strength to make the journey and for the safety of John's writings. He followed the soldier's lead and lifted the watering jar to his lips, pretending to take a drink. He felt slightly nauseated but pushed on.

The two men came to the location where they earlier encountered the snake. They stopped briefly to stare at the ground. The soil was still red but covered in a light film of dust. The snake body was gone; probably eaten by birds or another animal. In the harsh environment of this island, survival depended on basic instincts.

After several hours of walking, Tobias was beginning to drag his feet and stagger. They came upon the lone tree where they had stopped on the journey to visit John. Tobias crashed to the ground beneath the tree, gasping.

Gnaeus carefully studied Tobias and touched his forehead which was hot and dry. "You should be sweating. What's wrong with you? You look sick."

Tobias tried to smile, but his lips were cracked and flaky.

Tipping his jar to his lips, the centurion took a sip of water while watching Tobias out of the corner of his eye. Tobias repeated the same motion, even though he knew there was no water. He felt very sick and wondered how he was going to make it back.

Jumping to his feet, the centurion snatched the jar from Tobias. "What is going on here?"

Tobias hoarsely protested. "Give it back!"

"Did you drink all your water, you stupid old man?" The Roman turned the jar upside down and shook it. Something ratted inside the clay jar.

"What is this?" The centurion' suspicions heightened as he peered into the narrow opening but could see nothing. He inverted the jar and shook it even harder, but nothing came out. The soldier grabbed his own container and started to pour some of his water into Tobias' jar.

Tobias jumped to his feet and stopped the Roman. "No!" He screamed as he pulled on the clay jar.

"What is wrong with you? You're dying of thirst!" The soldier frowned, and then he got angry. "What's going on here? What's inside your jar?" He shook the jar in Tobias' face. "What is inside here? Tell me now, or you die right here!" The soldier rested his other hand on his sword handle.

Tobias slumped down against the tree.

Pushing the jar to Tobias' face, the soldier demanded, "What is so precious in here, you're willing to die for it?"

Tobias's eyes were red. "Something you would never understand."

The centurion yelled, "Tell me!"

Tobias buried his face in his hands. He asked YaHoWaH for a miracle because Tobias didn't want to lose John's writings. If he confessed, the soldier would probably kill him.

Taking Tobias' face into his large and callous hands, the soldier lifted it to look at him directly. "You had better start explaining before I lose my patience with you."

Tobias opened his mouth, but because his mouth was so dry, all he could do was hoarsely whisper.

"I've been watching you, old man. You take a drink only when I do, and you watch me. I've never seen you wipe your mouth or your lips wet. Plus, you tip the jar up too high," the Roman mocked Tobias by performing the same motion. "Like this. If you did it every time, your face would be flooded. I suspect there was never any water. Was there?" His voice was stern and demanding.

"No," Tobias mumbled.

"Are you completely out of your mind? This island will kill you. You cannot travel without water," the Roman said chastising Tobias.

"I . . . I . . . I ah . . . thought—" stammered Tobias.

The Roman stood and threw the jar at Tobias who deftly caught the clay jar and pulled it close to his chest.

"I should let you die right here." Walking a few feet away, the centurion shook his head. He walked back and pointed an angry finger at Tobias. "Your stupidity will get us both killed. What do you think Lieutenant Severinus will do when I arrive back without you?" He waited for this information to sink in. "I don't want to imagine it." He threw his hands in the air. "Why?"

The two men stared at each other in silence.

Exasperated, the Roman took his clay jar and opened it. He walked over to Tobias. "Open your stupid mouth, old man."

Tobias feared death was close, so he complied.

The soldier trickled water into Tobias' open dry mouth.

"Don't swallow, do you hear me?" demanded the soldier. "Now close your mouth and try to keep the water inside."

Tobias nodded.

The Roman kneeled close to Tobias and pressed his face very near. "Now, let the water seep ever so slowly down your throat, a tiny bit at a time. Feel the liquid wet every part of your throat. If you feel like throwing up, fight it."

Tobias let the wet liquid soak into every dry crevice. He fought the urge to vomit and slowly let the water trickle down his throat. When it was finally swallowed, he opened his mouth and gasped for air.

"Again!" demanded the Roman soldier as he trickled another measured amount into Tobias' eager and awaiting mouth. After he finished, the soldier sat down and watched Tobias. "You know what? I don't want to know what's inside your stupid clay jar, because if I do, then I'm involved in your foolish plan. This way, if you get caught, I can claim innocence, which will be the truth!"

Swallowing hard, Tobias said, "I am truly sorry."

Holding his hands up in the air, the Roman stopped Tobias. "Don't say another word." The soldier let his face drop and slowly shook his head. "Why? What did I do to deserve this?"

"Thank you, kind sir, for sharing your water," mumbled Tobias.

After a lengthy pause, the Roman stood to his feet. "How do you feel now?"

"Better, actually. Thank you again," said Tobias.

The centurion gave out a heavy sigh. "Get up."

Tobias struggled to get up from the ground, so the Roman grabbed Tobias' arm and helped him to his feet.

"Can you walk?" asked the soldier.

Without responding, Tobias slowly started down the trail. He could see their destination very far away. He was grateful the path was mostly downhill from this point forward. The sun was now moving to the west and was less intense.

Several times, the centurion stopped their progress. He would re-fill Tobias' mouth, trickling the water as before. "Now don't swallow. Just let it seep into your mouth slowly."

After this procedure had been repeated several times, Tobias started sweating again. His headache was less severe, and he felt better.

"You're sweating again. It is a good sign," said the soldier. He looked around. "We should be back before the sun sets. Do you think you can make it?"

Tobias nodded.

"Good. Let's keep walking," said Gnaeus.

With each passing hour, the air became cooler. A slight breeze came off the ocean and dropped the temperature further, bringing salty moisture with it. Tobias felt relieved and thanked YaHoWaH for the miracles of this day.

The two weary travelers arrived at the well near the port town. Both men hungrily drank the water, splashing it on their faces and clothes.

"Centurion! Lieutenant Severinus wants to see you immediately."

When Gnaeus turned, his captain stood inches away. He snapped to attention. "Yes, sir." He grabbed Tobias by his cloak and pulled. "Come."

When they arrived at the small white building, they found Lieutenant Severinus, as before, sipping wine and sitting behind his desk. Several other Roman officers milled about. Lieutenant Severinus stood, and Gnaeus snapped to attention.

The lieutenant studied the two men carefully. "Tell me, Centurion, how did you find the Christian, John?"

Gnaeus kept his chin held high. "He was remarkably well, sir, and still living in the grotto as before."

"And what did he and our shepherd guest talk about?" asked Lieutenant Severinus.

The centurion hesitated. "Sir, they discussed family matters. The prisoner, John, also prepared our dinner."

Lieutenant Severinus moved his face very close to Gnaeus. "Please, do tell me—elaborate soldier."

"Well, it was some fish John caught and the bread the shepherd carried."

The lieutenant quickly replied, "Not that Jewish flatbread? Did you really eat it?"

"After a long walk, we were hungry. It wasn't bad."

"I see," countered the lieutenant. He turned to Tobias. "Tell me, Shepherd, did you enjoy our little island of paradise?"

Tobias took his time to respond. "I am thankful you allowed me to see my brother, sir."

"And what have you brought back with you, Shepherd?" asked Lieutenant Severinus.

Tobias froze, staring at the lieutenant. His fingers tightened around the clay watering jar in his hands. "Excuse me, sir," he said nervously.

Gnaeus glanced at Tobias out of the corner of his eye.

Lieutenant Severinus smiled. "What did you learn, Shepherd."

Tobias' heart started beating again, and he relaxed a little. "This is a formidable island, sir, dangerous and frightening. I'm hoping one day John may be able to come home."

Laughter erupted in the room among the other officers. Lieutenant Severinus chuckled. "He should be dead."

Tobias didn't know how to respond.

Looking severe, the lieutenant pressed into Tobias' face. "Tomorrow, a merchant ship departs for Joppa. I want you off my island and on that ship. Do you understand me?"

Tobias nodded. "Yes, sir."

"This is not a request, Shepherd; I want you on the ship as they are leaving at sun up. Do not miss this boat or you'll find yourself a permanent guest; perhaps out there with your brother."

The officers in the room started chuckling again. Tobias nervously looked around at their faces and saw every man was staring at him.

Pulling his hand across his grey beard, Tobias replied, "I give you my assurance, Lieutenant Severinus, I will be on the boat first thing in the morning."

Lieutenant Severinus turned to Gnaeus. "And to make sure he does, this centurion will stay with you until you leave tomorrow. Isn't this correct, Centurion?"

Gnaeus snapped to attention and saluted, "Certe, sir."

"Now, get out of my sight, both of you. You stink!" The lieutenant dismissed them with a downturned hand flip.

Both men scrambled out the door. Once outside, the sky was getting dark. Gnaeus grabbed Tobias and roughly shoved him towards the boat docks. "Let's go, Shepherd. I guess I'm not getting my bath or a drink tonight."

As they walked, Tobias could hear the centurion grumble under his breath. Tobias stopped walking.

The soldier took several steps before he realized Tobias had stopped. He turned around. "What now?"

"May I buy you dinner and wine?" asked Tobias.

This caught the soldier off guard. "You have money?"

"Do you know of any good places?" inquired Tobias.

Gnaeus grinned. "You're paying, right?"

"It's the least I can do for you for saving my life today," responded Tobias.

"Well, as a matter of fact, I'm starving, and I know a place that serves great food," said Gnaeus with a small amount of frustration still in his voice.

Tobias held out his hand and smiled. "Please lead the way, sir."

The noisy small establishment was crowded with soldiers who happily greeted Gnaeus as he moved to an open table. When the soldiers spotted Tobias, the other Romans scowled. Tobias nervously watched them, watching him.

"Don't worry about them. They don't see much of your kind in here." Gnaeus laughed.

Tobias frowned. "Israelites?"

Gnaeus chuckled. "Or shepherds."

"They look as if they wish me harm," grumbled Tobias.

The Roman laughed. "They always look like that. Still, I suggest you don't spend too much time staring. They don't need much of an excuse to be angry, especially when they drink."

Tobias looked down.

Gnaeus pushed an empty cup toward Tobias and filled it with wine. "Here, drink."

With a half-smile, Tobias lifted the glass and let the liquid touch his lips, then set it back down.

"You don't drink, do you?" asked the centurion.

"I once studied to be a Pharisee, and I took an oath to avoid strong drink and certain foods."

Gnaeus studied Tobias for a moment. "Admirable, but crazy, Shepherd. The world is intolerable without wine."

Smiling, Tobias replied, "So you say, but men act crazy when they drink too much wine."

Gnaeus slapped Tobias' shoulder and laughed. "Well then, we mustn't drink too much."

Their food arrived, and the two men said nothing further as they ate. The Roman soldier drank vast amounts of wine throughout the meal, which consisted of various seafood delicacies including fresh lobster, fish, crab, and octopus. Tobias ordered water and quietly watched Gnaeus. He mistrusted the soldier and held up a piece from his dish. Tobias asked, "What is this?"

The centurion narrowed his eyes and studied the item. "I'm not sure, but it tastes great!"

Tobias looked at the round, cup-shaped and somewhat chewy item. "I don't think it tastes great."

In shock, Tobias watched Gnaeus snatch the item from his fingers and plop it into his open mouth. "Too bad, because I do!"

When they finished the food, the soldier ordered another bottle of wine to take with him. After Tobias paid for their meal, they walked back to the boat pier. It was dark with almost no activity around the docks, except sentry guards. As they approached the boats, they were stopped.

"Halt. What business have you, centurion?" asked one of the guards.

Gnaeus brushed the soldier aside. "He's with me. Step aside."

The sentry drew his sword.

Instantly, Gnaeus slapped the sentry across his face. "Put that thing away before I hurt you."

Stunned, the sentry pointed the sword at the face of Gnaeus. "Sir, you're drunk, and I will report you to the captain!"

Taking his hand, Gnaeus brushed the sword aside. "Go ahead, I'm here on orders by Lieutenant Severinus." Gnaeus was staggering a bit, so he grabbed at Tobias to steady himself. "This shepherd is to be on a boat for Joppa at dawn." His speech was starting to slur.

Still angry, the sentry stepped back and pointed. "The boat with two sails, on the end of the last pier, is the one you want. And you're still drunk, and I will report you to the captain."

Gnaeus pressed his face into the sentry's. "Go ahead, and when you get assigned to my detachment, I will make sure you regret your mistake."

For a short time, the two Romans let brawn control the situation, while they just stared at one another without flinching. Suddenly, Gnaeus slapped the sentry's shoulder, and he pushed the wine bottle toward the sentry. "Here, have a drink."

The sentry pushed the bottle aside and mumbled. "Foolish drunk!" as he walked away.

The centurion grabbed Tobias and plunged toward the last pier. Tobias steadied the Roman as they walked to the specific location. Looking around, they saw no one near the boat. Gnaeus placed one foot on the edge of the ship to look inside.

Instantly, a large, bald-headed man appeared, wearing a menacing look on his face. "What do you want?"

Caught off guard, the centurion stumbled backward and almost fell off the pier into the dark water. Tobias grabbed the soldier and held him in place. Gnaeus gave the bald-headed man a crooked smile.

"Good evening, my man, I am Centurion Gnaeus of the one-hundred-twelfth detachment, and under the service of Lieutenant Severinus, commander of this island."

Tobias was shocked that the centurion could remember the details with such accuracy while being intoxicated.

"And so?" replied the giant man on the boat.

Tobias took over the communications. "I am to travel back to Joppa, first thing tomorrow. Is this the correct boat?"

The giant nodded but stared warily at the centurion.

With his stupid grin, Gnaeus looked at Tobias then the giant and pointed at Tobias. "He speaks the truth."

The giant never moved. "Come back first light. No one boards until then."

Gnaeus snapped to attention. "Ita vero, Captain."

The giant never moved but shook his head in disgust.

"Thank you, sir. We will return in the morning," said Tobias as he steered the centurion back to the sentry post.

When they neared the end of their dock, where another long walkway connected all the individual boat slips together, Gnaeus stopped. He plopped himself on a large crate and patted the place alongside him.

"Right here, Shepherd. We will rest here 'til first light."

Tobias watched the soldier sway back and forth as he commanded their next steps. The centurion slowly rolled to his side and curled into a ball. The bottle of wine was tightly clutched in his hand.

He mumbled, "We will stay here until dawn." Seconds later, he was snoring.

Tobias smiled and slumped alongside the crate. He reached out and extracted the bottle of wine from the centurion's hands. Tobias corked the bottle and made himself comfortable. The water slapped alongside the various boats docked at the piers. Rigging jingled in the darkness as the ships swayed in rhythm with the small waves. Tobias could hear the water wash upon the sand nearby, lulling him to sleep.

While he slept, Tobias dreamed that an angel visited him and gave him instructions.

"Tobias, do not be afraid. You must carry the message of John to the people. Guard the words written and let no one see them until you have reached Arimathea."

"But it is many days of travel, and I must go by sea. How will I know I am safe?" Tobias argued.

The angel smiled. "Because Adonai has guided your steps and has great plans for you. Your journey will be smooth and quick. Remember to guard the writings in your hands," instructed the angel. "Now awaken Tobias, it is time to depart!"

When Tobias opened his eyes, the sun was beginning to rise, and the sky was shifting from blackness to a faint grey-blue. Still clutching the clay-watering jar in his hands, Tobias stood and saw the boat was preparing to set sail. He dashed toward the ship.

"Wait!"

Again, the giant man appeared. "Where is your soldier?"

Tobias pointed. "He sleeps."

The bald man grinned. "I'm certain."

A shorter, thin man came alongside the giant. He had thinning curly dark hair and a spotty beard. When he spoke, Tobias could smell rotting odors from the man who was missing half his teeth. He spoke a foreign language while talking with the giant, bald man.

He looked at Tobias warily and spoke with a heavy accent. "You have papers?"

Tobias nervously looked toward the slumbering centurion. "He is my escort," said Tobias.

"Bring here!" demanded the short man.

Tobias ran back to the centurion and began attempting to wake him. "Centurion, Gnaeus! Wake up! It's time for me to leave."

Slowly rising, the Roman soldier stretched and opened one eye. "What?"

"It's time for the boat to leave. I need you, now!" urged Tobias.

"All right, all right, I'm coming." The Roman centurion stood but was unsteady at first. Leaning forward, Gnaeus stumbled toward the boat. Looking at the giant man, he started to address the man with his formal introduction, but the bald man held up his hands.

"Not me. Tell the captain," he said looking at the short man standing next to him.

Gnaeus narrowed his eyes and studied the ugly man. "You're the captain?" He grinned.

Again, the short captain demanded, "You have papers?"

"I am Centurion Gnaeus of the one-hundred-twelfth detachment, and under the service of Lieutenant Severinus, commander of this island. Per his instructions, this shepherd is to be on your boat for Joppa."

The two men on the boat argued in their foreign language for a while. Then the captain threw up his hands and walked away. The giant explained.

"The captain says you need papers. How do we know if he is a prisoner or a free man?"

Gnaeus gained renewed strength and pressed into the giant man, "Now you listen here. I am a centurion, and I have strict orders to have this shepherd on your boat to Joppa. How about I seize your boat and cargo and have the lieutenant come down here and explain it to you personally? He might just even make you join the prisoners, as his guests."

The bald giant looked at the captain.

Motioning with his hand, the thin captain indicated Tobias could come aboard. "You stay up there." He pointed at the bow of the boat. "Be quiet and no trouble. You work when told."

Tobias nodded in agreement.

The captain quickly walked back to Tobias. "Twenty drachmae!" He held out his hand.

"But the journey to the island was only ten!" countered Tobias.

"No papers, I charge twenty!" the captain demanded. His hand was still extended.

Tobias retrieved three gold shekels. "This is all I have."

The captain deftly snatched them from Tobias' hand. Taking one, he bit into the side of the gold coin and saw teeth marks in the soft metal. He smiled displaying a mouth missing every other tooth. "You come!"

Tobias turned and shook the centurion's hand. "Thank you, kind sir. May YaHoWaH bless you."

Gnaeus smiled. "Thanks for dinner, Shepherd." He changed his expression to a serious tone. "Don't ever come back here!"

Tobias wasn't sure if the Roman was serious or not. "Yes, sir."

The Roman soldier spun on his heels and marched off the pier, never once looking back. He stopped briefly by the crate he slept upon, and drained the last contents of the wine bottle, before walking away.

As soon as the boat was untied from the pier, several men began unfolding the two sails. The wind snapped at the substantial fabric, and the men pulled on several ropes, lashing them to the sides. The craft lurched forward and rapidly moved out to sea.

Tobias crawled toward the front of the boat and tried to get into a comfortable position. After sitting down, he surveyed the ship and the various men working. Tobias counted eight men, including the captain. When he looked back at the shore, he was surprised to see the island quickly disappearing.

CHAPTER SEVEN

REVELATIONS

SOON THE BOAT AND TOBIAS escaped the inlet of Patmos. The wind increased, and rapidly the ship was skimming across the water. With the wind to their backs, the two sails swiftly carried them eastward.

The skies were clear, and the sun was hot, but the wind dissipated the effects quickly. Within six hours, the boat was clear of any small islands and heading into open seas. Nervously looking around, Tobias quietly prayed for a safe journey.

When the sun began to set, the winds didn't abate. Tobias overheard the sailors discussing the situation and wondered if they were in for a storm again. When the giant man walked past, Tobias inquired. "Is everything all right?"

The sizable bald man smiled. "Of course. Why do you ask?"

"The other men were talking about the wind. Is it a problem?" asked Tobias.

The giant frowned. "No, not at all. We don't normally get such a steady wind like this. Most times, it slows down when the sun goes down, but not tonight. It will be smooth sailing, and we will cross more distance with this wind. I just hope this holds for the night."

Tobias remembered what the angel in his dream said, and he quietly thanked YaHoWaH for the blessings of the wind. He looked down at the clay jar in his hands and wondered what was inside. The temptation to open it and find out was a strong urge. Tobias took a cord and lashed the clay jar to his body for safe keeping.

For almost four days the winds never diminished. The excitement of the crew was evident. They had never experienced such favorable winds and were amazed at their progress. The boredom of the trip wore on, and Tobias used the opportunity to sleep, even during the day.

Suddenly a crewmember called out. "Land, port side!"

Everyone in the boat gazed. When Tobias looked, he could see nothing at first. Several men were pointing. Then, slowly, the horizon changed from a thin blue-green line to a dark shadow, which began emerging from the surface. As the hour passed, the shadow rose higher and darker until Tobias could make out mountains. He turned to one of the crew members.

"Joppa?"

The sailor laughed. "No, but we are close. It is the island of Cyprus. Only two more days of this wind and we will be coming into port."

"But we have been at sea for only five days!" said Tobias.

The sailor smiled. "Yes, I know. The gods have smiled upon us. Poseidon has granted us a safe journey."

Tobias looked up to the blue sky. "Praises to Your mighty name, YaHoWaH. Thank You for granting us safe passage."

The boat continued past the island at a distance, and for hours the people on board watched the vast land mass drift by. By evening, the island was gone, and they were surrounded by open seas again. The next two days were tedious and took forever. Every hour someone would stand alongside Tobias and stare across the vast sea.

Straining to see any indication of land, Tobias would watch until his eyes were tired. Disappointed there was nothing, he would slump into his seat and close his eyes, giving his body more rest. The tension and anticipation were palpable, making the crew edgy. Near the end of day seven, a crew member who had climbed to the top of the mast cried aloud.

"Land! I see Joppa!"

The captain stood and peered off the bow. He then looked down at Tobias and smiled. "You bring us good luck."

Not able to see anything, Tobias wasn't sure if he saw land, but accepted the crew's proclamation land was imminent.

When the sun was setting, the elusive land had marginally moved closer. All through the night, Tobias kept staring into the dark, hoping the crew would see the lights of the homes along the shore, but it never changed. It wasn't until early daybreak when Tobias could see Joppa in the distance. By late morning, Tobias could make out familiar landmarks, and his excitement grew.

Arriving at the port of Joppa, the wind finally softened, and the boat slowly drifted into the harbor. The trip to Patmos had taken eleven days, but the return trip lasted only eight. The sailors were amazed.

The giant man turned to Tobias and exclaimed, "In all my years sailing, this is the first time we have crossed the sea in such a short time. Unbelievable."

As soon as the boat was tied to the pier, Tobias anxiously walked onto the dock and smiled. He was finally safe on land again and now only a day's journey away from his home in Arimathea.

"Brother Tobias!" a voice from the crowd yelled.

Tobias looked around and saw a familiar face smiling his direction. "Brother Markus." Tobias quickly walked toward the man. "What brings you to Joppa, my friend?"

Markus smiled. "YaHoWaH said I must meet you here and bring you home. Come, I have a cart waiting."

As the two men walked, Tobias asked, "A cart? You came here for me in a cart?"

Markus smiled again. "I had to purchase supplies, but two nights ago YaHoWaH came to me in a dream and said I must be here to meet you. As you can see, I'm here."

"Praise YaHoWaH. He is my provider, protector, and has kept me safe. I have great news from Patmos, where I was with John, one of the original witnesses' of Y'shua."

They stopped walking, and Markus looked surprised. "He is alive then?"

Tobias hugged his friend. "More than alive, he is writing and has sent messages to the believers in Judea." Tobias patted the clay jar strapped to his chest. "I have them stored in here!"

Markus frowned. "Inside the clay jar are messages?"

Tobias smiled, "I haven't read them yet, but I am anxious to get home to find out what John has for us."

"Then we must get you home quickly. But first, my wife says you must have supper with our family," assured Markus.

Tobias felt his body relax and broadly smiled. "This would please me, Markus."

The smell of garlic and leeks permeated the house when Markus and Tobias joined the family. For dinner, a lamb soup that consisted more of water than anything else was served. Subtle bits of lamb were chopped up and swimming in the soup. Warm, fresh bread was served when everyone sat down. Markus stood at the head of the table and quoted from Psalms, giving praise for all their blessings. He then turned to Tobias and asked him to pray over their meal.

After a relatively short prayer, everyone hungrily began to eat. Tobias smiled when he saw the five children enjoying their dinner. Suddenly, there was knocking at the door. The entire group sat in silence as Markus stood and walked to the door. A voice on the other side cried out.

"Markus, open up. I have a surprise for your family."

After unlocking the door, Markus opened it and saw a neighbor standing there holding a large platter in his hands. The man pushed his way in and walked to the dinner table. Steaming hot roasted lamb was piled on the plate.

"What is this, James?" inquired Markus.

His neighbor smiled. "We roasted a lamb this evening, and we have plenty to share."

Both Markus and his wife hugged their neighbor. "Blessings, James. And thank you."

Slapping Markus on the shoulder, James said, "Enjoy, friends," and then he disappeared out the door.

Without hesitation, the children began serving the lamb. Everyone was excited. For the next hour, the only sounds anyone heard were their wordless pleasure from the delicious meal. When everyone was full, the room returned to normal. The children cleared the table while their parents and Tobias sat to talk.

"So, Tobias, tell us of Patmos and John," prodded Markus. He turned to his wife. "Tobias has writings from the witness, John, and they're stored in his clay jar."

Tobias lovingly held the jar to his chest.

"And what has he written? Can you read it to us?" asked Markus' wife.

Tobias explained his adventure on Patmos. The couple laughed when Tobias told about the centurion and his last night on the island. He provided details about his time with John and the risk he took in bringing John's writings off the island. When he told about the incident concerning the snake, the couple was shocked.

"And you didn't get bitten?" asked Markus' wife.

"By the grace of YaHoWaH, I was protected my entire journey. I even had a dream in which an angel told me to keep John's writings safe and to make copies for the other believers. As you can imagine, I wish to get started right away."

Markus stood and grabbed Tobias' arm. "Then, by all means, let us get you to your home."

Tobias smiled at his friends. "Thank you for a wonderful meal."

Everyone hugged, and they walked Tobias to the door. "Shalom Tobias, go with YaHoWaH's blessings," said Markus.

"Thank you again. Shalom."

Tobias walked to his home, the home he wasn't sure he'd make the journey home to, and when he entered, the place smelled musty. Everything was as he had left it. So much could have gone wrong, and almost did, but here he was, safe again. Tobias sat at his table and carefully untied the clay jar.

After laying it on the table, he searched around for something with which he could break open the jar. He found a large round rock he had used as a weight for his writings whenever the wind would move things around.

Holding the clay jar in one hand, Tobias raised the rock, ready to strike a blow. He paused, adjusting the height of his hand, trying to determine if he was at the correct distance. Too high and the stone would shatter the jar and possibly destroy the documents inside. Too close, and the pot wouldn't break open. Finally, Tobias decided to start with slight hammering actions, in hopes the container would crack.

After several attempts, the only visible damage was tiny chips of clay splintering off. Tobias inspected the jar and could see no cracks. "Humph."

Tobias began attacking the jar again, but with slightly more vigor. The results were more of the same. Undeterred, Tobias raised his hand and struck the stone near the top. Instantly shards scattered everywhere. Tobias gasped.

Taking his fingers, he carefully pulled the loose pieces off and slowly opened the jar. When he looked inside, he saw multiple layers of parchment tightly rolled. In fact, there were so many layers, hardly any space was in the center.

Excited, Tobias chipped at the sides, creating more cracks. Like peeling a boiled egg, he slowly removed the thick clay away from the bundle of parchment. Meanwhile, Tobias prayed he wasn't damaging any of the precious documents inside.

With about half the jar broken open and a pile of loose shards strewn across the table, Tobias wrapped his hand around the roll of parchment and gingerly slid it free from the watering container. Some of the layers felt damp around the edges.

As Tobias held the giant bundle of parchment layers, his hand began to tremble. As he attempted to peel the first layer off, he heard a crackling sound, meaning the parchment might not be soft. He stopped immediately and set the roll down.

Speaking aloud, Tobias pleaded, "YaHoWaH, what should I do?"

He then spotted a large pot sitting in the cooking area. Tobias jumped to his feet and grabbed the container. He filled it with water and set it down. He then started a small fire. Resting the pot on top of the flames, Tobias waited impatiently.

He paced and kept watch on the pot, but nothing was happening. He fretted. "Boil water!" He added more sticks to the fire to increase the heat. Like a child just before Hanukkah, Tobias could hardly contain his excitement.

Slowly at first, the water began to form wisps of steam. He grabbed the roll of parchment and held it above the rising steam. The first layer started uncurling, and so he carefully pulled the sheet away from the bundle. Delirious with anticipation, Tobias could see John's writing. Setting the roll aside, he continued to steam the first layer until the page was supple.

He walked over to his table and saw it was covered in pieces of the clay jar. Taking his sleeved arm, he swept the clay shards on the table to the floor in one swift motion. Dust slowly filled the room, and he coughed. He then spread the layer face down on the table making it flat. Tobias needed a weight. Searching the room again, he kicked off his sandal in frustration and placed it on top of the parchment layer.

From around his home he gathered just about anything he thought could be used for weights. He ended up with his other sandal, plates, cups, and boards. He piled these items near his table. Running back to the steaming pot, Tobias began to delicately unravel each curled page, easing the loose parchment layers off, one page at a time.

He would dash to the table and spread the pages, weighing them down with the items he had gathered. Once the surface was full, Tobias fretted again. Then he checked the first page on the corner of the table and saw it stayed mostly flat when he removed his sandal. Tobias moved the layer to a nearby chair and checked the next piece of parchment. Repeating his movements, he was able to transfer about half the sheets onto the seat. He placed his smashing rock on the stack and started uncurling more layers from the roll of parchment.

As Tobias worked closer to the center of the roll, he found it took longer to unfurl the pages. After several hours, he was finally done. Multiple stacks of sheets were distributed on any surface he could see. He was tired, and his back was sore.

When he walked outside, the sky was ink-black, and stars dotted the heavens. The fresh air felt good. He sat down on a bench, leaned his head back, and thanked YaHoWaH for the miracle he'd just experienced. During the past hours, Tobias had refilled the pot with water multiple times, gathered more firewood and stoked it over and over. He estimated he had walked to Jerusalem and back in all the steps he took to perform his task.

After resting a long spell, he walked back into his house. He lit several oil lamps and arranged the stacks of parchment pages on the table. Taking the top sheet off one stack, Tobias inspected it in the dim light. He eyes were heavy, but he started reading aloud.

"When the Lamb opened the seventh seal, there was silence in heaven for about half an hour. I noticed the seven angels who stood before YaHoWaH were each given a trumpet. Another angel, who had a gold container for incense, came and stood at the altar. This angel was given a lot of incense to offer with the prayers of YaHoWaH's people on the gold altar in front of the throne. Then the smoke of the incense, together with the prayers of YaHoWaH's people, went up to YaHoWaH from the hand of the angel. After this, the angel filled the incense container with fire from—"

Tobias set the page down. Tears were welling in his eyes. "Oh, YaHoWaH in heaven, thank You for Your wonderful mercies and love. Thank You for Your Son, Y'shua the Messiah. Thank You for my long and protected life." Tobias extended his hands over the stacks of parchment pages. "Bless these words of Your servant, John. Find a way for him to be set free from Patmos. May Your words written here, bring men's hearts to You. May we honor Your Son's death by living our lives like Y'shua. May we spread these words to all the nations."

Exhausted, he trudged toward his bed. Crawling under the blankets, he pondered the words he'd just read. In a matter of minutes, he was sound asleep.

Tobias slept until late morning. He stayed in bed praying and wondering about the words he had read the night before. Suddenly, someone knocked at his door. He shuffled to the door and opened it to find his smiling neighbor.

"Markus! Greetings, my friend."

"And shalom, Tobias. I saw the lamps were lit well into the night here at your house. Did you sleep at all?"

Tobias smiled. "Yes, and I am still tired. Come, let me show you what John has written."

The two men walked over to Tobias' table, and Markus was shocked at the many large stacks of parchment pages.

"All this was inside the clay jar?" asked Markus.

Tobias nodded.

"And how did you get them out?" inquired Markus.

Tobias pointed to the floor, and Markus saw the clay shards everywhere.

"All this was in one jar, Tobias?"

Lifting a page from one of the stacks, he handed it to Markus and showed him the writing. Markus studied the page.

"What is this number for?" He showed the page to Tobias and pointed to the edge.

A tiny number was written in the corner, but Tobias hadn't seen it last night. He picked another page and looked, then another, and another. He looked up at Markus and smiled.

"John has numbered the pages. Now I'll be able to assemble them correctly!" Tobias was excited again.

Together, the two men sorted the pages. When they were finished, they found they had three separate manuscripts.

CHAPTER EIGHT

THE BEGINNING
OF THE STORY

FOR WEEKS, TOBIAS FOLLOWED JOHN'S instructions and made complete copies of everything John had given him. He would pour over the words of John and purposely ensure every word was written correctly. He toiled late into the night, often working by oil lamps until his hands were exhausted or he ran out of writing materials.

Markus and his family would come and visit Tobias and bring him food to eat. Each time, Markus would stop and read the pages, smiling as he poured over the story of Y'shua.

When Tobias had completed his third copy, he rested.

"What do you do now?" asked Markus.

Tobias smiled. "Now we hide the original in clay jars for safe keeping."

For several days, Tobias and Markus dug holes into the stone walls of Tobias' house. Very low to the floor, they carved out openings where the jars could be sealed and preserved. On the day the last pot was placed into the wall, Markus asked, "How do you know the writings will be safe, Tobias?"

Tobias smiled. "Because the jars and parchment are dry, and I have sealed the lids tightly with wax."

Markus seemed impressed.

"Only one more thing I must do, Markus," added Tobias.

"Which is?"

Tobias walked over to a pile of scrolls sitting on his table. He fished through the pile until he located the box. Trembling, he carried the box to the last opening left in the wall. Kneeling, Tobias gingerly opened the box and showed it to Markus.

"What is that?" he asked.

"This is the spike which held the hand of our Savior, Y'shua of Nazareth, the day He was crucified."

"Impossible!" said Markus in disbelief.

"No, it's true," said Tobias, "I was there and witnessed everything."

"May I touch it?" asked Markus.

Tobias carefully and respectfully held the box out.

Markus inspected every minute detail. "Incredible! So you knew Y'shua personally?"

Tobias nodded.

"But when did you meet Him?" asked Markus. "You must tell me the whole story!"

Tobias sat back and put his back to the stone wall. He looked up at Markus and smiled. "I was not called Tobias then. My given name was Nicodemus."

"Nicodemus?" asked Markus with skepticism.

"Yes. I was the son of Ziba, senior member of the Sanhedrin Council," explained Tobias. "I first visited Y'shua in the middle of the night."

Markus was puzzled. "Why at night? Were you afraid?"

Tobias sighed. "I wanted to meet the man whom many said was from YaHoWaH. He performed miracles and spoke with great wisdom, yet some folks in our council were not sure. For me, it was important I discover who this man truly was. Some in our council thought Y'shua was from the devil, especially Caiaphas and Annas. They wanted Y'shua dead. In fact, they are responsible for having Him killed. The night I met Y'shua, changed my life."

Markus asked, "What did you learn? What happened that night?"

With a crooked half smile, Tobias looked at his neighbor. "I went from a disbeliever to a follower of Y'shua. He is undeniably the Son of YaHoWaH, the Savior of man, and the King about whom David and the prophets wrote. He is El-Shaddai, Immanuel, and my friend. I look for His return every day."

Markus was excited. "I want to hear the whole story, from the beginning. Please share it with me."

Holding the spike in his hands, Tobias gazed at the stains. "I believe I can now tell my story. I was not appointed to the Sanhedrin Council, but my father was. I believe it was his dream to see me replace him when he died."

"Did your father believe in Y'shua?" asked Markus.

"Not at first. But just before he died, I believe he did. I wanted my own answers about Y'shua and not just the rumors of others. I had to see and hear the truth, so late one evening, I dressed in my finest robes and wore a large tunic as cover, to hide my identity. Being careful, I came to the home where I thought Y'shua and His followers were staying. Initially, when I knocked, no one answered, and I believed I had gone to the wrong house. Then I heard muffled voices inside arguing, so I kept on knocking. I wasn't going to leave that place without first getting the answers I so desperately wanted—"

CHAPTER NINE

THE UNWELCOME VISITOR

"WHO IS KNOCKING?" FRIGHTENED, JOHN forcefully whispered. "Everyone, be quiet."

"Don't answer, John. It could be soldiers or the temple guards!" Bartholomew urged in a hushed voice.

John stood and listened again as the soft knocking at the front door continued. "They're insistent," John whispered. He frowned and looked down at his close friend, the one they called the Teacher.

He reached up and took John's trembling hand. "Fear not, my friend. You have a new guest."

"But, what if . . . " John's voice trailed off.

John knew better than to question their leader. For several years, this man had been the companion to a group of twelve men now situated in this room. He was more than just a spiritual leader; He was their companion, a wise man, healer, and a charismatic speaker. He had chosen the handpicked men in this room to follow Him around the country. Other men and women had joined the group, and sometimes they would stay for a while, and then leave. The men gathered around were Peter and his brother Andrew, the brothers James and John. Then there were Philip, Bartholomew, Matthew, Thomas, James the son of Alpheus, Thaddeus, Simon the Zealot, and Judas, son of Simon of Kerioth. These men were from various background and vocations, yet none came from the elite of their society. Most of the religious leaders scoffed at the Teacher's selection of these men. Nonetheless, John was the closest friend, often spending time alone with Him to pray. Initially, John never really understood why he was nearer to the Teacher than any of the others.

The Teacher called John and his brother, James, *the Sons of Thunder*, not only because of their father, Zebedee and his booming voice but because these two men were quick to be defensive and to raise their voices in protest.

The other person close to the Teacher was Peter. He called him the *Rock*. Everyone assumed the name was tied to Peter's body because he was solid muscle and unmovable, especially when he had an idea stuck in his head, but Y'shua denied this and insisted it was for other reasons.

At the Teacher's insistence, they were meeting in another follower's home in the city of Jerusalem. The owners had retired to bed early. John surveyed the faces of his friends and saw mixed emotions. These men had much to worry about because, over the past several months, the threats to their leader's life were increasing. They feared for themselves as well as for Y'shua of Nazareth.

John resisted answering the door and had plenty of reason for the trepidation. When he looked at the Teacher, he could see that the man held none of John's apprehensions. The knocking grew louder. Slowly, John turned toward the main door.

Thomas quickly stood to his feet. "No John, please don't, I beg you!"

John ignored his warning and walked to the door. He paused, looking back at his friends once more. Everyone sat in a large circle with several plates of dried fish and bread in the middle. Small flickering oil lamps eerily lighted their faces. John saw a chorus of dread on each man. Long, dark shadows danced along the walls and disturbed John's senses. *The wine is fogging my brain.*

Meanwhile, the knocking persisted.

John gruffly whispered through the closed door, "Who is it that desires entrance at this late hour?"

A long pause ensued causing John's worries to heighten. John leaned his ear close to the door to listen.

The voice on the other side of the door was just slightly more than a whisper as it said, "I wish to visit with your Teacher. Please open the door. I need to remain anonymous to those who might see me out here."

"Do you know the hour?" John's nerve was bolstered.

"I do. It is an hour past the sixth watch and late. Now please, welcome me in." The voice was stern.

John knew by the man's answer he was someone well educated and with authority. It was clearly not some thief or beggar attempting to gain access, and it wasn't a Roman soldier. Still, John was tempted to tell the brazen individual to go away and come back at a more reasonable hour.

Suddenly John felt a hand touch his shoulder and warm currents of energy passed through his whole body. He jumped, turned quickly, and found himself face to face with Y'shua.

"Invite the man in. He is our guest, John."

"But—"

"Fear not my brother." The Teacher produced His warm smile. It was an expression which swept all fear from any man's heart instantly.

Y'shua had used this disarming smile numerous times before. Once, He was discussing religion and politics with a group of influential religious leaders of the Sanhedrin. Something He said upset them, and within seconds, they started collecting large rocks, intending harm.

Again, as in many times before, Y'shua produced His warm defusing smile, quickly causing all tensions to disappear. John remembered being in awe as the group of thirty or more leaders slowly dropped their stones and walked away. One minute they were anxious to stone their leader and the next—they dispersed into the crowd of onlookers.

John reached out and lifted the wood beam securing the door. He set it aside and slowly opened it a small crack. John braced the bottom edge with his foot, in case the person forced their entry. When John peered into the faint moonlit night, he could see a tall bearded man, perhaps his same age, standing patiently waiting. The tall man kept a watchful eye on the adjacent buildings and leaned in close as if to force his way into the room.

The hood of his robe was pulled over his head to shadow his face, but gold tassels were exposed along the lower edges of the man's inner garment. John's heart skipped a beat, and his body stiffened. This was not an average man standing in the doorway. John was all too familiar with a man dressed like this. Men of this man's position were powerful and ruthless. The men who wore gold tassels were high-ranking political and religious officials.

This was not a friend visiting or an individual needing the Teacher's healing touch. No, the man standing before John represented everything he hated about religion. John's muscles tightened; his hands tightly gripped the edge of the door.

"Why is he here and at this late hour?" John mumbled.

CHAPTER TEN

BORN OF WATER
AND SPIRIT

WHEN THE TEACHER BRUSHED AGAINST John, he again felt the unique energy surge through his body, and he shivered. Moving John aside and pulling the door open, the Teacher extended His hand to the man standing at the door.

"Greetings, Nicodemus."

The visitor stiffened and quickly scanned the streets. Y'shua took the visitor by the hand and led him to a bench near the door where a basin and pitcher of water rested inside the entrance. Nicodemus glanced warily at the other men gathered in the room.

Directing Nicodemus to sit, Y'shua bent over to remove the sandals from his guest's feet. Nicodemus quietly protested, but He softly smiled and continued to remove the man's shoes.

"Why are you doing this? I would never stoop to anyone below my station to do such a thing. This is the job of a servant," Nicodemus demanded.

Y'shua ignored the protests.

John's mouth dropped open as he watched the Teacher perform His tasks. John's thoughts struggled inside his head. *How can You stand to touch the man's feet, Teacher? Don't You know what this man represents?*

He could ruin us all. Looking across the room at his companions, John could see his friends were disgusted by their leader's actions, too.

After the Teacher washed the man's feet and dried them, He then poured water over the visitor's hands and wiped them with a fresh linen towel. Then Y'shua brought Nicodemus into the room where the other men were gathered. He had Nicodemus sit in the area where the men ate. Everyone, except John, shuffled away.

The room fell silent because the men were afraid of a Pharisee, everyone except the Teacher. Most of the men moved to the far side of the room and away from the gold-tasseled man. John sat on the opposite side of Y'shua, glaring at Nicodemus.

Y'shua broke off a piece of bread and shared it with His guest. He then grabbed a basket of fish and offered them to the man as well. For several minutes, the whole room watched in dead silence as the Teacher and Nicodemus ate their meal. John vaguely remembered seeing this visitor during the many street discussions with the Teacher and wondered why the man had come for a visit. He needed to know if Nicodemus was a spy for the council.

Nicodemus politely accepted a cup of wine from Y'shua, although he never drank any of its contents. John could hear his friends murmuring across the room, wondering and gossiping about their new guest. John frowned at his fishing partner, and instantly Peter quieted the men with a rebuke. For nearly a half hour, no words were shared, yet Nicodemus scanned the room several times. Watching the man, John wondered if the visitor came of his own accord.

Finally, John initiated the conversation. "You wished to speak with our Teacher, did you not say?"

Taking his flat palm and pulling it down his mouth and across his beard, Nicodemus took a deep breath. "Teacher, we, the men of the Sanhedrin, or at least some of our Pharisees—we think you may be a man of YaHoWaH. We understand this because we have seen the miraculous signs you perform, and no one can do these things if YaHoWaH was not involved."

John quickly realized some of the Pharisees were paying attention.

"Unfortunately, Your words confuse many in our company. We spend hours debating Your riddles. Some of us are convinced Your wisdom about our religious books must be from YaHoWaH because You confound our logic and speak with wisdom. Others think You're a madman or of the devil."

The Teacher smiled and took a sip of wine but said nothing.

"For what purpose are You here in Jerusalem? Do You have words of prophecy concerning our people? Why do You speak in riddles? Why do You antagonize and confront our authority?"

Y'shua nibbled on a small piece of fish and finally licked the oil from His fingers. "I am here to do the work of My heavenly Father and to guide men's hearts to the truth."

Nicodemus looked shocked and indignant. "Yesterday, a sage and pious man from the group of scribes visited You. Every citizen respects this wealthy man for his dedication to the laws of Moses. Yet, when he came to You to speak, You sent him away declaring he must give away his money to the poor and then follow You and Your men. Why?"

Smiling, Y'shua replied, "I'll tell you the truth, Nicodemus. No one can see or enter heaven unless they have been reborn."

The visitor stared blankly at the Teacher in disbelief. "Did You not understand my questions?" asked Nicodemus. "Once a man is born, he grows old, larger, into a man, he cannot fit back inside his mother's womb. Why would a man return to a woman's womb? Just so he may be reborn a second time?" Nicodemus shook his head in disbelief. "This is nonsense. I risked my reputation for this visit to try and understand You. Why are You still speaking in these ridiculous riddles?"

Y'shua smiled again and looked intently into the eyes of His new guest. "Again, I'll tell you the truth. No one can enter heaven unless they have been born of water and the spirit. A woman's body gives birth to another human body, but the Holy Spirit gives birth to a man's soul.

"Why are you so confused by My words, 'You must be born again'? The wind blows in various directions, but man cannot change its direction or even cause the wind to appear. Yes, you hear the sound the wind makes in your ears, but you have no idea where it came from or where it will go. Every person born of the Spirit is just like the wind."

"I don't understand what You're telling me. Your words are confusing, and I cannot comprehend their meaning. What are You saying?" asked Nicodemus. "Speak plainly."

John frowned and wondered himself what Y'shua was trying to say.

"Are you not a teacher of the religious books, Nicodemus? Do you not study them to pass on their meaning and wisdom to the next generation? Surely you understand the texts written down by your forefathers and that were taught to you in school for many years. Did not your teachers instruct you in their meaning and provide you with insight?

"What I'm telling you is the absolute truth." Y'shua swept the room with an extended arm and open palm. "We are telling everyone about what we know is correct about YaHoWaH. These men will provide testimony to the miracles I've performed for the sick, but still, you and the religious leaders cannot accept what you see and hear as being from YaHoWaH?

"I have been explaining the things of nature to you, and yet you have difficulty accepting or understanding these simple earthly concepts. Nicodemus, if you can't understand these worldly things, how on earth are you going to believe My words when I speak about YaHoWaH and the ideas of heaven?

"You see, no man has ever entered heaven, except the person who came from heaven. This person is the Son of Man. Me. You're familiar with the story of Moses who took his staff and turned it into a snake, slithering on its belly. He also lifted this snake into the air, and it became rigid like a staff again.

"Well, just like the staff of Moses, so shall the Son of Man be lifted into the air. Every person who believes I am the Son of YaHoWaH, sent here to save mankind, will eventually experience eternal life. Why? Because YaHoWaH loves this world and the people so much, He sent His only Son to earth for them to believe in Him. Those who believe, will not perish in the end but will have eternal life in heaven.

"YaHoWaH didn't send Me into the world to condemn the people. He sent Me here to save them from the final destruction and judgment. If anyone believes this information about Me, this person will escape the final judgment and condemnation. However, if they refuse to believe Me, it will be as if they had been judged already. They will bring condemnation upon their own heads because they refuse to believe I am YaHoWaH's Son and what I'm telling them."

John watched Nicodemus who seemed confused. Nicodemus blinked several times. He attempted to speak, but his speech sputtered.

John also sat quietly trying to absorb what the Teacher was saying and even he was having difficulty grasping the full meaning. Later, he must ask Y'shua about the exact meaning of the things shared.

"Nicodemus, I'll explain the whole of my message to you. The light came into this world, but evil men loved the darkness and not the light because they had selfish desires. People who love darkness also enjoy being evil, and they hate the light. The light exposes their evil deeds to other men, so they hate the light and love the darkness.

"Other men love the light. They seek the truth, and, therefore, they love being in the light. Their deeds are performed in the light so other men may see the truth and know that what these men are doing is because YaHoWaH is the light."

Deep furrows formed between the visitor's brows. "Some of Your words I comprehend. But unfortunately, I cannot grasp the full details of everything You've spoken. I will need further time to contemplate what You have shared."

To John, it was clear the visitor's mind was troubled, just trying to comprehend the complete meaning of the Teacher's words. John had to admit, even he was having difficulty with some of the concepts, but he would find an opportunity to speak to Y'shua in private later.

"Are You a crazy madman, or are You telling me the truth?" Without waiting for the answer, Nicodemus stood and walked toward the door but paused, looking down at the dirt floor.

Y'shua came up from behind and touched the visitor's shoulder. Nicodemus shuddered and his mouth dropped open as he turned to stare.

"I came to fulfill the words written in your law books and those that were written by the many prophets who have been witnesses to your people. I did not come to destroy their words, but to bring completion to their meaning. I am the light of this world."

Shaken to his fundamental core, Nicodemus appeared confused beyond his educational limits. Finally, Nicodemus pulled his hood over his head and wrapped his cloak tightly around his body to hide his gold-tasseled clothes. After staring intently at the Teacher, he quietly walked out the door and slipped into the darkness of night.

John watched Nicodemus walk away and disappear. He stood for a long time staring into the blackness of the street. Finally, John slowly shut the door and replaced the massive beam protecting the entrance.

CHAPTER ELEVEN

LET US DANCE
BEFORE ADONAI

SLEEP ELUDED JOHN AS HE tossed and turned on his sleeping mat. The conversations with Nicodemus repeatedly played out inside John's mind. Only one neatly trimmed oil lamp flickered in the room, producing a faint warm light. When John turned over, looking at the Teacher, he saw the man smiling back. Blankly staring at Y'shua, John wondered if the man could read his very thoughts. It was a little unnerving. As John started to roll back over, he saw Y'shua quietly arise and walk toward him.

Leaning down close to John's ear, Y'shua whispered, "I'm going out to pray. I'll return later."

John watched the Teacher disappear out the door, but then he quickly arose and followed Him out the door. It was not a night for sleeping and John wanted to speak privately with Y'shua. He quietly closed the main entrance and dashed down the dusty lane searching for his friend. The moonlit night gave the town an eerie bluish glow as John rapidly searched for Y'shua. John sprinted toward the Teacher's location. When he arrived at the corner, Y'shua was further down the lane and turning another corner.

Dashing forward, John arrived breathless to the corner, only to see the Teacher disappearing around another building. Frustrated, John ran with all his strength. For a long half hour, he played cat and mouse as the two men wound their way through the village. Arriving near the edge of the town, John paused and could faintly see Y'shua walking toward a river, which emptied into the lake. Finally, he ran and caught up.

"May I join you?" said John entirely out of breath.

"It would appear you have achieved your purpose."

John bent over at the waist, hands on his knees, and tried to catch his breath. Breathing hard, he could see Y'shua was not experiencing any symptoms of fatigue, despite His ability to stay ahead of John for the last thirty minutes. *How is this possible?* Instantly, the familiar currents of energy coursed through John's body as Y'shua touched his back. Abruptly, the exhaustion vanished. John raised his eyes and could see the Teacher bent over, grinning at John.

"Your determination pleases Me. You must have something important to talk about. Perhaps it was our conversation this evening with Nicodemus?"

"How do you do that? It's as if You're sometimes inside my head and know my very thoughts."

Ignoring John's question, Y'shua proceeded, "Come, My friend, we must talk." He then walked a short distance and sat on an outcrop of rocks along the river's shore. He patted a place alongside and motioned for John to sit. After a moment, John sat next to the Teacher.

"Y'shua, it is nearly impossible for me to place words on my feelings for You. I love You as if You were a blood relative and I admire Your wisdom. Something feels familiar concerning You, and at the same time, You are distant, unreachable. I feel safe around You even though it troubles me that You can read my thoughts. I also feel an absolute calm when I'm in Your presence."

John jumped to his feet. "But, why on earth did You invite that man into our house? And, of all the people in the world, how could You even tolerate touching his feet?"

Y'shua smiled. "His name is Nicodemus."

"I, for one, would have never touched his hands or feet. He represents everything I hate about our religion and its leaders. A Pharisee, of all people! I don't trust the man, and I don't care what his name is. You invited him in and treated him like he was one of our group—as if he was with us. How?"

"How long have you and Simon-Peter been friends?"

"Simon-Peter is like a brother to me, and I've known the man for nearly thirty years. Why do you ask?"

"Yet, you and I have known each other for hardly three years. Do you consider Me a brother?"

John's heart melted. "More if I could describe it. I distinctly remember the day I met You. I was present the day You were baptized by John the Baptist. Then the day I met You, we had a terrible fishing day. It started at three in the morning. My brother and me, Simon-Peter, and Andrew used two boats to set sail on the lake in the cover of darkness. Hours passed, and we had no fish. Each time we dragged our nets into the boat, we found snags, waterlogged stumps, and the occasional fish carcass for our efforts.

"When the sun had boiled our brains into senselessness, we rowed to shore because the wind was dead calm. Exhausted, we forced our bodies to perform the necessary chores of preparing our equipment for the next day. We had a reputation in the town for outperforming any other boat with regards to the capacity of fish caught.

"While we were washing and repairing our nets by the lake, You walked along the shore of the lake. A large gathering of people followed You as You spoke to them. When the crowd increased in size, they pressed in until You could not move. You were standing near the boat of Simon-Peter and Andrew, so You climbed into their craft. 'Would you please row slightly away from the lake's edge?' You asked.

"I listened to You speak from the boat to the people. I listened with fascination as You shared wisdom about the books of Moses and interpreted the words of the prophets. Your words were like salve to my cold heart bringing back fond memories of my father's teachings.

"When You were finished speaking, you asked Simon-Peter to move the boat into deeper waters and to cast their nets. Simon immediately protested. He said to You, 'It's a bad day to fish,' but You just smiled telling him to lower his nets once more. Within minutes, the net was so full of fish, it began to tear apart. Then Simon-Peter called out for our help, so we immediately dropped everything. I was impressed because even You worked by pulling in the overflowing catch. You stood alongside Simon and his brother, smiling and working.

"Suddenly, You looked at the four of us and said, 'Join me, and I will teach you how to fish like this for the hearts of men.' I saw a chance to redeem myself and fulfill a dream to become a religious or spiritual leader. I did not hesitate but gladly followed You. With minimal hesitation, James, Simon-Peter, and Andrew also joined me and we followed You.

"Although much has happened during this period, I do not regret my decision. I am confident I've learned more wisdom and insight by observing and listening to You. In fact, I've learned more than all my years in school. My understanding of history has changed, and I am now aware You are indeed sent from YaHoWaH and the promised prophet. You are the Messiah."

Y'shua rested His hand on John's shoulder.

"Then perhaps, Nicodemus could be a brother?"

John instantly went rigid. "Impossible! I'd rather make friends with a venomous snake than the likes of a man like him. The gold-tasseled men have the power to remove someone from their home, bar us from the temple of worship, or worse, have us stoned to death. They control the temple, our social laws, and set strict rules for every minuscule item of our daily living. They monitor how everyone washes their hands, prepares their meals, the hours when labor can commence, and interpret finite details of the religious scrolls. My own father detests the gold-tasseled men. He regularly fumes vitriolic statements concerning their kind of evil. 'Do not trust those men,' he warns. He also says, 'They are worthless scum, and yet they act as if YaHoWaH Himself appointed them master of everything. Pay no heed to these useless men or their ridiculous and meaningless rules. Honor YaHoWaH with your heart and do your best to follow the laws of Moses.'

"On the other hand, the Roman government rules the land and levies taxes, and we must pay them without failure. The Romans control the soldiers who can terrorize our communities. The fees we pay represents a hefty price, but at least we can live in a false sense of peace. So long as we obey the government's laws, we can live in relative calm.

"When I was around twelve years old, my father, Zebedee, taught reading and writing to the young men of the village. My brother and

I were his students. I learned a lot from that man. Plus, my father was well regarded by many people in town. One day, my mother became sick and died within months of her illness. The doctors were helpless and could not prevent her death. Immediately the neighbors and friends suspected sin in Zebedee's life.

"The painful loss of my mother was worsened by the burden of my father caring for a pair of sons and two daughters—all of us under the age of twelve. It was an impossible task, and he needed help. My father selected and arranged to marry a young girl nearly fifteen years his junior. Mary became his new wife and our mother. Unfortunately, the gold-tasseled men were upset with my father for not waiting the usual period of one year for mourning, nor did he consult with them regarding his marital change. Within days of his wedding, my father found himself stripped of his vocation as a teacher of students and our family was pushed to the outskirts of the town.

"We moved to a village in Galilee and lived with our cousin Saul and his wife Salome. They had no children, but Saul taught us how to fish on the lake. When we earned enough money, we set up our own business, Eventually, Simon-Peter and Andrew partnered with me and my brother to help each other out. The gold-tasseled men embarrassingly shamed my father and changed our whole way of life. I don't trust them and I don't like them."

"Simon-Peter has no family relations with you, still, you call him your brother. Why?"

John furrowed his brow. "Simon-Peter is a friend, and I consider him a brother because we would fight to the death to protect each other. He is the biggest of our lot with a head the size of two men together. He has a massive chest and shoulders, and his neck—the thickness of a tree trunk—it's barely visible. With one look, Simon-Peter could intimidate a mob of angry thugs. Even Roman soldiers are afraid of him. We quickly discovered, despite his intimidating looks, he was actually a gentle giant. I could ask the man for anything, and Simon-Peter would move heaven and earth to obtain it for me. We don't need to be blood-related to be considered brothers."

"Tell me, John, is Simon-Peter also from Abraham's seed, like you?"

John considered the words. "I suppose it is true."

"And so, you two are descendants of Abraham?"

"Your words seem reasonable, and so again, I must agree with You."

"Is Nicodemus a descendant of Abraham?"

John felt his body go rigid. Just the mere mention of the name caused John to well up with hate. He frowned. "If he is, what difference does it make?"

Y'shua moved closer and looked into John's eyes. He smiled. "I believe I hear music, we should dance!"

John jerked his head and watched the Teacher shed His outer cloak and begin to dance slowly. "I do not hear any music. Why are You dancing?" John asked.

"If you and Simon-Peter are from the seed of Abraham, then you two are brothers," said Y'shua while still dancing around John. "What does that say about the man, Nicodemus, if he also is from the seed of Abraham?"

John started trembling. He shook his head. "But . . . but, we are not brothers, we can't be?"

The Teacher removed his inner garment and began dancing again, wearing only His loincloth. Embarrassed, John scanned their location to see if anyone might be watching. They were alone.

"Are not the other men in our group also your brothers, John?"

"Yes, but—"

"I do believe I can hear the music getting louder, come dance with Me."

John clenched his fists at his sides and watched the Teacher dancing and jumping about. It reminded John of the story of King David in the Torah when David disrobed and danced this same way before YaHoWaH. John blinked several times. Y'shua reached out and grabbed John's hand.

"Surely you can hear the music. You must come and dance," He urged.

John stood stiff like a statute. "I will not dance. I cannot hear any music. Nicodemus cannot be my brother, can he?"

"And why not? Is he not from the same seed of Abraham as you, Simon-Peter, and the others?"

Tears began rolling down John's cheeks. *How can this be?* He placed his fists on his head and cried out in a hollow sound of anguish. "This cannot be possible, it cannot be so. Tell me this is not true!"

Smiling, Y'shua continued to dance in circles around John until John felt dizzy. He pulled John's outer cloak off and said, "Adonai awaits, you must dance."

John shook his head, confused. "What? Why?"

"Listen carefully, John, the sounds are there. The truth is knocking at the door of your heart."

John felt as if his head would explode. Despite the cold air of the night, John's body began to perspire and get warm. "If Nicodemus is my brother, then that makes every Pharisee my brother. That can't be right, is it?" John held his head with his fists.

"That is it, John, I believe you are beginning to hear the music, come dance."

John was so hot, he stripped off his inner garment and stood in his loincloth. His body was shaking, beads of sweat ran down his chest. *I do not want to dance. Why am I so hot? How can my enemies be my brothers?* John's thoughts streamed through his brain like a raging river, rolling and moving boulders of firm ideas he held in his head. "Is this what You meant when You said we must love those who hate us?"

Y'shua continued to dance. Holding John's rigid arm, He pulled to set John free. Suddenly, John leaned his head back and let out a loud tone, not quite a scream, but more of a long note or the start of a song. His body began to move awkwardly.

Laughing out loud, Y'shua encouraged John further. "Let the music flow through you, feel My Father's Spirit set you free."

"If we are all the children of Abraham, then every tribe, every Israelite is my brother," John exclaimed.

"Yes, John, dance with the music."

"And Samaritans, they are my brothers as well, are they not? They are children of Abraham, too!"

John started dancing wildly, jumping around in circles like the Teacher. His thoughts replayed the teachings of Y'shua. He remembered the sermons shared on the mountain in detail, recalling the parables, the words of comfort, the prayers, every aspect flooded through John. With clarity, he could remember all Y'shua's words, and for the first time, they made sense. He could feel his mind expanding, taking in ideas and concepts, his doubting confusion being pulled away like a cloth to reveal something hidden.

Using words from King David's Psalms, John began to sing songs of praise. He could hear music playing inside his head, tambourine, stringed instruments, the drums beating loudly. Tears of joy rolled from John's eyes as he leaped with joy, praising YaHoWaH, his provider, and protector. Completely unaware of his surroundings, John rejoiced with a loud voice.

After several hours, John could feel the tempo slow down, and the music start to fade. John had no recollection of the hour or how long he had been dancing and singing. Slowly John became aware of his surroundings. When things began to quiet down, he spun around very deliberately and surveyed his location. Y'shua was now gone and the morning sun was just below the horizon.

Despite hours without sleep, John felt invigorated. Looking down, he saw a small fire burning and two fish roasting over the hot coals. Warm, fresh baked bread sat on a large rock beside the fire, steam rising from the crust. John was famished, so he immediately started eating while looking around.

He called out, "Y'shua? Are You here?"

There was no response, only the river bubbling over the rocks. Off in the distant, he heard the sounds of cows, and a rooster crowing. On the rock outcrop where he and Y'shua sat earlier, he saw his inner and outer clothes folded neatly and stacked. When he picked them up, they were washed clean and stiff from being air-dried.

After eating the fish and some of the bread. John walked into the river and removed his loincloth. The water was quite cold, but he plunged his whole body into the river and quickly bathed. Shivering, John hurried back to the fire and dressed in his clothes. As he warmed his hands, he looked at the sky and could see the last stars fading with the rising sun.

Suddenly, John began to laugh, and it came from deep within his belly, a joy he had never experienced before. He felt freedom. Recalling his experience a few hours earlier, he remembered everything with clarity. He smiled to himself. *I must share this with Simon-Peter and the others.*

He bowed and prayed aloud. "Elohim of Abraham, Isaac, and Jacob, thank You for showing me the truth about who is my brother. Thank You, Adonai for sharing Your wisdom with me, for I am Your humble servant. Amen."

He slowly walked back into the village heading toward the home where his friends were probably waiting. A ram's horn sounded in the direction of the temple.

"Ah, the fifth hour of the day," he said to himself.

When he arrived at the house where he and the others were staying, John paused at the door. He could hear laughter inside. Finding the door unlocked, he eased it open. His friends were in a tight group, laughing, and talking with the Teacher. When He made eye contact, Y'shua broadly smiled. As John walked to join his friends, an arm reached out and wrapped tightly around his neck.

Simon-Peter squeezed.

"Simon, enough!" yelled John.

He could smell Simon-Peter's sweat, and he wrinkled his nose.

Simon relaxed his grip but kept the arm around John's neck.

"So, my brother, Y'shua says you were out dancing in the moonlight and singing the night away?"

John produced a sheepish smile. "It is an experience I shall never forget."

Simon smiled and shook his head. "The idea of you dancing half-naked and singing before YaHoWaH; I have to tell you, it is a sight I would love to see."

John pushed Simon-Peter away, and the group erupted in laughter.

CHAPTER TWELVE

SAMARITANS!

"ARISE, MY FRIENDS, THE TEACHER says we're leaving for Galilee." John walked over to each of his friends and shook them awake. "Quickly, the Teacher awaits."

Groggy and stretching, each of the twelve witnesses gathered their small belongings and stowed them in their bags. Peter rapidly packed then slung his satchel over a shoulder. Nearing John, he whispered, "It's just daybreak. Is there a problem?"

Scanning the room, John saw the men struggling to organize themselves during the early hour. "The Teacher wants to journey now. Dare I question His motives?"

Peter looked at the Teacher who was smiling and observing the frenzied witnesses. "Look at Him, He is always watching us. How long has He been awake?"

"He left in the middle of the night to pray. When I saw Him return hours later, He simply said it was time to leave."

"Well, moments are never dull with the Teacher are they, John?" A small grin appeared in the corner of Peter's mouth.

John's thoughts quickly returned to a couple of nights earlier. "No, I suppose not, Peter."

Vendors began setting up in the small markets, alongside the narrow paths between the buildings. As the Teacher walked, He greeted the early risers. Most of the sellers ignored the Teacher and His twelve witnesses as the vendors prepared their wares for sale. The Teacher stopped by a vendor and examined the fruits and dates. Instantly, the man produced a crooked smile.

"Fresh Barhi, Medjool, Deglet-Noor." The vendor lifted a small basket containing a mixture of various dates arranged into small piles. "Arrived yesterday from Egypt, please, try one."

Smiling, the Teacher placed a sample into His mouth. "They're sweet. I'll purchase two fists." He pointed to the dark Medjool dates.

From seemingly nowhere, Judas, son of Simon of Kerioth, appeared with a money bag in one hand. "How much?" he sneered.

Before the street vendor could answer, the Teacher deftly reached into the bag and withdrew three bronze Roman sestertii coins. Judas was bewildered as he watched the Teacher graciously pay the vendor and not ask for change.

Wide-eyed, the seller gazed into his hand. "Oh, thank you, sir. Thank you. Enjoy, and eat in good health."

While the market vendor stared at the coins, another seller came alongside and looked into his hand.

"Blessings Matthias, the market hasn't even opened, and already you've earned the measure for several days in one small sale."

Matthias faced the other vendor, tears starting to form in his eyes. "Yes, and this is exactly what I needed for the back taxes I owe to the Romans. Praise Elohim, He has heard my prayers."

When John overheard the vendors' conversation, he smiled.

The group journeyed a day and a half north of Jerusalem, arriving near Sychar. There the village of Samaria was nearly halfway between Jerusalem and Galilee.

James came alongside the Teacher. "Sir, typically we avoid contact with Samaritans because they are considered atheistic, or half-Jews. Why are we deliberately walking in this direction?"

"Watch and learn," said Y'shua.

They arrived at the well of Jacob, the grandson of the patriarch Abraham. There, the Teacher sat on short stone wall. The journey was hot and dry.

As Y'shua rested, he looked up and smiled. "Simon-Peter, take the men into the village and purchase something to eat."

Looking around, Peter saw tired and anxious men. When he looked in the direction of Samaria, a sour expression formed. The Teacher stood and touched Peter's shoulder, causing him to shudder. He twisted around, facing Y'shua.

"Our Samaritan brothers and sisters are from the same family, are they not?"

Peter began to protest. "So you say, but . . . "

"John and I will wait here for your return."

After a lengthy pause, Peter released a heavy sigh. "Yes, Y'shua."

The Teacher sat down and waited while the group disappeared down the road. He then closed His eyes and began praying. John reverently moved away and sat upon a large boulder, watching.

Between the long journey, the heat, and a little boredom, John was soon fast asleep.

Awakened by the sounds of a donkey braying and clanging harnesses, John sat up. He saw a Samaritan woman stop alongside the well. Strapped to the donkey's back were two large watering jars. As she untied a bucket with a long rope, she eyed the Teacher and John warily. She cautiously walked to the wall and was ready to drop the bucket into the deep well, when the Teacher spoke.

"May I have a drink?"

She set the bucket down. "I see you are a Jew, yet you ask me for a drink? I thought Jews had nothing to do with us."

"If you truly understood the gift of Elohim, and who is asking you for a drink, you would be asking Him, and He would give you living water."

"Sir, you have nothing to draw water with, and the well is deep. Where would you find this living water? Are you greater than our ancestor, great-grandfather Jacob, who gave us this well? Jacob, his sons, and his livestock, all drank from this well for over a thousand years. Generations of his family have come here to drink. Without a bucket, how can you offer me something called *living water?*"

John moved closer so he could listen to the conversation details. He was curious as to why Y'shua would speak with a woman, especially a Samaritan.

The Teacher extended His hand toward the opening. "Whoever drinks water from this well will get thirsty again. Anyone who drinks of the water I shall give him will never thirst again. The water I am offering will produce a fountain of living water springing up into everlasting life."

"Sir, please share this water with me so I may never thirst again. Besides, I'm tired of loading and hauling water to the village every day."

Y'shua smiled. "I'll tell you, first go and get your husband and bring him here."

Pausing, the Samaritan woman narrowed her eyes and hesitantly said, "I have no husband."

"When you say you have no husband, you speak the truth. For you have had five men as husbands and the man you're living with now, isn't your husband even though you live as if you're married."

Speechless, the Samaritan woman stared blankly at the Teacher. With a shakiness to her voice, she quietly said, "Sir, I suspect you are a prophet."

Y'shua smiled. "A prophet, yes, and sent to you by My Father in heaven."

"If You're a prophet, answer this. Our ancestors worshiped Elohim here on the local mountain. Yet, you Jews say Jerusalem is the only place where we ought to worship."

"Woman, trust Me when I say; a time is coming when neither on this mountain nor in Jerusalem, will you worship My Father, Elohim. You worship from what you think you know but don't really understand what you're worshiping. We worship what we know, for salvation is coming from the Jews.

"Now is the time when true worshipers shall worship the Father, Elohim, in spirit and truth, for the Father seeks the kind of people who worship him in this manner. Elohim is a spirit, and those who worship him must do so in spirit and truth."

The Samaritan woman frowned. "This is what I know, Y'shua the Messiah is coming. When He comes to us, He will explain every mystery, He will save and deliver us from our enemies. So, are You the Messiah, who is promised?"

"Yes, I am the one."

While the Teacher spoke to the Samaritan woman, the group arrived from the village. James elbowed Peter jutting his chin toward the Samaritan woman.

"Why is He talking with her? I wonder what she wants," he asked.

Peter shrugged.

Excited, the woman immediately left the donkey, watering jars, and her bucket behind. Running as fast as she could, she dashed for the village.

While watching the Samaritan woman run off, the group approached the Teacher. The men kept looking over their shoulder, watching the woman disappear. Several of the men extended small wrapped bundles.

"We purchased something to eat. Here, Teacher, have some."

Y'shua smiled. "I have food to eat of which you do not know."

"Who brought You something to eat?" asked Thomas.

"Did the Samaritan woman give You some food?" asked James

John looked at his friends and silently shook his head.

Peter asked, "Then where did You get Your food, Teacher?"

"My food is to do the will of Elohim who sent Me and to finish His work. Don't you always hear farmers saying, 'There are still four months before the harvest comes?' I'm telling you now, look at the fields for they are already white, indicating it is harvest time. The one who reaps gathers fruit for eternal life and will receive their just wages.

"This way, the one who reaps and one who sows will rejoice together. For the old saying is true, 'One sows, and another reaps.' I have sent you to reap where you have not labored, yet you have gathered from the labors of others."

As the men listened to Y'shua speak, they heard a crowd of people coming toward the well. Soon a large group of Samaritans from the village encircled Jacob's well. They recognized each other, but the town people only stared at the Teacher who was warmly smiling.

Out of breath, the Samaritan woman pulled on the arm of one man. With animated speech, she hurriedly explained what she had witnessed and heard.

"I was just visiting Jacob's well when I saw this Jewish man sitting there. We spoke about many things including living water. Most of all, He knew intimate details about my life and . . . " She pointed a finger at her man. "He even had information about you. I believe this is the Messiah! Come, you must meet Him."

"Has Photini, your woman, been drinking, Ephra?" someone asked.

"She must be drunk. She is rambling like a crazy person," said another.

Ephra ignored the gossiping villagers and stood alongside his woman. "Because Photini said You told her every detail about her life, we believe her testimony. You are the Messiah."

Suddenly, the folks from the village pleaded for Y'shua and His group to stay for a while. "You must come to our village and stay with us and eat with our families."

"Yes, kind sir, please,.You must stay here in our homes."

John and Peter stared at one another.

"We are Hebrews, and they are Samaritans, yet they are willing to have us stay in their homes?" asked Peter.

"Are we not strangers, no worse, enemies?" asked Thomas.

John smiled. "We must remember, they are brothers and from the same father, Abraham."

As the crowd walked back to the village, the Teacher casually spoke with everyone who asked questions. When they arrived, people gathered in the village square. Many sat on the ground and listened to Y'shua speak. They marveled at His words and wisdom. A few of those who were ill also received healing. The hospitality of the Samaritans was beyond their expectations, so the Teacher and His witnesses stayed for two days.

The Teacher spoke while John sat watching and listening when several individuals pressed close to Photini. "Now we believe. Not just because of what you told us, we believe because we have heard the truth ourselves. Indeed, this man they call the Teacher is really the Messiah, and we believe in Him."

CHAPTER THIRTEEN

THE DAY BEFORE SABBATH

"DOES NOT THE TORAH SAY, 'Adonai, YaHoWaH, will raise up for you a prophet like Me from among you, from your brothers; it is to Him you shall listen,'" said the father of Nicodemus, also a Pharisee of the Sanhedrin.

"That is foolishness, Ziba. The prophet Ezekiel says, 'Mortal man, tell the ruler of Tyre what I, the Sovereign Elohim, am saying to him, puffed up with pride, you claim to be a god. You say, like a god, you sit on a throne, surrounded by the seas. You may pretend to be a god, but, no, you are mortal, not divine.' Man is not equal to YaHoWaH. So to say so is an unforgivable sin," argued another Pharisee named Benjamin.

Many of the elders had gathered from various cities to take part in the annual discussions. The council would often meet weeks ahead of the Passover to haggle over matters of law. On this day, just before the Sabbath, the elders gathered to hear petitions of the court regarding legal issues for the citizens in and around Jerusalem. A lull in the line of petitioners appearing before the court opened the opportunity for the Pharisees to freely argue other matters. The subject of the Teacher came up, and a hot debate ensued.

Annas stood from his seat. "Leviticus says, 'Anyone who blasphemes the name of YaHoWaH must be stoned to death by the whole community of Israel. Any native-born Israelite or foreigner among you who blasphemes the name of YaHoWaH must be put to death.' This man, called the Teacher, claims to be the Son of YaHoWaH. Enough of this discussion about this Man and His blasphemy." Sitting down, Annas folded his arms, as if he were saying this was the final word on the matter.

Nicodemus, son of Ziba, stood. "Then what shall we do about this teacher called Y'shua of Nazareth. He has followers, a core group of men He calls His apostles, and His numbers grow with each passing day. His followers defy the authority of this council."

Ziba nodded and smiled. He was proud of how wise his son was becoming. Since Ziba was nearing eighty years and close to death, he wanted his son to replace him on the council of Pharisees.

Another elder spoke up. "Yes, what shall we do with this man who stirs up revolts. Have you seen the men following Him? That man, named Simon, is as strong as an ox. He frightens even the temple guards."

Joseph of Arimathea stood. "The temple guards are chosen for their looks, not their strength. They exercise their power through our authority."

Several in the room laughed and soon the men were quietly arguing. The high priests let the elders have a period of discussion, but soon they exerted their authority over the conversations.

Annas raised his hand, bringing the murmuring within the council chambers to an abrupt halt. "Cut off the serpent's head, and let the others scatter liked frightened sheep. This is what I say."

His proclamation was not lost on the men sitting around the room. Associations of the snake always represented evil and opposition to YaHoWaH. The room erupted in chatter again.

Caiaphas took his hard staff and slammed the end down on the stone floor, making a loud cracking sound. "In due time, gentlemen, in due time. I'm working on a plan as we speak. Soon we will end this rabble-rouser's dissension." In defiance, he refused to utter the Teacher's name.

Silently, heads slowly nodded in agreement.

Nicodemus had just recently been invited to join the council. He sat alongside an older man from the city of Arimathea by the name of Joseph who had befriended him. Seated around the room were others by the names of Gamaliel, Simeon, and Jonathan, nearly forty people in total.

Of all the people in the room, Nicodemus disliked Caiaphas the most. In addition to wearing a purple robe sewn with gold thread, Caiaphas had gold tassels inscribed with Scripture on the edges of his garment. Wearing an unspoiled, jewel-encrusted, white turban atop his head, Caiaphas thought he was of the same level as Moses himself as he administered edicts and assumed they contained the wisdom of Solomon. As high priest, Caiaphas was wealthy, powerful, and arrogant.

Nicodemus also detested how Caiaphas was cozy with Pontius Pilate, the Roman governor of Judaea. Caiaphas strutted through the synagogue with the authority of Abraham and expected devoted, almost worshipping, attention from everyone. Although short in stature, Caiaphas compensated for his height by ruling the court with an iron fist.

A temple guard entered the room in his ceremonial leather breastplate and uniform and cried out, "A petitioner wishes to approach the court. His name is Koresh."

After looking at Caiaphas, Annas nodded to the guard.

A slovenly man appeared before them. His soiled clothes reeked of onions, garlic, sweat, and old wine. The man removed his hat from his balding head and bowed before the council. His fat belly protruded under his shirt, and he rested his hairy fat arms across the midsection like a shelf. A soiled apron hung over the front of his clothes, and it was emblazoned with dried animal blood. Sallow-skinned, the man's dark eyes darted around the room as his lips curled upwards.

"Thank you, kind sirs." Koresh stepped toward the high priests, but two temple guards stopped him by crossing their spears in front of him. The ugly man snickered.

"State your business, Koresh," said one of the elders as he stepped near the man. As if seeking protection, the elder remained behind one of the guards.

Reaching inside his garments, Koresh withdrew his hands and leaned toward the elder. He grasped the elder's hand and shook it vigorously. "Thank you for hearing my petition."

The elder pulled his hand free and looked into his palm.

Koresh had deftly deposited three gold shekels, roughly several years wages, in the palm of this elder.

The elder displayed his open palm to Caiaphas.

Koresh chuckled. "You see, I uh . . . what I'm asking today, is . . . would this court grant me a divorce." Frightened and nervous laughter emitted from Koresh.

"And the grounds for this divorce?" asked Annas as he stood and walked over to the elder holding the coins. Annas plucked the gold coins from the elder's hand.

Koresh bowed his head, attempting to look solemn. "My wife is ill, dying really. I have needs. She is unfaithful to our bed."

"Lies!" cried out Caiaphas. Again, his hard staff slammed to the stone floor. He arose from his chair and walked over to Koresh.

Koresh protested, "I swear this on my mother's grave—"

Suddenly, from seemingly nowhere, Caiaphas' flat hand slapped Koresh across the side of his face.

Koresh cried out in pain and instantly massaged his red face. "But sir, I brought my tokens."

Caiaphas took his staff and tapped it against Annas' wrist causing the gold coins to fall on the floor.

"I implore you, sirs. Please accept my gift, for the divorce." Koresh bent over to gather the scattered gold coins. Crawling on the floor he reached out to grasp the first one, but Caiaphas stepped on his hand. Koresh cried out in pain.

"We will not accept your bribe," stated Caiaphas flatly. He kept his foot on the man's hand crushing it to the stone floor. Caiaphas then jabbed Koresh's shoulder with his staff, causing Koresh to look up. Tears forming in the corner of his eyes.

"Please grant me my divorce. My life is bedeviled," begged Koresh.

Caiaphas sternly stared at the man on the floor. "Close your foul mouth, Koresh. Did you not come to this court many years ago, begging to marry your brother's wife . . . Eunice was her name, if I recall correctly?"

"I did, but this was before she became ill and she denied—"

"Silence! Your father was an honest man and ran your inn with great distinction. Your older brother took possession when your father died, and he ran the inn as well with honesty, but not you. You cheat your customers, you water-down your wine and beer, charging high fees for every holiday."

"I . . . I uh, run a clean tavern, sir."

Ignoring Koresh, Caiaphas continued. "You greedily saw the profit of your family and seized your chance when your older brother died unexpectedly. Even though Eunice was older, and perhaps a bit loud in the mouth, you demanded this court grant you permission to marry the woman."

"It was before I found out what kind of woman she was—"

Again, the flat palm of Caiaphas slapped Koresh on the face. "You wanted the money, Koresh. And now your wife is ill, and you wish to abandon her so you can fill your lust elsewhere."

His face stung and Koresh took his free hand and massaged his cheek. "Not true. No, I would—"

Caiaphas leaned his whole weight with his foot atop Koresh's fingers, causing several knuckles to make a popping noise. Koresh winced in pain.

"You're disgusting, Koresh. Eunice has served you faithfully. You have your lustful eyes set on the dark-skinned Canaanite girl who works in your kitchen. What is she, perhaps fifteen?"

"You're wrong sir. I, uh—"

Caiaphas rapped his staff atop Koresh's head. "Koresh, do not think me a fool. I know you have had your way with his girl already, sneaking out by the wine barrels every chance you get, spilling your seed inside this loathsome woman."

"Traitors," cried out Koresh. "My employees must be spying on me. And they're lying, I assure you."

"You will go home and care for your wife, honoring the name of your brother and your family. When she has lived her full life, you will wait in mourning for one full year before you may have another woman. Do you understand me?"

Caiaphas removed his foot from the hand of Koresh. "Now, leave us and remove your disgusting stench with you. Find two unblemished ewes and bring them to the sacrificial altar on Sabbath to cover your sins with this Canaanite servant girl and for dishonoring your family. If you do not, you force me to exact righteous punishment as given in the Mosaic Law." Caiaphas sneered. "You could receive forty lashes with a rod for having relations with the Canaanite girl. Worse, she could be stoned to death."

Koresh shivered and looked mortified. "I accept my punishment, sir." He began walking backward, while massaging his sore hand, but glared at Caiaphas with defiance and hate in his eyes.

Taking his staff, Caiaphas rammed it into Koresh's chest. He doubled over, landing on all fours on the floor, coughing and gasping for breath. "There will be no divorce Koresh. Two spotless sacrifices tomorrow!"

Crawling backward, Koresh freed himself from the room but with regret eyed the gold coins scattered on the floor. When he was out of range from Caiaphas, he scampered out the door.

"Guard, gather those coins and wash them thoroughly. Then deposit them into my treasure box," barked Caiaphas.

"Yes, sir," replied one of the guards.

CHAPTER FOURTEEN

WORDS OF REBELLION

"BROTHER NICODEMUS, A WORD WITH you."

Joseph of Arimathea approached Nicodemus following the Sabbath services in the temple. During the discussions in the service, the scroll reading selected for the day was from Isaiah, near the end of the book. As the two men walked alone, they discussed the meaning of the prophet's writing.

"Tell me, what are your thoughts regarding the words of Isaiah when he says, 'He was condemned to death without a fair trial. Who could have anticipated what would happen to him?'"

"Is not Isaiah speaking about King David's children?" asked Nicodemus with weak confidence.

"Can I trust you brother? I see your eyes whenever Caiaphas struts about as if he were Abraham himself!"

Nicodemus stopped walking. He noted Joseph's shift in the conversation topic. He scanned their surroundings to ensure the two men were utterly alone with no one eavesdropping. "Why are you asking me these things, Joseph? I suspect what you wish to discuss would ruin us or endanger our families. Be cautious with your thoughts."

Joseph looked stern and lowered his voice. "I need to ask you; can I trust you?"

Taking his palm and dragging it down his beard, Nicodemus quickly contemplated his older friend's question. The two men had known each other for more than fifteen years. Nicodemus always looked up to Joseph because of his wisdom. Joseph was not one to pontificate with unnecessary words but wisely selected the thoughts he shared. Other Pharisees would always nod quietly whenever Joseph would share his rare wisdom with them. Still, Joseph was not part of the inner circle of Pharisees in Jerusalem but instead chose to remain in Arimathea.

"I will not break our laws, and YaHoWaH knows my heart. Again, why are you asking me this question?"

Joseph leaned in close to his younger friend. "Because, I want to openly discuss some things with you, but I need to trust my words will not condemn me. So again, I ask you, can I trust you?"

Nicodemus suspected Joseph wanted to discuss the Teacher. "And, can I trust you as well?"

Joseph held out his hand, and Nicodemus reluctantly connected his palm to Joseph's forearm.

"May YaHoWaH's judgment come upon me if I ever betray your trust," said Joseph.

Nicodemus now knew the topic was dangerous. "You have my word, brother. I am your friend, and you can trust me."

The tension immediately eased, and Joseph relaxed. "Come, let us walk to the river where we may sit quietly and relax."

Walking to the town's edge, the two men engaged in light banter about family, the weather, and political tensions. Nicodemus noted Joseph deliberately avoided the central theme of his thoughts. He could tell Joseph was extraordinarily cautious and as a result, knew he must choose his words carefully when responding to his friend. He decided to let the elder friend take the lead.

Joseph selected a large boulder along the water's edge and sat down, watching the lake in the distance. The fishing boats were tied down and idle for the Sabbath.

"There are no lakes where I live, so I find it peaceful to come here and be alone," said Joseph as he stared across the lake.

Nicodemus sat alongside Joseph. "It stinks of fish and sweat."

Turning to face Nicodemus, Joseph smiled. "Must you always find something contrary to say? Is not the view a beautiful example of YaHoWaH's creation?"

Nicodemus glanced across the lake. Motionless, soft pillows of white cotton hung silently in the dark blue sky. Purple mountains ringed the lake, and lush grass grew along the shores. Birds peppered the lake as they ate insects and dove for small fish. Small white caps floated across the lake as the prevailing wind swept down the north-eastern mountains and disturbed the water's surface. Quiet and serene, the lake was picturesque. Pragmatic as usual, Nicodemus finally replied.

"I suppose so."

Joseph laughed out loud, and Nicodemus narrowed his eyes.

"These are your words of wisdom on the subject? You suppose so? My friend, you do need to get your nose out of the scrolls and spend time communicating with YaHoWaH out here." Joseph swept his arm in a broad arc.

Nicodemus felt chastised unnecessarily. His response contained an icy edge. "I find YaHoWaH just fine in the Torah."

Joseph put his arm around Nicodemus' shoulder and smiled. "YaHoWaH is everywhere, my friend. Everywhere we look, the finger of YaHoWaH exists. Even when I look at you, Nicodemus, I see YaHoWaH at work."

"You do? How?"

"Because, Nicodemus, I see your passion for knowing the inner workings of YaHoWaH. You spend hours in the old writings, searching to know YaHoWaH. That's how." Joseph was smiling.

Nicodemus relaxed and said, "I see." But he didn't really.

Joseph shook his head in disbelief. "Must you always be so serious?"

"No!"

"Tell me, what makes you happy, Nicodemus?"

"Discovering the hidden truths in the Torah and revealing the secret meanings in the texts. Finding wisdom for everyday situations."

"Is not the world around us part of YaHoWaH's creation?"

"Of course!"

"Do you ever wonder why YaHoWaH made so many types of animals? Why YaHoWaH makes the weather change from one season to another. Are not the mysteries of the stars enough to confuse the mind? Are there not truths in YaHoWaH's creation we can discover, just like the words in the texts you study?"

Nicodemus dropped his shoulders. "I never thought of it in those terms. I suppose . . . " He gave out a heavy sigh. "You may be correct."

The two men sat and watched nature's activity occurring on the lake, pondering their individual thoughts. After a lengthy pause, Joseph broke their silence.

"The text read this Sabbath, from Isaiah, 'He was condemned to death without a fair trial. Who could have anticipated what would happen to him?' Does this sound familiar?"

Nicodemus thought on Joseph's question but could not understand his friend's meaning. "Not really. "

"When Caiaphas declares judgment over this man, the Teacher, and without a trial, are we not guilty of Isaiah's words?"

Nicodemus detested Caiaphas, but he loathed to rebuke the Pharisee leader publicly. He used a tactful approach. "Tell me more on your thoughts."

"I believe Isaiah was predicting circumstances surrounding this man called Y'shua of Nazareth, and not specifically about King David's immediate children."

Nicodemus tensed. He knew what Joseph was insinuating, but he didn't want to concede the argument.

"Elaborate, Joseph."

"Have you not witnessed the miracles this Teacher performs?"

"I have. So what is your meaning?"

"Are you serious, Nicodemus? Surely only a man sent from heaven could do the things this Teacher has done?"

Nicodemus thoughtfully contemplated the knowledge only he knew firsthand about the Teacher. Would he risk his reputation and disclose his information? He began to share his thoughts, but Joseph stopped him.

"Before you answer, my friend, please know I have arrived at my own understanding, independent of the counsel of Pharisees and Caiaphas, concerning this man Y'shua."

Nicodemus looked around nervously to reconfirm they were alone. "What we are about to discuss could easily condemn us to death. Are you sure you want to pursue this path?"

Joseph relaxed and knowingly smiled. "I knew it, you have something to share?"

"Perhaps."

"Nicodemus! Enough! Out with it already."

Nicodemus quickly scanned their surroundings and then hoarsely whispered, "I met with the Teacher."

Joseph's mouth dropped open. "When was this?"

Again, Nicodemus swept the area with his eyes. "Perhaps a fortnight past." He kept his face downward.

Joseph leaned back and stared at Nicodemus. His expression of shock slowly shifted to amazement. The younger man nervously glanced up but quickly dropped his eyes back to the earth.

Joseph leaned in close. "Please tell me everything."

"You can't be serious. What if, I mean, what would happen if . . ." Nicodemus' voice trailed off, too afraid to express his thoughts.

"The truth? I'm concerned about this man called Y'shua. Caiaphas is too comfortable with the Romans, and I suspect he is planning something evil. I believe Caiaphas is scheming to have this Y'shua of Nazareth killed."

"Joseph, you're speaking about the high priest! You should be more careful."

"Caiaphas is a pompous fool who controls the council through fear and intimidation. This is why I remain in Arimathea and avoid the politics of Jerusalem."

Nicodemus was emboldened by his friend's confession. "The Teacher was with His followers, and I visited them late one night." A disgusted expression appeared on Nicodemus' face. "You will not believe me, but He even washed my hands and feet like a servant, kneeling on the earth before me. It was repulsive."

Joseph stared speechless at Nicodemus.

"We then sat down to eat supper. All of the Teacher's followers were across the room glaring at me. I think they were afraid of me. Everyone except the one called John, he sat like a protective guard next to the Teacher."

"Tell me, Nicodemus, what did you talk about?"

Shaking his head in disbelief, Nicodemus attempted to share the conversations. "The Teacher spoke about being reborn. He said, for a man to get into heaven, he must be born again."

"You mean again from his mother's womb?"

"I said the same thing. The Teacher's speech was confusing and full of riddles. I've never witnessed another man like this in my entire life. He never directly answered my questions, but continued to speak in these bizarre parables."

Joseph crossed his arms, resting the fingers from one hand against his lips. He frowned. After a period of silence, he asked, "What is He like? Did you find Him engaging? Did He perform a miracle for you?"

"Are you listening to me? This Y'shua is either a madman from the pit of hell or a prophet. I'm bewildered. When He talks about the Scriptures, He speaks with authority and confidence. Not even Caiaphas does this."

For a long time, the two men sat in silence, pondering their thoughts.

"Tell me everything He said, Nicodemus. Tell it all."

"When I questioned His riddle, He spoke about trees and the wind."

"Nicodemus, you're too literal. Tell me exactly what this Teacher told you."

Nicodemus rubbed his temples. "He said we must be reborn with the breath of YaHoWaH, unlike when a man is born from the mother's womb, but in spirit, a spiritual rebirth. He used the words water and spirit and said YaHoWaH provides the Holy Spirit and rebirths a man's heart. He further insisted He was from heaven and born of YaHoWaH, allowing Him to perform miracles."

"But wasn't Y'shua born in Bethlehem? His mother is Miryam and His father, Joseph, was a craftsman. His brothers and sisters are known by everyone. How can He say He is from heaven?"

Nicodemus shook his head. "I don't know. Y'shua then spoke about the brass rod of Moses, which turned into a snake, but when Moses lifted the snake into the air, it turned into the rod again. Y'shua said He would be lifted up in the same way."

Joseph frowned. "How confusing, are you absolutely certain these are His words?"

"It's what I remember. Oh, Y'shua also said if we believed what He was saying, we could have eternal life. He talked as if He was the Messiah, but I'm perplexed about this man."

Nicodemus looked down on the sand at his feet. Exhausted, his head hurt more than the night he spoke with the Teacher.

Joseph placed his arm around his friend's shoulders. "Listen to me I believe this Y'shua of Nazareth is at least a prophet. I think we must search the Scriptures for all the references concerning the Messiah. I suggest you find what you can and I will do the same. When I return to Jerusalem in a few weeks, we can continue this conversation."

Finally, Nicodemus looked up and stared at Joseph. "I suppose it makes sense."

"I must tend to my metals business and travel for a few weeks, but when I return, I want to hear about your discoveries. Promise me we will continue our conversation."

Nicodemus pondered Joseph's question, drawing a hand across his beard. He started to grin. "I will study and either prove what this Y'shua says is false or find the truth."

Joseph patted Nicodemus' leg. "Come, Nicodemus, walk with me back to the synagogue."

CHAPTER FIFTEEN

THE SEEDS OF CHANGE

FOR WEEKS, NICODEMUS BURIED HIS face in the old scrolls. He poured over the words of the major and minor prophets and the Torah. Making copious notes, Nicodemus started seeing things he had never noticed before. References to the Messiah were hidden in many passages. The more Nicodemus discovered, the more determined he searched.

"You are spending a great deal of time in the scrolls, Nicodemus. What are you seeking with such fervor?"

Startled, Nicodemus jumped when the voice of his father broke the room's silence. He swallowed hard and felt a tightness in his chest. "Papa! I did not hear you behind me."

Ziba, looked over his son's shoulder and inspected the scrolls on the table. His wrinkled and bony fingers traced out his son's written words. Several manuscripts were stacked upon one another. He saw the notes his son had written. He squinted at the writing, trying to focus. "And what words are in Micah, Zechariah, Isaiah, and Daniel that have your interest?"

His son coughed nervously, trying to clear his dry throat. "My friend, Joseph of Arimathea, has challenged me."

As soon as the words escaped his lips, Nicodemus worried he disclosed too much, perhaps causing his father to further question his work.

Ziba, narrowed his eyes, staring at his son.

Nicodemus swallowed a hard lump in his throat. "Joseph of Arimathea is a good teacher." He forced a laugh.

His father stretched his arm and rested a hand on his son's shoulder. "Wisdom is knowledge from YaHoWaH. Joseph of Arimathea is a wise man, indeed." The elder's eyes watered as he relaxed his body. "You make me proud Nicodemus. I rejoice in the day you will replace me on the council."

Nicodemus hugged his father and kissed his neck. "Thank you, Papa, I love you. But, you still have plenty of life left in you. We have lots of time."

Ziba slowly shook his head and looked down. "Only YaHoWaH knows, my son. His blessings exceed my expectations already. If we could just cast off the heavy garment of Rome from our land, then we could truly be free again." He gave a heavy sigh. "This would be a good time for the Messiah to actually come and rescue us."

Nicodemus' heart leapt, and he almost blurted out what he had discovered in the scrolls, but caught himself. "Perhaps the Messiah is closer than we think, Papa."

Ziba looked up, a glimmer of hope in his eyes. "Only the Messiah's appearing could exceed the joy I have because of you, my son."

The two men embraced again.

As Y'shua traveled throughout the Galilee region, word from some of His followers arrived from Jerusalem. Simon of Caesarea ran up to the Apostles who were following the Teacher. Winded, Simon forced his way to the front of the crowd.

"John! You must be careful. My brother's son-in-law is a temple guard, and he said the Jewish Council is making plans to have the Teacher killed."

James passionately urged Y'shua. "Teacher, the Festival of Shelters is upon us. Perhaps we should not travel to Jerusalem at this time."

The others formed a tight circle around the Teacher and James. Thomas pressed the Teacher further. "James is correct. We will ignore the festival and remain safe here in Galilee."

Philip pushed everyone aside. "Leave this place and go to Judea, so Your followers will see the things You are doing. When people are doing good things, they don't hide what they are doing, especially if they want to be well known. Since You are doing these great miracles, let the whole world know about You!"

Suddenly, an argument broke out with each of the men trying to make their point. Some yelled above the chorus of voices.

Holding up His hands, Y'shua produced a warm smile, bringing the noisy group to silence. "The right time for Me has not yet come. Any time is right for you. The world cannot hate you, but it hates Me because I keep telling the leaders their ways are destructive. You go on to the festival. I shall not go but remain here. The right time has not yet come for Me."

Bewildered, the men glanced at one another and began murmuring.

John pulled on the Teacher's arm and whispered. "What do You mean the time is not right for You? Can You not, with one word, call down angels from heaven and crush the sanctimonious Jewish leaders?"

Y'shua placed His hands on the shoulders of John. He smiled and stared into John's eyes. "As always, you are passionate and speak the truth, My friend. But, again I say, My time has not yet come. Soon, but not now. We have more work to do before I must go. You will lead the others to Jerusalem for the festival. We will meet again at a later time."

John relaxed. "But, I'm not ready for You to leave us. I feel as if we have just started." He looked at the crowd gathered around them. "I'm worried we won't survive without You."

"Fear not, My friend. I will always be with you. The Holy Spirit will soon come and strengthen you when I am gone. For now, you must watch and listen."

"Always, Teacher. You know I am Your servant."

"Come, John, we must prepare the others for their journey."

With minimal fanfare, the Teacher's witnesses gathered their belongings and began their journey toward Jerusalem. Along the way, John listened to the men grumble among one another concerning the absence of their leader. Before long, Simon-Peter was encouraging the men to focus on the upcoming celebration.

"My friends, it's the Festival of Shelters, enough with the discouraging words. For me, I am looking forward to my mother's delicious, fluffy, and soft Callah. Oh, and her famous lamb meatballs and kugels!"

"Be quiet Simon. Now you're making me hungry," said Thomas.

Forcing his stomach out, Simon-Peter rubbed his big hands over the protrusion. "I can almost taste the scrumptious food now. For the next eight days, I am filling my belly with good food and wine." He grinned at his friends. "Then I am going to sleep all day!"

John shook his head and chuckled to himself. When they arrived in Jerusalem, the men split up, heading to individual relatives in the city.

Two days later, without warning, Y'shua set off for Jerusalem, walking alone. He encountered several travelers and stopped to visit with them, sharing words of encouragement and healing those who sought comfort. At the end of two days, He arrived at the hilltop overlooking Jerusalem. Deviating from the main road, He climbed an outcrop of rocks and sat down. Tears began to stream down His cheeks as He watched the city in the distance. "Father, Your will be done. Grant Me peace as I move toward Your destiny for Me. Protect the sheep You have given Me when I am gone. Amen."

Y'shua pulled His prayer shawl over His head and slowly walked into the city. Keeping His face hidden, He journeyed through the throngs of people who were intently pursuing their own agendas. Making His way to a specific home, and knocking on the entrance door, the Teacher was hastily welcomed. The master of the house embraced his guest.

"Rabbi, welcome. Come in, rest and refresh yourself."

Y'shua warmly smiled.

As the owner washed the Teacher's feet and hands, he said, "Your friends, John, Simon-Peter, and the others said You were remaining in Galilee, yet here You are. You are a welcomed guest in our home. Shalom."

"Shalom upon you, Joseph Bar-Nathan, and your whole household."

"Arise, Rabbi, Miriam has prepared fresh lamb stew and warm paratha bread." Joseph stood and walked toward the eating area.

"Perhaps later, friend. First I must spend time alone. May I use the room on the roof?"

"Of course, Rabbi. Please, join us when You are ready."

Y'shua touched Joseph's shoulder and smiled. "Thank you, My friend." He then climbed the small ladder and disappeared through the opening in the roof.

John and James stopped in the market and sat down for a bite to eat. They each ordered wine and waited for the server to deliver their request. When John spotted Nicodemus in the street, he nudged his brother, James.

Along with Nicodemus, they saw others of the Sanhedrin Council. The members were surrounded by temple guards in uniform. Folks walking the street gave the religious group a wide berth, avoiding eye contact.

"Spread out and find the man called Y'shua of Nazareth. Do so without disturbing the crowds. Go!" called out one of the Pharisees.

One of the guards took charge. "Yes, Annas." Immediately the temple guards walked away in different directions.

Annas grabbed the sleeve of one of the men walking nearby. The man had been intently eaves-dropping on their group, but when spotted, he tried to sneak away.

"Where is he, the one called Y'shua?" Annas asked.

Someone in the crowd yelled out, "He is a good man, this Y'shua. Leave Him alone."

"No," said another individual. "He is making fools of all of us. He cannot be trusted."

Annas looked around as people pressed into a tight circle. They cast their eyes away whenever Annas made eye contact. No one talked openly, but mumbled noisily.

Nicodemus scanned the marketplace and looked into the area where John and James were sitting. He narrowed his eyes. John and James quickly turned their faces and looked away.

"Here is your wine. Two denarius, please."

John placed four coins on the table. "We're thirsty, please bring us each another glass."

The server snatched the coins and walked back to the kitchen.

"Brother, do you think it is wise to sit here. What about them?" James pointed his thumb over his shoulder.

John stretched his neck and squinted into the sunlit market. The Jewish authorities were no longer there. He smiled.

"We're good for now. They're gone."

When the festival was nearly half over, Y'shua walked from the home of Joseph Bar-Nathan and Miriam and to the temple where He then began teaching the people who had gathered there. Among the various individuals in the temple area were men associated with the religious leaders. As they listened to His words, they were dumbfounded.

"How does this man know so much when He has never been to one of our schools?"

"He thinks He is a rabbi, but He is too young. Foolish man."

Y'shua looked up at the Jewish leaders and smiled. He spoke to them directly. "What I teach is not My own words, but it comes from YaHoWaH who sent Me. Whoever is willing to do what YaHoWaH wants will know whether what I teach comes from Him or whether I speak on My own authority. Those who speak on their own authority are trying to gain glory for themselves. But He who wants glory for the One who sent Him is honest, and there is nothing false in Him. Moses gave you the Law, didn't he? But not one of you obeys the Law. Why are you trying to kill Me?"

"You have a demon in You!" a scribe in the crowd answered.

"Who is trying to kill You?" asked a young Pharisee.

Nicodemus stood nearby and listened to the discussions.

Y'shua stared at the Jewish leaders. "I performed one miracle, and you were all surprised and annoyed. Moses ordered you to circumcise your sons, although it was not Moses but your ancestors who started the practice, and so you circumcise a boy on the Sabbath. If a boy is circumcised on the Sabbath so Moses' Law is not broken, why are you angry with Me because I made a man entirely whole on the Sabbath? Are not both actions considered work? Stop judging by what you see with your eyes, and discern the truth from what YaHoWaH has taught you."

Some of the people in the crowd acted surprised by the Teacher's wisdom and they began to argue among themselves. "Why are the authorities trying to kill this man?"

"Look, He is talking in public, and the authorities say nothing against Him! Can it be they really know He could be the Messiah?"

Another scribe chastised the crowd. "Did you learn nothing in school? When the Messiah comes, no one will know where He is from. We all know this Man comes from Nazareth."

Y'shua raised His voice. "Ah, but do you really know Me and where I am from? I have not come on My own authority. The One who sent Me, however, is pure truth. You do not know Him, but I know Him because I come from Him and He has sent Me here."

At once, the Jewish leaders were irritated. "You are a simple man from Nazareth. Now You boast of being sent from YaHoWaH?"

The leaders rushed toward the Teacher to seize him. As they were about to grab hold of Him, a crowd of onlookers encircled them with their mouths gaping open and staring.

A voice from the back of the crowd yelled out, "When the Messiah comes, will He perform more miracles than this Man has?"

Another individual said, "What laws did this Teacher break? He's made no threats against you."

Others began whispering supportive words about Y'shua and expressed displeasure with the actions of the Jewish leaders. The crowd then began to tighten the encircle around the small group of leaders. No one laid a hand on the Teacher.

Y'shua smiled, turned, and started walking away.

Annas rushed toward the leaders and the angry crowd. He stretched his arm over the knot of men, pointed a finger toward

Y'shua, and he called out, "Find the temple guards and then arrest this Man."

The Teacher stopped and faced Annas and Nicodemus. "I shall be with you a little while longer, and then I shall go away to Him who sent Me. You will look for Me, but You will not find Me because you cannot go where I will be."

"Where are You about to go so we shall not find You?" asked Nicodemus.

Another leader called out, "Will You go to the remote cities where our people live, and teach the Greeks?"

Another man from the Sanhedrin pulled on Nicodemus' arm, "He says we will look for Him but will not find Him, and we cannot go where He will be. What does He mean by these words?"

Nicodemus shrugged.

Y'shua smiled again, turned, and disappeared into the crowd.

When Nicodemus looked, he could no longer see Y'shua among the throng gathered in the temple square. The temple guards ran up to the leaders.

Annas grumbled aloud, "Where did He go? Find Him immediately."

The guards looked bewildered. "Who, sir? Where is he?"

CHAPTER SIXTEEN

THE MARCH TOWARD DESTINY

ON THE LAST AND MOST important day of the festival, Y'shua stood up in the synagogue and said in a loud voice, "Whoever is thirsty should come to Me, and whoever believes in Me should drink. As the Scripture says, 'Streams of life-giving water will pour out from His side.'

"When I am gone, the Holy Spirit will come to those who believe in Me. Once I am raised to the glory of My Father, then the Spirit will come."

Some of the people in the crowd heard Him say these things and said, "Perhaps, this Man is really the Prophet spoken of in the Torah!"

"I personally believe He is the Messiah!" exclaimed one man.

"What foolish talk this is! The Messiah will not come from Galilee!" spoke an elder rabbi hanging toward the back of the crowd.

Nicodemus stood nearby in the back of the synagogue and moved closer to the Teacher. He declared, "The Scriptures say the Messiah will be a descendant of King David, and He will be born in Bethlehem, the town where David came from. Tell us, were You born in Bethlehem?"

The crowd began arguing and screaming their various opinions, creating division among those standing there.

"This Man is from the devil, seize Him and take Him from the city to be stoned."

Yet no one in the crowd moved toward Y'shua.

Two temple guards observed and listened to the conversations between the crowd and the Teacher.

"Come, let us report our observations to the council," said one of the guards to Nicodemus.

The temple guards then left the area and regathered with the members of the council. Nicodemus followed them. When the guards gave their report to the Sanhedrin, the chief priests and Pharisees asked the guards, "Why did you not arrest Him and bring Him to us?"

The guards answered, "Nobody has ever talked the way this Man does! He speaks with authority and knowledge."

"Did He fool you, too?" the Pharisees asked them. "Have you ever known one of the authorities or one of the Pharisee to believe in this Man? The illiterate crowd does not understand the Laws of Moses, so they are under YaHoWaH's curse!"

Annas stepped in the middle of the group, hands in the air. "Listen to me, we will put an end to this madman soon enough."

Nicodemus raised his voice sharing his thoughts with the other Pharisees. "According to our Law, we cannot condemn someone without hearing from them and finding out what they have done."

Annas jabbed his finger toward Nicodemus and said, "Well, are you also from Galilee? Have you suddenly become one of His followers, too? Study the Scriptures, and you will learn no prophet has ever come from Galilee."

Frowning, Nicodemus tested the limits by pressing the issue further. "If this Man, Y'shua, is not the Messiah, then perhaps we might consider Him to be a prophet?"

An elderly rabbi stood up and shook his fist at Nicodemus. "I suggest you choose your words wisely, Nicodemus. Surely you are not duped by this Man's nonsense?"

"I'm simply saying we should give it consideration. I make no statement of fact, but I think we should consider the possibility this Man believes He speaks the truth. What if He is a prophet and we are the ones going against YaHoWaH's plan?"

The elder rabbi threw his hands into the air and scoffed. "I would be careful, Nicodemus. You speak of things you know nothing about. You are far too young and lack wisdom."

As the council continued in their arguments, Nicodemus dissolved into the crowd. He quickly returned to the synagogue and found the Teacher still speaking with the people gathered. He faced the Teacher who returned a warm smile and then Nicodemus sat down. Dumbfounded, he could not believe the extreme confidence Y'shua was displaying. *Do You not know these men are scheming and planning Your death this very moment?*

As He spoke with the people, the Teacher inched through the crowd, moving closer to Nicodemus. He then leaned over and whispered, "How are your scroll-studies coming along, Nicodemus? Did you discover anything enlightening?"

A shudder passed through Nicodemus as he blankly stared. He jumped to his feet and dashed from the synagogue. He wiped beads of sweat forming on his brow with a sleeve. Nicodemus shook his head and rushed home.

Hands shaking, he began unrolling his scrolls and he pulled his notes from a box where he had hid them. Muttering, he could not process the information fast enough nor could he arrive at any conclusions. Frustration overwhelmed Nicodemus as he read over his notes. "Why? What does this mean? Who is the Messiah? Help me, YaHoWaH."

He poured over the notes and the scrolls and furiously scrawled messages about his findings. Lost in his thoughts, Nicodemus started seeing connections he had missed before. Mumbling to himself, he began quoting Scriptures, which took on new meaning.

"In Deuteronomy it says, 'I will rise up for them a Prophet like you from among their brethren and will put the words of Elohim in His mouth, and He shall speak to them all that YaHoWaH commands. And it shall be, whoever will not hear the words of YaHoWaH, which He speaks in My name, I will require it of him.'

"And here in Isaiah, 'Then the eyes of the blind shall be opened, and the ears of the deaf shall be unstopped. Then the lame shall leap like a deer and the tongue of the dumb sing.' Is this not the same miracles this Y'shua is doing?"

Nicodemus jumped as someone suddenly knocked on the door. His breathing quickened as the banging continued. Nicodemus clutched his notes to his chest and stared. He quickly hid the scrolls and his summary notes under a covering. Just then, a familiar voice spoke from the other side of the door.

"Nicodemus, are you home?"

Frightened, Nicodemus jerked the door open and scanned the streets in both directions. He ignored his visitor and narrowed his eyes searching for anything out of place. Satisfied they were alone, and not being watched, he forcefully grabbed Joseph of Arimathea by his outer cloak and quickly pulled him into the house. Hastily, Nicodemus locked the door.

Joseph's voice was stern. "Nicodemus, stop! Are you crazy? What's wrong?"

"Were you followed?" demanded Nicodemus.

"What?"

Nicodemus repeated his question, enunciating each word. "Were you followed?"

Joseph walked over to the eating table and sat in one of the empty chairs. "Come, Nicodemus, sit with me. But first, why don't you tell me what's going on."

Hesitant at first, Nicodemus sputtered. "I . . . ah . . . I ah . . . I. . . " His words faded away as he began pacing.

After sitting in silence, Joseph finally reached out and pulled Nicodemus into a nearby chair.

"Stop pacing, Nicodemus. You're distressing me."

Frowning, Nicodemus finally began sharing his thoughts. He blurted out, "Because of my studying, I think the Messiah might possibly be Y'shua, the Teacher!"

Joseph blinked several times and then a smile slowly crept into the corners of his mouth. "Oh my, your studies have progressed rather quickly. Tell me, what proof do you have?"

Nicodemus jumped from his chair and pulled a weighty cloth away, uncovering his notes. He unrolled several scrolls. Excited, he poked a finger at the writing where he thought Y'shua fulfilled the Scriptures. "Surely you've arrived at the same conclusions. Look at what I found, and these words from the prophet Malachi!"

Joseph quickly scanned Nicodemus' handwritten notes. Periodically, he paused and glanced at the Scripture references in the scrolls. "I see . . . " Joseph slowly stood and leaned over the table. "Humm . . . " Stroking his beard, he narrowed his eyes and finally looked up at Nicodemus.

"Well, Joseph?" pleaded Nicodemus.

"When I started my own research, I wasn't absolutely certain the scrolls would support my thoughts on the subject, but—"

"Then you agree?"

Joseph rested his hand over his beard thoughtfully.

"Joseph! This is serious," demanded Nicodemus.

"I'm well aware, my friend. We will be marked for expulsion if we present this to our colleagues in the Sanhedrin."

Nicodemus' mouth dropped open. He fell backward into a nearby chair and nearly crashed on the floor. Joseph grabbed Nicodemus. He stumbled with his words. "I ah, I hadn't considered the outcome. We'll be ruined. No one will believe us."

"Hold your tongue, Nicodemus, your arguments are convincing, but I must warn you—"

"Then you don't agree with me?"

"I didn't disagree. I believe what I'm saying is we must be careful."

Nicodemus relaxed and dropped his head.

Joseph patted his shoulder, "You are far too serious, Nicodemus."

"How else can this Y'shua perform the miracles we've heard of, not to mention the wisdom He speaks? Is there any way to explain it? I know He talks in riddles, but even you must admit He baffles our wisest men on the council."

Joseph nodded slowly.

"So now what do we do?" asked Nicodemus.

"We? Are you suggesting we join with His followers?"

Nicodemus was taken aback. He wasn't prepared for Joseph's response. "You have another suggestion?"

Joseph sat back down and pondered. He rubbed his temples.

Nicodemus anxiously waited and fidgeted.

Joseph said nothing but scowled.

Nicodemus loudly sighed.

After a long pause, Joseph finally spoke. His words were thoughtful and calmly expressed. "I suggest we closely follow Y'shua and observe His actions and words further. Perhaps we will learn more."

Nicodemus let his shoulders slump.

Joseph stood, resting a hand on Nicodemus. "Be of good courage, this is an excellent start. We must get more information."

Nicodemus began to protest but decided against his actions. "I suppose you're correct."

"You must learn more about this Y'shua and be like His followers by listening carefully. You're not quite yet part of the inner council at the Sanhedrin. Perhaps, if you dressed appropriately, you might blend into the crowds following along."

Nicodemus looked up at Joseph, his eyes wide. "Are you suggesting I pretend to be one of His followers?"

"No, an observer."

"I must share something, which will put fear in your heart. When Y'shua was speaking at the synagogue earlier today, I was watching and listening. As He moved through the room, Y'shua inched closer and then leaned over and asked me how my scroll studies were progressing. It was as if He knew what I was doing."

"Seriously? He actually spoke to you and asked about your studies?" inquired Joseph.

Nicodemus nodded. "How did He know?"

Joseph contemplated this information. "Perhaps He was guessing."

Nicodemus threw his hands in the air in exasperation. "Guessing?"

The two men stared at each other and said nothing for a long time. Nicodemus began pacing again.

"What about one of His followers, the man named John, perhaps you could have discussions with him and ask more questions."

Nicodemus contemplated his friend's suggestion. He liked this idea better than pretending to be a follower of Y'shua.

"I'll try, but I make no promises."

Joseph smiled. "Good. Now, I must go and meet with the council over other matters. We will talk again soon."

Speechless, Nicodemus watched Joseph walk out the door and into the bright sunlit street.

CHAPTER SEVENTEEN

GUILTY!

EARLY THE NEXT MORNING Y'SHUA walked back to the temple. People gathered around Him as He sat down and began to teach them. While He was speaking, a tremendous commotion erupted in the outer courtyard. He paused and watched as a crowd of men roughly drag a disheveled woman into the area where He was sitting. Several teachers of the law and some Pharisees were responsible for the uproar and clutched the woman by her long hair. Thrusting her at the Teacher, they barked out their complaint.

"This woman was brought to You because she has been caught committing adultery!"

Immediately, the woman faced the ground hiding her tears.

With no respect in his voice, the oldest of the Pharisees looked down on Y'shua and said, "So You are called a *rabbi*. This woman was caught in the very act of committing adultery. In our law, Moses commanded such a woman must be stoned to death. Now, what do *You* say?" The Pharisee had a rock in his hand, and he shook it at Y'shua.

Sneering and laughing among themselves, the teachers of the law and Pharisees made hand gestures and yelling. Finally, they had Y'shua pinned into a corner, and they were savoring the moment.

Ignoring them, the Teacher bent over and began writing on the ground with His finger.

"Well, *rabbi*, what wise words do You have for us?" yelled one man.

"Yes, tell us the law doesn't work in Your favor," said another.

"She cannot be forgiven, we have the law on our side," demanded the older Pharisee.

Y'shua stood up. He looked at the mob of men who were accusing the woman and saw that many men had large rocks in their hands. Y'shua had no expression on His face, instead He held His open palm in the direction of the frightened woman.

"I'll tell you, whichever one of you has committed no sin may throw the first stone at her." Y'shua then squatted on the ground and wrote more words in the dirt.

An eternity passed as the accusers stood shifting their weight from one foot to another, staring at the Teacher. Some rolled the rocks over in their hands, debating their next actions. Suddenly, the oldest Pharisee threw his rock down. A small puff of dust kicked up as the big stone landed with a loud thud. The accused woman jerked from the sound but continued to stare down. With no further conversations, the men began dropping their rocks, one-by-one, starting with the oldest men first. Finally, the younger men released their stones and the angry mob slowly melted away.

When the Teacher looked up from His squatted position, the woman was still standing shamefully crying. He straightened up and smiled.

"Where did everyone go? Is there no one left to condemn you?"

Her voice was hesitant. "I have no idea, sir. There is no one left to stone me."

Y'shua cupped her chin with His hand. He looked into her tearful and terrified eyes and warmly smiled.

"Well then, I do not condemn you either. Now go, but it is time for you to stop sinning and to start making different choices for your life."

She gave a quick nod, then turning, the woman ran away.

Y'shua saw the teachers of the law and the Pharisees gathered in a tight knot a few yards away. He watched them arguing with one another and walked toward them.

John and Simon-Peter followed behind Y'shua, but John glanced down at the dirt where the Teacher had been writing. Y'shua had written the Ten Commandments as recorded by Moses. The command to not lust after a neighbor's wife was underlined. John smiled and followed his leader.

As Y'shua approached the Pharisees, the group stopped arguing and faced Him. "What words of wisdom do You now have?"

"I am the light of the world. Whoever follows Me will have the light of life and will never walk in darkness."

One of the Pharisees said to Him, "So, now You are witnessing on Your own behalf? What You are saying proves nothing."

"No, you're incorrect. Even though I do testify on My own behalf, what I say is true, because I know where I came from and where I am going. You do not know where I came from or where I am going. You make judgments in a purely human way. I, on the other hand, pass judgment on no one. But, if I were to pass judgment, My judgment would be true, because I am not alone in My actions. My Father, YaHoWaH, Who sent Me, is with Me. Is it not written in your Law that the witness of two men speaks the truth? Well, in the same way,

I have testified on My own behalf, and My Father who sent Me also testifies on My behalf."

"So, where is Your Father?" they asked Him as they looked around. "As rumor has it, You are nothing but a fatherless child."

"Unfortunately, you know neither My Father nor Me," Y'shua answered. "If you really knew Me, you would know My Father also. I will soon go away, and You will look for Me, but you will die in your sins. You cannot go where I am going."

Looking at one another, the Jewish authorities said, "He says we cannot go where He is going. Does this mean He will kill Himself?"

Y'shua smiled. "You belong to this world here below, but I come from above. You are from this world, but I am not from this world. This is why I told you, you will die in your sins. You will die in your sins if you do not believe I am, whom I say I am."

"And just who do You think You are?" they asked.

"You are supposed to be the educated and wise, yet you are not. I am what I have told you from the very beginning. I have so much to say about you, much to condemn you for. The one who sent Me, however, is truthful, and I tell the world only what I have heard from My Father."

With blank expressions, they stared at the Teacher. "You speak gibberish. Nothing You say even makes sense." Several men threw their hands in the air in a dismissive fashion.

"On the day, when you lift Me up, then you will know I am, whom I say I am. It is only then, you will know I have done nothing on My own authority, but I say only what My Father has instructed Me to say. You will also understand that He who sent Me is always with Me. He has never left Me alone because I always do what pleases Him."

Several bystanders yelled out, "Without a doubt, this is a Man from heaven."

"Yes, He is a true prophet," said another person.

"I, for one, believe He is telling us the truth," exclaimed an older man in the crowd.

"Why are you leaders so afraid of this Man?" asked someone.

Facing those who spoke their supportive words, Y'shua said to them, "If you obey My teaching, you are really My disciples, and then you will know the truth, and the truth will set you free."

Several of the Pharisees beat their fists against their chests. "We are the descendants of Abraham, and we have never been anybody's slaves."

Another person yelled out, "What do you mean, Rabbi, by saying 'we will be free?'"

Y'shua said to them, "I am telling you the truth, everyone who sins is a slave to sin. A slave does not belong to a family permanently, but a son, he belongs to the family forever. Therefore, if the Son sets you free, then you will be truly free. I know you are Abraham's descendants. Yet you are trying to kill Me because you will not accept My teaching. I talk about what My Father has shown Me, but you do what your father has told you."

The teachers of the law cried out, "Your words are from the enemy. We know who our father is, and he is Abraham!"

Smiling, the Teacher said, "If you really were Abraham's children, then you would do the same things he did. In all the times I have been with you, everything I have done or said is to tell you the truth. I speak what My Father, YaHoWaH tells Me, yet you are trying to kill Me. Abraham did nothing like this! You are foolishly doing exactly what your fathers have done."

Shaking their fists at the Teacher, they said, "Just who do You think You are talking to? YaHoWaH is the only Father we have, and we are His true children. The Torah tells us this, and they are words given to us by Abraham."

Y'shua pressed forward and leaned into their faces. "You see, this is an odd struggle. If YaHoWaH truly were your Father, well then, you would love Me because I came from YaHoWaH, and now I am here. I did not come on My own authority, but My Father sent me. Why do you have such difficulty understanding My words? I'll tell you why; it is because you cannot bear to listen to My message of truth."

Y'shua swept His hand over the group arguing with Him. "All of you are children of your father, the Devil. You follow the Devil's desires. From the very beginning, the Devil has been a murderer and never on the side of truth because there is no truth in him. When he tells a lie, he is only doing what is natural to him, because he is a liar and the father of all lies. But I tell the truth, and this is why you do not believe Me."

"Absolute nonsense. You're a foolish man with no formal education," yelled one teacher of the law. "Do not lecture us on the fine points of our law."

"Let Me ask you, which one of you can prove that I am guilty of sin? If I tell the truth, then why do you not believe Me? If someone comes from YaHoWaH, then they will listen to YaHoWaH's words. You, however, are not from YaHoWaH, which is why you won't listen."

Then an argument broke out with several of the leaders calling out insults.

"We're right, You are just like the heathen Samaritans."

"Yes, You have a demon inside You," a man cried out.

Y'shua replied, "I have no demon inside Me. Instead, I honor My Father, but you show no respect. I'm not asking for you to honor My position as the Father's son. But, mark my word, there is One who seeks to honor Me, and He judges everything in My favor. I always tell the truth. Whoever obeys My teaching will never die."

A Pharisee faced off with Y'shua. "See, we were right, You do have a demon inside You. Your words confirm it! You say, whoever obeys Your teaching will never die, yet Abraham died, and our prophets have died. If Abraham is dead, are You claiming to be greater than Abraham? Are You better than our prophets? Just who do You think You are? You're a simple man, and according to Your mother, You have no father."

After a pause, Y'shua smiled. "If I were to honor Myself, My honor would be worth nothing. The One who honors Me is My Father, the very One you say is your YaHoWaH. You have never known Him, but I know who He is. If I were to say I do not know Him, I would be a liar like you. But I do know Him, and I obey His word. Your father Abraham rejoiced because he was glad to see the time of My coming. Abraham saw it and was quite happy."

An elderly teacher of the law swiftly shoved his way to the front, shaking his finger up at Y'shua. "You are not even fifty years old, yet You have seen Abraham?"

Y'shua smiled broadly. "I am telling you the truth, before Abraham was born, I was."

Instantly, the group of teachers of the law and Pharisees grew extremely angry. They picked up stones to throw at Y'shua, but He turned and left the temple. In a matter of seconds, He vanished into the people standing nearby.

"Where did He go?"

"How can a man disappear like smoke, and so fast?" asked one of the Pharisees.

The oldest of the Pharisees frowned and produced an angry expression. He swept his eyes around the crowd and saw open-mouthed people watching his group. Making a wordless grunt, he stormed away with the others following close behind.

Nicodemus made mental notes of the conversations he witnessed. *Every time Y'shua speaks, He confirms what I know about this Man.*

As Y'shua walked away, John hurried and walked alongside his leader. He kept glancing up at His face but didn't say anything. His brow was creased.

Stopping, Y'shua stared at John. "Something troubles you, My friend?"

John looked around and saw the others in their group gathered around. The Teacher followed John's eyes.

"Peter, take the men to the market, we will join you shortly." He watched the men walk away and turned back to John. "Tell Me, what is on your mind."

John smirked. "You mean You don't know my thoughts this time?"

Y'shua grinned.

"Why did You let that woman go. She was guilty of breaking the law."

"So, you were ready to stone her as well?"

"No, I want to understand why You let her go without any punishment. I mean, doesn't YaHoWaH punish the wicked?"

"Have you ever done something wrong, and YaHoWaH didn't punish you?"

John thought about the question. "Of course, but perhaps it was a small sin or YaHoWaH was busy with something else."

Y'shua chuckled. "Did I not tell you, My Father knows the number of hairs on your head? Did I not say, He sees when even a small sparrow falls?"

At first, John struggled to speak. Finally, he shared his thoughts, "Are You saying YaHoWaH doesn't punish the wicked? If this is true, who does?"

"John, the rain falls on both the good and the bad. I do not judge men. Judgment is something My Father will do on the final day. I came to bring light into the world and to share the *Good News* to those who are lost, imprisoned, and hungry. I came to heal, not to destroy. I do only the things which My Father tells Me to do."

Pausing, John massaged his head. Suddenly, he smiled. "You are healing men. Not just from some ailment, but healing their souls. For some, You restore their sight or hearing. This woman, You were healing her heart, weren't You?"

Placing His hands on John's shoulder, Y'shua broadly smiled. "Are you hearing the music, John? Is it time to dance before Elohim again?"

John grinned. "I saw what You wrote in the dirt, the commandments of Moses. Is that why they dropped their stones?"

"No one is without sin, John. Only I can save man from his ultimate punishment. They could not act because they knew their own sins. Every sin is the same before YaHoWaH. None is greater or lesser than another."

John slowly nodded.

"Come, let us find the others, lest they think we have forgotten the way back."

CHAPTER EIGHTEEN

WITNESSING A MIRACLE

THE JEWISH LEADERS GATHERED IN the Synagogue and spotted a poorly dressed man briskly walking through the outer courtyard of the temple grounds. The Pharisees yelled at the man and stepped in front of him halting his journey.

"This is the Sabbath! No man is allowed to carry a mat on the Sabbath."

"But the Man who healed me told me to pick up my mat and walk." He showed them his worn, filthy mat.

Nicodemus asked, "What Man has healed you and given you these instructions?"

"I . . . I don't know His name," stammered the man.

"Where did this happen? Tell us now!" demanded another Pharisee.

"For the last thirty-eight years, I have been a crippled man. I have begged and asked my friends for help. Each day I lay by the Bethzatha pool, near the sheep gate, and wait for the Angel to stir the water. Did you know that when the water is moved, the first man to enter the water is healed of any sickness?"

The leaders scoffed. "Foolishness. You people believe in such crazy wives-tales. The wind moves the water."

"No, sir, it's true. I have witnessed it with my own eyes. Unfortunately, I couldn't make it into the pool fast enough, since I was a cripple. Every time, someone else who had assistance, or was less sick, would get into the pool ahead of me."

"And where are these people who have been sick, or experienced these miracles? Have they shown themselves to us so we may verify the results? No!"

"I speak the truth, sir. This Man came up to me and asked me if I wanted to be healed. I told Him of my plight and how I could not get into the pool fast enough to receive healing. He looked at me and told me to take up my mat and walk, so I did. It was a miracle, for my legs were like new!"

Nicodemus pressed the man further. "What was His name, this Man who healed you? Was He alone? Did He say anything else?"

Annas brushed past Nicodemus. "You fool! No one is allowed to work on the Sabbath. Carrying your filthy mat is work. You're breaking the law."

The man smiled. "Perhaps. But once I was a crippled old man, and now I am whole." The man started jumping around and dancing. "See, I am healed. I am like a young man again." He began singing praises.

The Jewish leaders shook their heads and walked away. "He is cursed. Leave him be."

Nicodemus lingered and continued to speak with the healed man. "Can you show me the One who healed you? Please take me to Him."

The man stopped dancing, looking thoughtful. "Why? Do you need a miracle, too?"

Nicodemus looked puzzled.

The man smiled. "Come with me, we'll see if he is still by the pool and healing others." He clutched Nicodemus by the arm and quickly ran back to Bethzatha. Struggling to keep up with him, Nicodemus ran until he was out of breath. He stopped but watched the man run ahead.

When Nicodemus arrived near the pool, Y'shua was smiling and speaking with the old man. Nicodemus stepped near enough to listen but stayed hidden near the corner of a nearby building.

"Ah, I see you are now completely whole," said Y'shua.

"Yes and look at me." The man started dancing again.

Y'shua laughed. He then placed a hand on the old man. "I warn you, you must be careful and avoid sin from now on, or something worse might happen to you."

The old man dropped his mat. "Thank you, sir." He bowed before Y'shua.

John spotted Nicodemus hiding. "Y'shua." John motioned with his chin. Y'shua smiled at Nicodemus who immediately darted behind a wall to conceal his face.

Just then, the old man ran off singing at the top of his lungs. "Y'shua healed me, praise be to YaHoWaH. Y'shua healed me, praise YaHoWaH."

"Shall I ask the old man to keep quiet Y'shua?" asked Simon-Peter.

He smiled and then started walking to where Nicodemus was hiding. Nicodemus spied Y'shua coming toward his position, and he quickly hid in a different shadow. He didn't look but listened.

When the twelve witnesses and Y'shua arrived at the corner, there was no one there.

The Teacher softly mumbled, "You cannot hide from My Father."

Y'shua's followers stared at their leader in amazement.

"To whom are You speaking, Y'shua?" asked Simon-Peter.

The Teacher softly smiled and walked away.

Still yelling at the top of his lungs, the old man who was healed ran back toward the Jewish leaders. Nicodemus quickly followed the man.

Standing in a tight group, the leaders argued. "This man from Galilee has broken the law and must be punished."

"Yes, He laughs in our faces and shows no respect."

Annas held up his hands. "Yes, yes, yes. We all agree He has broken the law. We must end this nonsense before all the people are completely deceived by this Man. But, we must have proof of His sins."

The old man nearly ran into the leaders.

"His name is Y'shua, and He healed me, praises be to YaHoWaH!"

Annas grabbed the man by the edge of his cloak. "Stop your jabbering you fool. Who do you claim has healed you?"

"Y'shua of Nazareth healed me," The old man said smiling and pointing in the direction where He had found the Teacher.

"And did He tell you to carry your mat?" demanded Annas.

"Of course! It is the first time in thirty-eight years I've been able to do anything for myself." The man could not contain his excitement.

A Pharisee pointed his finger at the old man. "You obeyed this Man, Y'shua even though you knew you were breaking the law?"

The smile slowly faded from the old man's face. Suddenly, his resolve returned. "If you had suffered these many years, as I have, you would do almost anything once you were healed so miraculously. What kind of YaHoWaH would heal a man as punishment?"

Annas brushed the old man aside and stormed off. "Ignorant peasant, you understand nothing. Do not suppose you can be a teacher to us. Now go away."

The old man ran off singing at the top of his lungs. "Y'shua has healed me, praises be to YaHoWaH. Y'shua healed me, praise YaHoWaH."

As his voice faded away, the Jewish leaders grumbled, wagged their heads and walked back to their council chambers in disgust. Just as they rounded a corner, they suddenly found themselves standing face-to-face with Y'shua. Simon-Peter and John quickly placed themselves on either side of their leader, arms crossed, wearing their meanest expressions. For a long time, no one spoke but stood frozen staring at one another. Nicodemus was instantly worried.

Y'shua produced His disarming smile. "My Father is always at work. Therefore, I must do what My Father tells Me and work, too."

The Jewish leaders began screaming, "Blasphemy, this Man is of Satan! You cannot work on the Sabbath."

Annas spit out his words. "How dare You. You have broken the law of Sabbath, and now You claim to be equal to YaHoWaH? Cursed are Your words."

"Kill him!" cried out several men.

Continuing to smile, Y'shua spoke to them. "This is the truth. Listen very carefully to what I am about to say to you. As I am YaHoWaH's Son, I cannot do anything on My own. I do only the things My Father tells Me. I am doing the same things My Father is doing. My Father loves Me and shows Me what to say and what to do. And guess what, My Father will show Me how to do greater things than healing a poor crippled man. When I do these new things, you will be truly amazed."

Several of the Jewish leaders began tearing at their clothes. They grabbed handfuls of dirt and threw it upon their heads. Others plugged their ears and screamed in agony. Nicodemus watched the leaders while standing behind them. His mouth dropped open as he listened to Y'shua lecture the Jewish leaders. He then faced the Teacher as he continued to lecture the leaders.

"Just as the Father raises the dead and gives them life, in the same way, His Son gives life to those He wants to. My Father judges no one, but He has given Me the full right to judge all men. Those who honor and respect My Father, they show the same respect to Me. Whoever does not accept Me does not acknowledge My Father who sent Me.

"I am telling you the truth, those who hear My words, and believe in My Father who sent Me, will have eternal life. They will not be judged but have already passed from death over to life.

"Listen, if you can, to this truth. A time is coming, yet it has already begun, when the dead will hear My voice, and those who listen to it will come to life. Just as My Father is the source of life, in the same way, He has made Me, His Son, to be the source of all living things.

"My Father has given Me the right to judge men because I am the Son of Man and from YaHoWaH. Do not be surprised by this; the time is coming when all the dead will hear My voice and come out of their graves. Those who have been obedient to My Father will live forever, and those who have done evil will be condemned and judged.

"Just remember, I can do nothing on My own authority. I judge as YaHoWaH tells Me, so My judgment is blameless because I am not trying to do what I want, but only what My Father, who sent Me here, wants Me to do. If I testify on My own behalf, what I say is not to be accepted as real proof. However, there is someone else who declares on My behalf, and I know what He says about Me is true.

"John the Baptist is the one to whom you sent your messengers, and he spoke on behalf of the truth about My Father. I do not need to have a human witness. I am only telling you this so you may be saved from yourselves. John was like a lamp, burning and shining, and for a while, you were willing to enjoy his light.

"But I have a witness on My behalf, which is even superior to the witness John gave. What I do—the deeds My Father gave Me to do—testify on My behalf and shows YaHoWaH has sent Me. My Father, who sent Me, also speaks on My behalf. You have never heard His voice or seen His face, and you do not keep His words in your hearts, for you do not believe in Me, whom YaHoWaH sent.

"You believe in your own righteousness and study the Scriptures because you think you will find eternal life through them. Do you not know these very Scriptures are speaking about Me? In your ignorance, you are not willing to come to Me so you may have life or even to seek eternal life.

"I am not looking for human praise. I know what kind of people you are, and I know you have no love for YaHoWaH in your hearts. I have come with My Father's authority, but you have not received Me. However, someone will come in his own power, and you will quickly accept him.

"You like to receive praises from one another, but you do not try to win recognition from the One who alone is from YaHoWaH. How is it even possible you could believe in My words? Do not think, however, I am the one who will accuse you of your sins to My Father.

"No, Moses, in whom you have put your hope, he is the very one who will bring accusations against you. If you had really believed Moses, you would have believed Me, because he wrote about Me. But since you do not believe what he wrote, how can you believe what I say?"

In a rage, the Jewish leaders rushed at Y'shua in a tight group to seize Him. Instantly, the wind picked up the sand, blowing it into the faces of the leaders, and blinding them. Stopping in their tracks, they briefly covered their eyes. As quickly as the wind appeared, it disappeared. When the Jewish leader looked around, Y'shua and His witnesses had vanished.

Nicodemus could not believe what he had just witnessed. Rushing home and bolting the door, Nicodemus began sweating as he placed his back against the door and closed his eyes, breathing hard. Thoughts raced through his mind as he tried to make sense of Y'shua's words. Suddenly, Nicodemus opened his eyes. Plunging toward the table containing his notes, he grabbed fresh parchment and ink. His hands shaking, Nicodemus took the writing stylus and began scratching down every word he had just heard moments earlier.

Stopping now and then, Nicodemus read over his words and made corrections. He continued to write everything, the speech playing over and over inside his head. When the stylus snapped, he tossed it aside and grabbed another. The ink jar went dry, and Nicodemus rummaged around half-crazed, looking for another fresh source.

Several hours elapsed before he finished. Slowing his pace, he carefully read over each of the pages. As he scanned the words, the voice of Y'shua resonated inside his head. Amazed, Nicodemus could not believe every detail had been captured.

Nicodemus dropped the pages, closed his eyes, and leaned his head back. He became acutely aware of a severe headache. He began rubbing his temples and moaned. "How can this Man be so arrogant? Is He equal to YaHoWaH, or something else? Can He really be lying, or does He speak nothing but the truth?"

Without answers, the stream of questions pounded inside Nicodemus' head. He was sick to his stomach, and he was tired.

Startled, Nicodemus jumped from his chair when he heard the ram's horn. The sound announced the sixth evening watch. He had fallen asleep while contemplating the words of Y'shua. Nicodemus remembered vivid dreams. Stumbling to his bed, he flopped himself down and curled into a ball. His head ached horribly. Nauseous, Nicodemus slowly rocked in the bed. Fighting the urge to be sick, he drifted off to sleep once again.

CHAPTER NINETEEN

SEPARATING SHEEP FROM GOATS

AFTER LEAVING THE JEWISH LEADERS, Y'shua traveled across Lake Tiberias—which is also called Lake Galilee. A large crowd of people followed Him because they had seen His miracles of healing the sick.

Nearby, was a small hill and Y'shua walked up and sat down with His witnesses. The time for the Passover Festival was getting closer. He spoke to the crowd and when He looked around, He saw a large group of people had gathered. Filled with compassion for the people who had journeyed to listen, He then spoke to one of His followers.

"Philip, where can we buy enough food to feed all these people?"

Philip answered, "For everyone to have even a small amount, it would take more than two hundred silver coins to buy enough bread."

Andrew, who was Simon-Peter's brother, said, "There is a small boy here who has five loaves of barley bread and two fish. But they will certainly not be enough for all these people."

"Make the people sit down on the grassy field," Y'shua told them.

There were about five thousand men, which did not include the accompanying women and children.

Y'shua took the offering from the small boy and gave thanks to His Father in heaven. He then divided the fish and bread into several baskets. When He was finished, He handed the baskets to his twelve witnesses.

"Serve the people who are sitting here."

Taking one of the baskets, Y'shua demonstrated to His followers by sharing the food with nearby people. Each person reached into the offered basket and received a portion of fish and bread. It took a long time for the people to eat and pass the food around, but everyone ate until they were perfectly content.

When the people were full, Y'shua said to His witnesses, "Gather the pieces left over. Please don't waste a bit."

When all the baskets were assembled and presented to the Teacher, there were twelve baskets filled with pieces of bread and fish. Everyone looked amazed and could not believe how much food remained.

Several people sitting near the witnesses stood up. One man shouted, "Surely this is the Prophet prophesied in the Torah, who was to come into the world!"

"This is a miracle. Like Elijah!" yelled another individual.

"You are the King promised by the prophets. Praise YaHoWaH," said a woman in a loud voice.

Y'shua watched the people and listened to them. The crowd was being worked into a frenzy and focusing on the miracle. Y'shua slowly moved away from the group. The people were engaged in personal arguments and didn't even notice the witnesses and the Teacher as they quietly withdrew from the crowd.

Disappearing over the next hill, Y'shua retreated to a solemn place. He spoke to His followers. "Please stay here. I wish to be alone and pray. I will return later."

Their mouths dropped open as the men watched their leader walk away. John began to follow, but Y'shua stopped him.

"Stay My friend. Comfort your brothers. Pray. I will return later."

His shoulders drooped as John watched Him walk away.

As the sun slowly melted into the horizon, Y'shua returned as promised. "Come; let us walk to the lake."

Along the shore sat a large fishing boat. There was no one around, and the fishing nets were missing as well.

"Climb into the boat. Sail across the lake to Capernaum."

Simon-Peter whispered in John's ear, "Whose boat is this? Are we stealing it?"

John looked intently into Peter's eyes, shrugged and shook his head. He then asked Y'shua, "Are You not coming with us?"

He smiled. "I will join you later. First, I must spend time with My Father."

The witnesses climbed into the boat and began rowing away from the shore. The crowd who had been fed began walking toward their direction.

"Go home. It is late," said Y'shua. He then turned and walked away toward a small distant hill.

As the witnesses drifted from the shore, they watched the people disperse. Moments passed and they struggled to move against an increasing wind. When John looked up again, he saw the Teacher was now gone. The craft had no sail, so the men exchanged seats, allowing fresh arms to row against a stiff wind.

The sun set quickly, and darkness enveloped the sky. Slowly, the stars appeared, a few at first, but then the whole heavens were filled with tiny specks of light.

Straining to see in the dark, John could not see the shore or any sign of Y'shua. The wind continued to increase until it was a powerful storm. Water began to build up into tall waves, with white caps forming all around the boat.

Andrew's arms were tired, so he changed places with Thomas. He then moved closer to his brother Simon-Peter.

"A storm is almost here. We are not more than three or four miles from where we started. We've been at this for several hours. Should we turn around and head back to shore and find safety from the storm?"

Simon-Peter looked anxiously toward John.

John tried to encourage his friends. "Stay the course, brothers. The Teacher said He would meet us in Capernaum."

Suddenly, the wind began to spray water from the white-caps surrounding them. The men worked harder, but they were not moving very fast. Despite years of experience at sea, the twelve men were starting to get frightened.

Matthew cried out, "What is that?" He thrust his arm off the side of the boat.

In the distance, a tall object slowly moved toward them. As it came closer, Judas, son of Simon of Kerioth, screamed in terror, "It's a ghost!"

The men quickly rowed as fast as they could, attempting to move the boat away.

"It looks like Y'shua, doesn't it, John?" asked Simon-Peter.

Through the wind and rain John strained his eyes. It did look like Y'shua walking on top of the water.

"Where is He going? He's walking right past us," screamed Bartholomew.

James, the son of Alpheus, stood up, cupping his hands around his mouth. He yelled as loudly as possible, "Teacher, don't leave us. We will perish out here. Save us, please!"

Y'shua turned and started walking closer. Some men were still petrified, and they were sure it was a ghostly spirit.

When Y'shua was almost to the boat, he smiled. "Don't be afraid, it is I!"

Simon-Peter stood up and yelled, "If it is You, Teacher, call me and ask me to walk on water to You."

Wide-eyed, James' mouth dropped open, "Are you crazy, Simon?"

"Come to me, Peter," said Y'shua.

Simon-Peter leaned over the edge of the boat and gently placed his foot upon the waves. It felt wet, but instead of his foot sinking into the water, it felt solid. He looked back at his brother and grinned. He then began to slowly walk toward the Teacher on top of the waves. Amazed, everyone watched and could not understand why Simon-Peter wasn't sinking. Large waves were dancing all around him.

When Peter took his eyes off Y'shua, he started sinking down and was about to drop into the sea. "Save me, Teacher!" he screamed.

At once, Y'shua reached out and grabbed Simon-Peter by the hand. Slowly He lifted him from the water until he stood alongside Y'shua. Wide-eyed, Simon-Peter looked around and immediately, his feet seemed stable again.

"Why did you doubt, Peter? Where is your faith in Me?"

Simon-Peter tightly wrapped his arm around Y'shua's waist with a death grip. The two inched closer toward the boat.

Matthew reached out and grabbed the Teacher's hand, pulling on Him. Everyone stopped rowing and helped the two people into the boat. Despite their exhaustion, the men were relieved to see Y'shua.

The moment they stepped into the boat, the wind ceased, and the lake's waters flattened into a peaceful calm. The bow of the boat then ran aground on the shore. When the men looked around, they could see the small village of Capernaum. The morning sun was starting to crest the horizon.

James stared at John and then Simon-Peter. "How is this even possible? We weren't even halfway across the lake, just moments ago."

Both men shrugged, looking perplexed.

Philip fell at the Teacher's feet, crying. "You are truly the Son of YaHoWaH. I lift my praises to Adonai."

Across the lake, the people who received the miracle feeding of bread and fish returned and began searching for the Teacher. It was early in the morning with daylight cresting the eastern hills. They met some others who were standing near the lake's shore.

"Where is the one they call Y'shua?" someone asked.

"When we were here yesterday, we saw Him walk over the hill in that direction. Only one boat was here at the time, but I am certain Y'shua did not get into the boat with His friends. His followers must have departed in the boat," answered a man as he pointed.

When those gathered around looked across the lake, they spotted several boats heading to shore. After beaching, the crowd rushed at the sailors.

"Where did you come from?" they asked.

"Did you see the man they call Y'shua. He was here yesterday."

One of the captains asked, "Y'shua was here? We have sailed from Tiberias because we heard He was here teaching."

An older man faced the captain. "It was a miracle. We were a large group sitting and listening to Him speak. When evening came, we were hungry, of course, but the only food we could find was a basket a small boy had. In it, he had a few fish and some pieces of bread."

Another man pushed his way into the conversation. "Then Y'shua blessed the food, and we started dividing it among us. Every man ate until he was full."

"You'll never guess what happened," said the older man with excitement in his voice.

A man in the back yelled out, "We collected twelve baskets afterward, and this was after everyone had eaten."

"Yes, yes, and all this from a small boy's lunch," said the older man.

The captain scratched his head. "Maybe there was someone else with food."

The older man held up his hands. "I witnessed this miracle with my own eyes. I'm telling you, this Y'shua is a great prophet."

"Where did He go?" asked the captain.

"We're not sure. When we saw your boats, we thought He had returned. His friends got into a boat and sailed across the lake last evening." A man pointed across the water. "In that direction."

"Then we must follow them. The town on the other side is Capernaum," said the captain.

In a manner of minutes, it was mayhem as men scrambled into the boats. Every vessel was filled to capacity, and the captain started pushing men out for fear of sinking. As the ships launched across the lake, the wind favored their sails. After several hours, they landed on shore in Capernaum.

Several of the men dove out of the boats before they touched the beach and started searching for Y'shua.

The newly arrived crowd and some sailors approached Y'shua as He sat in the synagogue, conversing with the people sitting around Him.

"Teacher, when did You get here?" they asked.

Y'shua answered them, saying, "I am telling you the truth; you are looking for Me because you ate the bread and had all you wanted, not because you understood My miracles. Do not work for the food which spoils, instead, work for the food that lasts for eternity. This is the food which the Son of Man will give you, because YaHoWaH, the Father, has put His mark of approval upon Him."

A man asked Him, "What can we do to obtain this food from Elohim? What does He want us to do?"

Y'shua smiled. "What YaHoWaH wants you to do is to believe in the One He sent."

"What miracle will You perform so we may see it and believe You? What will You do?" asked someone in the crowd.

Another man said, "Our ancestors ate manna in the desert, just as the Scripture says, 'YaHoWaH gave them bread from heaven to eat.'"

"I am telling you the truth," the Teacher said. "What Moses gave you was not the bread from heaven. It is My Father who gives you the real bread from heaven. For the bread YaHoWaH gives is Me, the One who comes down from heaven and gives life to the world."

"Most kind sir," they asked Him, "give us this bread always. The manna disappeared. Perhaps You can give us this bread you speak of."

"I am the bread of life," Y'shua said. "Those who come to Me will never be hungry. Those who believe in Me will never be thirsty. Now I said to you, that you saw Me but do not accept My words. But I tell you, everyone whom My Father gives Me will come to Me. I will never turn away anyone who comes to Me because I have come down from heaven to do not My will, but the will of My Father who sent Me.

"It is the will of My Father who sent Me that I should not lose any of those He has given Me. I will raise them all to life on the last day. For what My Father wants is for all who see Me, His Son, to believe in Me and then they should have eternal life. Those individuals, I will bring back to life on the last day."

The people started grumbling. "What do You mean when You say you are the bread that came down from heaven?"

"This man is Y'shua, son of Joseph, isn't He? We know His father and mother. How, then, does He now say He came down from heaven?" someone asked.

Y'shua answered, "Stop arguing among yourselves. Individuals cannot come to Me unless My Father who sent Me draws them to Me. On the last day, I will raise them to life.

"The prophets wrote, 'everyone will be taught by YaHoWaH.' Anyone who hears My Father and learns from Him comes to Me. This doesn't mean anyone has seen the Father. Since I was sent from YaHoWaH, I am the only one who has seen My Father.

"I am telling you the truth; anyone who believes in Me has eternal life because I am the bread of life. Your ancestors ate manna in the desert, but they died. I am the bread, which comes down from heaven, and as such, whoever eats of it will not die. I am the living bread that came down from heaven. If you eat this bread, you will live forever. The bread I will give you is My flesh, which I give so the world may live."

His statements started a heated argument among the people. "How can You give us Your flesh to eat? This is barbaric!"

Y'shua smiled. "I am telling you the truth; if you do not eat My flesh, and drink My blood, you will not gain life by your strength or work. Only those who eat My flesh and drink My blood have eternal life, and I will raise them to life on the last day. For My flesh is the real food, and My blood is the real drink. Those who eat My flesh and drink My blood live in Me, and I live inside them.

"My Father in heaven sent Me, and because of Him, I live also. In the same way, whoever eats Me will live because of Me. This is why I said, the bread that came down from heaven; it is not like the bread that your ancestors ate. They ate the manna, and then later died. Those who eat My bread will live forever."

Simon-Peter grabbed John by the sleeve of his cloak. "Do you understand what the Teacher is saying? It doesn't make any sense."

"This teaching seems too hard, John. Peter is right, how can you listen to these words? We are not cannibals eating the flesh of men," said James.

As he stared at Y'shua, John stroked his beard and replayed the words over in his head. "It's a parable, there is a deeper meaning."

Then the Teacher faced His handpicked twelve witnesses as if He understood their quiet grumblings. He got up and walked over to them. "Do My words make you want to give up?"

Instantly, they were worried. Every man shook his head. "No."

"What if you should see Me go back up to the place where I was before? What gives life is YaHoWaH's Spirit. Human power is of no use at all. The words I have spoken to you bring YaHoWaH's life-giving

Spirit. Yet there are some among you who still do not believe or understand Me."

John watched Y'shua as He scanned the people sitting in the synagogue. As the Teacher made eye contact with each follower, He would pause and stare, as if He knew who would believe and who would betray Him. The room then erupted in discussions among those sitting there. Suddenly, John's thoughts were interrupted.

"This is the very reason I told you, not a single person can come to Me unless YaHoWaH makes it possible for them to do so."

Right away, a large group stood up and walked out of the synagogue, grumbling and hurling insults as they stormed off.

"This man is crazy. I can't be associated with a madman who speaks of eating man's flesh. I'm done!" they complained.

After the dust settled in the room, John looked around and saw the twelve witnesses and a small group of people remained.

Y'shua smiled. "And you, would you also like to leave?"

Simon-Peter jumped to his feet. "Y'shua, where would we go? You have the words that give eternal life." He looked around the room at each of his friends. "We believe and know You are the Holy One, the Messiah, who has come from YaHoWaH."

The Teacher placed His hand on Peter's shoulder. "I selected the twelve of you for a reason, didn't I? Unfortunately, though, one of you is following instructions from the devil."

Every man looked at Y'shua in disbelief, except Judas who cast his eyes to the floor and looked ashamed. John noticed it but said nothing to his friends.

CHAPTER TWENTY

GATHERING EVIDENCE

NICODEMUS WAS SLEEPING SOUNDLY WHEN he was awakened by someone banging on his door.

"Nicodemus? I know you're in there. Answer me!"

Groggy, Nicodemus slowly lifted his stiff and achy body from the bed. The banging continued.

"I'm coming, hold on." Although his voice was raspy at first, Nicodemus' voice got louder with each word. More banging. "I said I am coming!"

"Open the door, Nicodemus; the council wishes to speak with you."

Yelling, Nicodemus screamed, "Enough! I said I'm coming!"

He unbolted the door and jerked it open.

"What?"

His visitors were taken aback.

"Well, out with it. I'm here now."

It was three of the temple guards. Two of the men stood with their mouths open. The leader demanded, "Annas wants you to report to the council; this very moment."

Nicodemus made a wordless sound. "Of course. Tell them I'm coming." He started to close the door, but the leader put his foot down and stopped it from shutting.

"Annas says we are to escort you there this instant."

Nicodemus thoughtfully processed their demands. "Give me some time, I need to gather my things." He again attempted to shut the door, but the temple guard wouldn't budge.

Nicodemus turned his back to the guards and gathered his papers and writing instruments and placed them in neat stacks. He was stalling, trying to determine why he was being summoned. Mumbling to himself, he then stored the jars of ink, grabbed his outer cloak, and followed the guards.

Marching like Roman soldiers, the temple guards encircled Nicodemus. When they entered the council chambers, Nicodemus could see the elders had been aggressively discussing matters. Some members of the Pharisees and Sanhedrin had splintered into separate groups.

"Ah, Nicodemus, thank you for joining us," said Annas.

Nicodemus muttered under his breath, "Did I have a choice?"

"Excuse me?" asked Annas.

"It sounded urgent. I came right away," replied Nicodemus.

"Excellent, thank you," said Caiaphas. "We have something special we'd like you to do for us."

Nicodemus scanned the chambers and spotted his friend, Joseph of Arimathea in the back of the room. A worried look crossed his face. Nicodemus turned and faced Caiaphas.

"I'm at your service, sir," he replied, but his voice was flat without emotion.

"Excellent. We would like you to go to this fatherless-liar and test Him. We know He has broken our laws, but we need more evidence to bring against Him. We are sending several men with you so we may get our answers."

Joseph of Arimathea gathered closer and asked, "If it pleases you, Caiaphas, I would like to accompany Nicodemus and the men as an observer."

"Excellent idea. Yes, I think this would be a good plan," sneered Caiaphas.

Mute, Nicodemus stood staring, processing his thoughts.

"Well, Nicodemus?" demanded Annas.

"I . . . ah . . . I . . . of course, sir. When?"

Caiaphas looked mean. "Immediately!" He took his large staff and pushed Nicodemus backward. "Go. Now!"

Nicodemus felt agitated over the disrespectful action, but then Joseph grabbed Nicodemus and moved him toward the door. Without emotion, Nicodemus looked at Caiaphas and Annas. "As always, I am at your service, sirs."

Joseph and Nicodemus walked away, and they glanced over their shoulders seeing four council members following. Nicodemus hissed under his breath.

"Such arrogance. What foolishness is this plan?"

Joseph wrapped his arm tightly around Nicodemus and pulled him in close. He whispered, "Not now, Nicodemus. We'll discuss this later."

✝

The next day, Nicodemus, Joseph, and the other Pharisees found Y'shua teaching in a nearby village. They noticed some of His followers were eating their food with hands considered ritually unclean and had not washed them in the way the Pharisees said the people should. They also watched the twelve followers purchase fruit from the vendors and begin to eat it without first washing the fruit as the law instructs.

One of the Pharisees watched in disgust. "Jews must follow the teaching of our ancestors. They should wash hands, cup, and bowls properly, and according to our laws."

The other Pharisees quickly nodded in agreement.

These two men approached Y'shua. "Why is it Your followers do not follow the teachings handed down by our ancestors, but instead they eat with ritually unclean hands?"

Facing the council group, the Teacher said, "You know, Isaiah was right when he prophesied about you! You're a bunch of hypocrites. Isaiah wrote, 'These people, says YaHoWaH, honor Me with their words, but their heart is really far away from Me. It is no use for them to worship Me because they teach human rules as though they were My laws!' You see, you set aside YaHoWaH's command and make the people obey your human teachings. You have a clever way of rejecting YaHoWaH's law just to uphold your own ideas.

"Think about this. Moses commanded, 'Respect your father and your mother,' and, 'If you curse your father or your mother, you are to be put to death.' However, you teach, if people have something, they could use to help their father or mother, and instead say, 'This is Corban,' which means, it belongs to YaHoWaH. Then you tell the people they are excused from helping their father or mother. In this way, the teaching you pass on to others cancels out the words of YaHoWaH. There are many other rules just like this that you follow."

Y'shua turned away from the council members and faced the crowds. "Listen to Me, all of you, and understand something. Nothing is coming into you from the outside, which can make you ritually unclean. Rather, it is what comes out of you that makes you unclean."

Y'shua then walked away and took His twelve men with Him into a nearby home. John tugged on the Teacher's sleeve.

Smiling, Y'shua asked, "What is it, My friend?"

John hesitantly questioned the words the Teacher just shared with the council members. "Are there not unclean and clean things we can eat, as Moses taught us?"

Y'shua stopped and looked into John's eyes. "You are more educated than the others." Looking at the other eleven witnesses, He continued. "Don't you understand? Nothing going into your body from the outside can really make you unclean. Because it does not go into your heart but into your stomach and then goes on out of the body."

Simon-Peter puffed up his chest. "Are you telling us, all foods are fit to eat?"

Smiling, Y'shua went on to say, "It is what comes out of you that makes you unclean. For from the inside, from your heart, comes the evil ideas which lead you to do immoral things, to rob, kill, commit adultery, be greedy, and do all sorts of evil things. Things like deceit, indecency, jealousy, slander, pride, and folly; all these evil things come from inside you and make you unclean."

Joseph of Arimathea turned to Nicodemus and grinned. "I like this Man. He's smart."

"What . . . by telling His followers to disobey the teachings of Moses?"

"No, Nicodemus. Think about His words very carefully. Can what you eat, turn you into an evil man? I don't think so. Or better still, did your supper last night, make you holy? I'll tell you, Y'shua's teachings are very wise."

Nicodemus dragged his hand down his beard and frowned. "If what you say is true, then why is there showbread on a reserved table in the temple? Is it not reserved for the temple priests and not for average men?"

"Ah, but didn't King David and his men eat the very same show-bread when they were starving? The scrolls record the story of them eating and surviving, no better still, David grew to be the greatest king of Israel!"

Nicodemus slowly nodded in agreement. "If what you say is true, then He makes folly out of the Laws of Moses."

"Nicodemus, listen to me. We're talking about food, not obedience to YaHoWaH. What this Y'shua says makes sense. Food makes us strong or weak, because the food is good or bad, not because of anything evil in the food itself. The showbread in the temple is there as a symbol, to remind us YaHoWaH fed His people in the desert with manna. This is why it never made David and his men sick nor did they die."

The other Pharisees traveling with Nicodemus and Joseph interrupted their discussion. "We must report back to Annas and Caiaphas regarding what we've learned here."

Joseph placed his hands on the shoulders of the men. "Yes, you must do exactly as you've spoken. Go quickly to Caiaphas, lest you forget the words you heard. Report to him immediately. Please tell them we, Nicodemus and I, will continue to follow this Man Y'shua and His followers. Tell Annas we will give our report later."

Gathering their belongings, the two Pharisees were buzzing with chatter, but quickly bid farewell and started their journey back to Jerusalem.

With distraught skepticism, Nicodemus looked at Joseph. "Do you think this action is wise? What if they tell them about our words as well?"

Grabbing his friend by the arm, Joseph rushed toward Y'shua and His twelve followers, who were walking down the road. "Come Nicodemus. We must catch up with them. I don't want to miss a word."

Surprised, Nicodemus was shocked by the zeal of his elder friend as he dashed forward. Suddenly, Nicodemus felt exhilarated.

Remaining near the back of the crowd and following the Teacher, Joseph and Nicodemus tried to blend into the followers by keeping their heads down and faces hidden. They discarded their formal cloaks and wore work clothing to match the people following Y'shua. They watched and listened to Y'shua but were also elusive in their conversations. A large crowd of one hundred plus people tagged along, so it was easy for them to blend in. When the group came to the town of Tyre, the Teacher asked the followers to remain in the village square while He retreated into a nearby house.

Moments later, the townspeople heard Y'shua was visiting. In a manner of minutes, the house where He was staying filled with crowds of visitors.

Suddenly, the people standing near Him divided leaving a wide opening. As they did, Joseph noticed a Gentile woman running down the clearing. The followers, Joseph, and Nicodemus joined the crowds.

"Kind sir, I beg you," she pleaded in a loud voice to Y'shua, "please heal my sick daughter."

Some of those standing nearby tried to quiet the woman, but then Y'shua appeared at the door.

"Sir, my daughter is sick with an evil spirit." The woman dropped to the ground and kissed the Teacher's feet. "I have traveled from a region of Phoenicia in Syria, and I beg You, please drive this evil demon from my beautiful daughter."

Y'shua answered, "Let us first feed the children. It isn't right to take the children's food and throw it to the dogs."

"Sir," she cried out, "even the dogs under the table eat the children's scraps!"

Y'shua smiled down at her. "Because of your answer, go back home. You will find the demon has gone out of your daughter."

Immediately, the woman arose and while bent at the waist, she started walking backward. She smiled. "Thank You, Sir, thank You. You are truly from YaHoWaH. Many blessings be upon Your head. Thank You for healing my daughter."

Nicodemus looked at Joseph. "How can she say thank you, her daughter isn't even here? How can Y'shua heal someone whom He has not seen?"

Dumbstruck, Joseph shook his head. "This is amazing faith. The woman believes the healing before she sees the proof."

Immediately, the noisy crowd was brought to abrupt quiet once again when another woman came running. She was quite excited.

"I rushed to the house where your daughter was lying in her bed. She is completely healed, and the demon has indeed gone out of her! She is up dancing and singing praises to YaHoWaH."

The crowd of people went crazy. They began to sing and dance in the street. "Hosanna, Hosanna. YaHoWaH is great! Hosanna, Hosanna. YaHoWaH is great!"

In the evening, Nicodemus and Joseph had trouble sleeping and talked long into the night. They watched with fascination as the people in the town took on a joyful attitude. Food appeared often and was shared among the followers of the Teacher. They carefully watched all the movements of Y'shua as He walked through the people, smiling and touching individuals. Around the last watch of the night, the people slowly drifted away heading to their respective homes.

A few hours later, when nearly everyone was snoring and asleep, Joseph saw Y'shua quietly leaving. No one was with Him as He silently stepped into the darkness and disappeared. Just before He vanished, Y'shua stared directly at Nicodemus and Joseph and then smiled. A shudder passed through both men.

"Do you think He knows who we are, Joseph?"

"I'm not sure, but it was as if He just looked into my very soul."

"Should we follow Him?"

Joseph slowly shook his head, "No, we must wait and see if any of His men follow."

Peering into the darkness, both men waited, but no one followed. After a long while, they finally relaxed.

Joseph whispered, "What do you make of today's events?"

Nicodemus was incredulous. "Joseph! We saw nothing. We have only the words of two women, Gentiles might I remind you. For all I know, they invented their story to impress the people."

Deflated, Joseph leaned his back against the wall where they were sitting. He let out a long slow sigh. "Perhaps, my friend, perhaps, but the people were surely convinced."

Joseph never took his eyes off the stars dotting the sky above, but Nicodemus slowly nodded in agreement.

Early the following morning, Joseph and Nicodemus were startled awake. In a fright, both men stared at the face of John, who was now bending over them.

"Come quickly. The Teacher says it's time to leave."

"What?" asked Nicodemus with a stunned voice.

John never hesitated but turned and quickly walked away.

Gathering themselves, Nicodemus and Joseph arose quickly and tried to remove the sleepiness. Stretching, Joseph groaned loudly. "I'm too old for sleeping on the ground. This is for younger men."

When they looked around, they saw Y'shua and His men ambling toward the edge of town.

"Come, Joseph, they're leaving."

As they started to leave, an elderly woman appeared in front of the two men. In her outstretched arms, she held a tightly wrapped bundle.

"For your journey. Something to eat. Go with YaHoWaH's blessings."

Befuddled, the two men just stared blankly at the woman. She smiled and stuffed the package into Nicodemus' hands. She then patted his hands with her leathery palms and scampered away.

Nicodemus was moved and choked on his words, "This from a total stranger. Come, Joseph, we must go now."

Nearly one hundred people were following Y'shua. Joseph and Nicodemus followed behind, saying nothing. The two friends didn't know what they were doing, but somehow fate was pulling them toward some unknown destiny. Several times Nicodemus and Joseph would look at each other as if they wanted to say something, but words escaped them. As they walked, they spotted Y'shua looking over His shoulder at them and smiling.

Wandering through Sidon toward Lake Galilee, they journeyed through a territory called Ten Towns. As they entered the village, familiar swarms of people gathered around. Soon, Nicodemus and Joseph found themselves in the middle of a large crowd of noisy people, but they were fortunately standing only mere inches from Y'shua.

Some of the people brought a man to Y'shua. The man's eyes were shut, and he was led along by several people who pushed others out of the way. The man's face looked upward toward the sky. As he grinned, he produced infant-like cries.

"Kind sir, please heal our friend. He cannot hear and can hardly speak. He has been like this since birth."

Another person standing alongside the deaf man said, "We beg You, sir, have mercy on this man! Just place Your hands on him, and he will be healed."

Taking the hand of the deaf man, Y'shua brought him a short distance away from the others. Both Nicodemus and Joseph stood with their mouths open as the Teacher placed His fingers into the man's ears. Then spitting into His palm, the Teacher wet His fingers tips, and He then opened the mouth of the sick man and touched his tongue.

The Teacher looked up to heaven, gave a deep groan, and said to the man, "Ephphatha."

Someone standing nearby asked, "What did he just say?"

John grinned. "He said 'open up!'"

At once, the man who was deaf, and unable to speak, started talking with no trouble at all. He smiled at Y'shua and said, "Praise YaHoWaH. I am healed!"

Again, the assembly surrounding the Teacher was buzzing with chatter.

"A miracle has just happened before our eyes."

"A prophet like Elijah has returned," various people exclaimed.

Y'shua looked thoughtfully at the crowd of people. "I order you to speak to no one regarding this."

His announcement had the opposite effect. People ran in different directions proclaiming loudly about the miracle they just witnessed. The people were utterly amazed.

"Everything this Man does is perfect," said one woman.

"He even causes the deaf to hear and the dumb to speak!" said a man.

Nicodemus turned to Joseph and saw the older friend smiling. "What do you find so amusing? This act was staged. The man wasn't really sick."

Joseph stared at his friend. "You really believe this is what happened, Nicodemus? I think we just witnessed our first real miracle."

"But how?" asked Nicodemus.

"Look around us Nicodemus, the people, and their reactions. How can you doubt the miracle? When they brought the man, he was mumbling nonsense."

Nicodemus folded his arms. "A great actor, that's all."

Joseph seized the arm of a passerby. "This man who could not speak, was he acting, or was he really unable to talk?"

The person frowned. "Are you serious? I've known James since he was born. He has never spoken before now. A sweet child, but mute as a rock." The man's eyes gleamed. "This is truly a miracle! I've never seen anything like this before. This man Y'shua is a prophet, from YaHoWaH." He shook his head in amazement. "Simply incredible. If I hadn't seen it with my own eyes, I would have never believed."

The man walked away, and Joseph turned to Nicodemus.

"Well?"

Nicodemus' mood softened. "Perhaps, just maybe this was a miracle."

Joseph wrapped his arm around Nicodemus and kissed him on the cheek. "I believe there is hope for you, my friend."

Nicodemus pushed Joseph away. "Stop it, you're embarrassing me."

CHAPTER TWENTY-ONE

CONVICTION

"JOHN, MAY WE HAVE A word with you privately?"

Nicodemus and Joseph barely slept through the night. The celebrations concerning the deaf and mute man gave the village something to rejoice. They approached John early in the morning before the other men had arisen.

John grimaced. "What do you wish to discuss?"

Simon-Peter saw the two outsiders speaking to John. He quickly joined them. "Is everything good with you, John?"

Nicodemus stroked his beard. "We wanted to speak privately with your friend."

"About what?" asked Simon-Peter, his eyebrows drawing together.

John put his hand on Simon's shoulder. "They're harmless, Peter. They just want to talk."

Simon-Peter hesitated for a long time staring at the two men as if they were spies. He tilted his head and made direct eye contact. "I'll tell you what, John, don't go too far. I want to stay close to you and if these two do anything which makes me nervous—well . . . "

John smiled. "Thank you, Simon-Peter. I'm sure we'll be fine."

"Nonetheless, I'll be keeping a close watch on you two." He jabbed his thick finger toward Nicodemus.

Joseph tried to smile. "We just have some questions and wanted to speak with John, but if it makes you feel more comfortable, you may join us."

Nicodemus quickly jerked his head toward Joseph. "I don't think it's necessary."

"Nonsense Nicodemus, we're just having a conversation."

Simon-Peter stood with his arms crossed, debating the situation. Finally, he said, "No, I'm fine, but I'll be standing right over there, watching."

John patted Simon-Peter's shoulder. "Thank you, brother."

As the three men walked away to a quiet place, both Nicodemus and Joseph glanced over their shoulders multiple times, only to see Simon-Peter standing, feet apart, arms folded, scowling.

John chuckled. "Don't worry, he'll be fine. He looks tough, but Peter is a gentle giant."

Nicodemus frowned. "He threatens and scares me."

John laughed. "He's good at it, too."

Finding a stone bench surrounding an olive press, the three men sat down.

John wasted no time. "I know you two have been following us since we left Bethany." He pointed at Nicodemus. "You, I know," he faced Joseph, "but I don't know who you are."

"I'm Joseph of Arimathea."

"I suppose you're a Pharisee as well, like Nicodemus?" John pointed with his thumb.

"Actually, I am an elder and counselor to the Pharisees and serve on the council of the Sanhedrin. Nicodemus is also on the council but is not currently a Pharisee. When he is older, he will replace his father."

John stared at the two men for a long time, making Nicodemus uncomfortable. "Why are you following Y'shua? Are you spies for the council?"

"No, no, no, of course not," protested Nicodemus.

"Y'shua is interested in you two. He's been watching you for several days. He said you would have questions and I should speak with you."

"How does he know these things before they happen?" asked Joseph in disbelief.

John ignored the query. "What are your questions?"

Joseph leaned in close. "The miracles, have you seen all of them? Are they real?"

Blurting out, Nicodemus added his own thoughts. "Or are they actors and part of some trickery?"

John frowned at Nicodemus. "They're real, and yes, I have seen hundreds of people healed of various infirmities."

"Truly, who is this Man?" asked Joseph.

"He isn't just a Man. He is the Son of YaHoWaH, and you know who He is. He's the Creator of the universe and Father to all men. The Teacher is bringing the light of wisdom to the world, saving men from the final destruction, and exposing the truth. He is the Messiah prophesied by Isaiah, Jeremiah, and even Moses."

"And you believe those words to be true?" asked Nicodemus.

"I know it!" John answered. "Y'shua has come to save men, not condemn them. He is the light of the world."

Joseph and Nicodemus sat back absorbing John's statements.

Finally, John leaned forward and looked grave. "The question is do you believe it? Are you ready to join us and follow Y'shua?"

"But Y'shua is just a man, born of flesh. How can He be the Son of YaHoWaH?" asked Nicodemus.

"Conceived by the Holy Spirit, his mother, Miryam, became pregnant while she was betrothed to her husband, Joseph. He never slept with her but honored what was promised through an Angel."

"She was a virgin? Are you saying she gave birth to Him without a father?" asked Nicodemus with skepticism while pointing at the Teacher.

"You have seen and heard Him yourself, have you not?" John asked.

"I must tell you, I am fascinated by His wisdom and knowledge," said Joseph. "No one on the council has this kind of wisdom or understands the Torah with such detail."

"I belie—" Joseph began to say, but Nicodemus cut him off.

"We are listening, watching, learning. We believe Y'shua has a gift from YaHoWaH, and we will decide later."

Joseph looked disappointed but conceded to Nicodemus.

John looked adamant. "Too many years studying the books of law have clouded your thinking. In time, you will understand."

Mute, the three men sat staring at one another for a very long time.

John finally broke the silence when he stood. "Y'shua says you may join our journey if you wish."

John turned and walked back toward Simon-Peter, leaving Joseph and Nicodemus alone.

"Tell me, Joseph, what are we doing here?" Nicodemus asked.

"Studying Y'shua of Nazareth. Learning. Deciding if this Man is from YaHoWaH and if He is who He says He is."

"I think, Joseph, you have your mind set already."

"And if I have?"

"What will we tell the council, Joseph? What will Caiaphas and Annas do when they find out you're a follower of Y'shua?"

"I believe it was you who tried to convince me this Y'shua was from YaHoWaH in the first place. So now, you are not so convinced?"

"For years, I have been training to replace my father on the council as a Pharisee. What will happen to me when they find out I've become a believer in a Man they have decided to destroy. Is our fate tied to Y'shua?"

Joseph scratched his cheek then placed his hands on Nicodemus' shoulders. "The council is trying to destroy the leader, not the followers. They believe if they remove Y'shua, His followers will scatter and be powerless. After all, Y'shua is the outspoken One who stirs the people."

"This man John seems rather confident. He speaks openly about Y'shua," stated Nicodemus.

"True, but we have heard nothing from the council about the followers of Y'shua or any plans to harm them, have we?" Joseph asked.

Drawing a hand across his beard, Nicodemus gazed at the twelve witnesses huddled together in discussion. They, in turn, kept glancing at Nicodemus and Joseph.

"At some point, we must report to the council what we have learned, lest we anger Caiaphas any further," said Nicodemus.

"Or not go back at all," said Joseph.

Nicodemus weighed his options. "I think we should follow for a while longer but go and report our findings later. We will then learn the fate of the followers of Y'shua."

"Agreed. So, what do you propose we tell John?"

Nicodemus saw the witnesses arguing among themselves. "I suggest we tell them the truth."

Joseph looked at the group and caught John's attention. After a few moments, John separated himself from his friends and walked over to Joseph and Nicodemus. After they explained their plan to John, he frowned.

"So you are spies for the Sanhedrin and will report on us when you return?"

"No! Surely, you must appreciate our predicament?" Nicodemus objected.

John contemplated the words of the two men. "What will you do then?"

Joseph quickly spoke. "We must maintain our positions and discover what the council plans for Y'shua. We personally believe Y'shua is from heaven and doing the work of YaHoWaH. Perhaps a prophet, we're not certain at this time. We must learn more. You and your friends have been with the Man for three years. It will take time for us to be your equals."

John narrowed his eyes. "I have watched many followers come and go for various reasons. There are twelve of us who are close to the Teacher and perhaps seventy or more who frequently travel with our group. I pray you will see Y'shua as the Son of YaHoWaH and become like us. I suspect you must unlearn everything the Sanhedrin has taught you and understand what you see and hear from a different perspective."

John turned and walked back to the other witnesses. Joseph and Nicodemus could tell he was explaining their conversation because Simon-Peter puffed out his chest and looked menacing.

Both Nicodemus and Joseph jumped when Y'shua approached them from behind unannounced.

"You looked worried," He said.

"Excuse me?" stammered Nicodemus.

Y'shua smiled. "I think Joseph is correct; you do spend too much studying the books."

Joseph chuckled, but Nicodemus gave his friend a scornful glance.

The followers journeyed to another small village very close to Jerusalem. As the Teacher walked along, He saw a man who had been born blind sitting by the main gate. It was the day of Sabbath, and Y'shua walked in the direction of the temple.

James asked Y'shua, "Teacher, whose sin caused this man to be born blind? Was it his own or his parents' sin?"

Y'shua answered, "His blindness has nothing to do with his sins or his parents'. He is blind so the power of YaHoWaH might be seen at work in the blind man. As long as it is the day, we must do the tasks of My Father who sent Me. The night is coming when no one can work. While I am in the world, I am the light of the world."

After the Teacher said this, He moved closer to the blind man. He then spat on the ground and made some mud with the spittle. He rubbed the wet dirt on the man's closed eyes and said to him, "Now go and wash your face in the Pool of Siloam."

Immediately, the man went with his friends who led him away. Nicodemus and Joseph trailed the blind man to see what would happen. The blind man washed his face. When he followed the Teacher's instructions, his sight was immediately restored.

"I can see! I see everything!" said the man.

His neighbors and all the people who had seen him begging at the gate started asking questions.

"Isn't this the man who used to sit and beg?"

"I believe he is the one."

A few other people argued against those people, "No he isn't. This man just looks like him."

The formerly blind man said, "Look! It's me. I'm no longer blind and can see everything. I see people, buildings, trees, and even children. I see all the beauty of YaHoWaH, Elohim!"

"But how is it possible you can see now?" the people asked him.

The man smiled. "There is a Man called Y'shua, and He made some mud, rubbed it on my eyes, and told me to go to Siloam and wash my face. So I went, and as soon as I washed, I could see."

"Where may we find this Y'shua?" the people asked.

Looking bewildered, he shrugged. "I don't know."

Joseph suddenly grabbed Nicodemus by his arm. "Come, Nicodemus, I have an idea."

Looking at the man who had been healed, Joseph said, "Sir, please come with me and my friend. If this is a miracle, we must show you to the Pharisees."

The man smiled. "Yes, yes, we must show them what YaHoWaH has done."

Nicodemus and Joseph quickly guided the man to the Sanhedrin Council chambers. Being recognized by their friends in the inner circle, the three people were immediately ushered into the presence of the council. Caiaphas saw Joseph and Nicodemus and stood to his feet. The teachers of the law, elders, and Pharisees began talking all at once, creating a din of noise.

Caiaphas slammed his staff to the stone floor, making a loud cracking sound, bringing everyone to silence.

"Come, Nicodemus and Joseph. Tell me about your travels. We are anxious to hear your report." Caiaphas looked around the room and produced a malicious smile. "What about this troublemaker of Nazareth? The other spies returned many days ago and gave us wild tales of this evil man."

The man who had been blind spoke up. "This Man called Y'shua is not evil, He has restored my sight. I was once blind, but I now see. Praise YaHoWaH."

Caiaphas slammed his staff to the stone floor again. "Be silent foolish peasant. Do not mention YaHoWaH in the same breath with this devil of a Man you call Y'shua."

The man looked confused. "Sir, I mean no disrespect, but Y'shua is sent from YaHoWaH, for He has performed a miracle."

Annas pushed his way to the front. "Tell us the truth. By what method have you received your sight?"

Taking his time, the man who had been healed explained the events. "Y'shua made mud from spit and dirt and applied it to my eyes. He then instructed me to go to the Pool of Siloam and wash my face. And now I can see."

Some of the Pharisees said, "The Man who did this work cannot be from YaHoWaH, for He does not obey the Sabbath law. It is forbidden to work on the Sabbath."

Nicodemus asked his colleagues, "How can a Man who is a sinner perform such miracles as these?" He extended his hand toward the formerly blind man.

Suddenly, a division arose among the teachers and Pharisees. They began fiercely arguing among themselves.

Joseph took the man's shoulders and asked him once more, "You say Y'shua cured you of your blindness. Well, what do you say about Him?"

The man's face brightened. "He is a prophet, of course!" was his answer.

Annas cried out. "This man cannot be telling the truth. No one can receive sight when they were born blind. What trickery is this?"

"Would you believe he was blind but now can see, if his parents were summoned?" asked Nicodemus.

Looking at the two temple guards, Annas commanded, "Go find this man's parents and bring them to us. Do not tell them why we want to speak with them. Do you understand?"

"Yes, sir," replied the guard. He left immediately with two men following.

After the guards departed, Caiaphas moved closer to Joseph and Nicodemus. He inspected them scrupulously, narrowing his eyes, as he looked them over. He scowled at the man who claimed he was healed of his blindness.

"You, go sit, over there." Caiaphas pointed with his staff at a small bench along the outer wall. "Sit there and be quiet while we wait for your parents."

The man beamed with pride, for he was now sitting among the leaders in the Sanhedrin. The room was silent as they watched the man obey his instructions. Everyone moved away from him and stood in a group whispering.

"Now, tell us, Nicodemus, what news do you report concerning this scoundrel of Nazareth?"

Nicodemus took a deep breath. Joseph smiled at Nicodemus and patted his shoulder.

"Joseph and I have been alongside Y'shua of Nazareth and about seventy other men who follow Him. We have listened to Him teach others and witnessed several healings. I must add, though, the information regarding some of the people healed was hearsay, in some cases."

Joseph interrupted. "Even though we did not know the individuals before their healing, the villagers were convinced and professed to witness the healing of these individuals."

Caiaphas dismissed Joseph's comment with the wave of his hand, "Foolish peasants will believe anything they are told. They're uneducated and ignorant."

"And tell me Caiaphas, what about this man?" Joseph extended his hand toward the formerly blind man sitting on the bench.

Caiaphas narrowed his eyes. "We shall see, won't we. We will hear the report of his parents first. So, did you learn anything else concerning this troublemaker? I heard separate reports from the teachers of the law that this Man openly defies the laws of Moses."

Nicodemus stroked his beard. "Did they indicate which laws had been broken?"

Scowling, Caiaphas said, "They said He did not follow the laws concerning the washing of food and hands. Furthermore, they said He blathered nonsense and never addressed their questions."

Nicodemus started to speak, but Joseph interrupted. "We were present for this discussion. Y'shua said it's not what you put inside your body making you unclean, but what comes out."

Caiaphas frowned. "He is now translating the laws of Moses and supposes to teach us? He is a craftsman from Galilee. How can He know more than the learned men within these walls?" Caiaphas extended his arms and swept the room.

Soft laughter swept through the men gathered around.

"He speaks with authority and wisdom. Never does He disgrace YaHoWaH, but He speaks only about doing good things," defended Joseph.

Caiaphas, his face beet red with anger, shook his staff at Joseph. "And are you now from Galilee, too? Are you becoming one of His followers? Do not be deceived by this devil. Soon He will no longer be a problem for us."

Nicodemus injected himself into the discussion, "What do you mean?"

Caiaphas snapped his attention to Nicodemus. "Careful how you speak to me, Nicodemus, you have not earned the right to question me; at least not yet."

When Nicodemus looked around the room, he focused on his father who wore a distraught and worried expression.

As the three men squared off in silence, a temple guard entered the space and called out, "The man's parents are here."

Turning his body to face the guard, Caiaphas softly spoke over his shoulder, "Nicodemus, we are not finished with this conversation."

The elderly and frightened parents were placed in the center of the council's chambers. Caiaphas motioned with his staff by pointing it toward Annas, who immediately moved closer to the couple and was joined by other leaders. A temple guard brought the formerly blind man over and placed him alongside.

"Tell us; is this man your son?" asked Annas.

The two parents glanced at the man and acted nervous. "Is our son in trouble?" asked the mother.

"Then he is your son?" questioned Caiaphas.

The man who had been healed of blindness was now grinning, anxiously working to interrupt the conversation.

"Of course." The two parents nodded in agreement and presented a demure posture. "We would recognize our own son," proclaimed the father.

Before Annas could ask his next question, the formerly blind man began talking excitedly. "Mamma, Papa, I can see you!" He lovingly took his hands and caressed his parent's faces.

Dumbfounded, the mother asked, "But how, my son?"

"The man called Y'shua restored my sight. Praise YaHoWaH . . ."

Instantly, Caiaphas slammed his large staff to the stone floor. The loud crack forced all eyes in the room to turn and face Caiaphas, who was now very angry.

"In these chambers, do not mention the name of the fatherless devil from Galilee."

"But, sir," pleaded the healed man, "can this not be a miracle from YaHoWaH?"

"Silence," screamed Caiaphas. "You are uneducated and foolish."

"What you say may be true, but without a doubt, I was once blind, but now I can see!"

Annas shook his fist at the three people being questioned. "Tell us the truth; was your son blind from his birth?"

The father placed his arms around his wife and son. "We have spoken only the truth about our son. He has been blind since the day he came from his mother's womb. His ability to suddenly see, after these thirty-some years, is a mystery for which we have no explanation. For years we blamed ourselves and thought YaHoWaH had cursed us, but I, for one, am filled with joy concerning his healing."

"How is it, then, he can now see?" demanded Annas.

The man's mother answered. "We know he is our son, and we know he was born blind. However, we do not know how he is now able to see, and we do not know who cured him of his blindness. Please ask him, he is old enough, and he can answer for himself!"

"Is it possible, Y'shua is the Messiah, and this is how I am healed?" said the formerly blind man.

The two parents instantly clasped their hands over their son's mouth. "Mind your tongue boy; we do not want to be expelled from the synagogue."

Caiaphas pointed his staff at the blind man. "Your parents are far wiser, and you should pay heed to their warning."

Annas grasped the son's cloak, near his neck and roughly shook him. "Make a promise before YaHoWaH you will tell us the truth! We know this Man who cured you is a sinner."

"I do not know if He is a sinner or not," the healed man replied. "One thing I do know, I was blind, and now I see."

"But what did He do to you?" Annas asked. "How did He cure you of your blindness?"

"I have already told you," he answered, "but you will not listen to me. Why do you want to hear it again? Perhaps you, too, would like to be His disciples?"

Shouting erupted from the leaders with one man calling out, "You stupid man, you know absolutely nothing. You claim to be a follower of a fatherless sinner, and we are the disciples of Moses. We know YaHoWaH spoke to Moses, but as for this Fellow, we do not even know where He comes from!"

The formerly blind man smiled. "What a strange thing to say. You do not know where He comes from, yet He cured me of my blindness! We know YaHoWaH does not listen to sinners, but He does listen to people who respect Him and do what He wants them to do. Since the beginning of the world, nobody has ever heard of anyone giving sight to a person born blind. I'd say unless this Man came from YaHoWaH, He would not be able to do such a thing."

Annas began yelling, "You were born and brought up in sin. How dare you attempt to teach us about the very things we have spent years studying."

The crowd of leaders surged toward the parents and their son and began roughly pushing them from the synagogue.

"Get out! Away from us, you fools. Go away, for you are all liars!"

"You are cursed like the sinner you follow."

In the commotion, Joseph pulled on Nicodemus and ushered him out another door in the opposite direction. Once outside, Joseph said, "Come, we will follow them and see what happens next."

The healed man and his parents scurried away to escape the council leaders' wrath. Joseph peered around the building and saw the three people running away.

"We must catch them, Nicodemus. Let's go!"

Eventually, the three members ran into Y'shua who was speaking with a crowd of children and their parents. When Y'shua saw the three people, He stood and asked the formerly blind man, "Do you believe in the Son of Man as the Messiah?"

Nicodemus and Joseph stood close by and listened intently. When John saw them, he motioned with his chin and Joseph acknowledged in return.

The healed man answered, "Tell me who He is, Sir, so I may believe in Him!"

Y'shua said to the man, "You have already seen Him with your new eyes. He is the One who is speaking with you now."

"Then I believe You, Master!" He then knelt before the Teacher.

Y'shua lifted the man to his feet and continued to speak with the followers. "I came to this world to judge so the blind should see and those who see, should become blind."

Then Joseph asked, "Surely You don't mean we are blind, too?"

Y'shua answered, "If you were blind, then you would not be guilty. Since you claim you can see, this means you are still guilty."

"Maybe we are the ones who are actually blind," mumbled Nicodemus.

"Perhaps, but rest easy, I have the ability to restore sight to the blind." Y'shua placed his hand on Nicodemus' shoulder and smiled.

Immediately, Nicodemus' body shivered from the current coursing through his joints, and his knees buckled. Both Simon-Peter and John grinned.

CHAPTER TWENTY-TWO

BECOMING SHEEP

"WHAT HAPPENED JOHN? I FELT as if my entire body was on fire."

"I think it is the power of the Holy Spirit, but I agree, Nicodemus, it cannot be described or explained."

"Does it happen every time Y'shua touches you?" asked Joseph. John shook his head.

A thick hairy arm wrapped around Nicodemus' neck. "Wait until He speaks your very thoughts out loud," Simon-Peter said laughing.

Nicodemus struggled to get free from Simon-Peter's grasp. "Wait, He can know my thoughts without me saying the words?"

Instantly, Joseph and Nicodemus dropped to their knees, unable to support themselves. Their legs felt like rubber. When they looked up, Y'shua was resting His hands on their shoulders and smiling.

"I only speak and do what My Father tells Me." He extended His hands. When Joseph and Nicodemus each took a hand from the Teacher, they were effortlessly lifted into a standing position. "Come, let us talk."

After supper in a friend's home, the small group of people following Y'shua gathered around. Approximately sixty people were crammed into the small house, with some folks on the outside and peering in through open windows. Inside, some stood, others sat on the floor. Y'shua reclined on a mat in the center. John rested alongside and nearly touched Him.

Discarding their worries about being part of the Sanhedrin, Nicodemus and Joseph no longer acted as if they were outcasts but found themselves comfortably rubbing shoulders with the followers of Y'shua.

The Teacher said, "What I'm about to tell you is the truth. Any man who does not enter the sheep pen by the gate, but climbs in some other way, is a thief and a robber. The man who goes in through the gate is the shepherd of the sheep. The gatekeeper opens the gate for him. The sheep hear his voice as he calls his own sheep by name, and he leads them out.

"When he has brought them out, he goes ahead of them, and the sheep follow him because they know his voice. They will not follow someone else. Instead, they will run away from such a person, because they do not know his voice."

The group of people gathered around looked confused. The parable the Teacher just spoke was not easily understood.

John asked, "Y'shua, Your words seem a little confusing. You speak of sheep, but I suspect You may be speaking about us, the twelve of us who follow You. Could You explain further?"

The Teacher said again, "What I told you is the truth. I am the gate for the sheep. All the others who came before Me are thieves and robbers, but the sheep did not listen to them. I am the gate. Those who come in by Me will be saved. They will come in, and go out, and find pasture.

"The thief comes only to steal, kill, and destroy. I have come so you might have life—life in all its fullness. I am the merciful Shepherd, who is willing to die for the sheep. When the hired man, who is not a shepherd and does not own the sheep, sees a wolf coming, he leaves the sheep and runs away. Therefore, the wolf snatches the sheep and scatters them. The hired man runs away because he is only an employed man and does not care about the sheep.

"I am the perfect Shepherd. As My Father knows Me, and I know the Father, in the same way, I know My sheep, and they know Me. I am willing to die for My sheep. There are other sheep, which belong to Me, which are not in this sheep pen. I must bring them, too. They will listen to My voice, and they will become one flock with one Shepherd.

"The Father loves Me because I am willing to give up My life, so I may receive it back again. No one takes My life away from Me. I give it up of My own free will. I have the right to give it up, and I have the right to take it back. This is what My Father has commanded Me to do."

Again, the people divided among the various meanings of these words. Many of them were saying, "He has a demon! He is crazy! Why do you listen to Him?"

Simon-Peter stood up and spoke with anger. "A man with a demon could not talk like this! How could a demon give sight to blind people?"

John got up and pushed everyone out except the group of witnesses, Nicodemus, and Joseph.

"It's late! Time to go home. Let the Teacher rest." John used his arms to usher people out the door.

Several people grumbled, but the room slowly emptied. For a while, those remaining just sat in silence. Y'shua scanned the room, making eye contact with each person. When he saw Joseph, Y'shua smiled.

"Teacher, may I ask You a question?" asked Joseph.

Every man sitting around was suddenly interested and waiting to see what would happen next. There were a few of the twelve witnesses who did not trust Nicodemus or Joseph, despite John's insistence otherwise. Y'shua stood and walked over to Joseph and sat on a stool next to the man. He looked into Joseph's eyes and smiled.

"You want to know why I call you My sheep."

Joseph raised his eyebrows and swallowed hard. "As a matter of fact, I do. Sheep are mindless animals needing constant care and a good watchful shepherd to manage them. Is this how You see us?" Joseph swept the room with his arm.

John and Simon-Peter wanted to know the answer as well so they inched closer to Y'shua.

"I am the *gracious watchful Shepherd*. The enemy, Satan, wants to devour those who are faithful to Me, like a wolf attacks the flock. However, I protect those whom My Father has given to Me. Listen to My words, learn, obey My teachings, and you will be safe from the wolf. Those who remain faithful will shepherd the ones who come later. They must be responsible for the new sheep."

"And what about the elders and teachers of the law?" asked Joseph. "Aren't they supposed to lead?"

Y'shua frowned. "Along the way, they forgot about YaHoWaH and started burdening man with their own laws and interpretations. They are no longer leaders, but men arguing over rules which would make a normal man crazy if he were to follow every detail they've written."

Nicodemus interrupted, "Then what are we supposed to do?"

Y'shua placed a hand on Nicodemus' shoulder and smiled. "Be sheep and listen to the *good and watchful Shepherd.*"

John spoke up, "Teacher, if You are willing to give up Your life for us, and we are Your sheep, then You must truly love us."

Y'shua stood and walked over to John. "My friend, with the exact same love My Father shows Me."

Simon-Peter rushed forward. "Then I am one of Your sheep!"

"As am I," said Philip.

Soon all the witnesses joined in unison and confirmed the same response while surrounding Y'shua.

Later in the night, as the room filled with the sounds of sleeping men, Nicodemus lay restless on his mat. Joseph grunted and rolled over facing his friend.

"You're not sleeping, Nicodemus. What troubles you?"

Nicodemus let out a heavy sigh. "Everything Y'shua says goes against the teachings I've dedicated my life to studying."

"Nicodemus! When we started searching the scrolls, it was you who convinced me this Y'shua is the Messiah. It appears you have changed your position and I am the one who is now convinced. Or perhaps I am wrong?"

Nicodemus sighed again.

John was nearby and rolled over facing the two men. He hoarsely whispered, "Every prophet, both the minor and greater prophets like Isaiah, foretold of the Messiah. Y'shua is the one whom they wrote about and the sooner you understand, the better it will be for you."

Joseph sat up on one elbow. He was shocked by John's under-standing of the old scrolls. "You're clearly educated, John. Why have I not heard your name mentioned in the Sanhedrin?"

John sat up. "It was a lifetime ago and unimportant now." His voice became angry.

"When was this, John? Have you studied the scrolls?" asked Nicodemus out of curiosity.

John gave his answer by first saying his reply in Hebrew, and then switching to Greek, followed by Roman, and finally Aramaic. "It is a long story and not worth speaking. But because of men like you, I went from a student preparing for a position in the council of Pharisees, to a lowly stinking fisherman. All this happened because my father needed a wife and mother to care for a brood of children, whose mother had suddenly died." John was agitated and jumped to his feet. He grabbed his outer cloak and stormed out the door into the darkness of night.

Speechless for a moment, Nicodemus stared at Joseph "I under-stood only half his words. How many languages did he use?"

Joseph lowered himself to his mat and stared up at the ceiling. He softly muttered, "He blames us! Why?"

"Blames us for what?" inquired Nicodemus.

Simon-Peter gruffly snorted, "For waking us all up! Now quit talking and go back to sleep."

Still puzzled by their conversation, Nicodemus pressed Simon-Peter for more answers. "Where do they go in the middle of the night? First Y'shua, and now John."

Simon-Peter rolled on to his side with his back to Nicodemus and Joseph. He whispered over his shoulder and sounded annoyed, "To pray and talk with YaHoWaH."

Dumbstruck, Nicodemus tried to comprehend the events of the evening. Within several minutes, Simon-Peter and Joseph were both snoring. Nicodemus sighed heavily and closed his eyes, but he could not sleep.

It was winter, and the Festival of the Dedication of the temple was being celebrated in Jerusalem. Y'shua was walking in Solomon's Porch in the temple when the people gathered around Him and asked, "How long are You going to keep us in suspense? Tell us the plain truth. Are You the Messiah?"

"I have already told you," said Y'shua, "but you don't believe Me. The deeds I do by My Father's authority speak on My behalf. Even with these things, you will not accept Me, for you are not My sheep. My sheep listen to My voice, I know them, and they follow Me. I give them eternal life, and they shall never die.

"No one can snatch them away from Me. What My Father has given Me is greater than everything, and no one can snatch them away from the Father's care. The Father, YaHoWaH, and I are one."

Like previous times, the people again picked up stones to throw at Him.

He said to them, "I have done many good deeds in your presence, which YaHoWaH gave Me to do. For which one of these deeds do You want to stone Me?"

They answered, "We do not want to stone You because of any good deeds, but because of Your blasphemy! You are only a man, but you are trying to make Yourself equal to Elohim."

He smiled. "Do you not understand the words written in your own law? 'YaHoWaH says, the law states, you are *gods*.' We know what the Scripture says is true forever. We know YaHoWaH called those people *gods*, the people to whom His message was given. As for Me, the Father chose and sent Me into the world.

"How, then, can you say I blaspheme because I said that I am the Son of YaHoWaH? Do not believe Me, then, if I am not doing the things My Father wants Me to do. But if I do them, even though you do not believe Me, you should at least believe My deeds. This way, you may know once and for all the Father is in Me, and I am in the Father."

Once more, the people tried to seize Y'shua, but He slipped out of their hands and disappeared into the crowd. He walked away from the city and journeyed to the Jordan River, to the place where John had been baptizing.

Nicodemus and Joseph traveled with the group that followed Y'shua. Along the way, they spoke with John and Simon-Peter. "John, last night you blamed us for your family situation. I don't wish to be insensitive, but we cannot comprehend why we are responsible," questioned Nicodemus.

John cast a suspicious glance at Nicodemus.

The others witnesses continued their journey, but Simon-Peter and the two new converts, Nicodemus and Joseph, stopped and focused their attention on John.

While keeping his eyes forward, John contemplated his response.

"I must tell you, brother, I too am curious about your past," said Simon-Peter. "You're closer to Y'shua than all of us, yet you don't say much either."

John stared at Simon-Peter and frowned. "When I was young, my brother James and I were students in our father's Chinukh. Father taught many students, and some of them were selected to join the bet ha-Midrash to further their education. As you two are both aware," John pointed his finger at Nicodemus and Joseph, "the gold tasseled men of the Sanhedrin are chosen from the best students in the bet ha-Midrash."

"Yes, we both followed this same education path," interrupted Joseph. "For years I have been an advisor to the elders and council, but Nicodemus' father is a prominent member. Nicodemus will one day replace his father on the council."

"*Would have* replaced my father. I doubt I will have the opportunity given my current status," said Nicodemus with an edge of sadness in his voice.

A small smile crept into the corner of John's mouth. "Then I suppose we have more in common than you know."

"So, what happened? Did you quit your education to follow Y'shua?" asked Nicodemus.

Joseph placed his hand on Nicodemus' shoulder. "If you remember, John said a family tragedy caused the change. Let's give the man time to share his thoughts without judgment."

John explained. "My mother passed away suddenly, leaving our father with the care of two boys and two daughters; all under the age of twelve."

"But this shouldn't cause any problems with your education," Joseph interjected.

"Our father could not be a rabbi and care for young children, so he sought a new wife," John said as he crossed his arms.

"Still, this is no reason for any sudden changes unless you didn't approve of your new mother," added Nicodemus.

"The gold tasseled men, like you, didn't approve of the new wife! They wanted my father to wait a year in mourning, but he could not manage the Chinukh and a growing family without the help of a wife. The gold tasseled men ruined our lives. They took the Chinukh from my father and threw us out of town. He was no longer a rabbi."

For a long pause, the four men stood gawking at one another. Then John turned and stormed away from the group. He walked straight toward Y'shua, who was waiting with a friendly expression.

"Amazing, I had no idea," said Simon-Peter. "I thought he grew up being a fisherman, just like my brother and I."

Joseph also surprised said, "Then you didn't know any of John's story, until now?"

Peter shook his head. "No, but it explains a lot."

"Does his father still have a Chinukh?" asked Nicodemus.

"His whole family are hardworking fishermen. I knew they moved to our village when we were young men, but I never knew where they came from, or what they did before moving."

"It's no wonder he hates us," mumbled Nicodemus.

"I don't think he hates us, Nicodemus; he dislikes what we represent," countered Joseph.

"But we didn't do this to him, and we certainly weren't on the council at the time either," defended Nicodemus.

Simon-Peter stepped near the two men, "But you're guilty by association."

"But, but, we had nothing to do . . . " stammered Nicodemus.

Peter walked away in a huff leaving Nicodemus with his useless defense of words. He then walked toward John and Y'shua.

After the group crossed the Jordan River, the Teacher and His followers camped in the place where John the Baptist had been visiting and baptizing. The area was near Jericho in a small village of Bethabara in Perea.

Many people joined the group, and they expressed their opinions concerning Y'shua to the other followers.

"John the Baptist performed no miracles," they said, "but everything he said about this Y'shua was true."

Many of the people who followed Y'shua were believers in John the Baptist and his message.

Late in the day, Y'shua stood and approached the witness, John. "I wish to be alone and pray."

John jumped to his feet. "May I join You?"

Before Y'shua could answer, Simon-Peter came alongside. "I want to come, too."

In a matter of seconds, all twelve witnesses gathered around and were wanting to join Y'shua. Just a few feet away stood Joseph and Nicodemus looking rejected as they stood alone but longing to be part of the inner circle.

The Teacher softly smiled. "Yes, you may come." He then turned to walk toward a small hill in the distance.

Before they could leave, Joseph pulled on John's sleeve. "If it's not too much trouble, may we come as well?" he begged.

The twelve followers formed a circle around the Teacher and walked in His footsteps.

Perplexed, John saw the others starting to leave and then stared at Nicodemus and Joseph. When he looked back at his friends, they didn't glance back to see if John was with them.

"Please?" plead Nicodemus.

After a sigh of resignation, John said, "The Teacher has invited you two. If it were up to me, I'd say no." John released another deep sigh. "Come but do not be too close. Oh, and no more of your questions; especially you." John pointed with his finger at Joseph.

Filled with excitement, Nicodemus and Joseph didn't hesitate but quickly walked to catch the group walking with Y'shua. John shook his head and muttered aloud to himself, "I hope I don't regret this decision."

After sitting on a large rock, the twelve witnesses gathered around Y'shua and squatted on the ground. Per John's instructions, Nicodemus and Joseph remained separate from the others, but near enough, so they could listen in. By being very quiet, they did their best to be nearly invisible to the others.

Once everyone was settled, Y'shua intently looked at each of His followers.

"I have a question for you. What are people saying about Me?"

James raised his voice above the others. "Some people think You're John the Baptist come back to life."

"Or Elijah!" shouted Philip.

"I've heard others say You're Jeremiah or some other prophet," said Matthew.

Y'shua frowned. "But, who do you say I am?"

At first, the men looked around at each other, but then Simon-Peter slowly stood to his feet.

"You are the promised Messiah, the Son of the living YaHoWaH. You have been sent from Elohim, Adonai."

Smiling, the Teacher said, "Simon, son of John, you are very blessed among men. You didn't discover this knowledge on your own or through any human means, but My Father in heaven has revealed this wisdom to you. This is why I will call you Peter. It means *a rock*."

Simon-Peter proudly crossed his arms and beamed with pride.

Y'shua continued and extended His hand toward Peter. "Upon this *rock*, I will build My community of believers, and the gates of Sh'ol Hades will not have any power to overcome it or stop it. I will give you the keys to the kingdom of heaven, and My Father will allow whatever you allow on earth. But He will not permit anything you don't allow here on earth."

Satisfied, Simon-Peter sat down as those near him congratulated him because of Y'shua's declaration.

"Now listen carefully to my next words," said Y'shua. "Soon I must travel to Jerusalem. While there, the Pharisees, the chief priests, and teachers of the law, who have been scheming for a long time, intend to do Me harm. Under their authority, I must suffer terribly. I will be rejected by all men and killed, but three days later I will come alive."

Instantly, Nicodemus stared at Joseph and swallowed a hard lump in his throat. "He knows, Joseph."

"How can the Teacher be so candid and speak with such calmness?" muttered Joseph.

When Y'shua stood, Peter pulled Y'shua aside. "Rabbi, You must not speak like this and in such devastating terms. Surely YaHoWaH would never let these things happen to You."

Y'shua frowned and pulled away, facing faced Peter. "Satan, get away from Me! You are in My way because you think like everyone else and not like My Father."

Peter instantly looked shocked. He went from being prideful to being embarrassed, within minutes. Hiding his face, he sulked and moved away from the group.

Nicodemus watched John and saw him wince. When he looked back at Y'shua he was casually conversing with other witnesses.

Speechless, Nicodemus tried to talk, but no words would come out of his mouth.

"He was so harsh with his reprimand of Peter. I don't understand," said Joseph, finally finding his own voice.

Y'shua then raised His voice above the murmuring group. "Listen very carefully to My words. If any of you want to be My followers, you must forget about yourself. You must be willing to face death and follow My instructions. If you want to save your life, you must be willing to give it away, even to death."

Saying nothing further, the Teacher allowed His words to settle into the minds of His followers. He looked into their eyes.

"If you give up your life for Me, you will discover real life. Eternal life. Let Me ask you, what will you gain if you own every worldly treasure, but see your life destroyed? What would you give up to get back your soul?"

Y'shua looked up at the sky and extended His arms. "I, the Son of YaHoWaH, will soon come in the glory of My Father and all His angels. He will reward all people for what they have done while living on earth; good or bad."

Y'shua studied the men gathered around. "Don't be ashamed of Me and My message among these unfaithful and sinful people you meet daily. If you are, I will be ashamed of you when I come in the glory of My Father and all His holy angels. I promise you, there are some of those standing here today who will not die before they see Me coming with My kingdom."

CHAPTER TWENTY-THREE

LAZARUS IS DEAD!

EARLY THE NEXT MORNING, THE twelve witnesses arose and began to eat. A reflective mood permeated the group as each man appeared to contemplate the information presented the night before.

"I will say this, Y'shua is unlike any man I have ever witnessed," said Joseph. "He can only be a prophet or man of YaHoWaH, and the last recorded prophet we know of was centuries ago."

"But are you willing to die with Him?" asked Nicodemus.

Joseph thought on the question. "If you were to ask me the same question two weeks ago, the answer would be absolutely not."

"Then something has changed your mind?" questioned Nicodemus.

Nodding slowly, Joseph said, "Yes. Without a doubt, Y'shua comes from heaven, and I'm beginning to believe every word He speaks."

Nicodemus toyed with his beard and stared off into the distance. His mind raced trying to make sense of everything he had witnessed for the last several weeks.

Joseph placed his hand on Nicodemus' shoulder. "I can no longer deny the truth."

Somewhat frightened, Nicodemus darted his eyes at Joseph. "You will surely die with Y'shua. Make no mistake; Caiaphas will destroy these men to stop them from spreading Y'shua's message."

Joseph lifted his chin. "Perhaps, but I can no longer remain blinded by the nonsense of the Sanhedrin."

Nicodemus began to speak but stopped. His confusion was overwhelming.

Joseph waited.

Finally, Nicodemus moved his shoulders back and stuck out his chest. "I have known the answer for a long time; I just didn't want to admit it. I have spent the last few weeks trying to convince myself Y'shua is just a clever man, a trickster deceiving these followers. But . . . "

"But, what?" inquired Joseph.

"I think it was my fears holding me back. The very thing I have dedicated my life to—to become a Pharisee like my father—is all I have ever wanted. Since I was a small boy, I have dreamt of being a Pharisee . . . " Nicodemus' voice trailed off as he looked away.

When he turned and faced Joseph, tears were welling in his eyes. "I'm not ready to die, Joseph, yet our fate is sealed if we follow Y'shua."

"My young friend, we are not going to die. Y'shua said we had to be willing to lay down our life, but didn't He also say that YaHoWaH gave Y'shua His followers and He would protect them?"

Nicodemus nodded, but didn't look convinced.

Joseph continued to encourage his friend. "Y'shua also said by following Him we would have eternal life. That doesn't sound so bad to me; in fact, I've never heard another prophet make this kind of promise!"

Nicodemus still looked sad. "The news of this will break my father's heart. It may be too much and kill the man."

"Nicodemus, your father is a sage elder. I think you may not be giving him enough credit."

Drawing his hand down his beard, Nicodemus wondered if his friend was actually correct. He played Joseph's words over and over inside his head, trying to make sense, but he could see only fear at the end of every road.

Joseph interrupted his thoughts. "Where are your notes regarding the Messiah, from the scrolls? Are they well hidden?"

"Of course, why do you ask?" Nicodemus now looked worried.

"When you originally showed them to me, I was of the same mind as you now. You must know your work is excellent and convincing, but I didn't want to accept it at first. But now, we have been listening to Y'shua, and all your writings are becoming very clear. I think if you go back and read your notes, you will discover what I'm saying is correct."

"No, you're right, Joseph. I have always known it, but it scares me to think we may be putting our lives at risk for this Man, Y'shua."

"For certain, we can never return to the Sanhedrin. That part of our lives is dead, and I am saddened by their blindness to the truth," stated Joseph.

"If Caiaphas has his way, we may feel more than sadness."

"Nicodemus, this is Y'shua, Son of Elohim, we are talking about. If He can perform miracles on the sick, surely He can save the likes of us?"

With pleading eyes, Nicodemus looked intently at his older and wiser friend. "For our sakes, I hope you're right."

As they were talking, a messenger came running into the camp. "Y'shua? Is Y'shua here?" he asked. He dashed from one cluster of people to another asking the same question. "Is Y'shua here? Are you Y'shua?"

Within minutes, the entire group following the Teacher was buzzing with activity and whispering. Then Y'shua, who had been off alone and praying, entered the camp.

"I am Y'shua, whom you seek."

The messenger fell at His feet. "Oh kind sir, Your good friends Mary and Martha have sent me to find You. Your dear friend Lazarus is very sick and is in need of You. They fear he is close to death. They have asked me to find You and bring You to them so Lazarus may again see You."

Y'shua knelt on the ground in front of the frightened messenger. "His sickness won't end in death. It will bring glory to Adonai, and His Son."

Relieved, the messenger stood and smiled. "Praises to YaHoWaH." He looked around at the other people who were encamped with the Teacher. "This is good news, yes?"

Y'shua smiled and took the messenger's hand. "Go back to My friends Mary and Martha. Tell them, and Lazarus, I love them with all My heart. I will be with them soon."

"You're not coming with me?" asked the messenger, seeming confused.

Continuing to smile, Y'shua urged the young man to run back to Mary, Martha, and Lazarus. "Go quickly and tell My friends I love them. I will follow later."

"But sir . . . I . . . ah . . . I . . . I don't understand," the bewildered messenger said.

The Teacher hugged the young messenger. "Greet them with this same embrace and tell them I love them. Now go, deliver My message."

At first, the young man hesitated, but after weighing Y'shua's instructions, he turned and ran back toward the city.

Grouped together, the twelve witnesses were talking when Nicodemus walked up to them. The men became quiet and gazed at the intruder.

"You need something, Pharisee?" asked Peter.

Nicodemus cringed, hearing the use of the formal word.

John smiled and embraced his fisherman friend. "Peter! This is our guest. What do you desire, Nicodemus?"

Peter scowled.

"A word, if you please," said Nicodemus hesitantly.

"Whatever you need to say to John, you may say it to all of us," demanded Peter.

Nicodemus saw the other witnesses gather closer. He looked over his shoulder and could not see his friend, Joseph. Returning his attention, he focused on John.

"I wish to apologize for my offensive comments earlier. On the one hand, we had no idea of your family's situation. On the other hand, neither Joseph nor I, nor my father for that matter, had anything to do with what the Sanhedrin did to you and your family. We are innocent. All my life, I have done my best to follow every letter of the law. I have dedicated my life to preparing myself to be an honest Pharisee, obedient to YaHoWaH, but I am not a Pharisee yet."

"You're guilty by association—" Peter began to say, but John interrupted him.

"Nicodemus, my friend Peter, is passionate. I suspect you have more you wanted to say." John smiled.

"For several months, long before we joined your group, Joseph and I have been searching the Torah for evidence of the Messiah. I have compiled a long list of notes where I have found Scripture giving testimony to His coming. For generations, students of the law have been seeking the Messiah and His appearance. At first, I could not believe this Y'shua from Nazareth was the promised Messiah."

"But now?" asked Peter with interest.

"Without a doubt, Y'shua is the Messiah, sent from YaHoWaH."

John broadly smiled. "And is this only your opinion? What does Joseph think?"

Nicodemus half smiled. "We are of one mind."

John reached out and embraced Nicodemus, who immediately stiffened his body, unprepared for John's warm display of affection.

The other men joined in hugging Nicodemus, but the man was unaccustomed and had never experienced anything like this.

"I need to say more," said Nicodemus as he wrestled himself free.

The group of men waited.

"The Sanhedrin, mostly Caiaphas, is set on destroying Y'shua. He has plans in place and seeks to bring Him harm. I fear for your safety—for all of you."

John rested his hand on Nicodemus' shoulder. "What about you and Joseph? Are not the men in the Sanhedrin angry with you, too?"

Looking around, Nicodemus found Joseph. He was being embraced by Y'shua. With his attention focused on the two men, Nicodemus faintly said, "We haven't told them yet."

✝

Two days after the messenger arrived with the news of Lazarus, Y'shua gathered the seventy-some people who were encamped.

"Now we will travel back to Judea, to the village of Bethany."

Simon the Zealot forcefully pushed his way forward until he stood in front of Y'shua. "Rabbi, the people there want to stone You to death! Why do You want to go back?"

The Teacher looked gravely at His followers. "Aren't there twelve hours each day? If you walk during the day, you will have the light from the sun, and you won't stumble. But if you walk during the night, you *will* stumble, because you don't have any light."

Confused, the men stared at one another.

Y'shua sighed. "Our friend Lazarus is asleep, and I am going there to wake him up."

Matthew asked, "Y'shua, if he is asleep won't he get better after his rest?"

The Teacher rested His hand on Matthew's shoulder and smiled. "I will be direct; Lazarus, is dead!"

"What?" asked James. "I thought You said he was sleeping?"

Y'shua shook His head. "I am glad I wasn't there because now you will have a chance to put your faith in Me. Come, let us go to him."

Thomas looked around at the other witnesses. "Come on. Let's go too; we might as well die with Him."

The group then followed their leader as they traveled past the city of Jerusalem, also known as the City of David. They then continued to the village of Bethany. A group of people met them on the road and saw Y'shua entering the village. "We know Mary, Martha, and Lazarus. We came from Jerusalem to comfort the two sisters whose brother has died. We are leaving to walk back home." Two people from the group ran back to the home of Lazarus and found Mary and Martha.

The group following Y'shua arrived at the home of Lazarus, and the people cried out, "Y'shua just arrived. He is walking through town this very moment!"

When Martha heard, she rushed out to await His arrival. Just before exiting the home, she looked at her sister, Mary.

"Are you not coming? Y'shua is here to comfort us."

Mary softly cried and never looked up. She shook her head. Several of the professional mourners began loudly wailing and surrounded Mary.

Martha wiped her eyes on an apron. Upon His arrival, she fell at Y'shua's feet and began to cry.

"Y'shua, I am glad You are here. If only You had come four days ago, my brother would not have died. Yet even now, I know YaHoWaH will do anything You ask."

Y'shua bent down and lifted Martha to her feet. He took His hands, brushed the tears from her face, and smiled. "Your brother will live again!"

"I know he will be raised to life on the last day when all the dead are raised to life. At that time Your kingdom will be complete, and we will be with You forever."

"I am the One who raises the dead to life!" said Y'shua. "Everyone who has faith in Me will live, even if they have died. But, just so you understand My meaning, everyone who lives because of their faith in Me, will never really die. Do you believe this, Martha?"

"Yes, Y'shua! I believe You are the promised Messiah and the Son of Elohim, YaHoWaH. You are the One we have been looking for, for many, many years. Our hope has always been in search of Your arrival in this world."

Martha began to weep again. Turning, she returned to the house and found Mary and brought her outside. "The Teacher is here, sister, He wants to see you."

Mary looked up. Her eyes red and swollen. "He asked for me?"

Martha nodded then hugged her sister. "Yes."

Mary looked up and saw Y'shua as the mourners gathered around her.

One of the women cried out, "Come, Mary we must go to your brother's tomb to cry."

Mary threw herself on the ground at Y'shua's feet. She began to sob loudly. She then pleaded with Him. "Oh Y'shua, if only You had been here, my brother would still be alive."

Mary and the mourners were all crying and lamenting the death of Lazarus. When Y'shua looked around and saw their grief, He was moved to tears. He leaned over and helped Mary to her feet and embraced her.

"Where have you placed Lazarus' body?" He asked.

Mary blotted her eyes with the sleeve of her dress and pointed. "Oh Y'shua, kind sir, come, and You will see."

When Nicodemus and Joseph looked at Y'shua, they saw tears falling down His cheeks. Joseph said, "See how much He loved His friend, Lazarus."

Nicodemus said, "He restores the sight to the blind. Why couldn't He have kept His friend Lazarus from dying?"

Y'shua continued to weep, but Mary took His hand and led Him to the cemetery, where Lazarus lay in a tomb. A large group of people followed, including the twelve witnesses and Joseph and Nicodemus.

In a small stone hill facing the graves, Mary pointed at a new tomb carved into the rock. A large wheel-shaped stone sealed the entrance.

The group gathered close around Y'shua and Mary, waiting.

Y'shua stared at the tomb for a long time.

Martha waited next to her sister Mary.

"Remove the stone from the entrance," Y'shua commanded.

The people were shocked.

Her mouth gaping open, Martha looked at the Teacher. "But Y'shua, You know Lazarus has been dead four days. The smell will be awful. His body is not fully decomposed."

Y'shua softly smiled. "Didn't I say if you had faith, you would see the glory of YaHoWaH, My Father?"

Mary and Martha stared at Y'shua. Finally, Martha called out to the men standing nearby. "You heard Him. Roll the entrance stone aside!" she demanded.

Wrapping a cloth around their faces, several men grunted and heaved the stone. At first, it wouldn't move, but eventually, the rock slowly started turning. Hurrying, the men quickly pushed harder and rolled the rock away from the tomb entrance. Once the opening was visible, the men quickly ran away in fear they would have to breathe the stench of the corpse.

Y'shua looked up, closed His eyes and faced the sky. He extended His hands in the air and began praying aloud. "My Father in heaven, thank You for answering My prayers. I'm saying this for the sake of the people so they will believe You sent Me here to this world. You are the Creator, You give life, You love Your creation, and I do Your will."

Facing the tomb, Y'shua cupped His hands around His mouth and yelled with a loud voice, "Lazarus, come out!"

After a few long seconds, the crowd of people gasped as the man who had been dead four days appeared at the entrance to the tomb. The body was wrapped tightly with strips of cloth, covering his legs, arms, and body. Even his face was completely covered.

Wide-eyed, Nicodemus' mouth dropped open. "Is this a ghost?"

Joseph was speechless. In fact, everyone standing was mesmerized and unable to move a muscle or speak.

Y'shua looked at the men who had rolled the stone away and said, "Don't just stand there, untie him and set him free."

The wrapped body stood frozen waiting. Hesitantly, two men approached and started removing the strips of cloth. They started with the hands and feet at first and then one of them slowly removed the wrapping from around his face. As soon as his head was uncovered entirely, Lazarus opened his eyes, and he blinked several times. He gasped, taking in a deep breath. When he saw Y'shua, he grinned. The men who were unwrapping Lazarus fell backward on the ground, crawling away on their hands and knees, trying to escape.

Martha and Mary plunged toward Lazarus and embraced their brother. Tears of joy streamed down their faces. Choking on her words, Mary stammered, "You're alive!"

Lazarus laughed. "Of course! Now, please take me home, I'm famished."

As the two sisters walked on either side of Lazarus, they locked arms refusing to let their brother walk alone.

Joseph grabbed Nicodemus by the shoulders and shook the man vigorously. "Did you and I just witness a miracle? Please tell me I'm not dreaming."

Dumbfounded, Nicodemus slowly nodded in agreement, but he could not speak.

Joseph pulled on Nicodemus' arm. "Come quickly. We must follow everyone. This was the most amazing thing I have ever seen."

Nicodemus stopped walking and spoke in flat tones. "This is undeniably a miracle, Joseph. Make no mistake." He shook his head slowly. "The man has been dead for four days, and we saw him come back to life." Nicodemus began to tremble. "The Sanhedrin cannot refute this. They must be made to understand the power of Y'shua, and acknowledge He is from YaHoWaH. Unbelievable, Joseph, absolutely unbelievable."

Arriving at the house, Nicodemus and Joseph looked inside. A crowd of people stood in the doorway and peered into the windows. They pushed their way to the window and glimpsed Mary, Martha, Lazarus, and Y'shua sitting at a supper table. All four were laughing and eating. Lazarus raised his wine glass and howled like a wild animal.

"It is a great day to be alive, Y'shua!"

While music played and people clapped in tempo, Lazarus jumped to his feet. He grabbed his sisters' hands and they all awkwardly danced together, twisting and spinning around the room. Y'shua laughed and clapped with the music.

Many other people had arrived when they heard Y'shua was visiting. Now, they wanted to see this Lazarus Y'shua had raised from the dead.

With a wide grin, Nicodemus spoke with excitement. "We have to tell Caiaphas and the Sanhedrin about this. We need to stop their plans from harming Y'shua. Once they hear about what we've witnessed, it will change everything." Nicodemus started walking. He stopped and yelled at Joseph, "Aren't you coming? We have no time to waste."

The two men started running down the road. Jerusalem was three kilometers away.

CHAPTER TWENTY-FOUR
ALL FOR NOTHING

THE TWO MEN WERE EXHAUSTED. They ran, walked fast, then ran some more. Out of breath, Joseph exclaimed, "Slow down, Nicodemus, I'm old and cannot keep up."

Joseph's face was flushed, and he looked sick. Nicodemus helped his friend sit down on a large rock alongside the road. He pulled his water bag from his shoulders and gave Joseph a drink.

Panting, Joseph expressed his gratitude. "Thank you, Nicodemus. I am no longer a young man. If we continue at this pace, you will kill me."

"I'm sorry, Joseph. Forgive me."

Joseph tried to smile. He reached out and patted Nicodemus' arm. "All is forgiven, Nicodemus. But from this point forward, we must walk. I do not have the strength to run any further. If you must, go ahead, and I will catch up."

"No!" exclaimed Nicodemus. "We will do this together. Now rest awhile."

Joseph nodded. "Thank you."

While Joseph rested, Nicodemus paced back and forth in the road. Joseph patted the rock. "Nicodemus, stop pacing. Please sit with me."

Reluctantly, Nicodemus complied.

Joseph tried to delay their journey. He began asking questions.

"We must construct our message to Caiaphas and the council. What are your thoughts, Nicodemus?"

Anxious, Nicodemus didn't want to waste another minute. He sighed heavily and stated the facts. "We tell Caiaphas the truth. The man Lazarus was dead, and we saw him come back to life. Caiaphas can be as clever as he wishes, but this is undeniably a miracle. We both witnessed it, along with a large group of people."

Joseph nodded approvingly. "I would like to make one sugges-tion. Before we tell about the miracle, perhaps we should explain to Caiaphas how Lazarus was dead four days. Plus, he had been placed in a stone tomb long before we arrived."

Nicodemus drew his hand down his beard, thinking.

"Is something bothering you?" Joseph asked.

"There are only three records in the Torah of someone coming back to life. Once with Elijah, once by Elisha, and once when a dead man touched the bones of Elisha. Both men were great prophets and men of YaHoWaH," said Nicodemus.

"What are your concerns then?"

Nicodemus looked cautious. "I fear Caiaphas will find a way to dismiss this miracle."

"Then we must convince him of the truth." Joseph stood. "I am rested enough, let us travel to the city and find the council."

When they arrived, the sun was setting, but they overheard peo-ple on the street discussing the miracle of Lazarus. Hurrying, they walked directly to the home of Caiaphas. After knocking, a servant came to the door.

"Greetings, Joseph, what brings you to my master's home at this hour?" The servant bowed before the two men.

"Tell me, is Caiaphas home and may we have a word with him?" asked Joseph.

The servant stepped aside and motioned toward a long bench in the inner courtyard. He looked deeply concerned. "Please have a seat. I must inquire with my master."

Many minutes later Joseph and Nicodemus could hear the shuffling of old feet and the distinctive tapping of Caiaphas' large staff. Caiaphas was dressed in an everyday, inner linen cloth garment. A royal robe of purple, with gold tassels along the edges, was hastily thrown about his shoulders. He scowled and appeared as if he had been asleep before their arrival.

Joseph and Nicodemus immediately stood.

"What urgent matter do you wish to speak of, Joseph?" Caiaphas examined the two men, and he sniffed noisily. "You smell like travelers and sweat." Caiaphas wrinkled his nose and made a face.

"Forgive the intrusion Caiaphas, but we have just rushed back from Bethany," said Joseph.

Caiaphas raised his bushy eyebrows but said nothing.

"As instructed, we were following the men associated with Y'shua of Nazareth," continued Joseph.

Caiaphas grunted.

"They had stopped along the Jordan River for several days. Then a messenger arrived concerning friends of Y'shua."

Nicodemus could no longer hold his tongue. "Y'shua's friend Lazarus was sick unto death and his sisters Mary and Martha wanted Y'shua to heal Lazarus."

Caiaphas narrowed his eyes at Nicodemus.

Joseph quickly regained control of the conversation by pulling on Nicodemus' shoulder. "Yes, Y'shua encamped by the river and spoke with the people for several more days after. On the fourth day, we journeyed to His friend's home in Bethany. Upon our arrival, we discovered Lazarus was already dead."

Nicodemus interrupted by blurting out his next comment, "Lazarus had been dead for four days!"

Caiaphas narrowed his eyes, took his staff, and pushed Nicodemus back. "Sit! I was not speaking with you."

Chastised, Nicodemus obeyed but was seething mad.

Joseph gave his friend a reassuring smile and then continued his story. "As my friend, Nicodemus, was saying, when we arrived in Bethany, Y'shua's friend, Lazarus had died, and was already buried in a stone tomb. Many visitors from Jerusalem came to visit Lazarus' sisters, Mary and Martha. Y'shua asked them to take Him to the chambers where Lazarus was buried.

"A large group of people followed Y'shua out of town to the tomb. His followers walked as well, and we joined along. Y'shua prayed to YaHoWaH in a loud voice and then He asked the men standing there to remove the stone covering the opening of the tomb. Martha protested because she said it would smell too bad since Lazarus had been inside for only four days. The men removed the stone as instructed."

Caiaphas made a face as if he could smell the stench of a rotting corpse. "This Man is insane. Why on earth do people follow Him?"

Joseph continued. "Several people backed away for fear of the smell, but not Y'shua, Mary, and Martha. Then Y'shua called out like this." Joseph imitated the Teacher by cupping his hands around his mouth. He called aloud, but not as loud as Y'shua. Joseph then repeated His command. "Lazarus, come out."

Pulling away from Joseph and hunching his shoulders, Caiaphas looked startled.

Nicodemus jumped to his feet, ready to take over the story, but Joseph cut him off by holding up his hands.

"Then, the most amazing thing happened. Lazarus appeared at the opening of the tomb. Standing still, he was wrapped tightly in his grave clothes. Y'shua then told the men to uncover Lazarus."

Nicodemus could no longer be still. "As soon as they uncovered his face, he gasped a deep breath, opened his eyes, and began speaking. The men standing nearest Lazarus ran away."

Caiaphas held up his hands. "Stop! No more lies!"

Joseph defended the retelling of the account. "We speak the truth. It is as we witnessed these events."

Nicodemus interrupted. "Furthermore, Lazarus went home with his sisters and Y'shua to eat supper. I watched the man eat, drink and dance as if his death had never happened."

Caiaphas shrank back, moving several steps away from his visitors. "Enough with your lies. This devil-man has cast an evil spell on you two." Looking frightened, he turned toward the house and yelled out. "Guards, come here immediately!"

Instantly, two temple guards appeared. "Yes, sir?"

Shaking, Caiaphas pointed his staff at Joseph and Nicodemus. "Arrest these men and take them to the Sanhedrin Council. Do it now!"

At first, the guards stood dumbfounded. Someone began to speak. "But, sir, these are members of the—"

Caiaphas rammed his staff into one of the guards. "Do as you are told. Arrest them and take them as I instructed. Gather the council together. Tell them it is urgent. Go!"

Mute, Joseph and Nicodemus went with the guards.

Along their journey, Nicodemus whispered to Joseph. "What will happen now? We did nothing wrong."

Joseph merely shook his head and shrugged.

The Sanhedrin Council chambers, noisy with argumentative conversations, went quiet when Caiaphas entered the room. Joseph and Nicodemus were led into the room, their hands bound, and both escorted by temple guards. The silent room at once filled with loud whispers.

Nicodemus' father, Ziba, moved to the center of the room and challenged Caiaphas. "What is the meaning of this?" he asked, pointing at his son and Joseph.

"They are possessed by a demon. They're speaking lies," defended Caiaphas.

Angry, Ziba stepped in front of Caiaphas and pointed his finger. "How dare you. These are men of YaHoWaH, learned scholars, men of the law. You have no right to accuse my son or our dear friend, Joseph of Arimathea, like this."

Turning, Ziba demanded, "Guards, release these men."

Caiaphas slammed his staff to the floor. "No! The heresy they speak is punishable by stoning. They claimed the fatherless troublemaker, has raised a man to life."

Narrowing his eyes, Ziba questioned his son. "Tell me the truth. What have you witnessed?"

Taking their time, his son, Nicodemus, and Joseph conveyed the same story they had told earlier to Caiaphas. When they finished, Caiaphas covered his ears and cried out. "Heresy and lies. Do we need further proof?"

A division began in the room, with some men siding with Caiaphas. Over half the people in the room sided with Ziba in protest. "We have known Joseph of Arimathea a long time. He has always spoken the truth. Ziba is also our friend and a man of YaHoWaH."

The room erupted in fierce arguments with each group shaking their fists at one another and yelling.

The din was broken when temple guards burst into the chambers. A noisy crowd of people entered with them. Without waiting for an invitation to speak, the people began calling out.

"A miracle has happened in Bethany."

"Lazarus is alive."

"Y'shua of Nazareth has raised a man from the grave."

"This Y'shua is a prophet from YaHoWaH."

Caiaphas slammed his staff to the floor. "Guards, stop this! Remove these people at once!"

Without delay, the temple guards began pushing the people out. Once the room was empty except for the Sanhedrin Council, the guards locked the doors.

Suddenly, someone cried out.

"Papa?"

When everyone looked, Ziba was on the floor clutching his chest with a pained look on his face.

"Papa, what's wrong?" Nicodemus, looked around the room, panicked. "Someone find a doctor!"

The scribes, Pharisees, and teachers of the law surrounded the stricken man and his son. Joseph bent down, took his rolled outer cloak and placed it under Ziba's head.

The older man reached up and grasped his son's neck, pulling him close into an embrace. Nearly whispering, he spoke his final words. "I believe you, my son . . . "

Then Ziba's arm dropped to the floor as he expelled the air in his lungs. For a long time, no one said anything or moved. Slowly, Joseph reached out and touched Nicodemus' shoulder.

"I'm so sorry."

"Oh, Papa. No." Nicodemus laid his head on his father's chest and wept.

Joseph reverently took his hand and closed the eyes of the dead man.

With a look of fierce anger, Nicodemus swept the room until he found the Chief Pharisee. He got up and lunged at Caiaphas, but Joseph grabbed him instead and held Nicodemus back.

"You! You murdered my father," he screamed.

Caiaphas withdrew and started shaking again. "He was old, Nicodemus. It is unfortunate timing."

"No, you brought this upon my father, and now he is dead because of you." Nicodemus pointed an angry finger at Caiaphas.

"I . . . ah . . . I . . . ah . . . I had nothing to do with his death." Caiaphas looked around the room for support.

Joseph held Nicodemus by his shoulders and guided him from the council chambers, but Nicodemus struggled. While they walked away, Nicodemus was filled with hate for the individual he felt responsible. "Caiaphas is the one born from the devil," he angrily hissed.

"Come, my friend," Joseph said as he pulled on Nicodemus.

Then four temple guards appeared and carefully loaded the body of Ziba on a litter. They solemnly carried him from the room.

Annas moved close to Caiaphas. "What should we do? This Man is working a lot of miracles. If we don't stop Him now, everyone will put their faith in Him. Then the Romans will come and destroy our temple and our nation."

Sneering, one of the other Pharisees said, "We must find a secretive way to arrest this Y'shua. Then we can find a way to end His life and this nonsense. But, we must not do it during Passover, because the people will riot."

Caiaphas then spoke up, "You people don't have any sense at all. Don't you know it is better for one person to die for the people than for the whole nation to be destroyed?"

After arriving at Nicodemus' house, he and Joseph locked the door. Nicodemus was in shock, so Joseph guided him to a chair at the table and poured a cup of water for him.

"Here drink this."

Nicodemus received the cup, looked at the contents, then set it down on the table.

Taking his friend by the shoulders, Joseph asked, "Where are your notes?"

"Excuse me?"

"Nicodemus, where did you hide your notes concerning the Messiah?"

Stumbling to the table in the corner of the room, Nicodemus pulled the heavy cloth back and pointed. "Why do you ask?"

Joseph made eye contact. "Because, Nicodemus, they are not safe here. I will carry them to Arimathea, where they will be protected."

Nicodemus shrugged and stumbled back to his chair. "I must prepare to bury my papa. Who shall I ask to help?"

Someone knocked on the door.

Joseph set the parchment notes down and covered them with the heavy cloth. He walked to the door and peered out. Recognizing the man, Joseph opened the door and warmly greeted the older Pharisee. "Gamaliel, it is good to see you."

The man rushed toward Nicodemus. "I'm so sorry for your loss. Many of us respected and loved your father."

Nicodemus slowly nodded.

"The temple guards have moved your father to your uncle's house. If you permit me, may I assist with the tahara?"

"Thank you, Gamaliel," said Joseph as he shook his hand. He then faced Nicodemus. "Go with Gamaliel to the home of your uncle. There you will conduct the tahara and prepare your father for burial."

"Where are you going?" asked Nicodemus.

"I will care for the other matters we discussed earlier. I will visit Arimathea and return as quickly as possible."

Nicodemus was still numb and stood gawking.

"Gamaliel, take Nicodemus with you. I will return in five to six days. Thank you again for your kindness."

Joseph pushed Nicodemus out the door and watched as Gamaliel guided Nicodemus down the road. Returning to the table, Joseph gathered all Nicodemus' notes and bundled them tightly with cords. Pausing at the door, Joseph looked back at the table. He then shook his head and walked away.

After leaving Bethany, the Teacher traveled to the town of Ephraim, which was near the desert, and He stayed there with His disciples. As He was traveling through Jericho, Y'shua spotted a small man in a tree, who was trying to get a look. The man, Zacchaeus, was so short he couldn't see above the crowds, so he had run ahead of the Teacher and climbed into the sycamore tree.

When the Teacher arrived at the spot where Zacchaeus was in the tree, He called out to him, "Zacchaeus, climb down from there. I want to stay with you today."

Zacchaeus climbed out of the tree and dashed toward Y'shua, smiling. Some of the people who knew Zacchaeus began grumbling amongst themselves.

"This man Zacchaeus is a sinner!"

"Why is Y'shua going home to eat with him?"

After arriving at his house, Zacchaeus wasted no time in gathering all his tax-collector and wealthy friends. He spent lavishly, serving excellent food and drink. Zacchaeus was so pleased with his guest, Y'shua, and impressed with His wisdom, and he was so excited the Teacher would spend time with him that he stood up at the end of the dinner to make an announcement.

"I want everyone here to know, I will give half of my property to the poor. And, I will now pay back four times as much to anyone I have ever cheated."

Y'shua smiled and said to Zacchaeus, "Today, you and your family have been saved, because you are a true son of Abraham. I came to look for and to save people who are lost."

"Then is YaHoWaH's kingdom about to appear, Rabbi?" asked Zacchaeus.

Y'shua told the people a story. "A prince once went to a foreign country to be crowned king and then planned to return home. But before leaving, he called in ten servants and gave each of them some money. He told them, 'Use this to earn more money until I get back.' But the people of his country hated him, and they sent messengers to the foreign country to say, 'We don't want this man to be our king.'

"After the prince had been made a king, he returned and called in his servants. He asked them how much they had earned with the money they had been given. The first servant came and said, 'Sir, with the money you gave me I have earned ten times as much.' The king said, 'Excellent, my good servant! Since you have shown you can be trusted with a small amount, you will be given ten cities to rule.'

"The second one came and said, 'Sir, with the money you gave me, I have earned five times as much.' The king said, 'Great. You will be given five cities.'

"Another servant came and said, 'Sir, here is your money. I kept it safe in a handkerchief. You are a hard man, and I was afraid of you. You take what isn't yours, and you harvest crops you didn't plant.'

"'You worthless servant!' the king told him. 'You have condemned yourself by what you have just said. You knew I am a hard man, taking what isn't mine and harvesting what I've not planted. Why didn't you at least put my money in the bank? Upon my return, I could have had the money together with interest.'

"Then the king said to some other servants standing there, 'Take his money away and give it to the servant who earned ten times as much.' But they said, 'Sir, this servant already has ten times as much!'

"The king replied, 'Those who have something will be given more. But everything will be taken away from those who don't have anything. Now bring me the enemies who didn't want me to be their king. Kill them while I watch!'"

John leaned in close to Y'shua and whispered, "Your stories are really messages about You, are they not?"

Y'shua smiled and hugged John.

When the men had finished the tahara for Ziba, they then placed his body in a new tomb. As they rolled the stone over the entrance, Nicodemus recalled the day Lazarus came back to life. He suddenly turned.

"I must go and find Y'shua."

As he started to leave, Gamaliel called out, "Where are you going, Nicodemus?"

He didn't stop but yelled over his shoulder, "To find Y'shua so he can bring my papa back to life!"

Puzzled, the people attending the service looked bewildered.

"What is he talking about?" asked his uncle.

Gamaliel shrugged. "I have no idea."

Running back to Bethany, Nicodemus went straight to the home of Mary, Martha, and Lazarus. There were some people still rejoicing over the news.

Half-crazed, Nicodemus ran up to Martha. "Where is Y'shua? I need Him now."

Martha was compassionate and concerned. "Sir, He left yesterday and said He would travel to Ephraim in the desert."

Nicodemus never bothered to thank the woman, but immediately ran in the direction of Ephraim. Along his journey, Nicodemus' mind raced. He replayed the day he saw Lazarus come to life, over and over inside his head. Nicodemus was convinced, if he could find Y'shua, his papa could live again. He ran, walked, rested, and pushed himself to unspeakable limits. Nicodemus did not even eat and instead pressed hard to reach Y'shua.

Upon arriving in Ephraim, Nicodemus began asking any person he met, "Have you seen Y'shua of Nazareth. Is He here?"

No one could help him. Several people suggested he go to the home of Zacchaeus. Exhausted and frustrated, Nicodemus heard more rumors, but was unable to find Y'shua.

Finally, as he reached the edge of the village, and after accosting every person he met, a woman carrying a water jar acknowledged she had met Y'shua. "He met with our local tax collector, Zacchaeus, and had dinner with the man. I believe Y'shua went on to Jericho with His followers."

"Thank you. Thank you," said Nicodemus and off he ran in the direction of the next town.

The road was dusty and long and required Nicodemus to ignore the needs of his body. Reaching his physical limits, Nicodemus was now going on day three without food or water. Delirious, he could see Jericho ahead and pushed his body forward, but he never made it. Stumbling, he lost his balance and fell to the ground in the hot sun. His face was red, and his lips parched dry. The skin was flaking off his lips, and his face was covered in dirt and sand. He eventually lost consciousness. Delusions flooded his brain as he thought he saw his papa, just before everything went blank.

CHAPTER TWENTY-FIVE

PASSOVER

LEAVING JERICHO AND EPHRAIM BEHIND, the Teacher and His twelve followers traveled to Bethphage and then He returned to Bethany on the Mount of Olives.

Six days before the Passover, the Teacher stayed in the home of Simon who had once had leprosy but was healed. A meal had been prepared for Y'shua and His twelve witnesses, so Y'shua had supper in his house. Martha was doing the serving, and Lazarus, who had been raised to life, was also there.

Y'shua was lying near the table, when Mary, the sister of Martha and Lazarus, took an expensive bottle of sweet-smelling perfume and poured it on the Teacher's feet. After breaking the bottle open, she also poured some of the fragrant liquid on Y'shua's head. Bending over His feet, Mary took her long hair and began wiping them. The sweet smell of the perfume filled the house. Some of the guests became angry and started grumbling.

Judas, son of Simon of Kerioth, complained, "Why such a waste? We could have sold this perfume for more than three-hundred silver coins and given the money to the poor!"

John looked at Judas. He knew Judas was dishonest because he had seen him carry the money bag and sometimes watched him steal coins for himself.

Some of the other guests started saying cruel things to Mary. But Y'shua held up His hands and smiled at the other guests.

"Leave her alone! Why are you bothering her? She has done a beautiful thing for Me." Y'shua then made direct eye contact with Judas. "You will always have the poor with you, and whenever you want to, you can give to them. But you won't always have Me here with you. She has done all she could by pouring perfume on My body to prepare it for burial. You may be sure, wherever the Good News is told all over the world, people will remember what she has done, and they will tell others."

Judas was embarrassed by the rebuke. An evil expression crossed his face as he stared at Y'shua and the other guests. Suddenly, he stormed off, angry, and disappeared into the evening light. John slipped out the door and quietly followed him.

Walking to Jerusalem, Judas marched straight to the Sanhedrin Council chambers. The temple guards met him at the door and recognized him as one of the followers of Y'shua.

"What do you want?" they asked.

"I wish to talk with the chief priests and the officers of the temple. I think I can help you arrest Y'shua," sputtered Judas.

John listened but couldn't make out his words.

Leading Judas into the main room, the guards withheld Judas from directly approaching anyone. Various leaders were engaged in heated arguments about Y'shua. The lead guard walked over to one of the Pharisees and whispered. That Pharisee stared at Judas, then grinned.

John snuck into a corner of the room, and hid in the darkness.

"Bring him here," said Annas in response.

Caiaphas joined Annas, and they both faced Judas. "What assistance are you offering to help us arrest your leader?" inquired Annas.

"I have traveled with Y'shua for almost three years. He is a disappointment. I thought He would help us overthrow the Romans, but all He does is just talk in riddles," answered Judas.

The Pharisees smiled at one another and began whispering.

Caiaphas asked, "And what would you do for us?"

Judas looked around the room and saw everyone was attentively listening. "My information should be worth something to you."

Sneering, Caiaphas stepped closer to Judas. "Of course. Deliver us this troublemaker, and we will give you thirty pieces of silver."

Judas rubbed his fingers together. "When?"

Annas put his arm around the shoulders of Judas, pulling him in close, as if he were their friend. "Start looking for an opportunity. Keep us informed when you're ready, and we will take it from there. Make sure there are no crowds around because we don't need further troubles. Shall we agree?"

Without a second thought, Judas quickly said, "I agree."

John strained to hear the conversation, but since he was far away, he didn't get the details.

Pleased he had made the correct decision; Judas stood taller and arched his back. He turned and walked back to Bethany.

When John saw Judas leave, he slipped out and trailed behind, making sure he was well hidden. Several times, Judas stopped, looked around, and then continued to walk. When he arrived, the village was settling in for the night. He found the home of Simon, the former leper, and saw the other witnesses still sitting with the Teacher. Judas quietly slinked into the room and sat down near an outside wall. John moved into the room and sat next to Peter.

Without any expression, Y'shua looked at Judas and nodded once. Judas forced a smile, but it seemed awkward.

John whispered to Peter, "He went to the Sanhedrin and spoke with Caiaphas."

Peter narrowed his eyes. "Why? What did they talk about?"

"I couldn't hear everything, but if Judas was with the Sanhedrin, nothing good can come of it."

The next morning, Y'shua and His followers continued their journey. As they were getting close to Jerusalem, the Teacher looked at John, James the son of Alphaeus, and Thomas. "Please go ahead of us to the next village. There you will find a young donkey, which has never been ridden, tied to a tree. Untie the donkey and bring it here."

"But, Rabbi, what if someone questions us?" asked Thomas.

Placing His hands on the shoulders of the men, Y'shua replied, "If anyone asks why you are doing this, say to them, 'Our Master needs it and we will soon bring it back.'"

The men ran ahead to a village just outside of Jerusalem. When they arrived, they spotted a young donkey colt tied to a tree next to the door of a home and facing the main street. While they were untying it, some of the people standing there asked, "Why are you untying the donkey?"

The owners of the home came out. "What are you doing with our donkey?"

John told the owners precisely what Y'shua said. To their surprise, the owners said, "Then take the donkey to your Master."

The disciples led the donkey back to the Teacher. They took their cloaks off and spread them over the donkey's back and helped Y'shua get on. Descending from the Mount of Olives, they led the donkey down the road, traveling toward Jerusalem.

It was almost time for Passover, and many of the Jewish people who lived out in the country had come to Jerusalem to prepare for the festival. They looked around for Y'shua. Then when they were in the temple, they asked each other, "You don't think he will come here for Passover, do you?"

The chief priests and the Pharisees told the people to let them know if any of them saw Y'shua, for they were hoping to arrest Him.

Suddenly, the people coming into the city recognized Y'shua riding on the young donkey. The people spread their clothes on the road in front of Him. Some pulled the branches of palms from the trees and spread them on the path as well. Trying to get Y'shua's attention, others started waving palm branches and yelling.

Following along behind the Teacher, people went along shouting, "Hosanna! YaHoWaH bless the One who comes in the name of the Adonai! YaHoWaH bless the King of Israel! Elohim, bless the coming kingdom of our ancestor David. Hosanna for YaHoWaH in heaven above!"

Several people asked the disciples, "Who is this Man?"

John answered, "This is Y'shua, the prophet from Nazareth in Galilee."

At first, the followers of Y'shua were confused by the crowds, but their feelings turned to joy. Quickly they joined in praising YaHoWaH. They also proudly shared among the people, "This is Y'shua of Nazareth, He has healed many people and brought Lazarus back from the dead!"

John yelled above the noise, smiling at Peter, "People of Jerusalem, don't be afraid! Your King is now coming, and He is riding on a donkey."

Peter clapped John's back and started laughing. "This is what we have been waiting for."

The people started shouting now even louder. "Blessed is the King who comes in the name of Adonai! Peace in heaven and glory to YaHoWaH."

The parade of people, with their singing and yelling, moved toward the gate of Jerusalem. The commotion they made caused even more people to join them. As Y'shua finally passed through the gate, a group of Pharisees stood in the shade, clustered together and scowling.

A Pharisee yelled at Y'shua, "Make Your disciples stop shouting!"

Y'shua stopped the donkey and smiled at the Pharisees. "If the people keep quiet, even these stones would start shouting."

The Pharisees looked at one another, horrified. "There is nothing we can do! Everyone in the world is following this Y'shua."

The rejoicing continued as the route of Y'shua took Him in the direction of the temple. He paused riding the donkey and handed the reins to Thomas. "You may return the foal to its owners. Tell them, 'YaHoWaH blesses their home and wishes to thank them.'"

With the temple in the short distance, Y'shua spoke to John, "Oh, poor Jerusalem. It is too bad because today your people don't know what will bring them peace! Now it is hidden from them. Jerusalem, the time will come when your enemies will build walls around you to attack you. Armies will surround you and close in on you from every side. They will level you to the ground and kill your people. Not one stone in your buildings will be left on top of another. This will happen because you did not see YaHoWaH had come to save you."

Several teachers of the law and Pharisees stood near enough to hear Y'shua speak these words. They instantly made note and started grumbling. "We must report this to Caiaphas immediately." John frowned when he saw their actions.

Some Greeks had come to Jerusalem to worship during Passover. John watched and listened to their conversations. Philip from Bethsaida in Galilee was near them when they turned to him and asked, "Sir, we would like to meet this Y'shua." Philip then told Andrew, and the two of them took the Greeks to the Teacher.

When Y'shua met them, he said, "The time has come for the Son of YaHoWaH to be given His glory. I tell you for sure, a grain of wheat falling on the ground will never be more than one grain unless it dies. But if it dies, it will produce overflowing amounts of grain. If you love your life, you will lose it. If you give it up in this world, you will be given eternal life. If you serve Me, you must go with Me. My servants will be with Me wherever I am. If you attend to My words, My Father will honor you.

"Now I am distraught, and I don't know what to say. But I must not ask My Father to keep Me from this time of suffering. In fact, I came into the world to suffer." Y'shua looked up at the sky. "So Father, bring glory to Yourself."

A voice from heaven then said, "I have already brought glory to Myself, and I will do it again!"

When the crowd heard the voice, some of them felt it was thunder. Others thought an angel had spoken to Y'shua. Then the Teacher told the crowd, "The voice spoke to help you, not Me. This world's people are now being judged, and the ruler of this world is already being thrown out! If I am lifted up above the earth, I will make everyone want to come to Me."

The crowd said to Y'shua, "The Scriptures teach that the Messiah will live forever. How can You say the Son of YaHoWaH must be lifted up? Who is this Son of YaHoWaH?"

Y'shua answered, "The light will be with you for only a little longer. Walk in the light while you can. Then you won't be caught walking blindly in the dark. Have faith in the light while it is with you, and you will be children of the light."

After Y'shua had said these things, He turned and walked away, taking His witnesses with Him. He went into hiding and worked a lot of miracles among the people, but they were still not willing to have faith in Him.

✝

The Pharisees loved praise from others more than they wanted approval from YaHoWaH, and they thought Y'shua was from the devil. One day John overheard the Pharisees speak to the people. "You are given orders not to have anything to do with anyone who has faith in Y'shua."

On the first day of the Festival of Thin Bread, it was time to kill the Passover lambs. Y'shua's twelve witnesses came to Him and asked, "Where do you want us to prepare the Passover meal?"

He said to Peter and John, "Go and prepare the Passover meal for us to eat."

They asked Him, "Where do You want us to prepare it?"

He told them, "As you go into the city, you will meet a man carrying a jar of water. Follow him into the house and say to the owner, 'Our Teacher wants to know where He can eat the Passover meal with His followers.' The owner will take you upstairs and show you a large room ready for you to use. Prepare the meal there."

So John and Peter then left, and when they entered the streets on the edge of Jerusalem, they saw the man carrying the jar of water as Y'shua had told them. After meeting with the man and explaining what Y'shua said to them, the man took them to a room above his home. They thanked the man and then started preparing the Passover meal.

John looked at his friend. "Peter, go to the market and purchase some bread and wine. I'll swing by the butcher's and see if I can purchase a cooked lamb. Meet me back here."

In the evening, after the sun set, the Teacher and His twelve witnesses gathered in the room where John and Peter had prepared the Passover. The men ate and were relaxing afterwards when Y'shua suddenly got up from the floor. The men in the room watched Him as He quietly prepared Himself. First, He removed His outer garment and wrapped a towel around His waist. He then put some water into a large bowl.

One by one, starting with Judas, Y'shua began washing and drying their feet using the towel He wore. When He came to Peter, he then asked, "Master, are You going to wash my feet?"

Y'shua answered, "You don't really know what I am doing, but later you will understand."

"You will never wash my feet!" Peter replied.

"If I don't wash you," Y'shua told him, "you don't really belong to Me."

Peter then exclaimed, "Y'shua, then don't wash just my feet. Wash my hands and my head."

The Teacher smiled softly. "People who have bathed and are clean all over, need only to just wash their feet. And you, My friends, are clean, except for one of you."

After washing their feet, Y'shua put His outer garment back on, and then He sat down again. He looked around the room and made eye contact with each man.

"Do you understand what I have done? You call Me your Teacher and Master . . . and you should, because it is who I am. And if your

Master and Teacher washed your feet, you should do the same for each other. I have set an example, and you should do the same for each other exactly as I have done for you. I tell you with confidence, servants are not greater than their master, and messengers are not more significant than the one who sent them. If you understand and do these things, then YaHoWaH will bless you.

"Now, I am not talking about all of you here in this room, for I know the ones I have chosen. But what the Torah says must come true because it is written, 'The man who ate with Me has turned against Me!'

"I am telling you this before it all happens. Then when it does happen, you will believe who I am. I tell you for sure, anyone who welcomes My messengers also welcomes Me, and anyone who greets Me welcomes the One who sent Me."

After Y'shua had said these things, He looked distraught and told His friends, "I tell you without a doubt, one of you will betray Me and will hand Me over to My enemies."

The men in the room looked shockingly at one another. One by one, they asked, "Surely, you don't mean me!"

"One of you twelve men, who enjoy the meal with Me from this dish, he will betray Me. The Son of YaHoWaH will die, as the Torah says. But it's going to be terrible for the one who betrays Me! That man would be better off if he had never been born."

The men sat there and just stared at each other.

John was sitting next to Y'shua during the meal, and Peter motioned for him to ask the Teacher which one would do this. Then John leaned toward Him and softly asked, "Y'shua, which one of us are You talking about?"

The other men sitting in the room started arguing about who would ever do such a thing.

Y'shua quietly replied to John, "I will dip this piece of bread in the sauce and give it to the one I was talking about." He then dipped the bread and gave it to Judas.

Judas said, "Teacher, I don't suppose you mean me?"

"So you say," He answered.

John watched in horror as Judas' face became dark and sinister. Y'shua leaned over to Judas and said aloud, "Judas, go quickly and do what you have to do."

After Judas took the piece of bread, he dashed out.

John wasn't sure he had actually understood what Y'shua meant. He leaned over and whispered to Peter, "Judas is in charge of the money. Perhaps the Teacher wants him to buy something they need for the festival?"

Peter whispered back, "On the other hand, maybe Y'shua told him to give some money to the poor?"

Y'shua then spoke to the others still sitting with Him. "Now the Son of YaHoWaH will be given glory, and He will bring glory to Elohim. After Elohim is given glory because of the Son, YaHoWaH will bring glory to the Son, and YaHoWaH will do it very soon. My children, I will be with you for only a little while longer. Then you will look for Me, but you won't find Me. I tell you just as I told the people, 'You cannot go where I am going.' But I am giving you a new command; you must love each other, just as I have loved you. If you love each other, everyone will know you are My witnesses."

Peter asked, "Master, where are You going?"

He answered, "You can't go with Me now, but later on you will."

"Master, why can't I go with You now? I would die for You!"

"Would you really die for Me, Peter? I tell you for certain, before a rooster crows, you will say three times you don't even know Me."

Peter seemed shocked and said nothing further.

CHAPTER TWENTY-SIX

A VERY LONG NIGHT

WAKING IN HORRIBLE PAIN, NICODEMUS vacillated between consciousness and the dream world. His ribs were tender and the mouth dry. Several times he cried out for his papa and Y'shua. Opening his eyes, the blurry images before him seemed far away.

"Yes, yes, rest easy my friend," came a voice from far away.

Nicodemus believed Joseph was standing over him, patting his shoulder in reassurances. As the room came into focus, he didn't recognize his surroundings or the people hovering nearby.

"Where am I?" Nicodemus asked weakly.

A middle-aged, bearded man came close and smiled. Standing next to him was a young girl, perhaps twelve or fourteen.

"You must rest. Your body has endured much," the man replied.

His daughter asked, "Will he die, Papa?"

Nicodemus' mind raced, trying to sort through the confusion.

The man patted his daughter's head, and smiled down at his daughter. "No, Sarah. He is now going to live and slowly get better." Facing Nicodemus, the man asked, "If I help you, do you think you can sit up?"

Nicodemus struggled, but every bone and joint felt out of place. He winced from the pain. The man put his arm behind Nicodemus' back and helped him.

"Grab those cushions, please," he said, pointing to his daughter.

The two of them worked hard, and eventually, Nicodemus was situated and sitting upright on the bed. His head pounded with a fierce headache. He reached up and massaged his temples and forehead.

The man brought a small bowl to Nicodemus' lips. "Here sip this. It is bitter herbs to help you feel better."

Famished and achy, Nicodemus graciously sipped the liquid. Coughing, he pulled away and made an awful face. "It tastes disgusting!"

The man laughed. "Yes, but you will appreciate the healing properties later. Please sip some more."

Nicodemus forced himself to continue drinking. Meanwhile, Sarah took cold, damp cloths and wiped Nicodemus' face and head. After a few minutes of care, Nicodemus held up his hand to stop their activities.

"Who are you, and where am I?"

"My name is Ananias. You are a guest in my home. Shalom."

"But where is this place? What is the name of your village?"

Confused, Ananias looked around the room. "Our home is inside Jericho."

Nicodemus closed his eyes tightly, trying to remember where he was last. "I cannot remember anything. I was walking and thought I saw a city in the distance, but I don't remember anything after." He tried to get out of bed, but the pain was intense. He held his abdomen and cried out.

"Easy, easy. You must not move so quickly." Ananias gently pushed Nicodemus back into bed.

Looking down, Nicodemus realized he was wearing nothing but a loincloth. "Where are my clothes?" He pulled a blanket up and covered himself, embarrassed.

"I'm afraid when I found you two days past, you were very close to death. Bandits had beaten you and robbed you of everything. You are dressed as I found you, almost naked." Ananias looked at Sarah and motioned with his chin that she should leave. She looked down and excused herself.

"Two nights past, I was praying on my roof when an angel came to me in a dream. He said I must go out and save you. He showed me the place where the bandits had hidden your body. You were near death and very far from the main road to Jerusalem."

"I was robbed? The events seem unreal. I—I . . . ah . . . I was looking for Y'shua." Suddenly everything was becoming clear, and he remembered more details. "I must find Y'shua." He tried moving again, but the pain stopped him. He cried out. "My father has died. I must find Y'shua of Nazareth so He can bring my father back to life!"

Ananias narrowed his eyes at Nicodemus. "What are you saying? You are delirious with pain."

"I must find Y'shua of Nazareth, so He can bring my papa back to life," repeated Nicodemus, but with more emphasis.

Ananias lifted the bowl to Nicodemus' lips. "You are still sick with the fever. Please drink some more." He frowned.

Nicodemus took a long drink then pushed Ananias' hand away. "You don't believe me, do you?"

"Sir, only a prophet from YaHoWaH could perform this kind of miracle. It has been thousands of years since the last prophet performed anything like this." Ananias stared at Nicodemus.

"I'm telling you the truth! My friend, Joseph of Arimathea, and I were traveling with Y'shua of Nazareth and His twelve witnesses. Y'shua's friend Lazarus was sick and died and his sisters Mary and Martha sent word for Y'shua to come help. We arrived in Bethany four days after Lazarus was buried in a tomb. But Y'shua told them to roll the stone away from the entrance. After calling out his name, Lazarus came out of the opening."

Ananias wrinkled his forehead. "How is this possible?"

Nicodemus became animated. "When Y'shua asked the men to unwrap Lazarus, he coughed once, opened his eyes, and he began talking."

Looking frightened, Ananias asked, "Was it a ghost?"

"No! Lazarus was alive! In fact, we witnessed the man singing, dancing, eating, and rejoicing afterward."

"Unbelievable!" said Ananias.

"This is why I must find Y'shua of Nazareth. My papa died, and I want Y'shua to bring him back to life."

Ananias softly smiled. "I have been hearing tales of a rabbi, healer, and storyteller, but I had no idea. Even the teachers of the law forbid us from discussing the matter, calling the stories lies."

Nicodemus steeled himself and sat upright. "I am part of the Sanhedrin and so is my friend, Joseph of Arimathea. My father was an elder Pharisee!"

"Then you must explain your recounting to the Sanhedrin Council. They should hear this matter immediately," declared Ananias.

Nicodemus slumped into bed. "We tried, but the high priest, Caiaphas, and Annas called us liars and tried to arrest us. Worse, they were going to stone us for heresy and blasphemy, but my father stopped them." Saddened, Nicodemus looked down into his bruised hands. "Now he is dead . . . " His voice trailed off.

Ananias patted Nicodemus' shoulder. "You must rest some more. I will pray and ask YaHoWaH to give me words of wisdom for you. There must be a reason why YaHoWaH brought you into our home."

Nicodemus nodded and realized he was more tired than he imagined. He was overwhelmed by his experience. Lying his head back, Nicodemus closed his eyes. He felt sick, and tears began to form in his eyes. "Thank you for your kindness; you and your family," he mumbled.

Ananias stood. "Rest easy and get well. I will return. Call out to Sarah if you need anything."

Without opening his eyes, Nicodemus thanked the man again. "May YaHoWaH bless you and your home."

Startled awake, Nicodemus was calling out his father's name.

Sarah came running. "Sir, how are you feeling?"

It was dark in the room, and Sarah took an oil lamp and made the flame brighter. It produced flickering shadows on the wall.

Ananias appeared, joining his daughter. "How are you feeling?"

Confused, Nicodemus asked, "What hour is it?"

Sarah looked perplexed and stared at her father.

"It is late; the middle of the night." He turned to his daughter. "Sarah, get some fresh water and bread."

"Yes, Papa."

Nicodemus sat up. The pain was less. He swung his legs over the edge of the bed and tried standing. Ananias quickly grabbed Nicodemus to steady him. Nicodemus looked down and saw bruising on his stomach and legs. He winced.

"You must do everything slowly. It looks worse than it really is," comforted Ananias.

Nicodemus laid back down, exhausted. "So you say." He shifted back comfortably into the bed just as Sarah arrived with nourishment. She handed the tray to her father while Nicodemus pulled the blanket up to hide his body.

"You will need your strength, please eat." Ananias helped him drink, then broke a piece of bread off and handed it to Nicodemus.

Between hungry mouthfuls, Nicodemus said, "I will leave in the morning. I cannot repay you at the moment. I can't find my money bag. I assume it was stolen as well?"

Ananias nodded slowly.

Sarah disappeared and returned with a warm bowl of lamb stew. "Here, sir. I prepared this today from our Passover lamb."

Nicodemus received the bowl, quickly shoveling spoonfuls into his waiting mouth. "This is delicious. Thank you . . . " His voice faded briefly. "Did you say Passover?" He stopped eating.

Both Ananias and Sarah said at the same time, "Yes."

They chuckled and then Ananias finished the sentence. "Passover is this Sabbath."

Nicodemus shook his head trying to clear his thoughts. "If Passover is upon us, then I must leave at first light."

"I don't think your body is completely healed—" Ananias started to say, but Nicodemus interrupted him.

"I will find a way. This is too important. Y'shua of Nazareth is the Son of YaHoWaH. I must stop the council from bringing Him harm. Caiaphas wants Him destroyed!"

Dismayed, Ananias stared with an open mouth. "You cannot be serious. How can they hurt a prophet from YaHoWaH?"

Nicodemus shook his head. "I don't understand it either."

Ananias lifted a bundle from the floor. "I have some clothes for you. They are not worthy of a Pharisee, but they are clean." He placed a small leather bag with a drawstring on top. "Here are five gold shekels, for your journey, please travel in safety."

Reluctantly taking the gift from Ananias, Nicodemus protested. "No, I cannot receive such a gift. The clothes are adequate."

"Nonsense, Nicodemus. You must take these as I have been instructed by YaHoWaH's angel." Ananias placed his hand on top of the bundle.

"How did you know my name?" asked Nicodemus, bewildered.

Ananias smiled. "The angel spoke to me again last night and gave me clear instructions." Ananias took his hand and placed it on top of Nicodemus' head. "Elohim, blessings on this man and take him safely to his home. Protect him and grant him peace as he shares Your words. Be with him, as his travels take him to far away places. Let him be a shepherd to those whom You call."

At daybreak, Nicodemus quietly got dressed. His body still ached, but he pushed himself to get ready for his journey. As he stepped into the first morning light, he stretched sore muscles. He then examined the clothes Ananias gave him. They were clean and stiff, and several patches dotted the hem and sleeves.

"May YaHoWaH watch over you."

Surprised, Nicodemus turned to see Ananias and Sarah standing in the doorway. "I didn't want to wake you. Please, I will repay you later."

"It is not necessary. YaHoWaH knows my heart." Ananias smiled.

"I cannot thank you enough for saving me." Nicodemus shook the man's hand.

With a sincere expression, Ananias asked, "Tell me, is this Y'shua of Nazareth, the Man you told us about . . . is He the Messiah, as spoken of in the Torah, or should we be looking for another?"

Nicodemus beamed. "He is the Son of YaHoWaH, the promised Messiah. I am certain of this. He is the promised One Isaiah wrote of. I believe He is the One many of the prophets wrote about."

"Then, how is it possible for men to bring Him harm. Didn't you say He performed miracles? Why would YaHoWaH allow His Son to be hurt by men?"

For a long time, Nicodemus stood motionless, processing the question. "I don't have all the answers yet. I am still learning. I just know what I must do now."

They continued to stare at one another for a long time. Finally, Nicodemus said, "Thank you again, Ananias." He looked down at Sarah. "And thank you both for your warm, generous hospitality."

Standing alongside each other, Ananias and Sarah hugged. Sarah asked, "Will he be all right, Papa?"

Ananias smiled and looked into his daughter's eyes. "Yes. He is going with YaHoWaH's blessings."

Several times, Nicodemus looked back toward Jericho as he walked down the road, watching the town slowly fade away. He worried about bandits but prayed silently for protection. So much time had passed, and he was anxious to find Y'shua.

He knew four days or forty days would not make a difference. If Y'shua of Nazareth could raise a man to life after four days, then no amount of time would stop this Y'shua. He had mixed feelings and wondered why the events had unfolded the way they had.

"How did Ananias find me, YaHoWaH?" Nicodemus asked aloud.

He also knew he must find his friend, Joseph of Arimathea. Together, they would stop the council from bringing any harm to Y'shua.

As he journeyed, Nicodemus gained renewed energy. With each step closer to Jerusalem, he quickened his pace. "Grant me strength, YaHoWaH, let me find Y'shua," he prayed while walking.

CHAPTER TWENTY-SEVEN

NO!

EARLY IN THE MORNING THE chief priests met hurriedly with the elders, the teachers of the Law, and the whole council, and made their plans. After Y'shua's arrest the previous night, the Sanhedrin had put Him in chains. Throughout the night, they questioned, interrogated, abused, and denigrated the Man.

The whole group rose up and dragged Y'shua before Pilate, where they began to accuse Him. "We caught this Man misleading our people, telling them not to pay taxes to the emperor and claiming He is the Messiah, a King."

Pilate questioned Him, "Are you the King of the Jews?"

Y'shua answered, "So you say."

Then Pilate said to the chief priests, "I find no reason to condemn this Man."

The chief priests started accusing Y'shua of many things. "With His teaching, He is starting a riot among the people all throughout Judea. He tells lies to the people, telling them He will establish a new kingdom. Is He seeking to depose Rome? He began in Galilee and now He has come here to work up the people against the emperor."

When Pilate heard this, he asked, "Is this man a Galilean?"

The Pharisees and council nodded in agreement.

So Pilate questioned Him again, "Aren't you going to answer? Listen to their accusations!"

Again, Y'shua refused to say a word, and Pilate was amazed. Pilate moved his face close to Y'shua. "These men," he motioned with his arm toward the council, "are here to have You condemned. Have You no response in Your defense?"

Y'shua remained silent.

Pilate then commanded, "Herod is also in Jerusalem at this time, and rules the Galilean region. Centurions, take this Man before Herod and ask him for his opinion."

Two armed soldiers brusquely grabbed Y'shua and pulled Him from the room. They marched to Herod's building with the Sanhedrin Council, grumbling the entire way, following close behind. Upon entering Herod's palace, the Romans relayed Pilate's instructions.

"Kind sir, we have been dispatched by Pilate with this Man who claims to be the King of the Jews. His Majesty, Pontius Pilate, desires your opinion regarding this Man called Y'shua."

The two soldiers roughly shoved Y'shua forward.

Herod was delighted when he saw Y'shua. "I've heard so much about You and wanted to see You personally for a long time. Tell me, will You perform a miracle for us?" he asked.

Y'shua remained silent.

Herod became upset. "I have asked You a question, and I am the ruler of the Jews. Did You not hear me?"

Still, Y'shua made no answer.

The chief priests and the teachers of the Law stepped forward and made strong accusations against Y'shua.

"He claims to be the King of the Jews."

"Yes, and He plans to tear down the temple, but claims He can rebuild it in three days!"

Everyone began laughing. Then Herod and his soldiers mocked Y'shua and treated Him with contempt. "Is this so?" said Herod. "Where are Your soldiers? What kingdom do You rule in? Where are Your workers and followers?" He started laughing.

Herod's soldier put an elegant purple robe on Y'shua. "Behold the king!" They then started making fun of Him.

When Herod regained his composure, he looked at the Roman soldiers. "Take this Man back to Pilate. He's an imposter and a nuisance. He is just another man and of no consequence. Tell Pilate today, we are no longer enemies, but I consider him a friend. Thank him for his consideration."

The Roman soldiers carried Y'shua back to Pilate. The Sanhedrin followed the soldiers, protesting during the walk. Several from the council reached out and slapped Y'shua calling Him names.

When the group returned to the governor's palace, the soldiers told Pilate what Herod had said.

Pilate looked at the council. "At every Passover festival, I am in the habit of setting free one prisoner the people ask for. Perhaps we shall see what the people want."

Jerusalem was packed with visitors from many different cities. Different languages were spoken at once as people crowded and pushed their way from one point to another.

Nicodemus scanned the busy streets, but as he did so, his head suddenly felt dizzy. His thoughts overwhelmed any reasoning, and self-doubt arose. Frantic, he scoured every avenue looking for Y'shua. He was confident he spotted the Man several times and he would come up behind an individual, grab their arm or shoulder and question them.

"Y'shua?"

Each time, an unfamiliar face would turn around and blankly stare back, unable to comprehend the interruption. Nicodemus performed this act several times with no success. Then a familiar voice called out.

"Nicodemus? Is it you?"

When Nicodemus looked around, he spotted Gamaliel. He lunged toward the man and greeted him. "Shalom, Gamaliel. It is good to see you."

Gamaliel frowned, looking Nicodemus over from head to toe. "What has happened to your robes, Nicodemus? And your face, you look as if you've been beaten!" He reached up and gently touched the healing sores on Nicodemus' face.

His questions were ignored. "Have you seen Joseph of Arimathea? I need to find him."

Deeply furrowed lines formed in Gamaliel's brow. "Are you well, Nicodemus? You left your father's burial so quickly and mumbled nonsense as you did."

Nicodemus looked up and scanned the sea of people around them. He spoke, but distractedly. "It is important I find my friend, Joseph. If you see him, tell him to meet me at my home."

"Of course, of course. I must tell you, Nicodemus, I am concerned for your welfare," said Gamaliel.

Nicodemus stopped searching and faced the man. "Excuse me? What did you say?"

"Nicodemus, you don't look well," the bewildered man replied.

"Nonsense. I feel fine. I must stop Caiaphas and the Sanhedrin from their plans," said Nicodemus, sounding frantic.

"What plans are those?" asked Gamaliel confused.

Nicodemus ignored Gamaliel's question. He shuffled into the crowds and started his renewed search for Y'shua. As he drew close to the temple, Nicodemus cautiously approached the area, watching for any members of the Sanhedrin. He hoped to meet Y'shua or a friendly face. Unfortunately, he didn't recognize anyone.

"Shalom, Nicodemus."

Nicodemus turned and faced a teacher of the law from the Sanhedrin. "Shalom, Eleazar." Nicodemus wasn't sure he could trust the man.

Eleazar looked at the clothes Nicodemus wore and his face. "You look rather like a peasant. What has happened to you?"

Nicodemus sighed heavily. "I was robbed and had everything stolen. I was visiting near Jericho and left for dead. A man found me and helped me recover. He loaned me these clothes."

Having seen Nicodemus searching, Eleazar's curiosity was stirred. "What or who are you looking for?"

"Where are the high priests, Annas and Caiaphas? I don't find anyone from the Sanhedrin here in the temple area," asked Nicodemus, trying to deflect the original question.

"Have you been absent from the city?" asked Eleazar.

Exasperated, Nicodemus became agitated. "I have spent several days healing. I just arrived a while ago."

"Then you don't know?"

"Know what?" pleaded Nicodemus.

"Caiaphas and the rest of the Sanhedrin had the troublemaker from Galilee arrested last night. All thanks to one of His followers by the name of Judas," said Eleazar somewhat arrogantly.

"What? Did you say they arrested Y'shua of Nazareth?" asked Nicodemus sounding appalled.

Eleazar narrowed his eyes. "How could you not know this? Aren't you a member of the council?"

Looking downcast, Nicodemus replied, "No, I am not. My father was, but not me."

Softening his voice, Eleazar touched Nicodemus' shoulder. "Oh yes, I heard about your father. I'm sorry for your loss."

Nicodemus looked up. "Thank you. Can you tell me, where is the council and Y'shua at this time?"

"So very much has happened in only one day. He was given to the Romans and will be crucified." Eleazar's comment was offhand and disrespectful.

Shocked, Nicodemus blurted out. "No!" He began backing away from Eleazar.

"What's wrong with you, Nicodemus? The blood has drained from your face."

Running away, Nicodemus bumped into several people, pushing them out of his way. His mind raced. *How can this be happening?* Nicodemus ran straight to his house. Arriving out of breath, he barricaded himself. When he saw the table where his notes once sat, he suddenly started to cry. Slumping to the floor, Nicodemus buried his face in his hands and sobbed. The news was unbearable.

Speaking to no one, he said aloud, "How can Y'shua bring my papa back now?"

The pain of losing his father, being robbed and beaten, and now having the prophet Y'shua of Nazareth arrested, was too overwhelming. For the first time in his life, Nicodemus felt utterly lost and alone. Bitter tears ran down his cheeks unhindered. Nicodemus looked up at the ceiling and cried out, "Where are You, YaHoWaH? If ever there was a time when I needed You, it's now!"

When Joseph of Arimathea arrived in Jerusalem, he walked directly to the Sanhedrin Council chambers. Other than a few temple guards, the only people left were the high priests.

"Ah, Joseph, Come, tell us of your news," said Annas.

Joseph looked around the empty chambers. "Where is everyone?"

Caiaphas spoke. "Resting. We had a very long and tiresome night."

Joseph narrowed his eyes. "I have just arrived from Arimathea. I'm afraid I don't understand."

The two high priests began to chuckle, which then led them to start laughing.

"I don't understand. What is so funny?" asked Joseph.

Caiaphas stood and walked over to Joseph. His expression was anger mixed with defiance. "Your Man, the one from Satan, He is condemned to die and remains with the Romans at this time. He is to be crucified."

"What? Impossible!" Joseph could not believe what he heard. "How?"

Caiaphas took the thick handle of his staff and tapped it against Joseph's chest. "With the help of His follower, Judas, we finally arrested the troublemaker."

Joseph was shocked. Speechless.

Annas walked over and joined Caiaphas. He sneered. "The trial lasted all night, but in the end, this Man's lies became obvious."

"But, but, what . . . " Joseph's thoughts faded away. He was numb and could not believe the ignorance of the religious leaders.

Caiaphas chuckled. "Now, now, Joseph. You must not worry. This one man has saved all of us. Now Rome will not be angry with us. One man's life, for the lives of many. It must be YaHoWaH's plan."

"YaHoWaH's plan? Are you serious? The only living prophet we've had in a thousand years, and One who raised a dead man back to life, and you're happy to send Him to His death?" Joseph was revolted.

With a fierce fire in his eyes, Caiaphas inched closer to Joseph's face. "Careful now, Joseph. You might guard your tongue. You're very close to speaking heresy."

Joseph was angry. "The only heresy I hear is being spoken from the leaders of this council seeking to destroy a Man of YaHoWaH. Since the Roman governor normally releases a prisoner at Passover, we will have to ask for Y'shua of Nazareth."

As he left, Caiaphas and Annas stared open-mouthed. Joseph yelled over his shoulder, "We will find a way to stop your nonsense." Just before Joseph was out of the building, he heard the chief priests arguing. He paused and hid in a dark corner listening.

Annas looked at Caiaphas and said, "What will you do now?"

Caiaphas grumbled, "What can Joseph do? He is nothing, but to be sure my plan works I have another step I must take."

"And what is your plan?"

Caiaphas called out, "Guards!"

Four temple guards immediately appeared. "Yes, sir."

"Watch Annas and learn." Looking at the chief guard, Caiaphas said, "Take my treasure chest, the one with the Roman coins in it, and bring it here."

Two guards ran off and returned moments later carrying a massive chest.

Caiaphas tapped the chest with his staff. "Tomorrow, you are to take this money and distribute it among the people in Pilate's courtyard. When the people gather near Pilate's palace, and he wants to release a prisoner, make sure the people cry out for 'Barabbas.' When he asks what shall be done with Y'shua, tell the people to cry out 'crucify Him.'" Caiaphas shook his fist when he gave them his orders.

"But sir, Barabbas is a notorious criminal and murderer," said the chief guard. "Are you sure this is—"

He was abruptly stopped by Caiaphas. "Just do as you are told. Distribute the money and get the people to cooperate. Start with those standing close to Pilate's porch and work your way through the crowd. Now go do what I've commanded you."

Two men hefted the chest, and the four guards started for the door.

"I want the chest emptied into the pockets of the people. Bring it back without coins," Caiaphas called out.

"Yes, sir," said the chief guard.

The guards disappeared out the door.

After the guards left, Joseph slipped out and dashed toward Nicodemus' house.

Joseph banged on the door and called out his name. "Nicodemus? Are you home?"

When he heard Joseph's voice, Nicodemus sprung from the floor and ran to the door. When he opened it, he hugged Joseph's neck. "Oh, Joseph. They've arrested Y'shua!"

"Yes, I know." He brushed past Nicodemus and walked into the room. "The council turned Him over to the Romans to be crucified."

"Why? What wrong did Y'shua do?" implored Nicodemus. "He only healed people and shared truthful words from the Torah."

"Caiaphas, Annas, and the others are jealous. I now know what Y'shua meant when He said they were blind."

Nicodemus looked at his older friend for advice. "What can we do to stop them? Y'shua is innocent and hasn't broken any Roman laws."

Joseph rested his hands upon Nicodemus' shoulders. "The Roman governor normally releases a prisoner at Passover, we will have to ask for Y'shua of Nazareth to be set free."

"And you think this will work?" asked Nicodemus.

"I'm not sure, but we must try. Have you seen any of the twelve witnesses?"

Nicodemus shook his head.

"What about John or Simon-Peter?"

Again, Nicodemus shook his head. "I've seen no one."

Suddenly, Joseph closely examined his young friend. Joseph narrowed his eyes and studied Nicodemus' clothes and face. He reached up and touched the scab on Nicodemus' face. "What has happened to you, Nicodemus? Did Caiaphas or his soldiers beat you? If he had a hand in this, I will personally take revenge—"

"No, no, no. I was robbed," Nicodemus explained.

Mortified, Joseph asked, "When? How?"

"After my father died, I ran into Gamaliel. He and some other men helped with the tahara and burial. Then I realized something. If I could find Y'shua, then perhaps he could bring my papa back to life, like Lazarus."

Joseph looked sad. "I'm sorry I could not be there for you."

"It is fine, Joseph. Did you protect my notes and scrolls?"

"Yes. The scrolls are concealed in several jars in my storage room. No one would know they were hidden in there," reassured Joseph. "But please, how did you get robbed?"

"I went looking for Y'shua. I ran back to Bethany, but He and His witnesses had left for Ephraim. I started my journey to the town but heard from a woman I met, that Y'shua was going to Jericho. By this time, I had gone several days without water or food."

Joseph nodded. "You were desperate to find Y'shua, I understand."

"But I never made it to Jericho. I remember seeing the city just down the road, but unfortunately, I never made it. I must have fainted from exhaustion. When I awoke, it was several days later, and I found myself being cared for by a man named Ananias and his daughter Sarah. The man said he was praying, and an angel came to him in a dream. He told Ananias where I could be found.

"I was beaten and stripped of my clothes and money. I was left for dead, hidden behind large rocks, and not near the main road, but Ananias came to me and found me. The man saved my life. I would have died, Joseph, if he had not saved me."

"How dreadful. Is this where your clothes came from?" asked Joseph.

"Yes, yes. Not only the clothes, but Ananias knew my name and said the angel told him who I was. He also gave me several gold shekels for my journey."

Joseph was surprised. "All this from a complete stranger?"

"Can you believe it? He and Sarah fed me and helped me recover. Then when I could, I departed for Jerusalem and started searching for Y'shua and you. This afternoon, I ran into Gamaliel, and he told me of Y'shua's arrest. I came home, not knowing what to do. I feel lost, Joseph."

Reassuring him, Joseph encouraged Nicodemus. "But you are alive and healing. YaHoWaH sent Ananias and Sarah to save you, and look—you and I are now together. YaHoWaH is good."

Nicodemus unenthusiastically nodded in agreement. "So, what do we do now?"

"We rest, and first thing tomorrow, when Pilate releases a prisoner, we start with the people in the governor's courtyard and encourage them to ask for Y'shua. We must find John and the other witnesses and have them join us. Come, we will visit my cousin's home and have supper with them. Then we will come back afterward and rest. Tomorrow will be a very long day and it's the day before Passover. We have much to look forward to. All is not finished yet."

CHAPTER TWENTY-EIGHT

CRUCIFY HIM!

THE DAY BEFORE PASSOVER AND the Sabbath and the portico of Pilate's palace was crowded with more people than the Roman soldiers had ever seen. A line of armed and menacing gladiator-like men created a barrier between the governor's platform and the sea of people surging forward.

Nicodemus and Joseph fought their way from the back of the crowd and toward the front. When they arrived, they were close enough to hear the conversations echoing from the stone porch.

Members of the Sanhedrin Council appeared before Pilate. When Pilate saw the group of Jews gathered and huddled together, he called his personal guard and motioned with his hand. "Laurentius, a word."

Tall and beefy, the soldier bent at the waist. "Yes, my legatus."

"What are these Jews doing here?" Pilate asked.

Looking over his shoulder and scowling, Laurentius commented, "A prisoner named Y'shua—I think He's some kind of healer or magician—they want to ensure you satisfy their wishes and eliminate the troublemaker from Galilee. They desire to see Him punished."

Pilate frowned. "Keep them away from me. I've had my fill of their religious nonsense. I'll allow them to stay, but I want no interference with my duties. Do you understand me?"

Striking his arm and fist across his chest, Laurentius stood to attention. "At your command, sir." Laurentius then quietly spoke to several soldiers and had them encircle the Sanhedrin Council members.

Pilate sat on the stone judgment seat. "Bring in the prisoners."

Y'shua Barabbas and Y'shua of Nazareth were dragged by their chains and placed in front of the governor. Both prisoners had been beaten, but Y'shua of Nazareth was wearing a purple robe, and the soldiers had made a crown of thorns and jammed it on His head.

Pilate raised his hand, and Laurentius and his men moved the Sanhedrin group closer.

Pilate addressed the council group. "You brought this Man to me," he pointed at Y'shua of Nazareth, "and said He was misleading the people and you want Him killed. Now, I have examined Him here in your presence, and I have not found Him guilty of any of the crimes. Nor did Herod find Him guilty, for he sent Him back to us. There is nothing this Man has done to deserve death, so I will have Him whipped and let Him go."

Immediately, the Sanhedrin group began screaming and arguing. The soldiers fought to contain the rowdy group.

"Sir, we have a law, and it says He ought to die because He claimed to be the Son of YaHoWaH, our God."

When Pilate heard this, he looked afraid. He stood and extended his hand. "This man Y'shua Barabbas is a murderer and is guilty of causing riots. On the other hand, I find no fault with this Man, Y'shua of Nazareth."

Immediately, the council group began shouting insults and shaking their fists. Pilate held up his hands. "Enough! Laurentius, clear these Jews out, now!"

After the room was quiet again, Pilate walked over to the two prisoners and gazed at them. "I will appeal to your people, and they will choose which one of you goes free today; the killer or a Messiah."

Turning, Pilate walked out to the platform overlooking the crowds. He held up his hands and waited for the noise to settle.

Nicodemus and Joseph looked up in anticipation.

"Citizens, in honor of your Passover festivities, it is my custom to release a prisoner back to you. Today it will be someone of your choosing. I have two prisoners. One is Y'shua Barabbas, who is a murderer and has caused many riots. The other is Y'shua of Nazareth. He is a man who is guiltless by my standards. So I ask you, which one do you want me to set free for you? Barabbas or Y'shua called the Messiah?"

Nicodemus and Joseph began screaming, "Y'shua! Y'shua!, Y'shua of Nazareth!"

Initially, many people around them joined in and cried out for Y'shua of Nazareth as well. Then other men from the crowd raised their voices even louder as they called out for Barabbas. Joseph and Nicodemus tried to counter the other people shouting, but they were quickly drowned out by the overwhelming crowd.

Pilate went back inside and asked Y'shua of Nazareth, "Where do You come from?"

Y'shua did not answer.

Pilate said to him, "Will You not respond to me? Remember, I have the authority to set You free or to have You crucified."

Y'shua answered, "You have been given authority over Me only because it was given to you by My Father in heaven. We call Him YaHoWaH and your people would refer to Him as God. But I tell you, the man who handed Me over to you is guilty of a worse sin."

Pilate looked disturbed by Y'shua's words. He went back out once more and tried to reason with the crowd. "Look, I will bring Him out here to you. I want you to see I cannot find any reason to condemn Him."

So Y'shua of Nazareth was brought out, wearing the crown of thorns and the purple robe.

Pilate said to them, "Look! Here is the Man! Do you want me to set Him free for you? Your religious leaders claim He is the King of the Jews?"

Joseph and Nicodemus again tried shouting for Y'shua, but men standing next to them roughly pushed Joseph and Nicodemus. "You two, keep quiet." One of the men extended his hand and showed them his Roman coins. "Unless you have more money than what we were paid, we will do as we were asked."

Joseph said to Nicodemus, "Caiaphas has bribed all these men. How can we compete against this many people?"

When the chief priests and the temple guards saw Y'shua, they shouted, "Crucify Him! Crucify Him!" Then the people started chanting the same words.

By crying even louder, Joseph and Nicodemus cupped their hands around their mouths and screamed with all their might. They yelled for Y'shua of Nazareth.

Then the whole crowd shouted louder, "Kill Him! Set Barabbas free for us!"

Pilate tried to find a way to set Y'shua free. He held up his hands and said to the crowd a third time. "But what crime has He committed? I cannot find anything He has done to deserve death! I will have Him whipped and set free."

Instantly, the crowds shouted back, "If you set Him free, it means you are not the emperor's friend! Anyone who claims to be a king is rebelling against the emperor!"

When Pilate heard these words, he took Y'shua of Nazareth inside once more.

When Pilate walked back out alone, he said, "He is your King! I must set Him free."

The crowd shouted back, "He is not our King! Kill Him! Crucify Him!"

Pilate shook his head and asked them, "Do you want me to crucify your King?"

The people answered, "The only king we have is the emperor!"

Suddenly the crowd became quiet. Pilate looked out and saw Caiaphas, Annas, and the entire Sanhedrin Council making their way through the people. Like Moses parting the Red Sea, the temple guards surrounding the religious leaders created a broad pathway for the Jewish leaders. As they neared Pilate's platform in the front, Pilate saw Caiaphas notice Nicodemus and Joseph and watched him scornfully glare at them.

"Get those two scoundrels out of here! They have no purpose for being here," barked Annas.

Temple guards began rudely pushing Nicodemus and Joseph, and soon others joined in. The crowd shoved the two men away from the front despite Nicodemus and Joseph protesting and trying to fight back. Once the two men were near the wall of the courtyard, several men blocked the gate, preventing Nicodemus and Joseph from re-entering.

"You have no right to do this!" shouted Nicodemus.

Joseph gently pulled on Nicodemus and moved him away from the gate. He had spotted several men in the crowd who appeared to attend to bring them harm if he and Nicodemus tried entering the courtyard again.

Pilate had Y'shua of Nazareth brought back out to the platform. When the crowd saw Him, the noise was at frenzy levels. Pilate held up his hands again. He wanted to reason with the people and find a way to set Y'shua free. "Tell me, what shall I do with Y'shua called the Messiah?" Pilate asked them.

In unison, the people answered, "Crucify Him!"

Pilate asked, "But what crime has He committed?"

Then the people started chanting at the top of their voices. "Crucify Him!" Their voices in unison grew louder with each shout until the whole courtyard resonated with their loud cries.

Pilate said to them, "You take Him, then, and crucify Him. I find no reason to condemn Him."

Suddenly the people began shoving each other and shaking their fists in the air. When Pilate saw it was of no use to go on, that a riot might break out, he motioned for his assistant, who carried out a basin of water. Pilate took some water, washed his hands in front of the crowd. Calling out in a loud voice, he said, "I wish to demonstrate I am washing my hands of this Man's blood. I am not responsible for His death. This is your doing!"

The people responded, "Let the responsibility for His death fall on us and our children!"

Pilate pleased the crowd and set Barabbas free for them. The people loudly cheered the decision. When the people became quiet again, he pronounced a death sentence on Y'shua of Nazareth, giving the people what they asked for. He then commanded his soldiers to crucify Y'shua.

Nicodemus was incredibly furious. "How can they condemn the Messiah? He is innocent!" He started for the gate, but Joseph stopped him. Nicodemus resisted, but then he spotted John standing by the wall with Mary, Martha, Lazarus, and another older woman who was sobbing. John was trying to comfort this woman. Moving to the outer courtyard, Nicodemus and Joseph rushed toward the familiar group.

Angrily, Nicodemus shouted at John. "Do something! We cannot just stand here and watch them murder the Son of YaHoWaH!"

John look shocked. "What do you think I can do?"

Frustrated, Nicodemus pressed John further. "I do not know, but just standing here is not helping. Where are the others and all His followers?"

John frowned. "They're hiding."

Joseph asked, "Perhaps we can find them and stop this madness."

John helped the older woman to her feet. "You may go, but I must attend to Y'shua's mother, Miryam."

Nicodemus was surprised as he had no idea who the woman was. Joseph helped John by taking Miryam's other arm. "Oh, I am so sorry, Miryam."

The crowd started cheering, and everyone turned to see the soldiers unshackling Barabbas.

Nicodemus screamed, "You stupid, foolish people!"

Several folks standing nearby gave him a menacing look. Instantly, Joseph grabbed Nicodemus and pulled him from the outer lattice wall. "Come, my friend, this is dangerous."

The crowd of people started chanting again. "Crucify Him!"

The group around Nicodemus watched as the Romans escorted Y'shua to the garrison area next to the palace courtyard. The men called all the other Roman soldiers to join them.

Y'shua's mother cried out. "Take me; I want to see my son."

The small group quickly moved along the outer wall until they could see into the Roman garrison yard. There they watched in horror as the Roman soldiers stripped Y'shua bare to His loincloth and shackled Him to a flogging post. A gigantic soldier began whipping Y'shua with a device containing nine leather cords that had multiple sharp pieces of flint braided into the whip. The Roman lashed at the back of Y'shua, pulling His flesh open with each jerk of the whip. Chunks of skin tore loose, leaving raw bloody trails in its wake.

Y'shua's body shuddered with each blow, but He never uttered a sound. This seemed to aggravate the flogger and so he intensified his blows. Violently shredded from the whip, Y'shua endured forty strikes. In a manner of minutes, His blood splattered everywhere and covered the stones all around His position.

The Roman soldiers removed Y'shua from the post, put a stick in His right hand, and draped the purple robe over His shoulders. They knelt before Him. "Long live the King of the Jews!" they mocked. They spat on Him and hit Him over the head with the stick.

Sickened by the sight, Nicodemus vomited then fell on the ground weeping. "Why, YaHoWaH, why? Please send Your angels to stop them!"

Y'shua's mother collapsed to her knees, lamenting over her son.

When Y'shua heard His mother's pitiful cry, He looked up at her trying to console her, but a Roman soldier roughly slapped Him across the face.

"What are You smiling at, Prisoner?"

CHAPTER TWENTY-NINE

FATHER, FORGIVE THEM

WHEN THE ROMAN SOLDIERS HAD finished mocking Y'shua, they took the purple robe off and put His own clothes back on Him. Then they led Him out to crucify Him.

Miryam pleaded with Nicodemus and Joseph. "Go, follow them."

The soldiers brought out a heavy wooden cross, crudely cut from huge timbers. Three prisoners were lined up, each given a cross on their shoulder. "Don't just stand there, fools, pick them up!" barked one soldier. "We're going on a small walk to crucify you."

The other soldiers made fun of the prisoners. For Nicodemus, the sadistic pleasure of the Roman soldiers was revolting.

Struggling under the weight of the cross, the prisoners stumbled or set the cross down so they could rest. A soldier quickly applied a boot to the prisoner's backside. With the snap of his whip, he yelled. "Get up! Die like a man, not some crying woman."

The crucifixion march ambled through the city moving to a small hill called Golgotha, or The Skull. All along the road leading to Golgotha people lined the streets. Some hurled insults, and others cried out support for Y'shua.

As they labored to walk, Y'shua lost His balance and tumbled to the pavement stones. Wincing from the pain, He tried to get back up but was unable to lift Himself and the weight of the cross. Nicodemus lunged forward to assist, but a Roman soldier blocked him.

A soldier standing near Y'shua yelled at a bystander. "You there, help this prisoner!"

Frightened, the man stood frozen.

The Roman grabbed the man by his arm and pulled him to the center of the road. "I said, pick up the cross!" When the man didn't move fast enough, the Roman hefted the cross onto a man's shoulder. "What's your name?"

"Simon of Cyrene," said the frightened man. He glanced at two wide-eyed young boys who were with him. "Remain here my sons, I'll return for you."

"Pick the cross up, you worthless dog of Cyrene, and help this prisoner," barked the Roman.

Nicodemus, John, and the others continued to follow closely behind Y'shua.

John assisted Miryam, Y'shua's mother. "Don't lose sight of them, please," she begged.

Simon struggled with the cross. Y'shua put His body under the wood and joined Simon from the opposite side. Reaching under the cross, He wrapped His arm around Simon's waist, and Simon did the same. Sharing the load, the two men carried the cross together. Y'shua's blood stains covered Simon.

"Shalom," said Y'shua as He looked over to His unwitting helper.

"Shalom, Rabbi, my name is Simon of Cyrene. News of You drew me here to Jerusalem, and I have traveled a great distance with my sons to find You. Although I never expected it to be like this."

Among the large crowd of people following Y'shua, were women who were weeping and wailing.

"Y'shua, call the angels and save Yourself!" cried one woman.

"Don't leave us, Y'shua. You are our Savior, and we need You!" implored another.

Y'shua stopped walking and turned to them. "Women of Jerusalem! Don't cry for Me, but for yourselves and your children. For the days are coming when people will say; 'How lucky are the women who never had children, who never bore babies, who never nursed them!' It will be the time when people will say to the mountains, 'Fall on us!' and to the hills, 'Hide us!' For if such things as these are done when the wood is green, what will happen when it is dry?"

A nearby Roman soldier took his whip and goaded Y'shua in the back. "Move along, we haven't the time for conversations."

When Simon of Cyrene and Y'shua arrived at the hill, the Roman detachment had already nailed the first prisoner to his cross. It was standing upright in a hole carved into the rock. The prisoner was crying out in agony.

Simon and Y'shua watched as a flurry of Roman soldiers toiled at their duties. After they stopped, the Teacher collapsed on the ground resting on all fours. He saw the Romans were working on the second prisoner who was fighting them. Two large soldiers stepped on each arm of the prisoner while another man pounded spikes into the prisoner's wrists. He started screaming. Three soldiers wrestled his feet together, and the soldier with the hammer drove the spike through the prisoner's feet.

As the Romans lifted the heavy cross and guided it to another hole in the rock, the wooden cross quickly dropped, landing with a loud thud. Every joint in the prisoner's body cracked, causing him to scream even louder.

The Roman soldier escorting Y'shua to Golgotha grabbed Simon's arm and yanked him away. Burying his face into Simon's, he yelled, "You're next citizen unless you move out of here. Now get!" He shoved Simon away.

As Simon walked backward, staring at the crucifixion spectacle, he bumped into John and Nicodemus.

"Oh, excuse me." He looked down and saw Miryam, the mother of Y'shua crying. He knelt down beside her. "You must be the Rabbi's mother. I'm so sorry for your pain."

Miryam reached out and patted Simon's blood-soaked arm. "Bless you for your kindness in assisting my Son."

When Simon of Cyrene stood, he looked intently at Nicodemus and the others.

Joseph said, "Thank you for helping Y'shua. What is your name?"

"Simon, my name is Simon, and I have come from Cyrene to celebrate the Passover." He looked a little panicked. "When the Romans forced me to help the Rabbi, I left behind my two sons, Alexander and Rufus. I now must go find them." Simon turned and ran away.

When the group with Nicodemus looked up, the Roman soldiers were nailing Y'shua to His cross. He was barely recognizable because He was now covered in dried blood and dirt. As the soldiers prepared to raise the cross, a messenger came running into the area.

"Stop! Wait!" he cried out. Something was in his hands.

The young messenger handed a notice to the commander. They spoke quietly. Then the commander called one of the soldiers.

"Valerianus, come here."

The soldier responsible for the prisoner's spikes walked over. "Yes, sir."

The commander handed him the notice. "This is from the governor. Nail it to the cross, above the prisoner's head."

"At your command, sir."

Valerianus then affixed the notice to the top of the cross. The sign was written in Hebrew, Latin, and Greek. The message said, 'Y'shua of Nazareth, King of the Jews.'

When he had finished, the soldiers hoisted the cross up and dropped it into a third opening carved into the rock. Y'shua was positioned in the center of the small hill with the other two prisoners on either side. As the cross fell into the hole, it jerked Y'shua's body.

Looking up to heaven, Y'shua cried out, "Forgive them, Father! They don't know what they are doing."

When Nicodemus made eye contact, he mumbled, "Forgive us, Y'shua."

With their arms outstretched, each prisoner pushed against their feet at the foot of the cross, filling their lungs with air. The exhausting exercise caused them to struggle with their breathing and chafe their exposed backs on the rough cross. Panting, their mouths were dry.

A young man with a bucket stopped below each man. Soaking a sponge in the bucket, the man would use a long stalk of hyssop to lift the sponge to the prisoner's lips. The bucket contained a mixture of wine and a drug called myrrh, a bitter substance with narcotic effects.

When the young man offered the sponge to Y'shua, He refused to drink.

It was nine o'clock in the morning when the Romans crucified Y'shua. After the soldiers were finished, they took Y'shua's clothes and divided them into four parts, one part for each soldier. They also took the purple robe, which was made of one piece of woven cloth without any seams in it.

The soldiers said to one another, "Let's not tear it. Let's throw dice to see who will get the robe." After they finished, the Romans sat there watching Him slowly die. They also allowed the bystanders to get a closer look.

Y'shua's mother, his mother's sister, Mary, the wife of Clopas who was also the mother of James the younger, plus Joseph, Nicodemus, Salome, and Mary Magdalene crept closer to the base of the cross. John began to comfort Y'shua's mother. Many other women who had come to Jerusalem with the Teacher had joined the large group. Nicodemus and Joseph saw the Sanhedrin Council walk up with Annas in the lead, so they withdrew, hiding their faces behind the group.

When Y'shua saw His mother with John standing there, He said to John, "She is now your mother, please take of her." Y'shua then looked at His mother and said, "Woman, this man is now your son, and he will watch over you."

The chief priests and the Sanhedrin Council inched closer to the cross and looked up at Y'shua and spotted the notice written on the cross.

Annas demanded loudly to the nearest Roman soldier, "Where did this notice come from?" Annas pointed with his staff above Y'shua's head.

The Roman towered over Annas and with a menacing expression scowled at the Jewish leader. "It was given by our Lord, Governor Pilate. Why do you ask?"

Annas shrunk back. "I was just curious." He did not appear pleased. He looked at a nearby temple guard and told him to inform Caiaphas of the notice. The guard then scurried away.

People passing by the cross shook their heads and hurled insults at Y'shua. "You were going to tear down the temple and build it back up in three days! Save Yourself if You are YaHoWaH's Son! Come on down from the cross!" They jeered and laughed.

In the same way, the chief priests, the teachers of the law and the elders made fun of Him. "He saved others, but He cannot save Himself!" They laughed.

"Isn't He supposed to be the king of Israel?" grumbled one of the priests.

"If He comes down off the cross now, perhaps we will believe in Him!" said another.

"He claims He trusts in YaHoWaH and claims to be YaHoWaH's Son. Well, then, let us see if YaHoWaH wants to save Him now!" mocked Annas.

"Let Him save Himself if He is the Messiah whom YaHoWaH has chosen!"

Then one of the prisoners started cursing Y'shua. "Aren't You the Messiah? Why aren't You saving Yourself and us from this horrible punishment?"

The other prisoner hanging there rebuked Him, saying, "Have you no fear or respect for YaHoWaH? You received the same sentence as this Man, but He has done nothing wrong. Both of us are criminals and deserve our punishment for what we have done. This Man, though, is innocent and doesn't deserve to be here." Then he looked at the Teacher. "Remember me, Y'shua, when You become the King."

Y'shua looked at the dying prisoner, smiled, and replied, "I promise you, today you will be in heaven with Me."

Helpless, Nicodemus, Joseph, and the others in their group stayed near the cross with Y'shua. A large crowd of people gathered to observe the spectacle. Some were there to deride Y'shua, but many others were there in support of the Teacher. There were many women in the group, but they only watched from a distance. They had followed Y'shua from Galilee and helped Him while He ministered to people. Among them was Mary the mother of James and John, and the wife of Zebedee.

The hour was noon, yet the crowds gazed at the sky and appeared frightened when suddenly, the sun quickly faded and the daylight vanished. Within minutes, the sky appeared as if it were past sundown with an eerie orange glow covering the area and animals curled on the ground in preparation for sleep.

For three hours, darkness covered the area, and it was strangely quiet.

At three o'clock, the sun reappeared, and Y'shua cried out with a loud shout, "Eloi, Eloi, lema sabachthani?"

Nicodemus looked at John and asked, "Did He cry out, 'Elohim, did You abandon Me?'"

Everyone in their group focused on John, but before he could respond, someone nearby yelled out, "Listen, He is calling for Elijah!"

Y'shua struggled to speak, and His breathing was labored. "I am thirsty."

The young man with the bucket and sponge ran over to Y'shua's cross. He started to dip the sponge in the liquid when another person stopped him.

"Wait, let us see if Elijah is coming to save Him!"

The young man lifted the sponge to Y'shua's lips, and He took a drink. Then with a loud, painful cry, He said. "Father! Into Your hands, I place My spirit!" Y'shua gasped one large breath and finally uttered His last statement. His words, "It is finished!" were spoken with His final breath. Y'shua then dropped His head and remained motionless.

With a loud booming sound, the ground beneath everyone's feet began to shake. Starting out slowly at first, the earth then began moving violently, knocking some individuals off their feet. As the earth shook, rocks split apart and birds noisily took flight, and the dogs nearby yelped and ran off. This earthquake lasted nearly a minute.

Several people fell to their face, believing the world was coming apart or ending.

The Roman army officer who stood nearby overseeing the crucifixion saw what was happening. Staring up at Y'shua, he said, "Certainly, this Man was truly the Son of God!"

Standing with the officer, the other ordinarily tough soldiers who observed Y'shua, witnessed the earthquake and everything else happening, and they were now terrified.

Positioned off to one side from the cross stood Annas and some men from the Sanhedrin Council. A breathless temple priest wearing a distinctive uniform came running up. He looked horrified. "Annas, the curtain veil between the Holy of Holies in the tabernacle has torn in half! I saw the ark uncovered and feared I would die!"

Annas grabbed the priest and shook him. "How is this possible? The curtain is heavy. Did it fall from the ceiling?"

The priest's eyes were wide with fright. "No, sir, it was torn in half, starting at the top and splitting to the bottom. It looked as if someone pulled it apart." Looking at the other council members, the priest continued. "The ground started shaking, and I witnessed the veil torn in half, then I started running to find you. As I ran past the field of the dead, I watched graves and tombs open up. Those who were once dead arose and began to walk around!"

"Stop!" cried Annas. "You're hysterical. You only thought you saw these things."

The priest argued with Annas. "I know what I saw. At first, I thought the same as you, but then several people who were in the graves walked up and grabbed me, asking me if I was alive."

"Show me. I don't believe you," derided Annas.

Nicodemus and the group watched as the council followed the priest and marched off. Looking around, Nicodemus and Joseph saw other people slowly drifting away.

Joseph pulled Nicodemus to one side and spoke quietly. "We cannot allow this man, Y'shua, to remain here on this cross."

Nicodemus' eyes widened as he stared. "What shall we do? The Romans always leave the bodies to rot in the sun, as a warning to others who might challenge their authority."

"Come, I have something in mind." Joseph tugged on his arm.

"What are we doing, Joseph?"

He was ignored as Joseph marched through the city. Eventually they walked directly to Governor Pilate's palace. Just before they were about to enter, Nicodemus jerked to a stop.

"This is your idea? We will be killed by the Romans or the council if they find out we're here."

Joseph dragged Nicodemus along and walked into the building. "It will be fine, Nicodemus. You must have faith."

At the main entrance, Laurentius met them. The imposing Roman soldier did not appear pleased at first.

Nicodemus swallowed a hard lump in this throat.

CHAPTER THIRTY
HANNAH THE WEAVER

RECOGNIZING THEM, LAURENTIUS RELAXED. HE extended his hand. "Joseph! It has been a long time, Citizen. How are you?"

Joseph tried to smile but appeared anxious. "I wish I were here for more pleasant reasons, but my friend and I would like to speak with the legatus, Pontius Pilate."

Giving them a sideways glance and narrowing his eyes, Laurentius took pause. "You appear concerned. Is there some way I may help you? As you can imagine, it has been a difficult day for the governor."

Joseph stepped near the Roman and almost whispered, "Laurentius, I would not insist, but the matter is of grave concern. I must make a request of our governor, and I fear he is the only one who can approve my appeal."

Laurentius frowned. "This has been a day filled with requests from the Jews. I fear my lord will not be pleased."

Joseph pleaded. "Laurentius, I implore you. This is very important."

"And who is this?" Laurentius pointed at Nicodemus.

Joseph relaxed. "Oh, forgive me. This is my dearest friend, Nicodemus." Joseph pushed his younger friend forward, but Nicodemus resisted.

Laurentius extended his muscled arm and hand. "Any friend of Joseph is also a friend of mine."

Nicodemus nervously shook hands with Laurentius and was shocked by the power of the man's grip. He nodded toward the Roman but said nothing.

"Please wait here. I will speak with my lord," said Laurentius. "I make no promises."

Several long minutes elapsed as the two men waited. Nicodemus started getting nervous. "Joseph, perhaps this isn't a good idea."

Before Joseph could respond, he and Nicodemus were interrupted.

"Joseph, it is you? How are you?" Pilate embraced Joseph while Nicodemus looked shocked. The two men shook hands.

"What brings you to my door on such an ominous day?" Pilate asked. "How is your business in Arimathea?"

"Thank you for allowing us to see you, sir," responded Joseph.

"Nonsense. You are welcome as always." Pilate turned to Nicodemus and saw the sores on his face. He frowned.

"Your Excellency, may I present my dearest friend, Nicodemus." Joseph pushed Nicodemus toward the governor.

Pilate cautiously greeted Nicodemus. "A friend of Joseph is accepted as one of our guests."

Nicodemus tried to smile, but he was too shocked at the comfortable atmosphere between Joseph and Pilate. "It is an honor to meet you, Pontius Pilate, sir." His words awkwardly tumbled out of his mouth.

"Are you ill?" asked Pilate, inspecting his face.

Nicodemus looked down at his feet. "I was beaten and robbed by thieves a few days past and left for dead."

"My friend is also with the Sanhedrin Council, but he is not quite a member yet. His father was a member until he suddenly died," added Joseph.

Pilate's face shifted to concern. "The council, you say?"

Nicodemus nodded slowly. He cautiously shifted his eyes from Pilate to Laurentius and back.

Pilate looked at Joseph. "No doubt you're aware of the trouble these Jews have caused me today, present company excluded."

"We are, kind sir. It is one of the reasons why we came to speak with you," answered Joseph.

Pilate gave them a sideways glance and furrowed his brow. "Are you with them?"

Nicodemus blurted out uncharacteristically, "Absolutely not! They are evil murderers!"

Both Joseph and Pilate looked at Nicodemus with surprise.

Nicodemus was embarrassed. "Excuse me, I'm sorry. I meant no disrespect, sir."

Pilate laughed. "I like you, Nicodemus, you're honest." Pilate turned and started walking to the inner part of the palace. "Come, we must sit and talk."

Following Pilate, Laurentius, Joseph, and Nicodemus trailed behind him to another room. Arriving near a large table, Pilate sat in an ornate chair at the head. Joseph and Nicodemus sat together on one side of the table, while Laurentius stood behind and near Pilate in a protective stance.

Pilate poured wine into three cups and offered it to his guests.

"Thank you." Joseph nodded.

"Yes, thank you," added Nicodemus.

After Pilate took a sip, Joseph also tasted the wine but set the cup back down. Nicodemus lifted the cup to his lips but set it down without drinking.

Pilate leaned forward. "Tell me, Joseph of Arimathea, what request is it you have of me."

"We've come to ask a favor, Excellency." Joseph looked at Pilate, then swept his eyes at Laurentius and Nicodemus.

Nicodemus appeared as if he might vomit. Beads of perspiration formed on his brow. *Joseph, why are you including me in this crazy plan?*

Joseph continued. "We've come to ask for the body of Y'shua of Nazareth."

Pilate sat back. "Laurentius." Pilate motioned with his hand.

Laurentius stepped forward and bent near Pilate, "Yes, my legatus."

"Send a runner and determine the fate of this Y'shua."

Laurentius stood upright, slapped his arm across his chest saluting the governor. "Certe." Spinning on his heels, Laurentius walked away.

"Tell me, Nicodemus, why are you opposed to your Jewish friends in the council?" asked Pilate.

Nicodemus sat upright. "They are not my friends. Their ignorance is inexplicable."

"And you, Joseph, are you in agreement with your friend?"

With a serious expression, Joseph nodded. "Yes, sir."

Pilate smiled. "I must say, your words and feelings will no doubt cause you much harm regarding the Jewish council. They argued rather strongly for the death of this man Y'shua. Out of fear the people would riot, I agreed and gave them Barabbas, but I found no fault in your Man."

"I'm afraid, sir, Nicodemus and I can no longer support their actions. As Nicodemus has stated, their ignorance is inexplicable," said Joseph solemnly.

"Then you do think this Y'shua is your King?" asked Pilate.

"Y'shua was—what I mean is—Y'shua was the son of YaHoWaH, our God. He was a prophet from heaven, but now they have murdered Him," interjected Nicodemus.

"But is it possible for men to kill a god?" asked Pilate.

Laurentius interrupted their conversation. "Sir, the Jewish council is here again to make another request."

Pilate jumped to his feet. "By the fury of Zeus, what in heaven's name do they want now?" Pilate looked at his guests. "We will continue our conversation. Please wait here." He then left them alone. He walked into the next room where Nicodemus and Joseph could hear everything spoken. Both men peered through a lattice window and could see the council members.

Caiaphas, Annas, and the Sanhedrin Council paced while waiting. When Pilate and Laurentius appeared, Caiaphas groveled. "Oh kind sir, we have but a few more requests."

"Out with it!" barked Laurentius.

Caiaphas tried to act polite. "My guard informs me a notice has been placed on the cross of this Galilean troublemaker, whom you have condemned to death."

"And what of it, Jew? It was you and your kind demanding He be put to death despite me finding Him innocent of any crime," snapped Pilate.

Caiaphas started to correct Pilate but stopped himself. "Well, the words on the notice are offensive to us. Perhaps you could consider our proposal. Rather than saying 'the King of the Jews,'" Caiaphas's upper lip curled, "you could see to it to have it say 'this man claims he is the King of the Jews?'"

Pilate never flinched or bothered to think about the proposal. Instead, the governor flashed a confident smile, leaned forward, and uttered, "I think not! What I have written stays written."

While contemplating his next words, Caiaphas made wordless grumbles.

Pilate quickly dismissed him. "Laurentius, we are finished here," announced Pilate. "Please escort this Jew from my palace."

"But I wasn't finished speaking," stuttered Caiaphas.

Laurentius fiercely stared at Caiaphas. "But his Excellency is! Now move along."

Caiaphas slammed his staff to the floor, and Laurentius never moved a muscle. Caiaphas slowly retreated. The small portion of the Sanhedrin followed him out the door.

Nicodemus snickered.

Annas moved forward a few steps. "It is the day before our Sabbath, and we would ask for the legs of the prisoners to be broken. This way, they may die faster and their bodies removed from the crosses. Our Sabbath is a holy day, and it would desecrate our Sabbath to have these men exposed."

At first, Pilate just stared at the man begging before him. "Laurentius, find a soldier to escort these Jews out of my home. Give the soldier directions to break the crucified prisoner's legs."

Laurentius saluted. "Sane quidem."

Pilate turned to walk away, but mumbled, "This day cannot end soon enough."

When he returned to the other room, he, Joseph, and Nicodemus discussed the requests by the Jewish council.

Then the runner returned from Golgotha and he explained the message the commander had given him.

Pilate dismissed the runner. "Thank you." Turning to his guests, he said, "I am sorry to report, but it appears your god—I should say, your prophet, Y'shua—may be dead."

Taking a piece of papyrus, the governor wrote out a message and closed the document with a wax seal. He then handed it to Joseph. "Give this to the commander. It gives him instructions to release the body, once the soldiers verify His death, to your care."

Joseph took the message but stared at it in his hand. "Thank you, sir."

Pilate placed his hand on Joseph's shoulder. "Please come and visit again but choose another day. I dread ones like this. Come when we can visit and talk." He turned to Nicodemus. "You are welcome to visit with Joseph as well."

Nicodemus nodded. "Thank you, sir."

"Now if you will excuse me, I must find my wife, have supper, and find a way to remove this day from my memory. I'm afraid it will require large quantities of wine and a warm bath to wipe away my thoughts. Laurentius, please show our guests out."

After exchanging pleasantries, Joseph and Nicodemus walked out of the palace.

Nicodemus looked at the note from Pilate resting in Joseph's hand. "So what do we do now?"

Joseph searched the streets and momentarily ignored his friend. "I'm sorry, what did you ask, Nicodemus?"

"What's next?

Joseph faced his younger friend. "We need the items necessary for the tahara—ointments, oils, myrrh, and spices. Do you need some money?"

Nicodemus was still numb, but quickly answered, "No, I have enough."

"Good. now, please go quickly and buy these things before all the shops close for Sabbath. Meet me at the burial gardens. I have a new tomb which was recently carved from solid rock. I had prepared it for myself, but we will bury Y'shua there instead. We must hurry," said Joseph as he pushed his friend down the street. "Sabbath starts soon."

Pausing briefly, Nicodemus digested Joseph's instructions before dashing off.

Joseph walked briskly toward Golgotha. When he arrived, the core group was still gathered near the foot of the cross. Miryam was still weeping, but now a Bedouin woman was kneeling beside her. Nearby, the Roman soldiers were busy cleaning up their tools.

The commander barked orders and seemed upset. "Has the world gone mad? We never make their deaths speedy." He cried out, "Valerianus, come here."

"Yes, sir," the soldier replied as he saluted his superior.

"Break the legs of the prisoners," the commander demanded.

"Excuse me, sir?" asked Valerianus.

"You heard me, our legatus, governor Pilate, has requested we break the legs of the prisoners so they may die quickly," lamented the commander.

Valerianus looked stunned. "By your command, sir."

So he went and broke the legs of the first man and then of the other man who had been crucified with Y'shua. When they came to Y'shua, the soldier saw He was already dead, so they did not break His legs. One of the soldiers, however, plunged his spear into Y'shua's side.

The commander looked at the runner. "Tell the governor, the legs of the prisoners were broken per his command, except for the one called Y'shua. Tell him this man was dead already, but to be certain, we drove a spear through His ribs and into the lungs. Inform him, we witnessed water and blood issuing out, verifying he is dead."

The runner dashed off and the Roman commander shook his head. "In all my days as a soldier, I have never seen a day like this."

Joseph walked up to the officer. "A word, commander?"

"What do you want, Citizen?"

Joseph handed the note from Pilate. "We will make burial arrangements for Y'shua." The soldier nodded and instructed the men to remove the body. As the soldiers struggled, the spike from the feet and one from the wrist of Y'shua snapped off when they tried to remove them, but the last nail pulled free. The Romans dropped the spikes on the ground alongside the cross.

As Joseph turned toward John, he could hear the Bedouin woman and Miryam speaking. The woman reached into her sack, which had been slung over her shoulder and retrieved a bolt of nearly white linen cloth. The weave was a meticulous herringbone and of exceptional quality. "I made this for the Messiah,"[1] said the woman as she outstretched her arms toward Miryam.

"Thank you, Hannah. We will wrap my Son in this."[2] Then the two women embraced. Miryam faced Joseph and John. Her eyes were swollen from crying. She extended the bolt of cloth in her hands.

Joseph leaned forward toward the women. "I have received permission from Pontius Pilate for the body of Y'shua. I have a new burial chamber prepared and will perform the tahara with Nicodemus. He is to meet me there." Joseph took the cloth from Miryam. He then produced a sack of money from under his belt and pressed it into Hannah's hand.

Hannah shook her head and frowned. "I have no myrrh for the body. Shall I go buy the burial spices?"[3]

"No, I have taken care of everything needed for His burial. We only lacked this beautiful shroud that you've made," said Joseph. "Please accept my payment for your excellent work."[4]

Hannah attempted to push Joseph's hand away, but Joseph released the bag, turned, and hurried away.[5]

Deep in thought, Joseph mumbled softly, "We need a cart and a few other materials." Inadvertently, he bumped into a young boy about twelve years old. "Oh, excuse me," muttered Joseph.

The boy looked up and smiled. "Joseph? Is it you?"

At first, Joseph tried to recollect where he knew the boy from. "Samuel? Are you Samuel Ben-Jacob?"

"Yes sir," the boy proudly stated.

Joseph retrieved several gold shekels from another money bag under his belt and held them out. "Samuel, I need some help. Would you like to earn these?"

Snatching the coins from Joseph's hand, Samuel responded, "Sir, what do you need?"

Joseph weakly smiled. "I need a cart to transport the body of Y'shua to the burial gardens, strips of cloth to tie the shroud, and a face napkin. Oh, and two workers will be necessary as well."

"Is that all, sir?" Samuel asked.

Joseph's mouth dropped open. "You remember my list?"

Samuel repeated it back word-for-word.

"Excellent, Samuel. Bring two buckets and meet me back here in less than an hour and there will be more money for your efforts."

Samuel smiled. "I'll be back in half the time." Instantly, he took off running.

Joseph smiled. "Thank You, YaHoWaH for such great luck." He moved back toward Golgotha. When he arrived, the soldiers were just lowering Y'shua's body from the cross. John was trying to help, but the soldiers brushed him aside. John pulled his outer cloak off and spread it on the ground. Joseph watched the scene with great sorrow.

"Please lay the body here," John pleaded while pointing.

The soldiers roughly dropped Y'shua on John's clothing and shrugged. "What a waste. It was a decent cloak too," they grumbled as they marched away.

Joseph and John immediately began wrapping the body in John's cloak. They tied knots into the ends of the robe near Y'shua's head and feet. Joseph removed his outer cloak and floated it over the body of Y'shua.

John's eyes bulged. "My clothing is simple and easily replaced, but yours is of fine quality."

Joseph put his hand on John's shoulder. "Take Miryam home and care for her. Nicodemus and I will perform the tahara. In three days, after we have been ritually cleansed, we will come and join you."

John embraced Joseph. "Thank you. You are like a brother, and we cannot thank you enough for your kindness."

"Y'shua is YaHoWaH's Son, a prophet, our Messiah. We must honor Him. Shalom, John. Blessings on Y'shua's mother."

Joseph watched John, Miryam, and the others gradually walk away. When he looked down, he noticed a long, bloodstained spike alongside two broken pieces on the ground near the body. First, Joseph looked around, and then he bent over to snag the nail. He tucked it inside the cloth along with the body of Y'shua. Moments later, young Samuel and two of his father's servants arrived with a cart. Two buckets and a large basket sat upon piles of fresh straw in the wagon.

"Excellent work, Samuel, but we must not waste a moment. The Sabbath will start at sundown. We must hurry."

Joseph bent down to pick up one end of John's cloak, and Samuel rushed over to help. The two servants took the other end of Y'shua's body, and between the four individuals, they lifted Him into the cart. In silence, they meditatively walked toward the gardens.

Mary Magdalene and Mary, the mother of another follower named Joseph, walked behind. One woman said to Joseph, "We desire to know the location of the tomb, and we have promised to tell the mother of Y'shua where her Son will rest."

Joseph nodded in silence.

CHAPTER THIRTY-ONE

TAHARA FOR Y'SHUA

JUST A FEW HOURS BEFORE sunset, Joseph, Samuel, and the two servants entered the burial gardens. Surveying the area, Joseph contemplated the scene. He brightened once he spotted Nicodemus resting on a nearby boulder.

Both men exchanged nervous smiles as they greeted one another. On the ground beside Nicodemus were several jars. A makeshift wooden table stood near the tomb entrance. Without speaking, Joseph and Nicodemus began their preparations. Joseph removed his inner garment cloak and set it aside.

Samuel and the two servants waited patiently nearby. The two women who had followed moved a short distance away and observed without interfering. Nicodemus removed his outer cloak, folded it and sat it on the rock where he had been sitting. Both men rolled their sleeves and tied their inner tunics tightly around their bodies allowing their arms to move freely.

When they were ready, Joseph motioned for the servants to bring the body. All five men assisted in removing Y'shua's body from the cart and carefully laid it on the wooden table. When Nicodemus saw Joseph's bloodstained, outer cloak lying over Y'shua, he was shocked.

"Joseph, this is your best royal cloak. It was expensive," Nicodemus lamented.

"Its value is far less than the Messiah it covers," voiced Joseph mournfully.

Nicodemus slowly nodded in agreement.

"Samuel, please bring the supplies," requested Joseph.

While Samuel carried the basket containing the other items requested by Joseph, the servants brought the two buckets. Removing the white linen shroud and other materials from the basket, Joseph carefully laid them on one of the nearby boulders.

"Please fill the buckets with water," Joseph asked while pointing at them.

The two servants dashed to a nearby well and returned with full buckets.

"What can I do to help, Joseph?" asked Samuel.

Joseph frowned. "You may sit and watch, but please be quiet and respectful."

Samuel and the two servants rested on nearby boulders and watched with reverence. Joseph and Nicodemus bowed their heads and quietly prayed. After their prayers, Joseph began chanting one of King David's Psalms. Both men stood alongside the wooden table and slowly rocked their bodies in rhythm, chanting.

After they finished their prayer, Nicodemus and Joseph began untying the knots in John's cloak. Nicodemus was distracted, so Joseph found the nail he had hidden earlier and secretly wrapped a piece of cloth around it. He then set it aside near his other garments. Then he and Nicodemus arranged Y'shua on His back. Joseph draped a thick piece of fabric over Y'shua's groin, and the two men removed His blood-soaked loincloth. They respectfully kept Y'shua's personal area hidden from view.

Starting with Y'shua's feet, the two men began washing the body of dried blood. They slowly and methodically progressed up the body, rinsing, and cleaning off dirt and crusted fluids. When they reached the neck, they stopped. With care, the men rolled the body to one side, with Y'shua's back to Samuel and the servants.

When Samuel saw Y'shua's flesh, he gasped.

Joseph and Nicodemus labored to remove many of the splinters jammed into Y'shua's skin. After they had removed them, they then tenderly washed the body, again beginning with the feet and moving up to the neck. Joseph delicately placed the loose flaps of Y'shua's flesh into their proper place, but it was apparent the skin would not be entirely sealed.

They then removed John's blood-soaked garment off the table and placed it into the basket. Another clean piece of linen was patted over Y'shua's shredded skin, and then they rolled the body onto its back.

Again, Joseph and Nicodemus began chanting another Psalm and rocking their bodies. After the Psalm they moved to Y'shua's head. Nicodemus held the face while Joseph struggled to dislodge the crown of thorns jammed into the skull. Once it was free, Joseph cast it into the basket with disgust. One of the thorns had stabbed Joseph's thumb.

Moving slowly, the men then washed the neck, face, and hair. The thickness of the dried blood made it difficult to remove all the sticky substance from the skin, but they did their best with the little time they had. Joseph looked up and saw the sun was nearing sunset.

"We must hurry, Nicodemus, we haven't much time."

Nicodemus tried to smile. "YaHoWaH will grant us the time we need. This is His Son, after all."

"True," said Joseph as he nodded. "Samuel, please bring us the three jars."

The young man and the two servants jumped to their feet, swiftly moving the jars near Joseph and Nicodemus. Astounded, Samuel stared at the body of Y'shua with an open mouth.

"We are finished with you, for now, Samuel. Thank you. You may sit and wait," said Joseph as he nudged the young man.

With difficulty, Samuel pulled himself away and walked unhurriedly to his place on the rocks.

Nicodemus opened the jar of oil and myrrh and cautiously poured half the contents over the body. He ensured the oil was evenly distributed over the skin. As he poured, Joseph took his hands and lightly massaged the liquid into Y'shua's abused skin. The body developed a warm glow from the oil. Once the front of the body was evenly covered, they rolled the body onto the side again.

The other half of the oil was spread over the back of the body. When Joseph and Nicodemus neared the shredded back, Joseph gently removed the fabric placed earlier and gingerly patted his flat palms on the torn flesh. He ensured the skin was not disturbed any further.

Next, Nicodemus opened the jar of expensive spices. Taking his hand, he reached into the pot and grabbed a large handful. Then he sprinkled the spices over the entire damp skin while Joseph lightly placed the material with his hand. When they finished Y'shua's back, Joseph took the linen shroud and unrolled it onto the table. He spread the cloth out, leaving the extra roll near the head.

The two men then cautiously rolled Y'shua onto His back so that He was flat on the linen cloth. Joseph painstakingly arranged Y'shua's head and hair, and then the two men repeated the application of spices to the front of the body. When they were finished, the men crossed the arms over Y'shua's groin and just under the cloth placed earlier.

Their third and final Psalm was sung, and when they finished, both men had tears falling from their cheeks.

"You know, Joseph, I hate them for what they have done to our Messiah."

"The Romans or the council?" inquired Joseph.

Nicodemus hesitated at first, thinking on Joseph's question. "I suppose both, but for entirely separate reasons. The Romans are ignorant savages and doing what they do best, by destroying human life. On the other hand, our so-called religious leaders are far worse because they condemned Him to death. He never harmed anyone, He only—"

Nicodemus choked on his words and could no longer speak.

"It is truly senseless. Just when I could see the potential for Israel to rise again as a nation, and have a true King, our hopes and dreams were snuffed out," bemoaned Joseph.

Standing in reverent silence, the two men waited, hoping for yet another miracle from the once-charismatic teacher.

Finally, Nicodemus spoke what both men were thinking. "How could YaHoWaH allow this to happen?"

Joseph shook his head and mumbled as if his thoughts were far away. "Didn't Y'shua say something to us about this day happening?"

Nicodemus searched his mind, trying to recall all the conversations of the past months. He quickly relived the journey they had taken, following the Teacher, listening to the Man speak, and the many lessons Y'shua taught the people gathered around.

Nicodemus frowned. "I do remember Him once saying, He must go away, but He would come back three days later, or something similar to those words."

"Yes, yes, yes. I remember the conversation, too. Did Y'shua not say He was going to die and come back to life?" asked Joseph.

Nicodemus scrolled through his memory searching for the words. "I don't think I was paying close enough attention. I'm sorry."

They stood in lengthy silence again.

Joseph finally broke their stupor by reaching for the napkin. He wrapped it around the face of Y'shua by cupping it under the chin and tying it to the top of His head. Then Joseph placed the triangle flap over Y'shua's face. He then took the linen cloth and unrolled the rest of the shroud, covering Y'shua's front. The beautiful linen cloth, made by Hannah, the weaver, was now enfolding the body of Y'shua. Joseph reached under the linen shroud and gently removed the piece of fabric covering Y'shua's groin. He placed it into the discard basket.

Reaching for the strips of cloth Samuel had brought, the two men secured the shroud tightly around Y'shua's body. Evenly spaced bands pulled the legs, thighs, and arms together, fastening everything in place. They then collected the cleaning rags and anything else loose, associated with Y'shua's body, and tossed them into the basket.

The evening light was quickly fading, and the two servants had built a fire. Joseph looked at the servants.

"Please discard the water in a safe area and burn the buckets in the fire, also the soiled materials. After we move the body into the tomb, burn this wooden table as well."

The servants nodded and rapidly obeyed their instructions. All five individuals then carried the body into the tomb and placed it on a bench carved into the rock cave. As Joseph and Nicodemus arranged Y'shua in a flat position, Samuel retrieved the basket and put it in the tomb. Joseph nodded his approval, and without asking, the servants and Samuel walked outside.

Joseph quoted words from Moses, from the day he died. It was a speech Moses gave just before YaHoWaH called him home to sleep with his forefathers. Then walking backward, the two men left the tomb, bowing before their fallen teacher.

Joseph called out, "Samuel, and you two, come and help us roll the stone into place."

All five men grunted and pushed on the massive stone. At first, it appeared as if the rock wouldn't budge. Then suddenly, it began to slowly move, rolling in front of the opening. As it closed off the tomb, the stone door stopped with a thud and trails of dust trickled off the rock face. For a few minutes, no one moved but instead stared at the sealed tomb, each individual feeling the weight of what they had just witnessed.

After a period of respectful calm, the two servants quickly dismantled the table and tossed it into the burning pit. The used buckets were already reduced to embers. The servants then gathered the straw from the back of the cart and tossed it into the fire and burned it as well.

Joseph untied his inner cloak and reached under his belt, retrieving a handful of gold shekels. He deposited five in each of the servants' hands. "Thank you for your service this evening." Then turning to Samuel, he smiled. "My boy, you have witnessed your first tahara. Here are five shekels for your hard work. Please tell your mother and father how I appreciate the loan of their servants, but even more, we are grateful for their fine son."

Samuel proudly smiled. "Thank you, sir."

Joseph laid his hand on Samuel's head. "Blessings, Samuel. May YaHoWaH grant you the desires of your heart. Now go in peace and enjoy your Sabbath with your family."

Samuel reached out and hugged Joseph in a tight embrace.

Joseph gently pushed the young man away. "Now go, or you will be late for Sabbath. Shalom."

Nicodemus and Joseph watched Samuel return toward town as the two servants followed lugging the cart. Nicodemus gathered his cloak and the empty jars. When they observed the area, the two women were no longer sitting nearby. The fire was slowly dying with a thin trail of white smoke lifting toward heaven.

Nicodemus looked up into the sky which, by then, was turning quite dark and faded stars began twinkling. Staring at his older friend, Nicodemus said, "We have touched a corpse. According to the law of Moses, we must now cleanse ourselves and offer a sacrifice on the third day."

Joseph smiled. "Yes, and there isn't enough time for us to prepare for the Sabbath now. Come along, my friend, and I will buy you supper at the inn run by the Greeks."

"I'm afraid we will not be able to attend Passover, the most important festival of the year," said Nicodemus.

Joseph slowly nodded.

"I must tell you, I would do it all over again for our Messiah. I owe Him my life," Nicodemus added.

"From this day forward, our lives will never be the same. Only YaHoWaH knows what our future will bring. But, this much I know, our time with Y'shua was far too short."

After the two men had eaten, Nicodemus bid Joseph farewell. "Good night, my friend, and shalom." The men embraced and walked to their respective homes.

As Nicodemus dragged his feet, he felt as if he were walking through thick mud. Each step required effort. If Nicodemus could, he would crawl into bed and sleep a century, for he was indeed exhausted. The past week felt like a giant weight around his neck.

Once he was home, Nicodemus climbed up to the roof. Black ink filled the sky, with occasional stars peering through the clouds. Before going up on the roof, he had retrieved fresh clothes and set up the materials needed for the cleansing ritual. Wrapping his soiled clothes into a satchel, Nicodemus began rinsing his body from head to toe.

Scrubbing briskly, Nicodemus wished he could wash away the shameful association of the Sanhedrin. Each new thought appearing in his head caused Nicodemus to confess more sins to YaHoWaH. He felt even dirtier going through the movements, and acknowledging his sins only increased his shame further.

After washing seven times, he dropped to his knees and wept bitter tears. Slowly he moved his body into a horizontal position. Burying his face to the roof he spread his arms wide and cried out to his Heavenly Father, begging for forgiveness. Nicodemus felt shame for his association with the very spiritual leaders which Y'shua of Nazareth had denounced.

While quoting a lamenting Psalm by King David, weariness consumed Nicodemus, and he quickly fell asleep. Sometime during his slumber, Y'shua visited him in a dream. Everything seemed real. He stood in a field surrounded by spotless lambs. Their wool was full and bright white. Y'shua appeared and smiled, moving through the sheep. He was as Nicodemus remembered when they first met, and not the corpse he and Joseph painstakingly cared for earlier in the evening. Y'shua then stopped in front of him.

"Tell Me, Nicodemus, what do you see?"

Nicodemus spun around. "I see hundreds of white sheep; more than I can count, Y'shua."

"They are in your charge. Can you tend your flock?" Y'shua asked.

"But, I don't own any sheep. Where did they come from?"

"They are in your charge. Can you care for your flock?"

"I know nothing about sheep, Messiah. What am I to do?"

"They are in your charge, Nicodemus. Feed the lambs."

Moments later, Nicodemus awoke, cold and sore. His skin felt numb. The sky was still dark, and he was shaken by his dream. Little by little, Nicodemus gathered himself and stood, stretching achy muscles. Shivering, he quickly dressed and made his way into the house. Stumbling in the dark, Nicodemus found his bed and curled into a tight ball, rapidly falling asleep.

The same dream reappeared.

A smiling and peaceful Y'shua stood among the many sheep gathered around. He extended His hand.

"Come, Nicodemus."

As he walked through the flock, Nicodemus touched individual lambs feeling the soft, tightly curled wool in his fingers.

Y'shua pointed. "What do you see now, My son?"

Nicodemus gazed where Y'shua indicated, and at first, saw nothing but more sheep. Then one of the lambs looked different. The face was dark, and it moved unlike the others. Nicodemus frowned, trying to understand.

Looking back, Nicodemus saw Y'shua was still staring at the unusually dark-faced lamb. Y'shua's face looked gravely concerned. When Nicodemus glanced back in the direction of the dark-faced sheep, he observed with shock as it attacked several lambs near the edges of the flock. The unique sheep wasn't a lamb at all but a wolf, and it was tearing apart innocent lambs, his lips red with blood.

"Do something, Y'shua!" Nicodemus screamed.

When Nicodemus searched for Y'shua, He was no longer around. Panicked, Nicodemus watched as the wolf, disguised as a lamb, attack another defenseless sheep. In a fit of rage, Nicodemus yelled and fiercely charged toward the dark-faced wolf. He had nothing in his hands to fight with but ran headlong at the attacking wolf.

In a sweat, Nicodemus suddenly awoke and was twisted in his blankets. He felt trapped and fought to release himself from the bedding. Once free, he jumped to his feet panting, staring at his messy bed. Finally realizing he was not in a fight for his life, but in his house, Nicodemus sat on the edge of the bed.

"What do these dreams mean, Adonai? Help me understand."

It was still late into the night, and Nicodemus was now frustrated and tired. He rolled over on the bed and tried to get comfortable. Lying on his back, Nicodemus stared into the darkness up where the ceiling should be. The scenes Nicodemus had just dreamed played over and over inside his mind. After a long while, Nicodemus fell asleep again.

Just before daybreak, the dream continued. This time, he was alone in the field of sheep. He called out for Y'shua and at the same time, kept a watchful eye for the dark-faced wolf. Both were now missing. When Nicodemus moved through the familiar flock of sheep, he neared the edge of the group when he spotted several lambs lying dead and torn to shreds.

Weeping for their loss, Nicodemus bent down and lifted one of the lambs pulling it to his chest. "Why, YaHoWaH, why?"

From behind Nicodemus, Y'shua appeared and touched Nicodemus' shoulder. When he looked up into the face of Y'shua, he saw He was crying as well. Then Y'shua reached out and touched the lamb in Nicodemus' hands. It was entirely restored and undamaged. The lamb struggled, so Nicodemus set it free, watching the lamb run and play with the other sheep. Then, like steam rising from a boiling pot, the scene slowly evaporated. When he awoke, Nicodemus stood next to his bed with his wool blanket dangling in his hands.

CHAPTER THIRTY-TWO

HE IS ALIVE!

THE NEXT DAY WAS THE Sabbath.

As Joseph walked the streets, he spotted the chief priests and the Pharisees meeting with Pilate again. He overheard Caiaphas and Annas had been initially rebuffed by the governor, but eventually, they'd convinced him of their need for a visit.

Joseph pleaded with Laurentius who then allowed Joseph to listen to their conversations from a hidden alcove.

"Tell me, Caiaphas, why is it you have spent so much time here in my palace? I grow weary of the demands you Jews place upon this office."

"Sir, with all due respect, we have but one more, small request."

Pilate crossed his arms. "So, out with it and let me attend to other important matters demanding my attention."

"Sir, we remember, while that liar was still alive, He said, 'I will be raised to life three days later.' Please give orders, then, for His tomb to be carefully guarded until the third day. This way His followers will not be able to go and steal the body, and then tell the people how He was raised from the dead. In our opinion, this last lie would be even worse than the first one."

Pilate rolled his eyes. "Tell me, are you asking about someone in particular?"

Caiaphas was incensed, but smiled anyway, "Sir, we refer to the prisoner we brought to you earlier." Caiaphas refused to speak his name.

Pilate grinned. "Ah yes, you must be talking about your king, Y'shua. King of the Jews is what I remember."

Several Romans standing nearby snorted and Caiaphas made a face indicating he was sickened by the reference.

Pilate smiled. "Laurentius, assign two men to satisfy their request."

Laurentius saluted. "Certe, legatus."

Pilate looked at his visitors. "Take the guard and go make the tomb as secure as you can. This is your last visit to my office. Please do not come here again!"

Caiaphas stuck his chin in the air and stormed from the palace, his minions following closely behind. When the council had departed Pilate, Laurentius came to Joseph.

"I'm afraid these men try the patience of His Excellency, the governor."

Joseph patted Laurentius' shoulder. "They are evil, self-serving, and pious men who do not serve YaHoWaH, my God."

"Then why do your people honor these men?"

"Good question, Laurentius. Thank you for indulging me."

"Good day, Joseph. Come and visit again, but as a good citizen, and not part of those Jews."

Joseph half smiled, turned, and walked out.

Caiaphas and Annas walked directly to the burial gardens and located the tomb where Y'shua lie. Joseph followed behind them but stayed well hidden. The Pharisees strung several royal cords across the stone covering and placed wax seals over the ends. They then instructed the Roman guards to keep watch until the end of the fourth day.

Joseph whispered, "Foolish men. May YaHoWaH punish your sins."

On day three of his cleansing ritual, Nicodemus dressed in his best robes then started walking toward the temple. In the distance, he witnessed a beginning trail of white smoke rising to the heavens. "Ah, the start of Shavuot. Thank You, YaHoWaH."

It was early, about the sixth hour. Along the way, Nicodemus passed several vendors selling a variety of animals deemed safe for sacrifices. Stopping by one stall, the seller had several yearling lambs for sale. He watched the young lambs jump and play, making bleating sounds in competition for attention.

"Are you looking for a sacrifice? All my lambs are spotless, and I will offer you a reasonable price," said the gleeful vendor.

Nicodemus selected a lamb and paid the vendor. When he lifted it into his arms, Nicodemus was instantly reminded of his dream. Guilt stabbed in his chest when Nicodemus glanced at the creature with its soft brown eyes staring back. It was then he realized the connection.

Sermons from Y'shua about sheep and sacrifice suddenly became very clear. Nicodemus remembered Y'shua's lessons and how He would be the sacrificial lamb for all of mankind. Nicodemus petted the lamb in his arms and spoke kind words to the animal as it licked his fingers.

Ambling slowly toward the temple, several excited women brushed past Nicodemus. He thought he recognized some of the women as followers of Y'shua. Their conversations were filled with enthusiasm as they rushed by in pursuit of some unknown goal.

"We must tell the others," Nicodemus heard one woman say as they ran.

Arriving at the temple, Nicodemus walked into the inner courtyard where a temple priest greeted him. Although Nicodemus had performed similar rituals many times before in his past, somehow it felt remarkably different this time. He was sad for his lamb and shuddered as if he was cold.

The priest carried a bronze bowl in one hand and a hyssop branch in the other. He then dipped the hyssop into the dish and sprinkled Nicodemus and the lamb. Walking in a circle, the priest ensured the purification water had touched everything. He set the bowl and branch on a table and took hold of a small knife. He placed a small pan below the lamb and held the creature in place.

"Place your hands upon its head and confess before YaHoWaH."

Nicodemus laid both hands on the lamb's head. "I have performed a tahara and touched a corpse. Three days have been spent as part of the cleansing ritual."

In a swift move, the priest slit the throat of the lamb allowing the blood to drain into the bowl. The yearling briefly struggled while the priest held firm, but then it lowered itself to the ground and closed its eyes. Motionless, the lamb was now dead, sacrificed for Nicodemus, and atoning for his sins. For Nicodemus, the connection of Y'shua being sacrificed for the sins of man became quite clear.

The priest took another branch, dipped it into the bowl, and sprinkled the blood over the burning altar, on the ground around the altar and around Nicodemus. He then lifted the lamb up to heaven and said a quiet prayer. When he was finished, he laid the lamb on the altar and allowed the flames to roast the sacrifice.

The priest and Nicodemus watched the smoke rise above the flames. Then the priest turned to Nicodemus.

"YaHoWaH has accepted your sacrifice. You are now clean. Shalom."

Nicodemus then gave a prayer of thanks, quoting from the book of Jeremiah, "We praise You, Adonai all-powerful! You are good to us, and Your love never fails."

A mixture of bitter and sweet tears stained Nicodemus' cheeks. On the one hand, he was happy to be cleansed, for he was fulfilling the Law of Moses. On the other hand, his grief for the death of his lamb and its connection to the loss of Y'shua were overwhelming.

Feeling numb, Nicodemus proceeded to walk back toward his home. While walking, a hand reached out and touched his shoulder.

"Nicodemus, my friend, how are you?" asked Joseph.

Nicodemus embraced his older friend. "I am now good, my brother."

"Great, because I have terrific news," exclaimed Joseph.

"Tell me, what is your news?" asked Nicodemus.

Joseph smiled and spoke in a whisper. "Y'shua is alive."

Shocked, Nicodemus stared at Joseph. "What did you say? I find no humor in your words."

"It's true. Several women, who were followers of Y'shua, went to the tomb this morning and Y'shua was gone. The shroud and wrappings were there, and even the face napkin was folded and set aside, but Y'shua was not there." Joseph was excited.

In disbelief, Nicodemus asked, "How is this even possible? Are you certain?"

"The women said the stone was cast aside like a giant tossed it from the doorway. It lay on the ground broken. If you remember, five of us struggled that evening to move the stone into place. What kind of power can toss a big stone, and so easily? I ran into John, and he confirmed everything. He even said Y'shua prophesied this was going to happen," explained Joseph.

"Come, Joseph, I want to see for myself," said Nicodemus as he started running in the direction of the burial gardens.

The following week, Y'shua appeared once more to His twelve witnesses at Lake Tiberias in Galilee. They had seen Y'shua twice. Each time, they were behind lock doors, yet Y'shua appeared without using the door.

Simon-Peter and his brother Andrew, Thomas called the Twin, Nathanael the one from Cana in Galilee, the sons of Zebedee, John and James, and Philip, were all together. They had finally gathered near Galilee because Y'shua had asked the witnesses to meet Him there. They waited by the lake until it was nearly evening.

Simon-Peter grew weary waiting and said to the others, "I am going fishing."

"We will join you," added John.

Therefore, the whole group went out in a boat, but all night they did not catch a thing. As the sun was rising, Y'shua stood at the water's edge, but the men in the boat did not know who it was.

He called out to them, "Fishermen, haven't you caught anything?"

"Not a thing," yelled Andrew.

Y'shua then said to them, "Cast your net out on the right side of the boat, and you will catch some."

So they threw the net out and could not pull it back in, because they had caught so many fish.

John said to Peter, "I believe the Man calling out to us is Y'shua!"

When Simon-Peter heard it was Y'shua, he wrapped his outer garment around his waist—for he had taken his clothes off—and jumped into the water. The other witnesses immediately rowed the boat to shore after pulling the net full of fish. They were not very far from land, about a hundred yards away, so it was a short distance. When they stepped ashore, they saw a charcoal fire with fish on it and some bread.

Y'shua said to them, "Bring some of the fish you have just caught."

Peter went aboard the boat and dragged the net ashore, full of big fish, a hundred and fifty-three in all. Even though there were so many fish, the mesh did not tear.

Y'shua said to them, "Come and eat."

The men thought they recognized Y'shua, but He looked different. Yet none of them dared ask Him, "Who are You?" because they were sure it was the Teacher.

Y'shua went over, took the bread, and broke it and gave it to them. He then divided the fish and shared it with the witnesses. From the time Y'shua was raised from the dead, this was the third occasion He had appeared to His close followers.

Once they had eaten, Y'shua said to Peter, "Simon son of John, do you love Me more than these others?"

"Yes, Master," he answered. "You know I love You."

Y'shua smiled and said to him, "Take care of My lambs."

A few minutes later Y'shua said to him again, "Simon son of John, do you honor Me with fond love?"

This time Peter was more forceful. "Yes, Son of YaHoWaH," he answered, "You know I honor and love You."

Y'shua said to him, "Care for My sheep."

John knew Peter felt guilty, for he had lied on the day Y'shua was arrested, telling several people he did not know the Teacher.

Finally, for the third time, Y'shua again asked, "Simon son of John, do you really love Me with the same kind of love I have for YaHoWaH?"

Peter became sad. It grieved him because Y'shua was asking the same question three times, and he was somewhat embarrassed. Peter told Him, "Y'shua, You know everything, and You know how I love You! Even, perhaps, more than any man here."

Y'shua looked at Peter, making direct eye contact, and said, "Then feed My sheep."

In agreement, Peter nodded slowly. When he looked around, everyone was staring. Peter was at a loss for words.

Y'shua smiled and placed His hands on Peter's shoulders. "I am telling you the truth. When you were young, you used to get ready and go anywhere you wanted to. But when you are old, you will stretch out your hands and someone else will tie you up and take you where you don't want to go."

John contemplated the words of Y'shua and realized He was speaking about the future of Peter's life. He was sure Y'shua described how Peter would meet his fate.

Then Y'shua said to Peter, "Follow Me!"

Peter pointed to his best friend. He knew John was closer to Y'shua than any of the other witnesses. He then asked Y'shua, "Master, what about this man? What will happen to him?"

Y'shua answered Peter, "If I want him to live until I come, what is it to you? You follow Me!"

Many of the witnesses then started whispering amongst themselves, believing John wouldn't die until Y'shua returned, as He had promised.

Y'shua looked at each of the men standing around and said, "Forty days after my resurrection, meet Me on the Mount of Olives. Tell all My followers to come and be present, for I wish to speak with them."

Then He instantly disappeared.

Y'shua appeared multiple times to various other individuals, including two people walking alone from Jerusalem to a nearby town. On many of those occasions, His followers touched Him and watched Y'shua eat while they enjoyed conversations with their Teacher who was once crucified.

Forty days following the resurrection of Y'shua, John and Peter sent word to Nicodemus and Joseph. They requested them to meet the witnesses on the Mount of Olives near Bethany. A large group of people gathered near the area where the Teacher had spoken many years earlier.

When Joseph and Nicodemus spotted John and Peter, they greeted one another. Peter was unusually subdued. They embraced one another.

"John, Peter, shalom," said Joseph.

John replied, "YaHoWaH's peace be with you as well."

Nicodemus was apprehensive. "Tell me, have you seen Y'shua? Is He really alive, like we saw with Lazarus?"

Both Joseph and Nicodemus were eager to know the answer to this question.

John smiled. "Without a doubt, we have seen and spoken with Y'shua, our Savior."

"And is this why we were summoned here today?" asked Nicodemus.

"It is. Y'shua has asked for us to be here so He may speak to His followers one last time," answered John.

"But I don't understand," said Joseph. "There is no record in the Torah of any previous prophet ever raising himself back to life."

Peter blurted out, "This isn't just any prophet; this is the Son of YaHoWaH!"

John calmed Peter by placing his hand on his friend's shoulder. "Peter is correct, Y'shua is not some ordinary man. He predicted His death and resurrection on several occasions. But we weren't listening well enough. From the time Y'shua taught us, I'm just beginning to connect the messages and words together."

"I recall some of the times Y'shua spoke about the future, but I must admit, I was so focused on the miracles, I missed the other details," added Joseph.

Peter grinned. "We each saw what we wanted to see, good or bad. Unfortunately, we weren't prepared for what was happening to the people."

"I agree, but at least Nicodemus and I were there to defend Y'shua in front of Pilate. The crowds were set against us. No matter how much we demanded they set Y'shua free, the people wanted the criminal Barabbas instead," said Joseph as he shook his head.

"Joseph is correct, Peter, where were you when all this took place?" questioned Nicodemus. "The only person we saw was John and the women who followed Y'shua."

Peter became angry but said nothing. Biting his lip, his eyes were downcast. He finally mumbled, "We were afraid the Romans would arrest us as well."

Joseph interceded. "Gentlemen, we are here because Y'shua is alive. Is this not great news?"

Suddenly, the crowd of people gathered on the mountain started loudly cheering. When Nicodemus and the group looked, they saw Y'shua standing on top of the hill. Y'shua's arms were outstretched, and He was smiling. John and Peter immediately ran up the hill and joined the other followers surrounding Y'shua.

It was a fantastic sight to behold for the Y'shua they had laid to rest just a few weeks earlier, was now standing before them very much alive. "See," said Joseph, "did I not tell you He was alive?"

Nicodemus stared with his mouth open and said nothing.

Most of the people standing around the mountain kept their distance from Y'shua because some were unsure. Some questioned if He was a ghost.

Following Judas' betrayal of Y'shua, he had taken his own life. After the son of Simon of Kerioth's death, only eleven witnesses remained. These eleven remaining witnesses tightly encircled Y'shua.

Then Y'shua spoke to His followers. "Foolish men, how slow you are to believe everything the prophets said! Was it not necessary for the Messiah to suffer His death and then to enter His glory by being resurrected?"

The eleven men gazed at one another, speechless.

Joseph and Nicodemus worked their way through the over five hundred people who had come to see the risen Y'shua. They wanted to be in front where they could hear the Teacher speak.

Staring at each of the eleven men, Y'shua gave them the following instructions, "Do not leave Jerusalem but wait for the gift I told you about, the gift My Father promised. The Holy Spirit is the comforter-friend I told you about, who will be present with you at all times. John baptized with water, but in a few days, you will be baptized with the Holy Spirit."

Then James, the son of Alphaeus asked, "Master, will You at this time give the Kingdom back to Israel, as promised by the prophets?"

Y'shua reached out and embraced His friends. "The times and occasions are set by My Father's own authority, and it is not for you to know when they will be. But when the Holy Spirit comes upon you, you will be filled with amazing power, and you will be witnesses for Me in Jerusalem, in all of Judea, Samaria, and even to the ends of the earth. Remember what I have taught you and love one another."

After quietly speaking with His close friends, Y'shua observed the crowd and smiled. Talking with a loud voice, He called out to the crowd, "All authority in heaven and on earth, and from My Father, has been given to Me. Therefore, go throughout the whole world and preach the gospel to every person you meet. Baptize them in the name of the Father, His Son, and the Holy Spirit. Teach them to obey everything I have commanded you.

"Whoever believes and is baptized in the spirit will be saved. Whoever does not believe is ultimately condemned. All believers will be given the power to perform astonishing signs and miracles. They will drive out demons in My name. They will speak in strange tongues. If they pick up snakes or drink any poison, they will not be harmed. They will place their hands on sick people, and these individuals will get well. Always remember My friends; I will be with you, even to the end of the ages."

As the group absorbed these words, they watched as Y'shua began to float upward, His arms spread open, and His eyes cast toward heaven. Y'shua's body glowed white and brighter with each second. Open-mouthed, the people stared as Y'shua rose higher and higher until He disappeared into the clouds above their heads.

For a long time, no one moved or spoke, and the people stared into heaven, expecting Y'shua to come back. Finally, two tall men, dressed in bright white, stood among the people looking up. Their faces were glowing. The people near the two men immediately gasped and moved away, fearing they were spirits.

One of the men spoke to the crowd. "Galileans, why are you standing there looking up at the sky? This Y'shua, who was taken from you into heaven, will come back in the same way you saw Him go to heaven."

Instantly, the two men also vanished.

Over the next few days, the companions of Y'shua frequently gathered to pray as a group. The women followers, along with Miryam the mother of Y'shua, and with His brothers, joined the group. Ten days after Y'shua ascended into heaven, they gathered in one room. Many other people who knew Him followed along and filled the room and area around the house. Joseph and Nicodemus were also there for a total of about one-hundred and twenty people.

The original eleven apostles were discussing the replacement for Judas, son of Simon of Kerioth when Peter stood up, making the announcement. "My friends, the Scripture had to come true in which the Holy Spirit, speaking through King David, made a prediction about Judas, who was the guide for those who arrested Y'shua. Initially, Judas was a member of our group, for he had been chosen to have a part in our work.

"But, when Judas concluded his betrayal, he discovered it brought him only horrible guilt; he then killed himself. As of today, eleven of us remain, but we should replace Judas with another. It is written in the book of Psalms, 'May his house become empty; may no one live in it.' It is also written, 'May someone else take his place of service.'

"So then, someone must join us as a witness to the resurrection of our Savior Y'shua. He must be one of the men who were in our group during the whole time the Master, Y'shua, traveled about with us, beginning from the time John preached his message of baptism until the day He was taken up from us to heaven."

Two men were proposed to the group, Joseph, who was called Barsabbas, also known as Justus, and Matthias. These two men were selected from the discussions.

Then John prayed, "Adonai, You know the thoughts of everyone, so show us which of these two You have chosen to serve as a witness. Let the man chosen take the place of Judas, who has gone to the place where he belongs."

Then the eleven drew lots to choose between the two men; the one chosen was Matthias. He was added to the group of eleven to replace Judas.

This day was also the day of Pentecost. All the believers were gathering together in one place. As they were praying, suddenly there was a noise from the sky, which sounded like a strong wind blowing, and it filled the whole house. Other people nearby and standing in the streets heard the noise and came running to investigate. A large crowd gathered around the house.

Nicodemus yelled out, "Look!"

Everyone saw what looked like tongues of fire which spread out from one central ball and touched each person there. The flames danced above the heads of the people in the room. People were all filled with the Holy Spirit and began to talk in other languages, as the Spirit enabled them to speak.

Jews living in Jerusalem and religious people, who had come from every country in the world, stood listening. They became excited because all of them heard the followers talking in their own languages.

In amazement and wonder, they exclaimed, "These people who are talking like this are Galileans! How is it, then, we hear them speaking in our own native languages?"

Different people called out, stating what country or city they had come from.

"We are from Parthia."

"I'm from Media."

"We come from Elam."

"We're from Mesopotamia."

"Judea!"

"Cappadocia."

"The three of us are from Pontus, and our friends are from Asia."

"We've traveled from Phrygia."

"Our city is Pamphylia."

"There are some of us from Egypt and the regions of Libya near Cyrene."

"We have come from Rome, both Jews and Gentiles converted to Judaism."

"Well, some of us are from Crete!"

"And we have traveled from Arabia, yet all of us hear them speaking in our own languages about the great things YaHoWaH has done!"

Amazed and confused, they kept asking each other, "What does this mean?"

Other individuals made fun of the believers, saying, "These people must be drunk!"

Peter stood up and in a loud voice began to address the crowd.

"Fellow Jews and all of you who live in Jerusalem, listen to me and let me tell you what this means. These people are not drunk as you suppose, because it is only nine o'clock in the morning.

"Instead, this is what the prophet Joel spoke about when he wrote 'This is what I will do in the last days, YaHoWaH says, I will pour out

My Spirit on everyone. Your sons and daughters will proclaim My message. Your young men will see visions, and your old men will have dreams. Yes, even on My servants, both men, and women, I will pour out My Spirit in those days, and they will proclaim My message.

"'I will perform miracles in the sky above and wonders on the earth below. There will be blood, fire, and thick smoke. The sun will be darkened, and the moon will turn red as blood, before the great and glorious day Adonai comes. Whoever calls out to YaHoWaH for help will be saved.'

"Listen to these words, fellow Israelites! Y'shua of Nazareth was a man whose divine authority was clearly proven to you by all the miracles and wonders which YaHoWaH performed through Him. You yourselves know this, for it happened here among you. All was according to His plan for YaHoWaH had already decided Y'shua would be handed over to you. Therefore, you killed Him by letting wicked men crucify Him.

"But, YaHoWaH raised Him from death, setting Y'shua free from death's power, because it was impossible for death to hold Him prisoner. Even King David said this about Him, 'I saw Adonai before me at all times. He is near me, and I will not be troubled. Therefore, I am filled with gladness, and my words are full of joy. Mortal though I am, I will rest assured in hope, because YaHoWaH will not abandon me in the world of the dead. He will not allow your faithful servant to rot in the grave. You have shown me the paths which lead to life, and Your presence will fill me with joy.'

"My friends, I must speak to you plainly about our famous ancestor, King David. He died and was buried, and his grave is here with us to this very day. He was a prophet, and he knew what YaHoWaH had promised him. YaHoWaH made a vow, He would make one of David's descendants a king, just as David was. David saw what God was going to do in the future, and so he spoke about the resurrection of the Messiah when he said, 'He was not abandoned in the world of the dead. His body did not rot in the grave.'

"YaHoWaH has raised this very Y'shua from the dead, and we are all witnesses to this fact. In truth, Y'shua has been lifted to the right side of YaHoWaH, His Father, and He has received from Him the promise of the Holy Spirit. What you now see and hear is YaHoWaH's gift, the Holy Spirit, which YaHoWaH has poured out on us. For it was not David who went up into heaven, but rather he said, 'Adonai said to my Master, sit here at My right side until I put Your enemies as a footstool under Your feet.' All the people of Israel, you now know for sure, this Y'shua, whom you crucified, is the One YaHoWaH made Master and Messiah in heaven and here on earth!"

When the people heard this, they felt ashamed and said to Peter and the other witnesses, "What shall we do brothers?"

Peter said to them, "Each one of you must turn away from your sins, and be baptized in the name of Y'shua the Messiah so your sins will be forgiven. When you do, you will receive YaHoWaH's gift, the Holy Spirit. For YaHoWaH's promise was made to you and your children, and to all who are far away, everyone whom Adonai our YaHoWaH calls to Himself. Therefore, save yourselves from the punishment coming on this wicked people!"

Many of the people gathered believed Peter's message and were baptized, and about three thousand people were added to the group of Y'shua's followers that day.

The believers of Y'shua spent their time learning from the twelve witnesses, taking part in the fellowship, and sharing their meals and praying for one another. Many miracles and wonders were being done by Y'shua's witnesses, and everyone was filled with awe. The believers continued together in close fellowship and shared their belongings with one another.

Many sold their property and possessions, and distributed the money among the other people gathered, according to what each one needed. Day after day they met as a group in the Temple, and they had their meals together in their homes, eating with glad and humble hearts, praising YaHoWaH, and enjoying the kindness of all the people. And every day, Y'shua added to their group, more people who were being saved.

CHAPTER THIRTY-THREE

Y'SHUA IS RETURNING

AFTER TOBIAS FINISHED TELLING HIS story of Y'shua, the morning light seeped into the windows as the sun crested the horizon.

Markus was initially speechless. "Tobias, I never knew this information. So, will you now write your stories of Y'shua? We who have never met Him need to keep the story alive."

Tobias nodded. "Perhaps, but I think the witness John has given us much more than I could ever write down."

Markus rested his hand on Tobias' shoulder. "Still, you should write down what you know. Others would like to hear what you've shared with me this night."

Tobias stared at the table of parchment stacks. "No, Markus, I must follow YaHoWaH's instructions. I must make copies and distribute them to the growing community of believers throughout all of Judea."

Sleepy, Tobias and Markus exchanged hugs.

"I must sleep a little. Tomorrow, please visit again."

"Thank you, Tobias, for now, I feel like I also know who Y'shua is. You need some rest, but I would like to come again tomorrow. Good night and shalom, my friend."

Tobias was exhausted and rubbed his drowsy eyes. "Shalom, Markus, and blessings upon you and your household."

Tired and sore, Tobias slogged off to bed. In no time he was asleep and remained so until late morning the next day.

Late in the afternoon, Markus stopped to visit again. "Greetings, Tobias."

Tobias was excited and animated. "Come in, come in Markus. I must show you what I've found."

The men sat down at the table and Tobias started with the center stack. His hand hovered over the parchment sheets. "This is the witness John's account of Y'shua." Lifting the first page, he began to read the words.

"In the beginning was the Word and the Word was with YaHoWaH, and the Word was YaHoWaH. The Word was with YaHoWaH in the beginning. Everything came into being through the Word, and without the Word, nothing came into being. What came into being through the Word was Life, and the Life was the Light for all people. The Light shines in the darkness, and the darkness doesn't extinguish the Light.

"A man named John was sent from YaHoWaH. He came as a witness to testify concerning the Light, so through him, everyone would believe in the Light. He wasn't the Light, but his mission was to testify concerning the Light. The true Light, which shines on all people, was coming into the world. The Light was in the world, and the world came into being through the Light, but the world didn't recognize the Light.

"The Light came to His own people, and they didn't welcome Him. But those who did receive Him, those who believed in His name, He authorized to become YaHoWaH's children, born not from blood or from human desire or passion but birthed from YaHoWaH. The Word became flesh and made His home among us. We have seen His glory—glory like that of a Father's only Son, full of grace and truth.

"John testified about Him, crying out, 'This is the One of whom I said, "He who comes after me is greater than me because He existed before me."'

"From His fullness, we have all received grace upon grace; as the Law was given through Moses, so grace and truth came into being through Y'shua the Messiah. No one has ever seen YaHoWaH. YaHoWaH's only Son, who is at the Father's side, has made YaHoWaH known to us."

Markus stared wide-eyed at Tobias. "Is John writing about the life of Y'shua the Messiah? His writing reminds me of the first book of the Pentateuch by Moses!"

Tobias vigorously nodded. "I agree with you, Markus. Hand me the last page in the stack."

Markus carefully pulled the bottom parchment out and handed it to Tobias. After studying the page, Tobias began to read.

"He asked a third time, 'Simon son of John, do you love Me?' Peter was sad because Y'shua asked him a third time, 'Do you love Me?' He replied, 'Master, You know everything; You know I love You.' Y'shua said to him, 'Feed My sheep. I assure you, when you were younger, you tied your own belt and walked around wherever you wanted. When you grow old, you will stretch out your hands, and another will tie your belt and lead you where you don't want to go.'

"He said this to show the kind of death by which Peter would die and glorify YaHoWaH. Then after saying this, Y'shua said to Peter, 'Follow Me.'

"Peter turned around and saw the disciple whom Y'shua loved. Now, this was the disciple who had leaned against Y'shua at the meal and asked Him, 'Master, who is going to betray you?' When Peter saw this disciple, he said to Y'shua, 'But Master, what about this man?'

"Y'shua replied, 'If I want him to remain until I come, what difference does this make to you? You must follow Me.'

"Therefore, word spread among the brothers and sisters, this disciple wouldn't die. However, Y'shua didn't say he wouldn't die, but only, 'If I want him to remain until I come, what difference does this make to you?'

"This is the disciple who testifies concerning these things and who wrote them down. We know His testimony is true. Y'shua did many other things as well. If all of them were recorded, I imagine the world itself wouldn't have enough room for the scrolls that would be written."

Tobias grabbed an ink bottle and stylus and turned the parchment over. As Markus looked over his shoulder, he watched Tobias write on the back, "The Good News of John, the witness." Tobias then returned the last page to the bottom of the stack and smiled to himself.

"Last night, Markus, I started reading from this other stack." Tobias pointed to the more substantial pile of sheets.

"I believe this is what John referred to as his revelation from YaHoWaH." Tobias picked up the top parchment from the pile and started reading.

"This is what YaHoWaH showed to Y'shua the Messiah so He could tell His servants what must happen soon. The Messiah then sent His angel with the news to His servant John. And John told everything he had seen about YaHoWaH's message and about what Y'shua the Messiah had said and done.

"YaHoWaH will bless everyone who reads this prophecy to others, and He will bless everyone who hears and obeys it. The time is almost here."

Tobias and Markus jumped to their feet and began dancing and singing praises. They both yelled, "Y'shua the Messiah is coming back!"

With tears of joy in his eyes, Tobias looked at his neighbor Markus. "I have made three copies as instructed by the angel who visited me."

Grinning ear to ear, Markus rested his hands on Tobias' shoulders. "We must distribute copies to all the believers."

"Yes . . . yes . . . yes. I have decided I will take one copy to those left in Jerusalem, and then perhaps I can meet with Paul and share this great news. Then I should ask the spiritual elders concerning the other copies."

Markus smiled. "Do you think we could change the attitudes of Rome if a copy was sent to the believers there?"

Tobias frowned looking determined. "These words will change the world, Markus. I know this because they burn with passion in my heart already."

THE END

An intersectional mixing of text from the following book was borrowed with permission from:

1 Harder, E. Ruth. *Hannah: Weaver of Life.* Russian Hill Press, 2015, pp. 294-295.

2 Harder, E. Ruth. *Hannah: Weaver of Life.* Russian Hill Press, 2015, pp. 294-295.

3 Harder, E. Ruth. *Hannah: Weaver of Life.* Russian Hill Press, 2015, pp. 294-295.

4 Harder, E. Ruth. *Hannah: Weaver of Life.* Russian Hill Press, 2015, pp. 294-295.

5 Harder, E. Ruth. *Hannah: Weaver of Life.* Russian Hill Press, 2015, pp. 294-295.

ACKNOWLEDGMENTS

I wish to acknowledge my wife Emily first. She is a huge fan and a terrific supporter of my writing and ministry. She is a precious and treasured gift from God, and I am humbly grateful for her.

I want to thank Linda Humes for her contributions to my writing and development of *Persuaded*. Her wisdom is greatly appreciated, and she was instrumental in directing me to re-write the manuscript—which involved a new, and better, opening to the book. Thank you, Linda.

During the several years it took to develop, research, and write *Persuaded*, I've come to rely on pastor friends for their input and advice. Among those are Robert Koch and Cid Cota (Assemblies of God), Lloyd and Monica Cook (Vineyard Church), and David Hinman (Vineyard/Disciple Making Movement-DMM). David also provided me with the concept of taking the message in *Persuaded* and bringing it to church audiences in a one-man show. Thank you all for your wisdom and help.

Among the contributors from the Northern Arizona Word Weavers group, there are too many to list. This group is led by Alice Klies who provides inspiration and encouragement for many developing authors. Thank you, Word Weavers, for your positive remarks and support.

I would like to extend a big thanks to the Jerry Jenkins Writers Guild (jerrysguild.com). Each week, Jerry Jenkins provides fresh information to writers around the world. He has an expanding library of information and downloads. I cannot emphasize enough the value of being a member of his guild. Through the knowledge I've learned, my writing has improved. Readers of my works have noticed the improvements. Thank you, Jerry, for broadcasting your knowledge.

Persuaded is possible because Dr. Sam Lowry and the team at Ambassador International have provided their support. I wish to include Anna (COO) and Hannah (Creative Director), who have endured through this project with me. Thank you all for helping me achieve another published book and working with me again. I wish this company the best of success in the years to come and thank them for their perseverance.

I wish to extend a special thank you to Daphne Self who provided excellent feedback and editing skills in the final version of *Persuaded*. I appreciate you.

With each published book, my base of readers and followers grows. It would take many pages to list your names. Know this—thank you for partnering with me, for providing reviews, emails, and calls of support.

For more information about
David Harder
and
Persuaded
please visit:

www.DavidHarder.com
www.twitter.com/davidcharder
www.facebook.com/David.Harder.Author
www.instagram.com/davidcharder

For more information about
AMBASSADOR INTERNATIONAL
please visit:

www.ambassador-international.com
@AmbassadorIntl
www.facebook.com/AmbassadorIntl

*If you enjoyed this book, please consider leaving us a review on
Amazon, Goodreads, or our website.*